REMINDERS OF HOME

An evocative and charming Edwardian family saga

DOMINIC LUKE

Brannans Family Saga Book 5

Joffe Books, London
www.joffebooks.com

First published in Great Britain in 2023

Cover art by Jarmila Takač

ISBN: 978-1-80405-814-5

Oh yet we trust that somehow good
Will be the final goal of ill
To pangs of nature, sins of will
Defects of doubt, and taints of blood;

That nothing walks with aimless feet;
That not one life shall be destroy'd,
Or cast as rubbish to the void,
When God hath made the pile complete;

That not a worm is cloven in vain;
That not a moth with vain desire
Is shrivelled in a fruitless fire
Or but subserves another's gain.

In Memoriam LIV
Alfred, Lord Tennyson

CHAPTER ONE

She trudged along the lane in the silence of the night, infinitely weary, her bags hanging heavy from her arms. A waxing moon glimmered faintly behind a pall of grey-dark clouds. The July countryside was wreathed in shadow.

As she walked, scenes from the last few days played in a loop in her head, as jerky and grainy and chimerical as a cinematograph. She faced again the matron of the hospital. The familiar stony face regarded her coldly across a large and cluttered desk.

'Really, this is most inconvenient. To leave now when we are at our very busiest. I find it incomprehensible.'

'My cousin is dead,' Dorothea had explained yet again, mechanically, knowing it would do no good. 'My cousin has been killed in action. We grew up together. He was like a brother to me. My poor aunt, his mother, will need me.'

'*We* need you. Your country needs you. What about your duty to king and country? Though perhaps I shouldn't expect *you* to understand, with your divided loyalties, Nurse Kaufmann.'

Kaufmann, Kaufmann, always Kaufmann. She had, at times, this last year and a half, almost grown to hate the name. It singled her out. It was the mark of Cain. But — oh!

— it was *his* name, it belonged to *him*. How could she ever hate anything that was *his*?

'All the same,' Nettie Thomson had said — Nettie Thomson, the one real friend she'd made in all these months, 'wouldn't it make things easier to change just for now? You could use your maiden name.'

But that wasn't allowed. It was against the law. Someone like Nettie Thomson wouldn't understand, someone who'd never had any dealings with the police except perhaps to ask directions in the street, someone whose name was not known to them, whose movements were not controlled. Nettie Thomson had no idea what it was like to be an alien in the land of your birth.

'Now then, Mrs Kaufmann, let me see.' The loop in Dorothea's head moved on. She was with the police inspector now, the police inspector who had been scrupulously polite in a way that had set Dorothea's teeth on edge. 'You want a permit to travel, I understand. And what would be the purpose of your journey?'

'My cousin is dead. My cousin has been killed in action.' She had repeated the same lines. She had repeated them over and over, these last few days. But they were words, just empty words. How could she believe them? How could it be true? How could someone as young and strong and vital as Roderick be dead?

All too easily. She knew that well. She had seen it. She had seen what war did to men. She knew how fragile a thing the human body was.

She had tortured herself ever since the news came, knowing so much and so little. How had Roderick died? Had it been instantaneous? Had he been blown to smithereens in a single moment? Or had he died slowly and in agony, had he suffered as she'd seen men suffer during her time nursing? Perhaps he'd been carried alive from the field of battle. Perhaps someone had done their best to save him. It might, for all she knew, have been the enemy who came to his aid. Had German nurses cleaned his wounds? Had a German doctor tended him? Perhaps Johann—

'Oh, don't, Doro, don't! It's horrible enough, without letting your mind run riot.' Nettie Thomson, slim and slight in a neat nurse's uniform, had looked at her anxiously just a few hours ago. 'I wish I could come to the station with you. I wish I could. But that old battle-axe the matron . . .' Nettie had shrugged, and then she'd had to go, dashing off to do her duty to king and country, dashing off because there were never enough minutes in the day.

Dorothea had finished packing her bags. She had left, for the last time, the little room with the bare boards and the row of beds divided by curtains; the room she had shared with four others, three of whom were strangers still. Stepping out into the dreary streets of south London, she had lugged her bags up the hill to the tram stop. In due course she had reached Euston. It had been swarming like an anthill. She had struggled onto an overcrowded train. A Tommy had been so kind as to give up his seat for her. The Tommy's name, she'd discovered as the train got under way, was Ernest Grimshaw. He was from Bolton; he was going home on leave. He had told her his life story as the train stopped and started, inching through the north-west suburbs and out into the verdant countryside. He'd told her about his mam and his dad and his sisters and his little brother and the street where they lived and the mill where he'd worked before volunteering for the army. He'd chattered in his Lancashire accent, open and unaffected, leaning against the window, whilst the other people in the carriage pretended not to listen. In all his talk he'd said not one word about the war.

She'd warmed to him, so free-spoken and friendly. But, of course, she'd not been able to help but wonder if he would have given up his seat so readily had he known her name was Kaufmann and that she had a German husband — that she was, in fact, German herself, for a woman couldn't be English if she'd married a foreigner: the law didn't allow it. Even a woman who'd never left England's shores was considered an alien under those circumstances, never mind one who'd lived in Hamburg for two years until the summer of 1914.

Dorothea had wanted to tell Ernest Grimshaw all about it. She had wanted to tell him her life story in return: how she had no father or mother, how she'd lived the greater part of her childhood in a big house in Northamptonshire with her aunt and uncle and two cousins, how she'd met on holiday in Switzerland a young German, how she'd gone on to marry him and to move to Hamburg. She had wanted to explain that the outbreak of war had found her on a visit to her old home, that she'd been apart from her husband for nearly two years since then, and that she questioned every day her decision to stay in England — but would she have been any better off in Germany? She had wanted to tell Ernest Grimshaw all this, but she hadn't dared. What might he say, do? Not just him. The others in the compartment, too. The rather prim, elderly lady. The fat man in a bowler hat. The worn-looking woman with a small boy on her lap. There'd been others whose faces she had barely registered. She had so wanted to repay Ernest Grimshaw's kindness by being as open and friendly and honest as he had been. But she had not dared take the risk.

It was this which had gnawed away at her these last two years, slowly sapping her spirit. To be so suspicious went against her nature; to always fear the worst of people made life mean and miserable.

She had sat isolated in the crowded compartment, while Ernest Grimshaw, yawning, having exhausted every detail of his young life (except the war), had found a space to sit on the floor. He had fallen asleep as the journey went on and on. His head had nodded, and then slipped sideways, to rest against her skirt. She had felt the gentle pressure of his cheek on her knee. She had looked out as the train crawled onwards, the sun dipping down, the countryside bathed in golden light. She had seen woods and fields and gentle hills, a winding canal, haymaking in some of the meadows. And all the time she'd been thinking, *He will never see this again, England in July, high summer*. For he was dead. Roderick was dead.

Dusk had come. Dorothea's mind had gone wandering back to another train trip sixteen years ago, this very same journey when she was eight years old, being taken by her papa from poverty in London to the grandeur of Clifton Park, where he had abandoned her to be looked after by an aunt and an uncle she had never heard of. That had been a journey into the unknown. This hardly seemed less so. She felt as if she had been away an age, even though she had visited Clifton as recently as two months ago. But Roderick had been alive back then. He'd been alive and on leave. And she had not known that she would never see him again.

The train had neared Welby at last. Ernest Grimshaw had woken as she stirred, the train slowing.

'I'm so sorry to disturb you, Private Grimshaw.'

'That's all right, miss. I were only snoozing.'

He'd helped her with her bags, then leapt agilely back into the carriage and swung the door shut. The train had pulled away, the locomotive disgorging great bursts of white smoke into the night sky. It had trundled out of the station and over the bridge and faded into the dark, heading for Duncan's Hill Tunnel. Standing on the empty platform, she had watched it go. A wave of utter desolation out of all proportion had swept over her, to have taken her last leave of Ernest Grimshaw when he'd been so kind, when he'd looked so very young and innocent sleeping with his head resting against her knee. She wondered how long it would take him to reach Bolton. She wondered if his mam and his dad and his sisters and his little brother would sit up waiting. She imagined how excited they would be to see him again, their dear Ernest. But she knew she would never learn anything more of his life story.

Welby station had been dark and deserted. It really did seem the middle of nowhere at that hour. She had not realized quite how late it was, still not used to the clocks having changed. There'd been no one to meet her. Her telegram must have miscarried. Or maybe they'd given up waiting, the train so delayed. And so she'd set off walking, just as she'd done sixteen years ago with her papa on a cold December evening. Back then, as now, she'd been dead on her feet. She'd fallen asleep as she walked, and her papa had picked her up and carried her. There was no one to carry her this time. She had to go on alone.

She reached now the crest of a rise and stopped to look ahead, putting her bags down. The moon, which had been blurred by thin cloud as she walked, shone out brightly for a moment. The road ran on, down from the rise and into the village of Hayton where no lights showed. The battlemented tower of St Adeline's was stencilled black against the night sky. The empty silence all around was broken only by a whispering breeze in the hedgerows and, faint and some way off, the enigmatic chirring of a nightjar.

She shivered. She picked up her bags and hurried on. Soon she reached Hayton's outlying buildings, Maybank perched above the road, home of the village doctor, and then the ostentatious but rather faded elegance of the Red Lion. She walked along the deserted High Street. Here was the village green and the sycamore in full leaf, grey in the dim moonlight. She turned aside, taking the path that ran alongside the churchyard. It led to a shortcut across the fields. She stumbled a little on the uneven ground, but it could have been pitch dark and she'd still have known her way.

She trudged across Row Meadow. It seemed to her that she must be the only waking creature in the whole of the wide and empty night. On and on she trudged, on and on, head down, half-asleep, no end in sight. Perhaps there really *was* no end. Perhaps she was fated to walk in the dark forever.

Her head jerked up. She ventured into the deep darkness beneath the trees of the Pheasantry. She emerged as if from a tunnel. Gravel crunched under her feet. And there it was, the wide facade of the house with all its blank windows, the house she'd called home for so many years. It was wrapped in webs of shadow, now that the moon was hidden once more.

Almost it looked abandoned, forgotten, a ghost house. She baulked at the thought of climbing the steps and ringing the bell. Such a jangling at this hour would be enough to wake the dead. She made her way instead round to the right. In a daze, tired beyond enduring — tired from her journey and from the relentless routine of the hospital — she passed under the archway that led to the stable yard. If she couldn't get in by the side door (it had always been kept unlocked at night in the old days), then that would be the end; she would only have energy enough to curl up in one of the stables and sleep, sleep, sleep. There were no horses to disturb her. They had all been taken away.

But the side door opened when she tried it. She made her way blindly along the little passage, tripping over her own feet and dropping her bags with a clatter. She left them where they fell, feeling her way forward. Her hand fumbled for the handle of the inner door. She opened it and stepped through.

For a moment she wavered, her tired brain trying to decide what to do next. There was a heavy silence.

Then came a scuffling noise. A dim light bobbed up the back stairs from the basement. A rather tremulous male voice hailed her. 'Hello? Who's there? Who is it?'

A man in a nightshirt appeared. He held a candle in one hand, was brandishing a poker with the other.

'Mrs Kaufmann? Is it you?'

'Crompton! Oh, Crompton!'

'Why, we'd given you up, Mrs Kaufmann! We thought you weren't coming! You've never walked all the way from Welby, have you?'

'I walked, yes. It was very dark.'

It was dark still, the candlelight muted, flickering over Crompton's rather worn, middle-aged features. Why were the electric lights not working? Ah, of course: the generator would be off at this time of night.

Dorothea swayed where she stood. Things began to happen in a blur. Suddenly she was down in the kitchen, Crompton coaxing some life into the embers in the range.

Mrs Bourne was also there with her hair in a net and wearing a voluminous dressing gown. Dorothea gaped. In all her years at Clifton, she had never seen the self-respecting housekeeper in such a guise.

'Some warm milk, Mrs Kaufmann.'

A glass was pressed into her hands. She gulped from it. She felt as if she hadn't had anything to eat or drink for an age.

Next thing she knew, she was climbing the back stairs, dragging herself up, up.

Mrs Bourne opened a door. 'I had this room readied for you, Mrs Kaufmann: your usual room.'

'My bags! I've lost my bags!' A sense of panic gripped Dorothea. But there, huffing a little, was Crompton, weighed down with them.

The door softly closed. She was alone now, alone in her own room, the room off the nursery that had been hers for twelve years growing up: precisely half her life. Her dear room, where she felt safe, where once she'd been happy, long ago, before the war.

She scrabbled in her bags, one last effort. Here it was, the photograph of Johann in a simple silver frame. She kissed it gently, then propped it on the bedside table and blew out the candle. Too exhausted to get undressed, she fell between the crisp, white sheets and sank immediately into oblivion.

* * *

She surfaced from a long, deep sleep, to find brightness seeping through the curtains. She felt a sense of peace, blessed peace. She lay there and savoured it, cradled in the lap of luxury.

But a moment later Dorothea furrowed her brow. All thoughts of peace in times like these were illusory. And something must have woken her. What?

Struggling to sit up, she saw in the doorway a girl in her early twenties wearing a maid's uniform and carrying a tray.

'Oh, miss, I didn't mean to disturb you. I thought you'd be up by now.'

'That's all right, Daisy. Have you brought tea?'

'Tea and a bite of breakfast, Miss Dorothea. They've had their breakfast downstairs long since. You've been asleep hours and hours.'

As Dorothea settled herself and accepted the tray, she said, 'How are you, Daisy?'

'Very well, miss, thank you for asking. Here's your tea. There's toast and porridge — an egg too — and bacon. Cook made it all special like.'

'Dear Cook! I've missed her! I've missed you all! Stay a moment, Daisy, whilst I eat. Tell me all the news. How's your family? How's everyone in the village? I feel quite out of touch.'

'Mam and Dad are just the same, they never change. Our Billy's out in France, of course. Our Jem's still at the same factory, the one in Lawham. He's making soldiers' boots . . .'

Daisy sat perched on the edge of the bed, which would have earned her a sharp rebuke from Mrs Bourne had she been caught, but to Dorothea it seemed quite natural, just as it seemed natural to be called *Miss Dorothea* instead of *Mrs Kaufmann*, Daisy not able to break the habit.

Daisy heaved a heartfelt sigh. 'Oh, miss, isn't it awful about Master Roderick? This place has been ever so quiet since we heard. You hardly dare breathe, somehow. And Tilda says—'

'Tilda?'

'Tilda Johnson, miss, the new housemaid.'

'Of course. I was forgetting. I met her in May. But go on, Daisy. Go on.'

'When the telegram came, Tilda says, Mrs Brannan just sat there sewing and never said a word. She just sat there sewing and sewing, as if nothing had happened. Oh, miss, I'm so glad you've come, I can't tell you! Everyone is miserable as sin: the mistress, Miss Eliza, Mrs Roderick. No one hardly says a word and I get in such a quiver!'

At this point, the door flew open, and in came Miss Eliza herself: Roderick's sister Elizabeth, aged sixteen. She flew across the room and flung herself into Dorothea's arms. Daisy only just rescued the tray in time.

'Doro, Doro, where have you been?' Eliza was crying, sobbing, overwhelmed by her emotions, as she so often was.

'I came as soon as I could, dearest Eliza.'

Dorothea wanted to offer some comfort, but what could one say? There was nothing to say. Nothing would take the pain away. Nothing would bring Roderick back.

She cradled her cousin in her arms, stroking her beautiful fair hair, waiting for the storm to subside.

* * *

Later, in the morning room before lunch, Eliza sat so stiff and formal, blank-faced, that it was difficult to believe she was the same girl who'd been sobbing her heart out upstairs. But there was always a commanding sense of decorum in the presence of Mrs Eloise Brannan. To Dorothea's eye, her aunt appeared all but unchanged, unless she was a little paler than usual. Poised on the chaise longue and dressed in mourning, Aunt Eloise was a widow in her early fifties who was now also bereaved of her only son.

'The circumstances of his death are not entirely clear.' Aunt Eloise spoke calmly, crisply. 'I wrote at once to ascertain the facts, of course. I wrote to his fellow subalterns. I wrote to his superiors. I await their replies. If necessary, I shall put an appeal in the newspaper. We must know every detail.'

Why, thought Dorothea, why was it so important to know? She herself was only too happy *not* to know. She'd seen at the hospital how it was possible for men to survive all manner of wounds. They lived with terrible amputations and the most appalling deformities. What, then, did it take in order to prise life away from them? Dorothea did not want even to think about it.

She wondered if Roderick's wife, Rosa — now his widow — also wanted facts, or if she too would rather be spared. Heavily pregnant, Rosa was silent, seemed distracted. She was not in widow's weeds, but then she'd always been somewhat bohemian in her ways.

'There can be no funeral, of course,' Aunt Eloise continued. 'The government makes that impossible, by their callous refusal to bring home the dead. But we must have *something*, some sort of ceremony. A memorial service, I thought. I will need your help, Dorothea, in arranging it.'

'Of course, Aunt.' Why else had she come back to Clifton, if not to help?

'Do you know,' said Aunt Eloise after a pause, and as if suddenly remembering a point of utmost importance, 'when Roderick was here last, I noticed he had grey hairs. Just imagine. Grey hairs. And he was only twenty-three.'

* * *

Dressing for dinner: it was like stepping back a hundred years. Dorothea felt positively profligate, sat at her dressing table, fiddling with her dark curls, wasting precious time on her hair when there were dressings to change and bed pans to empty, floors to mop, sheets to change, and an endless round of cleaning. But not here. Not at Clifton. Here, there lingered a vestige of an earlier way of life, of which dressing for dinner had been a part.

She wondered how the men on her ward were getting on, Nettie too. She wondered if the hospital was coping with the flood of new cases which had just begun pouring in as she was preparing to leave (to desert her post).

She threw her hairbrush down and got impatiently to her feet. What did it matter how her hair looked? It was not important.

But it was not time yet to go downstairs. She went instead next door, to the day room of the nursery. Strictly speaking, her bedroom too was part of the nursery, but even after she'd grown up she'd never moved to a bigger room on the floor below, and now, whenever she returned to Clifton, she liked, for old times' sake, to stay in the room she still thought of as her own.

The day room was quiet, devoid of all life, apart from the parrot, mournful in its cage, its feathers rather ragged-looking and faded; Roderick's daughter, Katherine, nearly two, was already in bed. Dorothea walked slowly around, reacquainting herself with the big nursery table, the shelves packed with toys and games, the rocking horse with a film of dust on it. In this very room, less than two months ago, she had sat and talked with Roderick on the final evening of her short visit (she had been granted a few days absence from the hospital in the special circumstances of Roderick's leave). As now, she'd been dressed for dinner, Roderick too. He'd been sitting at the big table, a tall and handsome figure, his dark hair brilliantined, his dark eyes impenetrable. She remembered the smell of his aftershave and the way his fingers had drummed on the scrubbed surface of the table.

Dorothea crossed to the barred window. It was still daylight, which seemed odd at this hour (but the clocks had changed, she kept forgetting about the clocks). Brightness lingered on the horizon away to the right, where the sun, out of sight, was sinking below the rim of the earth. The view was entirely familiar to her, the land here at the back of the house sloping away to where the canal was all but hidden in its shallow valley, Ingleby Wood a green blur on the rising ground beyond.

The world as seen from the nursery window looked peaceful, bucolic — completely unchanged.

'It's hell, Doro. It's bloody hell out there.'

Roderick's voice in her head sounded very real. Almost she felt that if she turned round she would find him there, large as life. And why not? He'd liked to have his own way; he'd always hated anyone getting the better of him. Perhaps he would outwit even death — if anyone could, it was Roderick.

She didn't turn round, her eyes fixed on the view; whether this was because she was afraid of facing Roderick's ghost, or whether she didn't want to confront the day room undeniably empty, she could not say. She wondered what it was that had brought them both up here on that evening two months ago. Pure chance, no doubt. Yet it seemed to her, looking back, that it had been preordained.

She'd joined him, sat at the table. The lamp in one corner had given out a dim light which dwindled into deep shadows in the further corners. Roderick had talked to her in an extemporary way, as he sometimes did, opening his heart — or a part of it, for no one on earth had ever seen all of Roderick's heart.

'It's hell out there, Doro, I can't tell you. Mother hasn't the first idea. As for Rosa — well, Rosa *tries* to understand, but she always sees things how she thinks they *should* be, and not how they *are*. You're the only one I can properly talk to. I don't have to pretend with you. Maybe it's because you're a nurse and you've seen something of what it's like, you've seen what it can do to a man.'

He had grown a moustache since joining the army and he'd taken to smoothing it with his fingers, exactly the way his late father — Dorothea's Uncle Albert — had done. This unconscious imitation had made her smile as she watched him two months ago, but now, in the implacable silence of the day room, the memory was almost unbearably poignant.

'Let's not talk about the war, Doro. Let's not.'

He'd got up abruptly from the table where he'd been sitting and he'd wandered restlessly around the room, fiddling with the toys on the shelves, doodling on the blackboard with a stick of chalk.

What was it he'd drawn?

She turned to look, forgetting her fear of the empty room, but the blackboard had been wiped clean and all trace of Roderick's scribble was gone. She felt a sharp pang at this loss. She wanted to cling to every last vestige: it seemed desperately important.

Trying to reconstruct, word for word, their conversation of two months ago, she found it all disjointed in her mind, as if she'd not been paying proper attention. And perhaps that was partly true. Half her mind had already been back at the hospital, where she'd been due the next day. And always, everywhere, more than half her mind was with Johann; she never stopped thinking of Johann. But how she wished, now, that she'd focused more on Roderick that evening! It would not have cost her much, to have given all of herself for those few, fleeting moments.

He'd turned away from the blackboard, shaking his head. 'Lord, Doro! Do you remember? Do you remember growing up here in the nursery? Do you remember what it was like? What hopeless little idiots we were — well, I was, anyway. You — you always had more idea of things, even as a kid. Look at this place! It's as if nothing has changed! I expect even my toy soldiers are still somewhere about. And old Polly goes on forever. Here's Nanny's chair. Funny how it's still *Nanny's* chair, when Nanny went away years ago. Dear old Nanny!' Those last three words had been laced with irony, and he'd grinned: a rather savage, wolfish sort of grin.

His grin had faded. Running his hand back and forth across the headrest of Nanny's chair, he'd said, 'We were in the Ypres sector a month or so ago—' (The war had intruded. *Let's not talk about the war*, he'd said, but he'd seemed to find that impossible — unlike Ernest Grimshaw.) 'We had a hot time of it, I don't mind telling you. Had to be ready to stand-to at any moment, day or night. The trenches were in an atrocious state — and small wonder, when the Hun strafed them to kingdom come at every opportunity. I remember one bombardment in particular: the worst of the lot it was, as if the end of the world had come. As I cowered in my dugout like a rat in a sewer, I found myself sucking my thumb. Can you believe it? I was actually sucking my thumb! Poor old Nanny thought she'd cured me of that forever. Apparently not.' He'd added insouciantly, 'The Hun could learn a thing or two from dear old Nanny.'

Dear old Nanny. But Nanny had done her best by her own lights, even though that meant not sparing the rod. It was Roderick who'd borne the brunt. He'd been, in those days, what Nanny called 'a handful'. Dorothea's eyes still watered when she recalled some of the beatings he'd taken. She'd been full of concern for him afterwards but Roderick — strong-willed, a boy with all a boy's bravado — had brushed her solicitude aside, cultivating a stiff upper lip.

But two months ago, out of the blue, here in the day room, he'd suddenly said, 'She was a brute, Doro. An absolute brute. I know you won't have it, and you only ever see the good in people, but Nanny . . .'

Leaving the sentence hanging, he'd come back to the big table and sat down again opposite her. He'd begun to caress the table edge with the palm of his hand. Looking unseeingly round the room, he'd said, very hesitantly, 'Sometimes I . . . I think that Nanny . . . I think she might have stunted my growth in some way. I don't mean on the outside. The bruises always healed. But inside . . . inside there's something that—' He'd broken off abruptly and he'd given a snort of disdain. 'I'm talking rot, of course. Absolute rot. This is what happens when your brain's been rattled by the Hun artillery.'

His wandering eyes had come to rest on his own hand as it caressed the table edge and he'd seemed to make a conscious effort to keep it still. Without looking up, he'd said softly, as if to himself, 'Why does one dwell on all that's unpleasant? Why not remember the times when one was happiest?' He'd glanced at her with those dark, impenetrable eyes. 'Do you remember our holiday, Doro, just you, me and Eliza? We went to Switzerland, to that little place — what was it called? A village halfway up a mountain. Anderdorf. That's it. It was called Anderdorf. I liked it there. I liked climbing the mountains. I don't think I've ever been happier than when I was climbing the mountain peaks above Anderdorf. Or perhaps . . .' He'd frowned down at the surface of the table, following the grain of the wood with a fingertip. 'Perhaps "happy" isn't the word. Perhaps there's a better way of putting it. "At peace". Yes. That sounds right. I was at peace.

'I still think about that holiday. Sometimes, when I'm up to my knees in mud and my ears are ringing from the Hun bombardment and I'm surrounded by death on every side, I find myself remembering the silence, and the cold clean air, and the night sky above the Alps, a sky ablaze with stars.'

Anderdorf, thought Dorothea. Anderdorf, where she'd met Johann and her life had changed forever. How odd that Anderdorf should have had such significance for Roderick too. She'd never known he felt like that about Anderdorf.

It seemed somehow incongruous that Roderick should have hankered after silence and stillness.

She saw him in her mind's eye as he'd been two months ago, digging his thumbnail into the table, making a groove, all his attention focused on it. Suddenly he'd sat back, frowning so hard that his eyebrows met above the bridge of his nose. 'Don't get the wrong idea from all this blather, Doro. It's really not so bad out there. It's not so bad I can't stick it. I'm not likely to let myself down — or you, or Mother, or Rosa. After all, I've known worse. If I survived school — if I survived Nanny — I can survive anything.'

To all appearance, he'd been deadly serious, comparing school and Nanny to the front line; but there'd always been times when Dorothea found it impossible to tell if he was joking or not.

'Yes, it's true, I was bullied at school,' he'd added, confirming what she'd long suspected, but which he'd never admitted before in so many words. 'You've no idea what little savages boys together are. No doubt it did me good. It was character building, I expect. But I don't know why I'm telling you all this. I'm not making much sense.' Slouched in his chair, arms dangling, he'd looked at her across the expanse of the table. 'You have a way of drawing people out of themselves, Doro — like an enchantress. I'm sure there's never been a girl like you.'

Even now, two months later, she still couldn't make her mind up if he'd been mocking her or not. Perhaps both. He'd always been a contradictory boy.

On a whim, she went over to the toy shelves and searched amongst the clutter. Yes, here they were still, he'd been right: his toy soldiers. She remembered great battles across the whole of the table, all his soldiers lined up with careful precision before he set about massacring them with great sweeps of his arm. Now it was real men, and not toy soldiers, being massacred across the Channel.

Roderick had seemed indestructible. In October last year, he'd been in the thick of the fighting at the Battle of Loos, until he was wounded and invalided home. By happy accident, he'd landed up at her hospital in south London. Pale and dirty, his arm and shoulder swathed in blood-soaked bandages, he'd appeared half-dead, but he'd healed remarkably quickly, been sent to convalesce, and re-joined his regiment less than three months later; when last she'd seen him, here at Clifton on leave, he'd looked as good as new. Nothing, it had seemed, could keep him down. He'd even said as much, that evening in the nursery.

'Do you know, Doro, I have this feeling I'll pull through. I really think I shall. I've as good a chance as anyone.'

He'd been wrong.

She was tempted to think that some sort of presentiment had brought them together in the nursery that evening, two months ago. But Roderick would have scoffed at such an idea. He'd never believed in signs and portents. Why, then, had he opened his heart to her? What had prompted him to speak as he'd done that evening? Had he been trying to tell her something? What had he wanted of her?

She had the strangest feeling there was unfinished business between them. It would now remain unfinished forever.

As she replaced the box of soldiers on the toy shelf, she heard the distant sound of the gong. It was time to go down to dinner.

* * *

'"We look not at the things which are seen but at the things which are not seen; for the things which are seen are temporal but the things which are not seen are eternal."'

Hayton's old vicar, usually so genial, was today suitably solemn, his venerable voice ringing out in the half-empty church. Fitful sunlight glowed through the stained-glass windows. The congregation, all in black, listened with heads bowed — all except Aunt Eloise, who sat tall and straight, staring ahead, unflinching. Dorothea, beside her, shivered. It was always cold in St Adeline's. Even at the height of summer it was cold. The only time she'd known it warm was the day of her wedding four years ago.

Four years. It felt more like forty. But it had been this very same vicar who had married her. She drew comfort from the fact that he was still here. It was good to know that some things didn't change in this changing world. Also, he'd known Roderick since Roderick was a boy, and that made a difference today.

'I would like now to read, if I may, a few lines from a letter of condolence sent by Roderick's commanding officer.' There was a moment of hush as the vicar carefully unfolded a piece of paper. He held it reverently. 'Major Braithwaite writes, "Lieutenant Brannan was one of the finest young men it has been my privilege to lead. He was an exemplary officer and a shining example in the battalion. I hope at this time of bereavement it will be of some comfort to you to know that, to the last, he never failed in his duty, and that his courage under fire was always of the highest."' The vicar paused, then said, 'And now, if I may ask you all to stand . . .'

There was a sound of shuffling. The organ struck up. Music echoed. Voices were raised in song. The music, the sound of the singing, the words of the hymn, brought tears to Dorothea's eyes.

The day thou gavest, Lord, is ended,
The darkness falls at thy behest;
To thee our morning hymns ascended,
Thy praise shall sanctify our rest.

The hymn ended. The music died away. In the sudden silence, there was a loud sobbing at the back of the church. Heads turned to look. Drying her eyes, Dorothea glanced round too. A solitary figure was sat right at the back, in the very last row, dressed in a plain black frock. It was Susie Carter, Dorothea realized, from the village. Once a housemaid at Clifton, Susie was now married to one of Dorothea's oldest village friends, Nibs Carter. It was odd that she should be so upset. But it just went to show that even a brassy girl like Susie had a heart. People should not be so quick to judge.

Aunt Eloise had also looked round and, as they both turned back to the front, Dorothea expected to see on her aunt's face a look of cold disapproval at the interruption: such an unbridled display of emotion. Instead, Aunt Eloise appeared pensive, almost puzzled; this was so unexpected that Dorothea took another glance to make sure she hadn't been mistaken, but the fleeting expression was gone: Aunt Eloise's features were now frozen in place, a mask concealing her inner feelings. Dorothea felt sure she must have imagined that it had ever been otherwise.

The service came to an end. The congregation filed slowly out through the porch, to gather in the bright sunshine on the path. Nobody seemed quite sure what to do next. There was to be no interment, of course. Dorothea wondered if Roderick might have an anonymous last resting place somewhere in France. By all accounts, his body had never been found — perhaps because there was nothing to find. Dorothea had seen at the hospital how even one small fragment of shrapnel could cause unthinkable injuries, ripping a man to shreds; but here, today, in this sleepy and unsuspecting corner of Northamptonshire, she kept this knowledge to herself.

She surveyed the little gathering, the people who'd come to remember Roderick. Mrs Somersby of Brockmorton Manor was as elegantly dressed as ever, but appeared a little withered beneath the wide brim of her hat; she was accompanied by a daughter and her daughter-in-law. Colonel

Harding of Newbolt Hall was with his unmarried elder son, and his younger son's wife; but Lady Fitzwilliam had come alone from Hayton Grange. These seven represented what the village would term 'the quality'. From the village itself there was the headmaster and his wife, the aged Miss Evanses who lived on the green, Mrs Adnitt from The Hawthorns, and one or two others. There was no sign now of Susie Carter.

Few of Roderick's friends and acquaintances had been able to come at such short notice. One who'd managed was an object of discreet but general interest, being a man in uniform: he seemed somehow symbolic of so many others. After searching her memory, Dorothea was able to identify him as one of Roderick's Oxford contemporaries, a Mr Gerry Milton — or Lieutenant Milton, as the pips on his shoulder now proclaimed him to be. She remembered him vaguely as a rather shy and reticent boy; to all appearance, he'd not changed much, for he was stood a little apart and alone. As no one else seemed inclined to make an effort, Dorothea felt it was beholden on her to do so, and she made her way across to speak to him, trying to recall when it was they'd last met — she felt sure it must be three or four years ago at the very least — but her thoughts were interrupted by the unmistakeable booming voice of Colonel Harding, which rose high above all other muttered conversations.

'He's on the run now, the Hun. We've got him on the run. This latest attack has well and truly knocked the stuffing out of him. Next stop Berlin, you mark my words. Berlin before the year's out.'

'He's wrong, you know,' said Lieutenant Milton quietly as Dorothea joined him, thereby relieving her of the need to make any opening remarks. 'It won't end this year, or the next. You'll find that the men at the front are much less sanguine than people here at home.'

She learned that Lieutenant Milton was on convalescent leave after a bout of trench fever. A stroke of luck, he said, otherwise he'd not have been able to come today.

'I wouldn't have wanted to miss it, a chance to say good-bye. I was rather cut up when I heard about Roddy. He was always so . . . so full of life.'

'Had you seen him recently, Lieutenant Milton?'

'Well, no, not for a while, to tell the truth. I write to him sometimes — wrote to him, I should say. I had a reply from him once, a while back; just after he'd been wounded at Loos, it was. Rather a shambles, he said, Loos, but he couldn't wait to get back out there. That was just like him, I thought.'

'Yes, it was, wasn't it,' said Dorothea. The Battle of Loos, by her calculation, had been at least nine months ago. One letter from Roderick in nine months: that, too, was just like him.

'He was not the sort of fellow one would easily forget,' said Lieutenant Milton, 'though I'd not seen much of him since Oxford, and even at Oxford I never felt that I . . . that I really knew him. I'm not sure that *anyone* really knew him — knew all of him, I mean. He always struck me as someone who had what one might call . . . hidden depths.' Lieutenant Milton gave an embarrassed little laugh. 'It sounds rather silly, put like that. And he was the least silly person I've ever met. Well, it's been nice talking to you, Mrs Kaufmann, but if you'll excuse me, I have a train to catch and I really must pay my respects to Roddy's mother before I go.'

Lieutenant Milton moved away to join the queue of people waiting to offer their condolences to Aunt Eloise. Shy and reticent he remained, but he'd changed nonetheless: there was a quiet self-reliance about him that she didn't remember from before.

Dorothea suddenly realized that she'd not yet spoken with old Lady Fitzwilliam, who'd always been kindness itself, and she turned to look for her. She found her way blocked. Mrs Adnitt was there, dour in black.

Dorothea began to say, 'Hello, Mrs—'

The words died on her lips. Mrs Adnitt leaned forward until her face was only inches away, then she hissed, 'Hun-lover! Traitress!'

21

It happened in the blink of an eye. One moment Mrs Adnitt was there. The next she'd gone. Dorothea was left reeling.

She was used, after two long years, to being singled out. She was used to hostility, whether veiled or otherwise. She'd been aware even today of people watching her, of looks cast in her direction both calculating and unfriendly. Colonel Harding had made it particularly obvious as they filed out of church, deliberately turning his back on her. But this was different. It was different, seeing the hatred burning in Mrs Adnitt's eyes and her lips twisted with loathing, the hissed words dripping with poison. That it should happen here, in Hayton — that it should happen today of all days, Roderick's day — made it all the more hurtful. And yet no one seemed to have noticed.

Dorothea was aware of her legs buckling. She was sure she would fall. She felt terribly alone.

Suddenly, there was someone beside her, an arm holding her up. A voice said, 'Dearest Dorothea! Roderick would be so glad you're here!'

It was Rosa. She was talking very loudly, as if making an announcement.

'Roderick was always so proud of you. He often said as much.' In an undertone, Rosa added, 'Take no notice of that spiteful old witch. Don't give her the satisfaction,' before addressing the world at large again: 'The way you nurse our brave men, the way you nursed Roderick—'

'Oh, but I . . . I didn't . . .' stammered Dorothea. 'He was on a different ward, he—'

'This lot don't know that,' murmured Rosa. 'It was the same hospital, that's all that matters.' She wrinkled her nose. 'What a crowd of mealy-mouthed hypocrites! If Roderick were here, he'd be tearing strips off them, for the way they've treated you today. Come on. Let's get away.'

Rosa led Dorothea down to the lychgate, forging a way between people lingering on the path, staring them down defiantly. Her big, distended belly made her appear rather ungainly, but she did not seem in the least self-conscious. With her head held high, and dressed today in mourning, she was particularly striking; her olive skin and dark eyes, and a judicious touch of make-up, gave her almost an exotic look.

Dorothea began to recover from the first shock of her encounter with Mrs Adnitt. She was distressed by the trouble she was causing. 'Oh, Rosa! This is all wrong! I should be comforting *you*! He was your husband.'

'Never mind all that. I'm just glad it's over. We can wait for Mrs Brannan in the motor.'

* * *

They arrived back at Clifton. Aunt Eloise swept up the front steps; Eliza trailed after her. Dorothea waited for Rosa. As Rosa levered herself out of the car, she grimaced.

'What's wrong?' Dorothea took Rosa's arm as, earlier, in the churchyard, Rosa had taken hers.

'Nothing's wrong. I felt dizzy for a moment, that's all.' Nonetheless, Rosa allowed Dorothea to help her indoors.

'Are you sure you're all right?'

'My feet ache, my back aches — those pews are most uncomfortable. And I expect I stood around far too long after the service.'

'I'm sorry. I should have realized.'

'It's my own fault. I didn't think to go and sit down. Church has a sort of numbing effect, don't you find?'

'Oh, but it was a lovely service.'

'Pure hagiography. So pious. So false. There was nothing of Roderick in it.'

Rosa lowered herself onto the settee in the drawing room. Dorothea sat down next to her. She would rather have sat by the window, but it wouldn't have felt right to take a seat on the other side of the room when it was just the two of them.

As she set about taking off her hat, Dorothea was at a loss how to respond to Rosa's scathing words. Rosa often came across as irreverent and hard-headed; there was nothing soft or maternal about her, even when heavy with child. It almost seemed unfair that she should be the one with a daughter, and another child on the way.

Dorothea froze in the act of removing the last hat pin, as she realized where her thoughts had led her. It was horrible, unworthy, to be jealous of Rosa's good fortune — especially when Rosa had been so kind. Dorothea could only imagine that her encounter with Mrs Adnitt had shaken her more than she'd supposed: it had been the last thing she needed, after the intense emotions of the memorial service.

Rosa, oblivious, continued, 'It was all so sanctimonious, painting an image of perfection. I'd rather remember Roderick as he actually was — the man we knew. If it had been left up to me, I'd not have had a memorial service at all, but Mrs Brannan insisted.' Rosa took a deep breath, held it, then suddenly burst out, 'To sit in church, thanking God for his life — it was a farce! What about his death? Do we have God to thank for that, too?'

Rosa fell silent, staring distractedly at the decorated screen in front of the empty fireplace. She'd come across today as an aloof, almost lonely figure — all the more so as none of her friends or family were in attendance. Aunt Eloise was the one who'd attracted all the sympathy, the one around whom a crowd had gathered outside the church. But Roderick had meant more to Rosa than to anyone else: he had been her husband.

And now she was grieving for him. Her austere, almost savage remarks came out of this grief — although there might be some justice in what she'd said about the memorial service; there was reason to think Roderick might have agreed with her: he'd always scorned all humbug and sanctimony.

Turning her hat round and round in her hands, Dorothea tried to think of something she could say that might bridge what she thought of as the gap between her and Rosa. All that came to mind were some lines from an old hymn, the one about God moving in mysterious ways.

Behind a frowning providence
He hides a smiling face.

But Rosa would find no comfort in that.

In the end, it was Rosa who broke the silence, making an effort to shake off her reverie.

'What will you do now? Go back to nursing? They call you auxiliary nurses "VADs", don't they? "Voluntary Aid Detachments". It sounds like some sort of utensil. But that's how women are seen, how they're spoken of: as objects.'

Dorothea didn't quite know how to respond to this, so she said instead, 'I would have liked to go back to nursing.'

There was no question she'd be needed, with the Somme battle still raging. But she couldn't forget the matron's words during their last, difficult interview.

You have let me down very badly. I find your behaviour both dishonourable and inexcusable. I will make it my business to see that you never work in any hospital ever again.

'I would have liked to go back, but I rather think I've burned my bridges where nursing is concerned.'

'They won't have you? Such a waste! Your husband — is he still working as a doctor?'

'Yes, he's a doctor in the field, treating wounded soldiers.'

'It must be hard, being apart from him. Roderick and I, we also spent a lot of time apart. After we married, he had his last two terms at Oxford and then, no sooner did he graduate than the war broke out and he joined the army.' Rosa paused, as if choosing her words. 'Don't you feel, sometimes, that you'd prefer to be in Germany? At least you'd be nearer your husband.'

'I'd see very little of him, with him working away, so I'd not be much better off. Hamburg is my home, of course, and I'm bound to return sooner or later, but I'm not sure how welcome I'd be right now.'

'Yes, I see. I don't imagine the English are particularly popular at present.'

'That's what Johann was worried about, if I went back.'

'All the same, it couldn't be much worse than the way you're treated here.'

'Johann doesn't know that.'

'You've not told him?'

'He has enough to think about.'

'And so he imagines you are safe and well, whereas in fact — well, that ghastly woman — what is her name?'

'Mrs Adnitt. But — honestly, Rosa — not everyone is so unkind.'

'It only takes one or two people to make one's life a misery.' Rosa sighed. 'Oh, this war! It's like a nightmare from which one never wakes. And the longer it goes on, the less hope there seems of it ever ending — and all because the Germans . . .

'But I don't suppose you feel that way. And you're right not to. The Germans aren't to blame, not the ordinary Germans, living ordinary lives. They have no more say in their government's folly than we do in ours. The man who killed Roderick, he was simply obeying orders. It's the people who give the orders, they're the ones who are really to blame. I know this, I know it very well; I know it in my head, I know it in my heart. Yet I can't help but feel . . . bitter. I feel very bitter towards that man, the one who killed Roderick.' Growing heated, Rosa exclaimed, 'I hate this war! I hate it! I hate the way it's made me question everything, all my cherished beliefs. I used to think the world could be changed for the better, I was convinced of it. I used to believe in a brighter future. But now . . . I don't know what will become of us now. We can't go back, I know that much: we can't go back to the way we were.'

Dorothea didn't disagree with what Rosa was saying — most of it, anyway — but she thought it best to change the subject; as Nettie Thomson would have said, there was no point in torturing yourself.

'How are you feeling now? Are you still dizzy? Perhaps you'd like some tea.'

'No. No tea.' Rosa hoisted herself off the settee. 'I think I'll go and lie down.'

Watching Rosa make her ungainly way out of the room, Dorothea would have liked to believe that a new rapport had developed between them. If she'd never felt entirely at ease with Rosa, thought Dorothea, then that was a failing on her own part, she was sure of that; she would usually get on with anyone given time. As for any jealousy she might feel of Rosa as a mother — that was just silly. Childlessness, in her present circumstances, was more of a blessing than anything. She and Johann were both still young. There was plenty of time for children later.

At first glance, Rosa seemed an odd choice as Roderick's wife: unconventional, opinionated, she had opposing views to Roderick on all manner of subjects, and they'd often been at odds. Aunt Eloise, certainly, had hoped for a very different sort of daughter-in-law. But if Roderick had married any of the girls of whom his mother approved, he'd have got bored in no time. As he'd often said, Rosa kept him on his toes.

But Rosa was wrong to call the memorial service pious and false: Dorothea felt that, today of all days, it was Roderick's good side which ought to be at the fore. That was not to deny there'd been another side to him; Dorothea couldn't help thinking of Gerry Milton, and the letters Gerry had written to Roderick, and the single, solitary letter sent in reply. But undoubtedly the good had outweighed the bad. How else could he have inspired such loyalty in Milton? Nor was Milton the only one.

Dorothea's eyes came to rest on the bundle of papers heaped on the low table before her. Here was another reminder of Roderick, some of his personal effects that he'd left with a fellow subaltern before he went up the line that last time. They'd been sent on and had arrived, fittingly, that very morning. There was nothing very intimate, nothing unexpected: a silver cigarette case, some letters from home, a notebook.

Dorothea knelt by the table and turned the pages of the notebook. It was filled with jottings in Roderick's large, sloppy scrawl, mostly notes on the duties and responsibilities of an army lieutenant. The pains he'd taken in making the notes was telling. It was 'just like him' — as Gerry Milton might have said — to have wanted to make a success of his promotion; to be not just a good lieutenant but the best.

She looked at the pencilled jottings; she traced, with her finger, the curves of each rough-written word. Turning the last page of the notebook, she found tucked inside the back cover a loose leaf folded over. She opened it up. Written on it were several incomplete and disjointed sentences.

> *My dear Raynes —You probably won't remember me*
> *Dear Tommy: we seem to have lost touch*
> *Dear Raynes*
> *Dear Captain Raynes*
> *I thought I'd drop you a line*
> *I was thinking of you the other day*
> *— do you remember, Tommy, the legendary Cricket Cup semi-final against Conway's, in the summer term of 1908? That was quite a day. That was the best day of—*
> *I wish*

The last letter *h* trailed away across the page.

Dorothea furrowed her brow. Hadn't there been a boy called Raynes during Roderick's school days? He'd been rather an object of hero-worship, if she remembered correctly. Not that she'd taken much notice, especially when talk turned to cricket. Roderick had been passionate about cricket. She found it impossibly dull.

What had made Roderick want to write to Raynes after all this time? There was something out of character about the hesitation and uncertainty of the abortive openings, set down one after another and not crossed out. It made her doubt that the letter had ever got written, let alone sent.

She folded the paper and put it carefully back in the exact place where she'd found it.

* * *

She could not sleep. She sat in bed with the lamp on, going through the letters she'd received from Johann during their two years apart. They seemed very few, and they were all so crabbed and cautiously written, subject to the censor's heavy hand. Johann's words, his handwriting, the paper on which he'd written, each battered envelope: she examined every detail. As she did so, Johann took shape in her mind. The sound of his voice. The touch of his hand. His clear blue eyes. His shy yet discerning smile.

She put the letters aside. She reached for the picture on her bedside table. She looked at it in the dim lamplight, Johann with his blond hair swept into a side parting, his nose slightly snub, facing the camera with a steady gaze. How handsome he was! The most handsome man she had ever met. Also the kindest and the gentlest and the bravest, more honourable than anyone. And he'd chosen her, of all people: he'd chosen plain old Dorothea Ryan, who came from nothing and had nothing. How proud she was to be Frau Kaufmann! Let people say what they would, let a thousand Mrs Adnitts hiss their vitriol in chorus, she would never be ashamed to bear his name, never.

She raised the photograph to her lips and kissed it. Then she put it back on the bedside table, and turned out the light.

CHAPTER TWO

Dorothea, in the gardens, was sat on a bench beneath the pergola near the ornamental pond, trying to compose a long-overdue letter to Nettie Thomson in London. But where to begin?

It was a warm afternoon, but rather overcast. Roderick's dog, Hecate, lay at her feet. Her pen was poised to write but there was a phrase lodged in her head, distracting her. It was, perhaps, something the dear old vicar had said at the memorial service more than two weeks ago.

In the midst of life we are in death . . .

In the midst of life, death. And yet, thought Dorothea, in the midst of death, there was also life, for Rosa had given birth hard on the heels of the memorial service: Roderick's son was already a fortnight old. Aunt Eloise had wanted him named after his father. Rosa thought that morbid. The boy should not be so burdened. He was not a replacement for Roderick, but a person in his own right. She had decided to call him *Laurence*.

Aunt Eloise was most unhappy about the name. She was aggrieved, too, that Rosa resolutely refused to wear black. Also chalked up against Rosa's name was her temerity in smoking a cigarette from a packet Roderick had left behind on his last leave. To smoke one of Roderick's cigarettes was sacrilege. Aunt Eloise wanted everything of Roderick's preserved untouched. This had been spelled out to Rosa in no uncertain terms.

Eliza had been much upset by the furore over the cigarette. 'Why is Mama so horrible to Rosa all the time?'

But Dorothea could see both sides. 'They are very different people, with different ways of doing things. It will take time for them to get used to one another.'

'I have got used to Rosa. Why can't Mama? I like Rosa. Rosa talks to me. She *listens* to me. Mama treats me as if I am a child.'

Rosa had said something similar on the subject of Eliza. 'Mrs Brannan wants to wrap her in cotton wool. But if Eliza is ever to learn about life, she must be allowed to make her own mistakes.'

We are a house divided, Nettie.

(Dorothea framed the words of her letter, seeing them as they would appear on the page.)

We are each of us grieving — and grieving alone. Aunt Eloise keeps up appearances, as might be expected. Eliza mostly stays in her room. As for Rosa—

What could one say of Rosa? At first, she'd seemed to be coping remarkably well, but just lately there'd been a change. She complained of being tired all the time, she had no interest in anything; even the new baby seemed to bring her little joy.

'Mrs Roderick's not right,' Daisy had said with a shake of her head. 'She's not right at all.'

Poor Daisy! These last few weeks had been the straw which broke the camel's back.

'I used to like my work here, miss. This used to be a nice place to work. But now — I've had enough. I can't abide the big house no more.' She'd set her jaw, defiant. 'Zack

Hobson's asked me to marry him, and I've said yes. I don't care what me dad says, or anyone. I'm handing in me notice and I'm marrying Zack, and that's all there is to it.'

Aunt Eloise had sighed on hearing the news. Since the start of the war, servants had done nothing but leave. How many was it now? She'd quite lost count. The situation was becoming impossible.

> *Everything seems to fall on me, Nettie. I am needed here more than ever. I sometimes think that Clifton wouldn't go on at all, if I wasn't here.*

Dorothea put her hand to her mouth, yawning. It wasn't only Rosa who felt tired much of the time. Recently Dorothea had found it difficult to sleep. She looked back now with envy to the night she'd arrived, when she'd fallen into bed and slept undisturbed for hours. Ever since, her nights had been haunted by dreams of the hospital: of mud and blood and open wounds, of amputated limbs and broken bodies, of her aching feet at the end of every shift, of the agonizing screams of men having their dressings changed.

She shook her muzzy head. Brooding on it would get her nowhere. She had to be sensible, practical. At the very least, she could finish her letter.

But when she looked down, she found that she hadn't even started it. The paper was blank: she hadn't written a word.

She took a deep breath, gripped her pen. With an effort she wrote:

Clifton Park
Hayton
Northamptonshire
6th August 1916

Dear Nettie

There she stopped, staring at the date. The sixth of August. The sixth of August, already. Which meant she'd been back nearly a month. Tomorrow was Bank Holiday Monday. The Sunday before the bank holiday was traditionally the day of the village fête. Not this year. This year, the fête had been cancelled.

Dorothea had never known it happen before, but the fête committee — of which Aunt Eloise was an integral part — had been unanimous. The fête would not go ahead, as a mark of respect for Roderick, as a reflection of the general mood. With the war entering a third year, there was no place anymore for fun and frivolity, there was no time for such things; everyone was far too busy. The nation had to be kept on its feet. Food must be grown, coal must be cut; there was not a minute to lose. Army boots were desperately needed — uniforms too — in order to kit out an endless parade of new recruits: conscripts now, rather than volunteers. Guns were churned out in ever greater numbers. There were never enough bullets and shells.

Food, coal, shells, men: the war's greedy maw devoured them all.

A soft and muted whimpering interrupted Dorothea's increasingly fevered thoughts. She looked down at the dog by her feet. Hecate was stretched out flat, with her head resting between her front paws. She whimpered again, as Dorothea leaned down to stroke her.

'What is it, Hecate? What's wrong?'

'She's sickening for summat, Mrs Kaufmann.'

Dorothea looked up. Smith had appeared unnoticed. He came limping around the pond with a spade in his hand. He was a young man of twenty, assistant to the old gardener, Becket.

'She's been out of sorts all this week — longer,' Smith added.

'What is it, Jeff? It can't be old age. She's no more than ten.'

'It's as if—' Smith hesitated, eyes focused on the dog. 'It's as if she knows, Mrs Kaufmann. It's as if she knows her master won't be coming home no more.'

'Oh, Jeff! Do you really think so? But how could she?'

Watching Smith, in his oversize cap and grubby trousers, crouch down to fondle the dog's ears, Dorothea wondered if what he said might have a grain of truth in it. Roderick, she was sure, would have scorned the very idea. But Roderick had not always got things right. Roderick had thought he'd be coming home at the war's end.

'Poor thing.' Smith continued to fondle the dog's ears. 'Poor old thing.'

Hecate whined softly and feebly wagged her tail.

* * *

Bank Holiday Monday also happened to be little Katherine's second birthday. The day after, her father would have turned twenty-four.

'I had thought of sending him a cake,' said Aunt Eloise on the day itself.

Dorothea was alone with her aunt in the drawing room after lunch. She was reading the newspaper, the casualty lists. She always went through the names one by one. It seemed to her the least they deserved.

Bradford, Bradshaw, Bridges

The close-packed lines of print took up a whole page in the paper.

Collett, Colyer, Cooper

She wondered about them; who they'd been, what they'd been like, where they were from. She wondered who was mourning them.

Davies, Davies, Dugdale, Evans

It was five weeks now since the start of the great Somme battle, and still the long, long lists kept appearing. Colonel

Harding's bullishness on the day of Roderick's memorial service had so far proved groundless, just as Gerry Milton had predicted. The Hun was not on the run. There was no end in sight. Lately, in her more unguarded moments, Dorothea had found herself wondering if the war would *ever* end.

Dorothea looked up from the newspaper at her aunt's mention of the cake. Aunt Eloise, all in black, was standing at the French windows with her back to the room. She had been silent up until now.

'Roderick always enjoyed Cook's cakes and puddings. Greengage tart: that was his favourite. I wonder. Should we have greengage tart at dinner this evening? It's not too late to tell Cook. But . . . I don't know . . . perhaps it wouldn't be right.'

For Aunt Eloise to be so hesitant, so undecided, was unexpected, disconcerting. She'd been standing there, too, for some considerable time, simply staring out of the window, which was also out of character. Usually, she kept herself busy. The house — as she so often said — did not run itself. And even if she took a break from the endless routine, she would invariably be found reading or sewing.

Dorothea put the newspaper aside, sensing that her aunt had more to say. Aunt Eloise stood framed in the window, upright, immaculate. Her frock, with its narrow waist and flared skirt, its lace edging and bishop sleeves, was redolent of the fashions of twenty years ago, but nothing ever looked dated on Aunt Eloise. There was something timeless about her.

'I . . . I have been thinking about that girl. The way she behaved at the memorial service. So very distressed. Hysterical, even.'

'Do you mean Susie Carter, Aunt?'

'Yes . . . yes . . . the Hobson girl. Her name was Hobson, when she worked here. She married that young man — Carter — oh, it must be nearly two years ago now, not long after the war began. Quite a sudden marriage, it was. Very sudden.'

'Sudden, but not unexpected. Nibs set his cap at Susie long ago.'

'The marriage was very sudden,' Aunt Eloise repeated, almost as if she hadn't heard Dorothea. 'Not long before, there was a fight; they came to blows.'

'Who did?' asked Dorothea, confused.

'Roderick, of course, and the Carter boy.'

'Oh. I see. Well, I can't say I'm surprised. There never was any love lost between them. I've no idea how it all started, I could never get to the bottom of it, but they fought like cats and dogs when they were boys, and nothing I ever said made any difference.'

'But this wasn't when they were boys. This was two years ago, just before Hobson got married.'

'Two years ago? I'd have been here then, but I don't remember anything like that. How strange.' But there'd been other things on her mind in the summer of 1914, with war looming and a decision to make: whether or not to attempt the journey back to Hamburg.

Aunt Eloise continued, 'Carter laid an ambush. He set upon Roderick just outside the village, on the Welby Road. Roderick . . . he . . . he looked terrible. Cuts and bruises. A black eye.'

'Now you mention it, I think I do remember the black eye. He came off his horse, he said.'

'Not his horse. It was Carter. Carter did it. They . . . they fought over Hobson.' There was a slight pause, then Aunt Eloise added, 'Carter discovered that Roderick — that Hobson—' She left a deliberate silence, full of meaning.

'Roderick and . . . and Susie?' Dorothea felt sure she had misunderstood.

'Roderick told me himself,' said Aunt Eloise, 'on the day of the fight.' Slowly she turned to look at Dorothea. Her face — there was barely a wrinkle; she did not look her age — was expressionless. 'There is a child. It was born, I believe, rather early in the marriage.'

'Surely you don't think—'

But it was obvious this was exactly what Aunt Eloise was thinking. Dorothea gaped.

'Did Roderick — did he know?'

'I don't believe so. The child was never mentioned. Perhaps it never occurred to him. It never occurred to me, not until . . .' Aunt Eloise paused, as if pondering something. 'Perhaps it would be more accurate to say that I never *allowed* myself to think about it. But since the memorial service . . . well, if the child is Roderick's . . . his flesh and blood . . .'

'But that can't be right, Aunt. It *can't* be.'

'I must know the truth either way, Dorothea. I have to know.'

'And . . . and then what?'

'I should want to see the child, of course.'

Dorothea had a sudden vision, horribly real, of Aunt Eloise descending on the village and sweeping up to the Carters' front door. She saw her aunt and Susie Carter haggling over a squalling infant and engaged in a grotesque tug-of-war. Her blood ran cold when she thought of Nibs Carter, and what he might say or do.

Nibs was Hayton born and bred. Surly, some people called him, and sullen. He'd terrorized Dorothea when they first met as children — she'd found him scrumping apples in the orchard. Later, he'd worked for a time in the Clifton gardens. She'd got to know him and, yes, to like him. He could be blunt — rude — but you always knew where you stood with him. She liked to think that after all this time he had a grudging respect for her. It would only ever be grudging, because that was how he was. He worked, these days, as a labourer on a local farm.

A sense of panic gripped her. A direct confrontation between Nibs and Aunt Eloise was something to be avoided at all costs. So desperate was she to avoid it, she found herself promising to—

She was not sure quite what she'd promised. To go to Susie Carter. To ask about the child. But to what end? It was too late, however, to back out. Aunt Eloise was already leaving the room; she seemed to think it was all decided.

Dorothea couldn't sit still. She jumped up and walked back and forth, she looked out of the window. She saw a peaceful, sunny, summer afternoon. But Clifton seemed to be under a cloud. A terrible weight of responsibility was bearing down on her, and there was no one she could turn to for help. Johann was too far away, Eliza too much of a child, and it would hardly be seemly to talk to Rosa of her own husband's infidelity. (The child was — how old? Not old enough to have been conceived before Roderick's marriage. Did Rosa know or suspect anything of this? But there was nothing to know! Of course there wasn't! It was all a misunderstanding — wasn't it?)

If only Nettie Thomson wasn't so far away! Nettie had been such a comfort in recent months. But Nettie was in London, and the letter Dorothea had begun on Sunday lay on her dressing table upstairs, unfinished and unsent.

Dorothea could see no way out. She had to do this, she had to discover the truth. And she had to do it alone.

* * *

Dorothea, at the edge of the village, turned off the Lawham Road and walked briskly down Back Lane, which ran for some way between leafy hedgerows. On one side was Seed Meadow, now cropped of hay, on the other Square Field awaiting the harvest. Where the hedgerows ended and the lane began to curve to the left, the first buildings appeared: small stone cottages on both sides of the road, workmen's cottages, two-up, two-down. In the first of these on the right, the Carters lived.

Dorothea slowed, stopped. Fresh doubts assailed her. What if Aunt Eloise was mistaken? She must be mistaken. But Dorothea knew that her aunt would not rest until she was sure one way or the other. There was no point delaying; it was best to get it over with.

Nonetheless, Dorothea hesitated a moment longer, looking all round. The lane was empty, not a soul in sight. She was glad of it. She felt as if she was about to commit a crime, and she didn't want any witnesses.

She forced herself to go on.

There was a little garden, long neglected, in front of the Carters' cottage. An uneven path led up to the front door. On the doorstep, Dorothea hesitated one last time, looked guiltily over her shoulder. The lane was still empty, the morning warm and bright, but away beyond Rookery Hill clouds were massing.

Taking a deep breath, she rapped on the door, then waited. Muffled noises came from within, so she knew there was someone home. After what seemed a very long time, the door abruptly opened. Susie Carter stood there, barefoot, in a threadbare dress. Strands of mousey hair hung limp over her face.

'Hello, Susie.'

'Oh. It's you, Miss Dorothea. I thought you'd gone back to London.'

'No. I'm still here. May I come in?'

'If you want. But I've washing to do and I must get on.'

Dorothea closed the front door and followed Susie into the back room. Here there was an old stove, some cupboards, a few shelves with pots and pans, and a big sturdy table with half a dozen dilapidated stools tucked under it. Water was boiling in a copper, puffs of steam escaping from under the lid. Washing was piled on the table. On the flagstone floor was a deep wooden tub full of soapy water. Next to it was a tin bath for rinsing, and a pail of cold water. The back door was wide open but even so the air in the room was hot and sticky.

Susie went straight back to what she'd obviously been doing, manhandling a tall, roughly made dolly with her red, swollen hands, grinding away at washing in the tub.

'What a lot of washing!' Dorothea winced at her words. So false — just like her reason for being here.

Susie appeared not to notice. 'I take in washing to earn a few pennies. Lucky for me there's folk in the village too proud to do their own laundry. Not that I'm ever short of washing on my own account. There's me and Jake and Nibs, there's Ned and Dixie too, and I still do Clover's things, even though she's not here no more.'

'Clover's moved out?' Dorothea seized on this piece of news, shying away from her errand. 'I didn't know that. Where has she gone?'

Susie was panting as she strained at the dolly. 'Clover got took on at the Grange by Lady Fitzwilliam. More fool her ladyship! I can't see as Clover will be much of a kitchen maid. Thinks she's Lady Muck, does Clover. Likes to be waited on hand and foot.'

Clover, and her twin brother Dixon (Dixie), were the youngest of Nibs's siblings. Dorothea racked her brain for something she could say about Clover, to keep the conversation going, but nothing came to mind. She felt she was trespassing here. And, to add to her discomfort, she had noticed as soon as she entered the room a child sat on the flagstones in one corner playing with some pebbles: a barefooted boy about eighteen months old, dressed in a faded shirt, and trousers too short for him with string for braces. She was mortified to catch herself inspecting the child, searching for any resemblance to Roderick. There was nothing. The boy was like his mother, with a round face and mousey hair. Despite his chubby cheeks, he looked rather pasty and his nose was running.

Up until now, the child had been quiet, engrossed in his game, but he seemed suddenly to sense that he was being watched. Studiously ignoring Dorothea, he picked up two of the largest pebbles and began to bang them together, chanting in a loud voice, 'Aye-ee, aye-ee, aye-ee, aye-ee!'

Susie snapped, 'Stop that, Jakey!'

The boy wrinkled his nose and then, with a flash of anger, he threw the pebbles across the room as hard as he could. A shiver went up Dorothea's spine: for a split second, the boy had looked exactly like Roderick in one of his tempers, fierce and impatient with blazing eyes.

The moment passed almost at once. Dorothea began to doubt what she'd seen. She'd been shaken by it, nonetheless.

Anger drained from the boy's face and he raised his arms, entreating. 'Mummy! Mummy!'

'Shush, Jakey. Stop whittling. Mummy's busy.'

'Is he Roderick's child, Susie?'

The question seemed to come out of nowhere. Dorothea almost looked round to see who had spoken; the voice was not hers. It couldn't be.

There was a sudden, yawning silence; they were all frozen in place. Then the boy began to whimper, and the spell was broken. Dorothea was appalled. All her careful plans, to work up to the question diplomatically — all her plans were in tatters. She dared not look at Susie.

All three of them spoke at once.

'What did you want to go and ask me that for?'

'Oh, Susie! I'm sorry! I'm so sorry!'

'Mummy, Mummy, Mum-meee! Aye-ee, aye-ee, aye-ee!' Jake's whimper rapidly rose to a wail.

Susie raised her voice so she could be heard above the noise. She said sharply, 'Who is it, then? Who's been tattling about me?'

'No one, Susie. Please forgive me. It was a terrible thing to ask.'

'Someone must have said summat.'

'It's just that Aunt Eloise—'

'Mrs Brannan? What's *she* got to do with it?'

'Aunt Eloise has got it into her head . . . She saw you at the memorial service . . . But it's silly, a silly idea. She's made a mistake, that's all.'

Dorothea experienced a rush of relief, absolutely convinced now that Aunt Eloise had got it wrong.

Susie was standing with her hands on her hips. She eyed Dorothea defiantly. 'There int no mistake. Jake is Master Roderick's.'

'Susie! Oh, Susie! But are you . . . are you sure . . . are you quite sure?'

'Well, of course I'm sure!'

'But how can you be? I don't understand! What about Nibs?'

'If yer asking whether Nibs knows, if that's what yer asking, well, yes, he knows. Oh, he knows, all right.'

They faced each other, Dorothea at a loss for words, Susie too it seemed. Dorothea was only dimly aware of her surroundings: of Jake on the floor gaping up at them, of steam puffing out from under the lid of the copper, of the trees outside rustling in a sudden gusting breeze. Her mind was struggling to make sense of what she'd just heard.

At length, Susie looked away. She began toying with the handle of the dolly. Neither angry nor defiant now, but entirely passive, she said, 'Nibs knew it weren't his child I were carrying, he always knew that. He asked me whose it was, went on at me till I couldn't stick it no more, so I told him.' She faltered. 'I'd never seen him in such a state. I thought he'd kill me. He dint. He went after Master Roderick instead. He tried to kill Master Roderick.'

The fight on the Welby Road two years ago. So it really had happened; Aunt Eloise was right about that too.

The signs were obvious in retrospect. Dorothea remembered clearly the evening Roderick had come down to dinner with cuts and bruises and a black eye. The story he'd told — that Conquest had thrown him — was so unlikely, she couldn't understand why she'd ever believed it. Roderick would never have let a horse get the better of him, even so haughty an animal as Conquest. Dorothea could only imagine she'd been so wrapped up in her own affairs that her judgement had gone to pot.

Conquest had been taken away, requisitioned months ago, and Roderick was now dead. This was his legacy, this muddle and confusion.

'If . . . if Nibs really knew . . .' Dorothea hesitated, trying to pick the right words so as not to offend, but Susie butted in.

'If Nibs knew, why was he fool enough to marry me —
is that what yer want to know?'

'Oh, Susie, no—'

'He made out as he was saving my good name. Huh!
As if I've ever had a good name in Hayton! I'll tell you why
he married me. He wanted a skivvy. He wanted someone to
look after him — to look after his brothers and sister, and
all. The two eldest girls, Becky and Milly, they kept house to
start with, after their mam and dad both died, but then they
both got wed, and Becky moved away, and Milly got a kid of
her own, and that left Clover the only girl, and she's next to
useless. So Nibs fetched me in, Nibs married me. And don't
I wish as he never had! Miserable as sin, he is. And here's me
having to take in washing to make ends meet. A bed of roses,
I don't think!'

Susie wasn't being fair. Yes, Nibs could be dour,
Dorothea was only too aware of it; she knew, too, that he
rubbed people up the wrong way, and had a temper on him.
But there was no mistaking his feelings for Susie. He'd been
'stuck' on Susie for years. He'd persisted with it even when
Susie blew repeatedly hot and cold. Nibs held firm to the
things he believed in.

'Now, Susie, you know that Nibs isn't all bad, and I'm
sure he's done his best for you, for Jake too.'

'But I don't love him. I never loved him. I never loved
him the way I loved Master Roderick. I always loved Master
Roderick. Loved him straight off, my first day at the big
house. I was only a kid, just thirteen. Master Roderick was
so much older. He never even looked at me. Then summat
changed. That hot summer we had, the summer before he
went off to college: that's when things changed.'

'But that was years ago, Susie!'

'Five year since. I weren't yet seventeen. I'd never been
with a boy. I never had, neither, whatever folk might say —
and I know what they say, the way they tittle-tattle about me.
It's all lies. I've only ever been with Master Roderick, and
with Nibs. And Master Roderick was me first. Oh, I know

what you're thinking. But I weren't as green as all that. I knew nothing could come of it. I knew Master Roderick dint love me. I weren't the first girl he'd had, neither. He never let on, but I could tell. I used to think he'd go off me, the way he must have gone off them others. I used to think he'd forget all about me, him being away at his studies so much. But every time he come home, we started up again. I think he had a taste for me. He had a real taste for me.'

Susie seemed almost glad of this opportunity to say all this, to tell someone all about it. Perhaps it afforded her a sense of relief more than anything, getting it off her chest.

Dorothea was astounded. She told herself that Susie must be lying. But Susie had no reason to lie. That was just clutching at straws.

It seemed to Dorothea incredible: all that going on, Susie and Roderick, right under her nose, and she'd never even noticed! Why had she never noticed? She'd not moved to Hamburg until a year later, if Susie was telling the truth — a year after it began.

Dorothea suddenly heard in her head, clear as a bell, Gerry Milton's words on the day of Roderick's memorial service: *I'm not sure that anyone really knew him — knew all of him, I mean.*

A truism, she'd thought. The sort of thing people always said on such occasions. She ought to have realized how accurate a description it was.

'Everything changed when *she* came,' added Susie, and Dorothea, jolted out of her train of thought, said, 'She? Rosa?'

'He ought never to have wed her. She weren't right for him.'

'But he would never have married you — you said as much yourself.'

Hearing her own words, Dorothea was mortified by how callous they sounded — yet that didn't make them any less true.

'He might a-done,' said Susie, obstinate, and contradicting what she'd said earlier. 'He might have wed me, if *she'd* not put the screws on him. She got her baby on purpose, that's what she did. She got her baby on purpose, to trap him.'

'Rosa wouldn't do that, she's not like that!'

'She weren't good to him like I was. He told me that himself. She weren't affectionate with him, because of the baby growing inside her. He needed some loving, so he came to me.'

'Do you mean . . . ?'

Shocked, Dorothea wanted not to believe it, but she knew it must be true: Jake was living proof, for he couldn't be much more than eighteen months old.

'He was married, Susie. Roderick was married. Oh, how could you, when he was married? Had you no self-respect?'

Susie glared at her defiantly. 'I'd a-done anything for him, anything. I loved him.' She paused, looked almost triumphant, but then her face slowly crumpled and tears brimmed in her eyes. 'He was so tall and strong and nice-looking. I loved him more than anything. And now . . . now he's gone. He's gone, and I'll never see him no more, not never!'

Susie sobbed, her tears beginning to fall, and Dorothea felt suddenly contrite — for speaking so sharply, for doubting Susie's word. Where was her compassion? And people called Susie hard-nosed and unfeeling! How little they knew. How little anyone really knew of anyone else.

Jake, on the floor, was watching his mother closely. He began to cry too (he at least had some sympathy). Before long, he began to wail.

Dorothea was galvanized by this sudden crisis, but before she could do anything a sudden gust of wind blew a flurry of rain in through the back door.

Susie threw up her hands. 'Now look! It's pouring, and I've me washing out.'

This emergency trumped all others. Susie dashed outside, Dorothea hot on her heels. In the small back garden, sheets, pillow cases and clothes of every description were draped over several washing lines slung from hedge to hedge, or else from hooks in the cottage wall, and all hoisted high on wooden props. The sky had clouded over completely whilst Dorothea was talking with Susie; the rain looked set to continue for some time. Dorothea got to work, helping Susie gather the washing.

As they ran back and forth, little Jake used his arms as levers to push himself into a standing position and he tried to follow them into the garden. He didn't like the rain, however, and retreated to the doorway. Susie, staggering in with an armful of clothes, nearly sent him flying.

'Get out from under me feet, Jakey!'

Dorothea dumped another bundle of clothes onto the table and then scooped Jake up out of the way, just as Susie came dashing in with the last of the sheets. Dorothea pushed the door to with her foot.

Jake weighed less than she'd expected. He wriggled in her arms, frowning up at her. She found herself, once again, looking for any resemblance to Roderick. Had she imagined it, that fleeting glimpse earlier? She rather felt she had. But whether Jake looked like his father or not, he was Roderick's child: there seemed little doubt of that.

Dorothea managed a shy smile. Why she should be shy of a boy of eighteen months, she could not say. Jake stopped wriggling and a look of puzzlement came over his face.

Susie was spreading the half-dry washing all around the back room of the cottage. Dorothea said to her, 'Did Roderick know about Jake?'

Susie didn't pause in her work, calm again now, and detached. 'I told Master Roderick I might be in trouble. I'd missed my time, and I'm always regular. "It might be anything," says he, "you can't be sure." But I knew. I could feel it, somehow. "Let this be a warning to us," says he. "We've had our fun, but now it's over." "It don't have to be over," I says, "it don't have to end." But he wouldn't have it. "I've a wife, Susie, and a child on the way. I have to think of them now." He dint have no choice, see? She'd got him where she wanted him.'

'And did he ever . . . meet Jake?'

Susie shook her head. 'Jake were born March following. Master Roderick had gone in the army by then.' Gathering up some more of the half-dry washing, Susie continued, 'When he were sent home wounded, I went up the big house to see him, but Mrs Brannan were there like a guard dog, and Nibs followed me up and fetched me away. Nibs said afterwards that if Master Roderick so much as looked at Jake, he'd be sorry he had. He'd wish the Germans had got to him first, by the time Nibs had finished with him. I've not been near the big house since.'

Susie went into the other room. Dorothea cradled Jake in her arms. She realized now that Roderick had told his mother some of the truth, but not the whole truth. He'd told her about his liaison with Susie, but he'd not mentioned the baby. He must have known he was Jake's father, but he'd done nothing about it. Had he washed his hands of his son altogether? Some would say Roderick was more than capable of it, but Dorothea wasn't so sure. Perhaps he'd thought about Jake. Perhaps it had weighed on his conscience. The pity of it was, she would never know.

Dorothea hadn't forgotten her promise to Aunt Eloise. She felt brave enough to face up to it, now that Susie wasn't with her in the room. Taking a deep breath, she called out, 'Would you mind very much, Susie, if I took Jake up to Clifton for an hour or so?'

There was a sudden silence in which her words seemed to echo through the tiny cottage. Then, slowly — almost reluctantly, it seemed — Susie reappeared, framed in the doorway between the rooms. She looked at Dorothea with suspicion. 'Take him to the big house? What for? Why would you wanna do that?'

'Aunt Eloise — Mrs Brannan — now that she's pieced it all together, now that she's realized that Jake is Roddy's child, she would like to see him.'

Susie's expression hardened. 'Oh, she would, would she? And why should I let her? What's she ever done for me?

Seven years I slaved up the big house, and never a smile, never a look, did I get from her. She thought I were trash, did Mrs High-and-Mighty Brannan. They all thought I were trash, Bossy Bourne and the rest of 'em, looking down their noses.'

'Oh, Susie, I'm sure they didn't. I know I never did.'

'No, miss, you dint. But you had yer favourites, all the same.'

This barb stung. It stung all the more because Dorothea had to admit there was some truth in it. Susie had never exactly been the easiest person to get on with.

But that was no excuse, Dorothea chided herself.

Susie grew almost wistful for a moment. 'I do miss it sometimes, working up the big house. Nibs says I were no better than a slave, but it weren't all bad. Me and Sally Kirkham, we had some larks! She were a right one, Sally — clever too. Old Bossy Bourne were always trying to catch us out. She put pennies under the carpets or down the back of the chairs to see if we'd find 'em and hand 'em in. She used to inspect the dirt we swept. Sally were wise to it all. She could sniff out them pennies like nobody's business. And she learned me how to save some dirt from one day to the next, so I'd always have some to show if ever I skimped. Oh, she were a clever one, that Sally, right clever.'

'I never knew anything about that,' said Dorothea wonderingly. 'About the dirt, I mean, and the pennies. Nobody ever told me.'

'Why would they, miss? Yer not one of us. Yer one of *them*.' Susie shrugged, dismissive, then crossed to the table, gathering up the last of the washing; but her mind was obviously elsewhere and she paused, staring at the steaming copper. 'Sally came to see me afore she went away. Told me about the factory where she were going, the money she'd be earning, making bombs and whatnot. I'd half a mind to go with her. But—' Susie slowly turned and her eyes came to rest on Jake, cradled in Dorothea's arms. 'I couldn't leave him behind. And I couldn't have took him with me.' She met Dorothea's gaze, hugging her armful of washing, and once again her expression hardened. 'I know what you think of me. I can see it on yer face. I int ashamed. I int ashamed of loving Master Roderick. I int ashamed of wanting something better. So you can think what yer like. It's no skin off my nose.'

'Oh, Susie, I would never . . . I don't . . .'

Susie was silent for a moment, and impassive, observing Dorothea's embarrassment, then she said rather harshly, 'Your trouble, miss — yer too soft, too soft by half. You want the whole world to get on together, you want to be everyone's friend, but that int the way things work, and you can't change it just by wishing.'

Susie's voice, by the time she had finished speaking, had softened, tinged with something almost like pity. She didn't wait for a reply but took the last of the washing into the next room.

Dorothea suddenly felt very tired. Why had she come here? She wasn't wanted; she was doing no good. There'd been a time when she prided herself on bringing people together but these days she found herself, more and more, having to take sides. If you were for England, you had to be against Germany; if you refused to condemn Germany, then you betrayed England. And so it went on, for or against, for or against.

She was tempted just to leave. But she'd made a promise to Aunt Eloise, and she couldn't back out now. She stayed where she was, waiting, Jake now quiescent in her arms.

When Susie finally came back from the other room, Dorothea made one last appeal. 'Please, Susie. Will you let me take him? You can understand why Aunt Eloise wants to see him. He's Roddy's child, and Roddy is gone.'

Dorothea half expected to be met with a blank refusal. Instead, Susie seemed caught in two minds.

'She . . . she won't want to keep him or nothing, will she? She won't take him away, and say I'm not fit?'

'Jake belongs with you, Susie. I'll bring him straight back, I give you my word. Whilst we're gone, you can finish your washing, without him under your feet.'

Susie looked at Dorothea, looked at Jake, looked away. She pushed her lank hair off her face. Then — brief, abrupt — she nodded, before disappearing once more into the other room.

* * *

Dorothea found Aunt Eloise in the parlour, the room Roderick used to call 'Mother's Lair'. Aunt Eloise was sat at her bureau, but did not appear to be working. Dorothea set the child on his feet. He clung to her skirts, a scrap of skin and bone in tattered clothes, with bare feet and a snotty nose.

'Here he is, Aunt. Here's Jake Carter. I . . . I'll wait next door.' Dorothea had to prise the tiny fingers away from her skirt.

In the breakfast room, Dorothea walked round and round the oval-shaped satinwood table. She tried to tell herself she'd done no harm, but she couldn't help feeling she was in the wrong. She'd twisted Susie's arm, she'd stolen Jake away, and for what? What good would it do Aunt Eloise to see the child?

Time was ticking on. She had to get the boy back to his mother. It didn't help that it had taken much longer to reach Clifton than she'd expected. As she carried Jake down the Carters' garden path and out into the lane — the rain had turned to drizzle by then — she'd been hailed by a trumpeting voice.

'Miss Doppoppy! Miss Doppoppy!'

Mercy Bates had been lumbering and lolloping up the lane. They called her in the village 'the dibby girl'. She was not so much of girl these days. She was a hulking woman in her thirties, but she still had the mind of a child. Dorothea had known her for years. Said to have been fathered by one of the Cardwell brothers, both now dead, Mercy had lived for a long time with her two maiden aunts at the post office. When they passed on, she'd been taken in by another aunt, Mrs Atkin, the blacksmith's wife, and that was where she still lived.

Dorothea had always been a great favourite with Mercy.

'Heh-ro, Miss Doppoppy!'

'Hello, Mercy. What are you doing out in the rain? You should be indoors where it's dry.'

'Ha ha ha! Ha ha ha!' Mercy pointed. 'Is it yourn baby?'

'Jake's not a baby — are you, Jake? But you must know him, Mercy. He's Mrs Carter's little boy.'

Mercy shook her head. She peered at Jake. Jake turned his face away. Mercy shuffled this way and that, trying to get a good look at him, but Jake refused to meet her eye and he buried his face in Dorothea's shoulder.

'We have to go now, Mercy.'

It had taken precious time to effect a parting. In the end she'd had to be firm.

'I'll see you another day. Go and shelter from the rain now, there's a good girl.'

As she neared the Lawham Road, Dorothea had glanced back and seen Mercy still standing in the middle of the street in her shapeless frock, her shoulders slumped and a look of crushing disappointment on her face. Dorothea felt unutterably cruel. But what else could she do?

Halfway to Clifton, Jake had suddenly decided he wanted to walk. She'd soon seen that, on his unsteady legs, it would take them an age to get anywhere. She'd scooped him up once more. He'd protested loudly. All the way up the long, tree-lined drive, he'd squirmed and wriggled, until her arms were aching and the front of her summer coat was wet with his snot and spittle.

If Jake carried on in the same way when she came to take him back, she couldn't see that she'd ever get him home.

The parlour door opened. Aunt Eloise emerged, leading a very meek-looking Jake by the hand.

'Thank you, Dorothea.' Aunt Eloise hesitated in the doorway as she went back to the parlour. She looked round briefly. 'I know I can rely on you, Dorothea, if . . . if there's ever anything he needs . . . if there's ever anything. I know I can rely on you.' She went into the parlour and closed the door.

Dorothea looked down at the boy. She did her best to muster a smile. 'Let's get you home now, Jake.'

His face creased into a scowl. He bunched his little fists. Meek no longer, he said, 'No!' He puckered his mouth, defiant. 'No!'

Dorothea's heart sank.

* * *

She knocked on the Carters' front door, but it wasn't Susie who answered, it was Nibs.

He was twenty-six, lean and strong, if not particularly tall. He looked dusty and sweaty in his work clothes. His face was tanned from being so much out-of-doors. There was a faded white scar barely to be seen on his forehead. His mouth was a little lopsided, though it only really showed when he smiled. He was not smiling.

'What *you* doing with *him*?'

'I . . . I . . .' *I stole him away. I betrayed you.*

Susie appeared, elbowing her husband aside. 'Miss Dorothea took him whilst I finished the washing.'

Susie reached out to reclaim her son, but Nibs barred her way with his brawny arm. 'What's going on?'

'Not here, Nibs,' said Susie quietly. 'Not on the doorstep.'

After a second's pause, Nibs nodded curtly at Dorothea. 'Yer best come in, then.'

Dorothea entered the cottage, Jake still in her arms. The front room, with its bits of furniture and washing spread everywhere, seemed very small and cramped. Nibs filled the place with his brooding presence, somehow appeared taller, burlier, and menacing. His younger brother, Edmund (Ned), was also present, and he got to his feet as they came in. He had on a well-worn shirt and waistcoat. The frayed right cuff of his shirt was tucked up where his hand should have been, the hand he'd lost in a farming accident a number of years ago. A third brother, the youngest, Dixie, sloped away up the narrow stairs like a ghost.

Susie did her best to pour oil on troubled waters. 'Like I told yer, Nibs—'

Nibs cut her short. 'Yer lying. I allus know when yer lying.' He swung round to face Dorothea. 'Where you been with him?'

A small white lie might have saved the situation. Dorothea couldn't manage even this. But she didn't dare tell the truth either — not with Nibs looming over her.

He gave her a long, hard look. 'I know where yer been. Up the big house. That's where yer been. You took him up the big house. What did yer wanna go and take him there for?'

Dorothea quaked, unable to speak, certain he could see right through her.

His expression slowly darkened. He suddenly rounded on Susie. 'You! Yer gone and told her, ant yer. Yer bleeding well gone and told her. Who else yer told, whilst you was at it? All round the village, is it, that the lad's not mine? A right bleeding mug I'll look, taking on another chap's bastard!'

'What you on about, Nibs?' Ned stared at him, puzzled. 'You saying yer not Jake's dad? Who is, then?'

Nibs ignored him. Glaring at Susie, he snarled, 'Yer done this on purpose, to show me up. Yer a bitch.'

Ned thrust himself forward. 'Don't you go talking to Susie like that!'

'Mind yer own fucking business.' Nibs turned his rage on his brother. 'I'll speak to her however I bleeding well choose. You take care of yer own woman — oh, I were forgetting, yer int got one. Huh! Who'd have yer, a bleeding cripple?'

Ned flushed angrily and the brothers squared up to each other, eyeball to eyeball. Dorothea could feel Jake cringing against her; she tried to shelter his ears from the worst of the language.

It was Ned who stepped back. Frowning, he said, 'Why d'you have to be such a nasty bugger, Nibs?'

Jake chose this moment to make his presence felt; his voice swiftly rose to a deafening howl. The sound spurred

Susie into action. Ignoring everyone else, she took the boy from Dorothea and carried him, kicking and screaming, into the back room. Ned, after a moment, followed. He flung the door shut behind him.

Left alone with Nibs, Dorothea tried desperately to think of something to say. If she couldn't put things right all at once, she could at least make a start.

But the words wouldn't come. What was wrong with her?

Nibs prowled this way and that, like a caged animal. 'Look at the state of this place! Bleeding washing all over, so's a chap can't sit down.' But he was too worked up to have sat still for long. 'I'd like to get my hands on him, for what he did to her.' (*Him* was obviously Roderick: the way Nibs spat the word out made that clear.) 'But I can't touch him. He's dead. He's bleeding well dead. As for *her*—' He made a noise that was halfway between a groan and a growl. 'I wish to goodness I'd never clapped eyes on her.'

'Oh, Nibs! You don't mean that!'

'It's ote to do with you. You know ote about it — you know ote about *me*.'

'But you've got it wrong, Nibs. It wasn't Susie who told me about Jake. Aunt Eloise worked it out for herself.'

He swung round, ignoring the question of Susie's culpability and turning his fierce, dark eyes on Dorothea. 'Why'd you do it? Why'd you take *him* up *there*.' (This was a different *him*, the word this time drawn out and dwelt on, meaning Jake.)

'Surely you can see that Aunt Eloise—'

'He's mine. She can't have him.'

'She doesn't want—'

'You tell her that. Tell her from me.' He took a step towards her, fists raised.

She couldn't help but flinch. But though she'd been afraid for Ned just now, she wasn't afraid for herself. She knew Nibs would never hit a woman, least of all her. He'd said a moment ago that she knew nothing about him, but she knew enough.

He dropped his fists, as if he was aware of what she was thinking. His rage drained away. In a bleak voice, he said, 'Go. Get out. Just get out.' He turned away, dismissive, but almost at once wheeled round and burst out savagely, 'I thought you was different. Yer not. Yer as bad as the rest of 'em — all those bleeding toffs, sticking their noses in. Think you can do whatever you want, you lot. Think the likes of us don't count, 'cause we've got nothing, and you've got it all. You make me sick, the lot of yer.'

He bundled her to the front door.

'Get out me house, and don't bleeding well come back.'

He slammed the door in her face.

She felt hopeless and wretched as she made her way up Back Lane. She'd kept her promise to Aunt Eloise, but at what cost? Nibs would never forgive her. How angry he'd been, and how bitter! So cruel to Susie, and to poor Ned. And it was all Roderick's doing. Roderick had made this mess.

Men were all the same, Dorothea said to herself, growing angry. Men were impossible, intractable. There seemed to be something inside them that was always fighting against their better nature. Even Johann wasn't perfect.

But Johann didn't pretend to be. He had his faults, and he wasn't too proud to admit it.

'I am always so grumpy, *liebling*. I can't think why you put up with me.'

Oh, but he was such a dear! Far from being grumpy, he was the most even-tempered man she'd ever met: he only ever got annoyed with himself, never with her. He was the one and only person in the whole world she could entirely rely on. And it was at moments like this, when she was all at sea, that she missed him the most.

Why wasn't she with him? She was not wanted here. Mrs Adnitt, Colonel Harding, the matron at the hospital — they'd all made it plain. And now, even an old friend like Nibs had turned against her.

But would she have been any better off in Germany? After they were married, she and Johann, his family had welcomed her with open arms. But that was before the war, before Johann's cousin, Gerhard, was killed in action at Verdun (Johann had written to tell her). The French had killed Gerhard, but the French were allies of the English, and the English — what was it Johann's younger brother, Siegfried, used to say about the English? That England plotted to stifle the Reich, to encircle her with enemies. That England refused to accept Germany as a great nation. That Germany must stand up for herself.

'What stupid talk, Siggi!' Johann had chided him. 'Where do you get such ideas?'

Siegfried had laughed then, as if it was all a joke. It did not seem so funny now, two years into the war.

As she toiled along the Lawham Road, spots of rain in the air, Dorothea couldn't help thinking that the place she wanted to go back to could not be found in Germany, any more than it could be found in England. The place she wanted to go back to was the world as it had been before August 1914.

But that world had vanished beyond recall.

* * *

Alone in the morning room after breakfast, Dorothea braced herself to face the daily paper with all its grim news (the news was always grim), and the latest casualty lists. Gone were the days when she'd find the paper in pieces, having been pored and picked over by Rosa, Eliza, Aunt Eloise — Roderick too, when he'd been home. Gone were the days when the war was still fresh and of interest. No one bothered much with the paper now. Dorothea always found it in pristine condition.

Her eye was caught by the date on the front page: Saturday, the second of September. Two months since the beginning of the Battle of the Somme. Two months since Roderick's death. And it was three weeks already since she'd brought Jake Carter to Clifton for his one and only visit. Aunt Eloise had not spoken of him again, as if she considered the matter closed.

Dorothea wondered whether Rosa had any inkling of Roderick's infidelity. If she did, she gave no sign. But it wasn't always easy to guess what Rosa was thinking, and just lately she seemed strangely indifferent to much of what was going on around her.

The war, meanwhile — as the newspaper made clear — was spreading like a canker, contaminating one country after another. Roumania was the latest to be sucked in, taking the side of the Allies. Greece, the newspaper hinted, might well be next.

Dorothea sighed, listlessly turning the pages of the paper; as she did so, there was a soft tap on the door and a moment later the housemaid Johnson sidled into the room.

Dorothea was glad of the interruption. She put the paper aside. 'Hello, Tilda. Do you want me?'

'Beg pardon, ma'am. It's Smith, ma'am.' Tilda Johnson, who'd never known her as *Miss Dorothea*, always addressed her as *ma'am*. 'Smith wants you to go to him. It's important, he said.'

'Thank you, Tilda. I shall go at once.' Anything was preferable to the newspaper.

She found Jeff Smith in the stable yard; this was a rather melancholy place, now that all the horses had gone, the groom too. Hecate was at Smith's feet.

'Oh, Jeff! Is . . . is she . . . ?'

'I found her like this. She's dead, miss.'

'Oh, poor thing!'

'There weren't nothing I could do. She just faded away. Pining, she was.'

'I'm sure you did your best.' Tears sprang into Dorothea's eyes. 'We must make a grave for her. We can do it together. But first I have to tell the others.'

She went back into the house. All was still and quiet. The morning room was deserted, as she'd left it. There was no one in Aunt Eloise's parlour, nor in the library where Rosa could often be found. But as Dorothea began to climb the stairs, she heard voices up ahead. The voices grew louder: shrill, angry voices, shattering the peace of the house.

The voices were coming from Roderick's room, the room he'd shared with Rosa. The door was wide open. Dorothea looked in from the corridor.

She couldn't remember the last time she'd seen Roderick's room. Before she moved to Hamburg. Before Roderick was married.

Rosa had made some changes when she moved in. Dorothea knew this, because Aunt Eloise was still very much aggrieved about it: desecration, she called it. Seeing the room for herself, Dorothea could understand why. The walls were now orange and purple and emerald green. Much of the furniture had been brightly painted and daubed with swirls and dots and clumsy-looking patterns. It was all very . . . was *modern* the right word? Perhaps *bohemian* better described it — the sort of thing Roderick had always scoffed at. It was a wonder he'd put up with it. Then again, perhaps it wasn't really so surprising, knowing how contradictory he could be. In many ways entirely conventional, there'd also been a rebellious streak in him, and he'd liked sometimes to shock people, to shake things up. Was that why he'd accepted the 'desecration' of his room? Or was it his feelings for Rosa that had led him to embrace the changes? Never had the old truism about opposites attracting been so borne out as with Roderick and Rosa.

All these thoughts passed though Dorothea's mind in an instant, and were just as quickly forgotten as she took in what was happening. Rosa was grabbing armfuls of clothes out of the wardrobe and piling them on the bed, whilst Aunt Eloise tried to block her way.

'For the last time. Put those clothes back. Put them back where you found them. Put them back *at once*.'

'I don't see why I should. They're Roderick's things. Roderick doesn't need them now. It's a waste, leaving them to moulder, when there are people who could make use of them.'

Rosa dodged round Aunt Eloise and flung more clothes on the bed, before returning to the wardrobe.

'Everything must be left as it is!' cried Aunt Eloise sharply. 'Nothing must be changed. *Nothing.*'

'Why? Why, why, why? It won't bring him back!'

They were like different people, thought Dorothea: they had changed out of all recognition. Rosa, after weeks of lethargy, appeared to have worked herself into a sudden frenzy, whilst Aunt Eloise was raising her voice in a way that had never been known, that her aunt would normally have considered vulgar. As Rosa pushed past her mother-in-law with another bundle of clothes, Dorothea even grew afraid that they might come to blows. Nothing seemed impossible, the way they were acting.

Stepping into the room, Dorothea tried to come between them. 'Aunt . . . Rosa . . . please . . .'

They took no notice. Aunt Eloise — tall, unbending — faced Rosa, who clutched the clothes to her chest as if shielding herself, a gesture that Dorothea found oddly reminiscent of Susie Hobson on the day of the revelation about Jake. Neither woman gave any ground, and they were saying the most irrational, the most hurtful, things imaginable: *ranting* was the word that sprang into Dorothea's mind.

Aunt Eloise accused Rosa of being no sort of wife, of only marrying Roderick for his money, of being ready to abandon him and run off with 'the Russian' ('the Russian' — Mr Antipov — had been a friend of both Roderick and Rosa; they'd met him at Oxford).

Rosa answered none of these charges. She hit back instead. She said that Aunt Eloise was mean, malicious and spiteful; a frustrated old woman who manipulated everyone around her: she took advantage of Dorothea, squashed Eliza, had done her best to make Roderick selfish and spoilt — and she'd even murdered her own nephew. Oh yes, Rosa knew all about it, she'd heard the story in the village: how the poor, crippled boy had been locked in the attic and starved, all so that Mrs Brannan could get her hands on his inheritance — Clifton Park itself.

As Rosa grew ever more overwrought, Aunt Eloise seemed to go the other way, to recover at least some of her usual composure. She waved Rosa's tirade away as if she was swatting a fly. 'What nonsense! You are being hysterical.'

To Dorothea, it was like watching tumultuous waves crashing against a hard and impervious breakwater; but whilst Aunt Eloise stood firm, Rosa was now showing signs of crumbling, the force of her onslaught beginning to ebb.

'Roderick would never have allowed you to talk to me like this!' Rosa sobbed, clutching the bundle of clothes ever tighter.

Immensely superior, and as if looking down from a great height, Aunt Eloise seemed almost triumphant.

'You know nothing about what Roderick would have allowed. You know nothing about him at all. You? You were only ever his wife. He was my son . . . my . . . *son* . . .' Aunt Eloise's voice cracked, as if she too was about to crumble, but she gathered herself at once, and in tones so icy it sent a shiver up Dorothea's spine, she said, 'If you find it so disagreeable here, then I suggest you leave. It's not as if you are wanted.'

With that, Aunt Eloise swept from the room, Dorothea shrinking against the door to let her pass. Dazed by what she'd witnessed, Dorothea for a moment didn't realize what Rosa was doing. Focusing once more, she saw that Rosa had abandoned the bundle of clothes she'd been holding — had simply dropped them on the floor — and was now dragging out a large bag from under the double bed.

'Rosa! What are you doing?'

'What she said I should. I'm leaving. I can't stay here — not now.'

'But Aunt Eloise didn't mean it. She's upset — you both are. You both said things you shouldn't have. Please, Rosa, stop and think. Where would you go? What about the children?'

Rosa turned her tear-stained face towards Dorothea. Dorothea was jolted by the sight. Rosa looked stricken, vanquished — it was terrible to see in a woman usually so strong and self-assured.

'You don't understand. I'm not leaving because of Mrs Brannan. I'm leaving because of me. What use am I? What use am I to my children? There's nothing left. There's nothing inside me. Nothing at all.'

'Dearest Rosa, you are still in mourning—'

'It's worse than that, far worse. The children . . . I . . . I can't love them anymore. I've tried and I've tried, but I can't, I can't do it.' Rosa extended an unsteady hand, beseeching. 'Will . . . will you look after them for me?'

'Of course I will, I'll always—' Dorothea stopped herself: she was responding to Rosa's irrational behaviour, instead of talking sense. 'You can look after your children yourself, Rosa. This is your home, you belong here.'

'I don't. I don't and I never have. It was a mistake ever to have come. It was a mistake to have married Roderick. Roderick didn't love me.'

'Of course he did! How can you say that he didn't? You and Katherine, you meant the world to him.'

'I don't know. Perhaps you're right. Perhaps he did love me. He loved me despite himself.' Rosa wiped the tears off her cheeks, perfunctorily. 'He'd much rather have loved someone else — someone more suitable — someone like . . . like *you*.' Rosa's eyes grew wide. 'But he did love you, didn't he! He loved you all along — only he never knew it.'

'No!'

The very idea was absurd: Dorothea found it grotesque to think of Roderick having those sorts of feelings for her.

'You're mistaken. You're quite mistaken.'

'Am I?'

Dorothea took a step back. It seemed obvious now that Rosa had taken leave of her senses. There was no reasoning with her. But Aunt Eloise was no better. What had happened to everyone? It was like living in a madhouse.

Dorothea turned and stumbled from the room.

* * *

'Hello! Hello! Hello!'

The raucous voice, repeating the same word over and over, brought Dorothea back to herself; it was like surfacing from deep water. She slowly became aware that she was curled up in Nanny's chair in the nursery. The parrot, Polly, was eyeing her through the bars of the cage.

'Hello! Hello!'

How long had she been sat here, lost to the world? She couldn't even remember what she'd been thinking about — if she'd been thinking at all.

'Hello!'

'Oh, Polly! What a mess! But I expect you've seen it all before, you wise old thing!'

Polly had been a part of the nursery for as long as anyone could remember.

'Yes. You're quite right, Polly. I am being silly, hiding away up here. I can at least *try* to put things right.'

Dorothea got to her feet. First things first. Rosa must be stopped from running away in a moment of madness. How? Well, if Aunt Eloise could be persuaded to retract her words, that would help. Aunt Eloise was eminently sensible, a pillar of rectitude. She would surely see, looking back, that what had happened was wrong.

Dorothea hurried downstairs. She tapped gently on the parlour door and then went in, not waiting for an answer. She stopped dead. Aunt Eloise was on the sofa — not so much sitting as splayed there, as if she'd collapsed. And perhaps that wasn't far from the truth, for her face was grey and drawn, and she was breathing heavily, her bosom rising and falling. In Roderick's room she had seemed indomitable, strong as granite. Now she appeared spent, utterly defeated, as if that last effort had cost her everything.

This was so completely unexpected that Dorothea, for a moment, struggled to take it in.

Aunt Eloise raised a feeble hand. 'D-D-Dorothea . . .' Her voice was little more than a whisper.

'It's all right, Aunt, I'm here.'

Spurred into action, Dorothea found herself perfectly calm and proficient, the way she'd learned to be at the hospital. She pulled the cord to summon help. She made Aunt Eloise comfortable. She placed a pillow under her aunt's head. She pulled the cord again. No one came. Reluctant to leave her aunt too long on her own, she ran out of the parlour and across the breakfast room. In the hallway she bumped into Crompton, coming belatedly in answer to her summons.

'Oh, Crompton, it's Mrs Brannan. She's not well. Send for the doctor. Send for Dr Camborne.'

'At once, madam.'

As Crompton hurried away, Dorothea caught sight of Eliza, standing like a statue halfway up the first flight of stairs.

'Eliza. Please go and sit with your mother. I must find Mrs Bourne and the medicine chest.'

'No! No, I won't!'

'Eliza, please—'

'I heard them arguing, Mama and Rosa. I heard them shouting. Mama has gone mad, Rosa too. You are all mad. I hate you. I hate you all. I hate this place, as well. I hate Clifton, I hate it. I wish I was dead, like Roddy.'

She turned and fled up the stairs, leaving Dorothea dumbfounded in the hallway.

* * *

Later, after Dr Camborne had been and gone, after Aunt Eloise had been settled upstairs in bed, Dorothea went outside for a breath of air, standing on the front steps, listening to the breeze sighing in the cedar tree. Dr Camborne had been reassuring. Aunt Eloise's collapse did not appear to be a symptom of anything serious, merely the result of exhaustion and the effects of her bereavement (Dorothea had not mentioned the clash with Rosa). The doctor had ordered complete rest. He would call again tomorrow, to see how the patient was, and to prescribe a sleeping draught if necessary.

Dorothea had left Mrs Bourne to fuss over Aunt Eloise (if a woman as correct and ceremonious as Mrs Bourne could ever be said to fuss). Going to Rosa's room, she had found it empty, the bag gone. She had then knocked on Eliza's door. Eliza had told her to go away. Standing now on the front steps, Dorothea felt as bone-weary as if she'd just finished a long shift at the hospital.

She was about to go back inside, when she felt something touch her hand. Looking down, she thought for a moment it was Hecate. Then she remembered with a jolt that Hecate was dead. Hecate was dead, on top of everything else. This animal was Circe, one of Hecate's pups, now three years old.

Dorothea knelt to stroke and pet the eager animal. 'Hello, Circe. Hello, you lovely thing.'

Roderick had chosen the name. He had chosen which of Hecate's pups to keep. He had told her all this in one of his irregular but ebullient letters to Hamburg.

'Oh, Circe!' She smiled at the dog through sudden tears, and Circe, wagging her tail, licked Dorothea's face with a warm, wet tongue, wonderfully alive.

CHAPTER THREE

A letter came from Germany, but not addressed in Johann's hand. It had been forwarded, as usual, via Switzerland: the owner of the Gasthaus where she'd first met Johann, and where they'd later stayed during their honeymoon, kindly acted as a go-between in her correspondence with Germany. As she opened the envelope, she realized that the writing belonged to Dr Kaufmann, Johann's father. The letter was in English. In Hamburg, Dr Kaufmann had often spoken to her in English. 'It is good practice for me, I think.'

> *Dearest daughter,* she read. *My heart breaks as I write this letter. It is my sad and painful duty to tell you that our beloved Johann—*

Dorothea's eyes galloped across the page. She read faster and faster, skipping words, then whole phrases, picking out others.

> *. . . the English dropped a bomb on his field hospital . . . a bomb from a Flugzeug . . . no words can express how much I—*

The letter fell from her fingers. There were spots before her eyes, she felt dizzy, blood was throbbing in her ears. Dr Kaufmann . . . what he'd written . . . what he'd told her—

No. No. Johann couldn't have gone — he wouldn't. He wouldn't just leave her.

But how odd, she thought. How odd that Dr Kaufmann should write *Flugzeug* instead of *aeroplane*, when his English was so good. How odd to find this one fragment of German mixed in with all the English.

A bomb, she thought, from the air. Like the bombs dropped by the Zeppelins. They'd been back recently, the Zeppelins: they'd dropped bombs, rumour had it, on a town up north. 'An industrial town', the newspapers had described it circumspectly. Dorothea had wondered if it might be Bolton. Bolton was an industrial town. It had at least one mill — the mill where Ernest Grimshaw used to work. Ernest Grimshaw had been going home on leave when she met him. But that was a long time ago. He'd be back at the front by now — if he wasn't dead.

If he wasn't dead.

She clutched her head with both hands. Such a terrible pain! And it seemed so very bright in the morning room, unbearably bright. She shielded her eyes, looked down at the letter on the floor where it had fallen.

A Flugzeug, she thought. A bomb from the air.

Oh, but it was so unfair! It was so unfair of God! He'd taken Roderick. Why take Johann too? Why?

God made no answer.

Where was He?

St Adeline's, she thought. If God was anywhere, that was where He'd be.

She jumped to her feet. She hurried upstairs to fetch her coat, to put her boots on. The house seemed oddly deserted. It was as if everyone was hiding from her. But she didn't want to see anyone. How could she explain? How would she ever find the words?

A Flugzeug. A bomb from the air.

If only she could be rid of this headache! The pain was too much to bear! But she was going to St Adeline's. She'd find God there. God would explain. God would take away the pain.

As she hastened across the space of gravel in front of the house, she thought she heard someone calling her name. She didn't look back. She broke into a run. She took the path that led through the Pheasantry and out across the fields to the village.

* * *

Haltingly, she walked along the nave. The church was as silent as a sepulchre. Dim light seeped in through the stained-glass windows. Shadows were heaped in the recesses.

She stood at the altar rail and looked at the golden cross. She waited, shivering. How cold it was! But it was always cold in here. Even in high summer it was cold. (But summer was over. It was October now.) Once only had she known it warm, on the day of her wedding four years ago. Roderick had walked her up the aisle. And here, right here — on this very spot — Johann had been waiting for her. She remembered the sunlight glinting in his golden hair. She remembered how grave and handsome he'd looked, dressed in a frock coat, and with his tall hat in his hands.

Here. It had all happened here.

But it seemed like a dream, a fairy tale. This alone was real: the chill air, the shadows, the emptiness; a place of cold stone and dead wood, of trinkets, meaningless trinkets.

Footsteps echoed behind her; she thought at once of the genial vicar. Such a lovely old man. So friendly. So familiar. Ten years he'd been at Hayton. He, it was, who'd conducted Roderick's memorial service three months ago. And it was he who had married her to Johann in the summer of 1912. Surely she'd find some comfort in seeing him again, in knowing that some things didn't change in this changing world. The vicar would tell her where God was. The vicar would account for the Flugzeug, the bomb from the air.

She turned, eager, desperate, thankful—

But it wasn't him.

It wasn't him.

'You're not . . . you're . . . not . . .'

It was a man in a dog collar, yes. But a young man. A rather thin and pale man, who looked unsure of himself, who looked as if he knew nothing about anything.

He spoke. 'How do you do? I hope I'm not disturbing you. My name is—'

'I wanted Reverend . . . I wanted . . .'

'I'm afraid he's ill at the moment. I am standing in for him. I'm the new curate. My name is—'

'But I . . . I . . .' She stood wringing her hands, the disappointment threatening to crush her.

'Is something wrong? If there is anything I can do . . . ? I'm Owain Morgan.'

'I came to . . . to find God. To ask him why . . . why . . . God has taken everything. He's taken everything I had.'

'Everything? Are you quite sure?'

Sure? Was she sure? What manner of question was that?

She was rocked on her heels by sudden hatred: fierce, overpowering hatred. She hated this young man, who ought to have been the genial old vicar but wasn't. She hated this man more than she'd ever hated anyone.

Nothing remained now. *Everything* had changed in this changing world.

Choked with rage, she couldn't speak. She wanted to seize the golden cross and hit, hit, hit—

Shaking, and breathing heavily, she edged along the aisle, keeping her eyes on the man who shouldn't have been there. She had to get away before the rage took over — before it took over completely.

'Please,' he said, holding out a hand. 'If there's anything—'

She brushed past him. She broke into a run. If she ran fast enough — far enough — perhaps she would escape her hatred, her headache too.

She pushed open the heavy wooden door and took to her heels.

* * *

'Doro! Where have you been? We were so worried!'

Eliza was there in the hallway as Dorothea let herself in by the front door. Aunt Eloise was there too, holding the letter, the letter from Germany. (A Flugzeug. A bomb from the air.)

'My dear.' Aunt Eloise took her hands. 'I am so sorry. So very, very sorry.'

'Where have you *been*, Doro? Where have you been all this time?'

Running, running, running. She had outrun her headache, and her hatred too, but there was no escaping this, the letter from Germany and the news it contained, the news that was written on Aunt Eloise's face and on Eliza's, the news that was undisputedly real. There was no escaping it.

There was no escape.

He was dead, he was dead, he was dead.

* * *

The house lay under a pall. Roderick was gone. Rosa had fled. Hecate's body lay buried in the gardens awaiting a memorial stone. In the dining room, Aunt Eloise was gaunt all in black, Eliza was pinched and pale. The servants looked different too, as if they were worn down with care.

Crompton, serving lunch, stopped by Dorothea's chair. 'I'd just like to say, Mrs Kaufmann, on behalf of us all downstairs—'

'Yes, Crompton, yes.'

She ate her lunch, biting, chewing, swallowing, forcing herself to do what now seemed so pointless. Aunt Eloise, with immeasurable dignity, slowly spooned her soup. Eliza sat with her head bowed.

* * *

Dorothea looked at her reflection in the three-folded mirror on the dressing table in her room. She expected to see white hair, she expected to see wrinkles. She felt old, so very old. She saw instead black curls and smooth cheeks. She was only twenty-five. But age meant nothing, appearances meant nothing. Inside she was old. She would always be old now. She would never be young again.

She put her hand on the German letter to remind herself. A Flugzeug. A bomb from the air.

It dawned on her that the letter must have been opened and inspected before it was delivered. The censor would have read it. The censor would have read Dr Kaufmann's words, read them dispassionately, aloof. The censor had known of Johann's death before she did.

The thought of a stranger touching, opening, reading this letter made it seem sullied, unclean. She dropped it with a shudder.

* * *

The house was a mausoleum, a tomb. Any moment now, the last stone would be levered into place, sealing the entrance, cutting off all light and life forever. Dorothea grabbed her hat and coat. She ran downstairs. She made it just in time, just before the tomb was sealed. But once outside she stood beneath the cedar tree, at a loss. Where could she go, what could she do?

She walked in the gardens without purpose. Clouds swirled in the grey autumn sky. There was a blustery breeze. The ground was wet from recent rain. A slightly sunken place in the lawn near the mulberry tree was where Hecate was buried. Smith had dug the hole. He'd jumped in, to gently lift the body down, then afterwards he'd carefully covered it with earth and replaced the turf.

Did Johann have a grave? Where was it? Who had dug it?

Meaningless questions. To think of Johann, buried, it wasn't right.

She trailed along the cinder paths. The bee hives stood silent. Apples lay rotting in the long grass of the neglected orchard, plums too; they squelched under foot as she walked over them unheeding. Faded cabbages in the untidy vegetable garden had gone to seed. Runner-bean plants drooped dying on their poles. Behind the privet screen in one corner, withered vegetation had been piled high on the festering compost heap.

She did not linger in the gardens, lest she run into Smith or the aged gardener, Becket: Becket, who'd worked at Clifton for half a century. Becket was growing deaf. You had to raise your voice and repeat yourself. *He is dead. DEAD.* Words she did not want to say even once. Nor did she want Becket's pity or his condolences. She'd heard it all before. She'd heard it a hundred times, these last few days.

Days? Or — how long had it been? She'd lost all track of time.

She broke into a run, though she had no reason to hurry. She ran along the stony lane past Becket's cottage. The lane faded into a grass-grown bridleway across the fields to Brockmorton. But Dorothea turned aside, took a branching path to the right that climbed the long, green slopes of Rookery Hill.

Her steps slowed as she toiled to the very summit. A rising wind surged and seethed through the stand of poplars that stood tall against the leaden sky. The autumn landscape was spread below her. There was a man at work in the big field called Horselands, halfway between Clifton and the village. Sturdy great horses, which at this distance looked as tiny as children's toys, were pulling a plough, turning the rich, dark earth made heavy by rain.

But somewhere beyond the horizon, in the greedy fields of France and Flanders, it wasn't rain soaking into the soil, it was men's blood.

* * *

Walking. Walking again. Every day she went walking. This time, she was walking down Clifton's long drive that ran between lines of tall evergreens, and was disfigured by ruts and pot-holes full of water, and by weeds encroaching at the margins.

As she walked, she reasoned. There must be some mistake. Johann wasn't dead. He couldn't be. She'd know if he was dead. She'd *feel* it. So perhaps he'd merely been wounded by the bomb from the air. Or perhaps the bomb had fallen on an entirely different hospital. Any day now, she would receive a letter in Johann's neat, compact hand. He would explain the misunderstanding. He would tell her he had been alive the whole time.

Why had Dr Kaufmann written to her, why repeat such unfounded rumours, why be so cruel?

He would not be so cruel. Dear, kind Dr Kaufmann — who'd welcomed her as the daughter he'd never had — would not write such terrible words unless he knew them to be true.

But how had he found out? How had the news reached him? Had there been a knock on the door, a telegram? She pictured him, white-haired, with a white beard and whiskers, reading the telegram with his spectacles on the end of his nose, the way he read the newspaper every morning. And then—

What then? Her imagination failed her.

Her wavering feet slowed and stopped. She'd reached the end of the drive. She'd reached the end of her thoughts, too. There was no reason to go on, no reason to go back either. She stood where she was, numb and purposeless.

The drive opened out onto the Lawham Road. Left was the way to the village, which was hidden by a fold of the land. To the right, the road ran down towards the canal. There was no one in sight, no sound except the wind in the trees. She watched the branches tossing and swaying. Every so often, she caught a glimpse of something all but hidden in the thicket: the little round cottage called 'the Gatehouse', which she'd forgotten about until now. But how could she have forgotten? She'd always known it was there.

She thrust her way into the thicket, ducking under the low-hanging branches. The gamekeeper had once lived in the Gatehouse, but he was long gone, and the cottage stood forsaken now, shadowed by the overhanging trees, and with moss and ivy growing up the walls. The windows were broken. There were dead leaves and old birds' nests in the gutters. The little garden had ceased to be a garden, choked by trailing brambles and the withered remains of summer weeds, littered with fallen twigs and drifts of dead leaves.

Dorothea walked slowly round the deserted building, trailing her hand on the stonework. She peered through the jagged windows, saw nothing but darkness. She remembered her first sight of the place, years ago, just a few weeks after her arrival at Clifton. She'd been running away. She'd decided to go back to London and search for her papa. Needless to say, a penniless girl of eight, she'd not got very far. But though her plan had come to nothing, she'd not given up hope that one day she would see her papa again.

She'd clung to this idea for many years. In all that time, her papa had never come back, and she'd not been able to track him down. Bit by bit, all hope had died. It was sixteen years since he'd abandoned her at Clifton on a dark winter's night. She knew now that she would never see him again. He was gone for good, and she would never know what had become of him; he'd be forever a loose end, one of life's many unsolved mysteries.

So foolish — so futile — that fond hope of seeing him again. She had deluded herself; she'd wasted years on it. She would not make the same mistake twice. She would not allow herself to hope, when all hope was vain.

There was no muddle, no misunderstanding. Johann was dead.

Dead.

She turned away from the Gatehouse and began to retrace her steps. Rain started to fall. The rain was blown this way and that by the breeze. She barely noticed.

Inch by inch, with head bowed, she trudged up the drive.

* * *

Another day. How many now? She had lost count. It didn't matter.

Her booted feet waded through the leaf litter in Ingleby Wood, the only sound in a desolate silence. The odour of fallen leaves, and of the mould beneath, rose round her in the still air. Mist drifted amongst the trees. Some of the trees were bare already; on others fading foliage still clung, dull brown on the oaks, pallid yellow on the maples. Only the strangling ivy was still green, twisted round and round the tree trunks. Where there was no ivy, a brown fungus grew on the bark like congealed blood. Through the topmost branches, there was a glimpse of louring sky, grey and sombre.

Walking heedlessly, she tripped over an out-thrust root, stumbled a few paces trying to keep her balance, then came to a halt. Right at her feet, half-hidden in withered bracken, was the shrivelled corpse of a bird, a cock pheasant. It was a mass of matted feathers. The once proud colours were now drab and dull. Its legs were like sticks, the claws curled up. The beak was half-open, as if frozen in the act of taking a last, gasping breath. The eye sockets were empty.

She stood staring down at the meagre remains. This, then, was the fate of all life. To die and lie forgotten. To crumble into nothing.

She shivered suddenly all over. A breeze was getting up. The mist was swept away. Thrusting her ice-cold hands deeper into her pockets — she had forgotten to put on her gloves — she turned her back on the dead bird and went on at random, with no aim in mind. She shuddered every so often but she was barely aware of it, was barely aware that she was walking at all.

The breeze strengthened. It soughed through the tree-tops, filling the silence. She reached the wood's end. She struggled through an old, overgrown hedge, a tangle of brambles. The thorns snatched and tore at her. Doggedly, she kept going; she wrenched herself free and burst out into the open, and found herself by the canal. A bitter wind was whipping along the towpath. Withered leaves from the wood behind her whirled through the air, and were scattered across the rippled surface of the murky, grey-brown water. On the opposite bank was a long-disused and overgrown meadow that sloped gently up and away from the canal. At the top of the rise, half a mile distant or more, Clifton stood square and grey, a grim bastion of cold stone: austere, forbidding — yet diminished at this distance, when seen against the wide, leaden sky.

She turned her back on the biting wind. Huddled inside her coat, she trudged along the bleak towpath that followed the sweeping curves of the canal. Ingleby Wood was left behind; Clifton faded into the folds of the land. Hambury Hill drew ever nearer, hunched beneath torn and tattered clouds.

She came to Broadstone Tunnel, where the canal burrowed into the hillside. A brick-built arch framed the gaping entrance: a gateway to nothingness.

She turned hurriedly aside, toiled up the old track by which horses had once been led from one tunnel entrance to the other. As she reached the brow of the hill, the swirling clouds were suddenly rent asunder, unmasking for a fleeting moment the setting sun as it sank, slow and ponderous, towards the rim of the earth, big and round and orange and crimson, glowing intensely but giving no warmth; it stained the cloud-strewn sky with angry colours like dying embers. She stood unmoving as the gusting wind eddied round her, her layers of clothes no defence against its cold, searching fingers. The lurid sun shone out brightly for a moment, then the scudding clouds drew a veil over it, and the smouldering colours of the sky faded rapidly into a drab, grey dusk.

The old horse track continued across the broad hilltop, up and down over the long, flattened ridges of a windswept meadow. She followed it only a little way, then turned aside and climbed over a gate. She stumbled down the steep hillside, with the canal now somewhere away to her right. At the foot of the hill was a wide ploughed field. She went on without stopping.

Her boots were soon clogged with mud. They grew heavier and heavier, weighing her down. Every step became an effort, her skirts trailing in the mire. The wind was gusting full in her face. Her cheeks ached from it. And now snow began to fall out of the leaden sky. Clumsy-footed, heavy-legged, numb with cold, she plodded on like an unthinking beast of burden.

The snow grew to a whirling blizzard so that she was half-blinded by it. Everything seemed to be disintegrating around her, dissolving into chaos. Summer was forgotten, lost in the distant past. Autumn, in all its bitterness, had withered to an end. Now began the endless winter of the world. Spring would never come again.

* * *

She had the letter from Dr Kaufmann, and all the letters she'd received from Johann since August 1914, too few and too circumspect, written with half an eye on the censor. She had the photograph of him in the silver frame, another photograph in her purse of the two of them together. She had a silk scarf he'd bought her, and a brooch, and her wedding ring. And there was a picture postcard of the church of St Nicholas in Hamburg that he'd given her on the day she left for England. On the back he'd written: *To my darling wife. Enjoy your trip to England. Come back safe and sound. From your loving husband.*

She laid all these things on her bed. Her mementoes. Her memories. Sacred relics. More precious than gold. They had to be kept safe at all costs. If she perhaps had a box to put them in: that would help protect them. A wooden box with a lid, and a lock and a key. Might there be such a thing in the village shop? She would go and see. She would go right away.

A sudden sense of urgency gripped her. She threw on her outdoor clothes. In the doorway of her room, she hesitated, looking back. There were her sacred relics, spread out on the bed. Unprotected. At risk. She must fetch the box. She must fetch it without delay.

She ran downstairs and out by the front door. She was halfway across Horselands before it occurred to her that she should have told someone where she was going. Wasn't it nearly lunchtime; wouldn't they be looking for her? No. No. Lunch had come and gone — or was that yesterday she was thinking of?

She shook her head. The box. She must fetch the box.

She ran on, across ploughed Horselands, across Coney Close, across Row Meadow: silent, empty fields under a shroud of grey sky. As she neared the village, her eye was caught by the square tower of St Adeline's, with its grey stone battlements. She had not been to church since the day Dr Kaufmann's letter arrived. How many Sundays had passed since then?

She turned to her left and slowly opened the little side gate that led into the churchyard, almost as if she was being lured there against her will. She walked a few steps towards the church, then came to a halt. She couldn't bring herself to go in. What was the point? God was not there. God was nowhere. God had abandoned the unhappy world.

She lingered, looking round. Graves, graves, graves: graves on every side. Some standing straight, others leaning, a few fallen flat. She'd seen them often down the years. She must have read nearly every weathered inscription, at one time or another. But never until now had she truly understood what these stones represented.

So many dead. So many to mourn. So much sorrow.

She trailed slowly round the churchyard, looking at the headstones, touching them. Here was Uncle Albert's last resting place, with its plain and simple memorial. And this was Richard's grave: Richard Rycroft, Aunt Eloise's nephew and erstwhile heir to Clifton Park. The house and the estate had been held in trust for him until he came of age. But poor Richard had never made it to twenty-one.

Rosa, in September (it seemed like another world), had accused Aunt Eloise of locking Richard in the attic and starving him to death — something she'd picked up in the village, no doubt. Such lurid tales often did the rounds; there was seldom much truth in them, and this was no exception. Richard had not starved. Afflicted by a withered leg and fragile health, he'd succumbed to diphtheria at the age of fourteen.

Richard. One of her first friends at Clifton. Suffering with diphtheria herself at the time of his death, she'd not been well enough to attend his funeral. Once the worst of her illness was over, she'd wanted to see where he was buried. Just as today, she'd left the house without telling anyone and walked across the wintry fields. On this very spot, she'd lain down and rested her head on the newly turned earth; it had been hard as iron from the frost. A dozen years ago. A dozen years ago, almost to the day.

Panic gripped her. Almost to the day? Was it, then, December? Had she missed Richard's anniversary? She'd never missed his anniversary! Even in far-off Hamburg, she'd always lit a candle in memory of her dear friend.

But it couldn't be December — could it? Her mind groped, trying to count the days and weeks. But thinking of Hamburg had brought Johann back to the forefront of her mind. She'd come to the village with only one aim. She mustn't let herself be side-tracked.

She followed the main path and let herself out of the churchyard by the lychgate. She hurried across the green and into the shop. The bell jangled as she opened the door. It was gloomy inside on this gloomy day.

A man loomed up behind the counter, a man in his early forties, burly and thickset with flecks of grey in his beard. It was Mr Cheeseman. He was brother-in-law to the young shopkeeper, David Cardwell, who'd been killed the previous year at Loos, on the very same day Roderick was wounded.

Stony-faced, Mr Cheeseman said to her, 'Now just turn round and take yourself off.'

'But—' The wooden box. Her sacred relics.

'We don't want no Germ-Huns here,' he declared, 'and that includes you. Them Germ-Huns killed my boy. I won't serve 'em here.'

He was talking not of his brother-in-law, but of his son Johnnie. News of Johnnie's death had reached the village in August.

Dorothea was thrown into confusion. What did any of this have to do with her? All she wanted was a little wooden box with a lock and a key.

Before she could summon up the words to explain, a voice spoke out behind her.

'Now then, John Cheeseman. There's no call for that sort of talk.'

Dorothea had thought herself the only customer. She'd not heard anyone else come in. But here, large as life, was Mrs Turner, marching up to the counter. Mrs Turner was mother to the former housemaid, Daisy; Dorothea had known her for years. A plump, rosy-cheeked woman, she was much of an age with Aunt Eloise, but no two women could have been more different: one the mistress of Clifton Park, the other wife to a farm labourer and living in a two-up, two-down cottage on Back Lane.

Mrs Turner stood shoulder-to-shoulder with Dorothea. She said to the shopkeeper, 'Your boy's dead, John, and I'm sorry. Of course I'm sorry. He was my own blood. But you've no right to take it out on Mrs Kaufmann. You know very well that Mrs Kaufmann did everything she could to get Johnnie out of the army, after he went off to fight at fifteen. It's none of her fault if they never sent him back like they ought.'

'You mind your own business, Molly Turner. No one asked you to stick your nose in. It has ote to do with you.'

'Others have suffered, John, not just you.'

'Her, you mean,' said Cheeseman, glancing darkly at Dorothea. 'I've heard what she's been saying, but it's a filthy lie. The English don't drop bombs on hospitals. It's them Germ-Huns what do that. Any road, her old man, he only got what was coming — the dirty, rotten Germ-Hun.'

'Wait till our May hears about this!' Mrs Turner spoke sharply. 'She'll have summat to say about this performance, mark my words.'

'Always got summat to say, has May. Don't mean I have to listen. I'm her husband. I say what's what. And I want that Germ-Hun out this shop.'

'It's May's shop, if you want to be like that about it. It's May's, now that David's gone — and don't you forget it.' Mrs Turner turned her back on him. She took Dorothea's arm. 'Come, Mrs Kaufmann. We know when we're not wanted.'

Dorothea resisted for a moment. A box. A wooden box. Oh, but what did it matter? Her sacred relics, they were nothing but a few scraps of paper, a lifeless photograph or two. They wouldn't bring him back.

She yielded to Mrs Turner, allowed herself to be led, stumbling, out of the shop. Now that her quest had come to nothing, she had no purpose in life, and nowhere to go, and she wilted, her knees buckling.

'Sit you down a minute, dearie. You've gone white as a sheet.'

There was a bench on the green, beneath the bare and twisted branches of the sycamore; it was no more than a plank, nailed across two sawn sections of a tree trunk. They sat here side by side.

'I . . . I'm sorry. So sorry.'

'What's that, dearie? What are you sorry for?'

'Johnnie. I . . . I did my best.'

She'd written letters, canvassed support. But not everyone had applauded her efforts. Why shouldn't the lad fight for his country, some people said, if it was what he wanted? He might only be fifteen, but he was a shining example. What was it she hoped to achieve? Denuding the army of fine young fellows like Johnnie Cheeseman would only benefit the Germans. Ah, but wasn't she married to a German? Well, then. Well.

'I did my best.'

'Of course you did. There's no one could have done more. But the army wouldn't let him go. If anyone's to blame, it's John Cheeseman himself. He drove the boy away, being too hard on him. Always thrown his weight around, has John Cheeseman. Ask our Pippa, she'll tell you — and she's his own sister!'

Pippa, of course, was married to Mrs Turner's son, Jem, and thereby the Turner and Cheeseman families were connected. But also, the wife of the man in the shop, May, was somehow connected to Mrs Turner. A cousin, was she? Or — no — Mrs Turner's niece? Dorothea furrowed her brow, trying to remember. Time was, she could have drawn up family trees for half the village without stopping to think. Why was it suddenly so confusing? What was wrong with her?

She looked round in bewilderment, half expecting the green to have changed out of all recognition, because she felt so strange and out of place. But the green was the same as ever, a triangular space of grass with the sycamore midmost and an old well in one corner; the High Street was on one side, School Street led off at a right angle, and a path connecting the two formed the third side of the triangle, passing in front of a big, ivy-fronted house where the Miss Evanses lived, aging spinsters. It was as familiar to her as Clifton itself. For years, the village had been like a second home.

Home. What did *home* really mean?

She'd always thought of it as a particular place: Hamburg or Clifton or London (she'd lived in the East End as a little girl, her and her papa, in ever-worsening poverty). But as she sat here on the green, she suddenly realized that the old proverb had it right: *home is where the heart is*. And her heart was with Johann, always would be. Wherever Johann was, that was home. Now he'd gone, she had no home. There was no place on earth for her.

She looked across the High Street to the churchyard, where Uncle Albert was at rest, Richard too. She thought of the frosty day in December 1904, when she'd sought out Richard's grave and lain down on it. If only she could find Johann's grave, she would lie down there and never get up. She would lie there forever.

She remembered what it had been like to lie on Richard's grave all those years ago — the frost-hardened earth digging into her, the cold seeping into her body. In a strange coincidence, Mrs Turner had found her that day too, just as she'd happened to be in the shop a moment ago. Mrs Turner had raised her up off the frozen ground, had taken her hand, had led her to the Turners' little cottage. Dorothea remembered sitting in front of the fire drinking hot sweet tea, while Mrs Turner talked to her easily, friendlily — in exactly the same way as she was talking now while they sat here on this bench. Mrs Turner had always been kindness itself.

Dorothea suddenly felt guilty, for she'd not been listening at all; she'd barely heard a word of what Mrs Turner was saying. She did her best to pick up the threads.

It seemed that Mrs Turner was still talking about Johnnie Cheeseman.

'. . . Just sixteen years old, no more than a boy — it's a crying shame is what it is. And poor May, to have lost her son as well as her brother, somehow it don't seem fair.' Mrs Turner paused, as if she sensed that Dorothea was suddenly paying attention. 'How are you feeling, dearie? You don't look quite so peaky now. So pale, you were. I thought you was going to pass out.' Another pause; then, hesitantly, 'It's true what they're saying, then? It's true about your husband? Well, I *am* sorry. He weren't one of us, I know, but it's a wicked waste of a life whether or no.'

Dorothea had already realized, from what Mr Cheeseman had said in the shop, that the village knew about Johann's death. But she didn't want to talk about it — couldn't — felt their knowing was a gross intrusion, wanted only to escape from them. A sense of panic rose up in her.

At that moment, there was a sound of running footsteps and a boy appeared from the direction of School Street. He came racing across the green towards them.

'Well, now, here's our Dicky-boy,' said Mrs Turner. 'He's been to the butcher's for me. A good lad, he is.'

Dorothea saw a rough-hewn, lumbering youth, his cap skew-whiff and his arms too long for his jacket. He skidded to a halt in front of them, out of breath from running.

'Mr Lines got no bacon, Granny, nor no beef, neither. Got next to nothing, he says, and what he's got folk can't afford. Might as well shut up shop, he says, for all the good he's doing. He dint half go on. I had to stand and listen to him for best part of a hour.'

Mrs Turner burst out laughing. 'Get on with you! You've not been gone five minutes. Sit down a bit. I'm here with Mrs Kaufmann. Your uncle's been showing himself up again, saying all sorts in the shop. He were downright rude to poor Mrs Kaufmann.'

'Uncle John?' said Dick, as he plumped himself down on the bench. 'Oh, no one never takes no notice of Uncle John. I don't.'

The boy stole a shy glance, and Dorothea wondered if he remembered her. She'd always felt she had a special connection to Dick Turner. By chance, she'd been present when he was born, and it was she who'd suggested his name: she'd had in mind, of course, her friend, Richard Rycroft, heir to Clifton. Dick had been no more than eighteen months old when Richard died. That December day, when Mrs Turner had found her lying on Richard's grave, Dick had been there too, Mrs Turner minding him whilst his mother got on with dressmaking, a sideline of hers. Sat by the fire in the Turners' cottage, Dorothea had held Dick in her arms. He'd felt warm as toast after the cold churchyard. He'd been sucking his thumb and watching her; after a while, he'd smiled.

He had the same shy look on his face, sat here on the green all these years later.

Dorothea couldn't remember when she'd seen him last. He'd been a page boy at her wedding, but that was four years ago. If she'd seen him since, it had slipped her mind, but she'd never forgotten him. He'd grown up a lot from the boy she remembered. He must be fourteen now: fourteen, Richard's age at death. Dorothea had always thought that nothing could ever hurt as much as losing Richard. She knew better now.

'Dick's been working down Manor Farm since the summer,' said Mrs Turner, 'same place as his granddad.' (Dick's granddad — husband to Mrs Turner — had worked at Manor Farm as long as Dorothea could remember.)

'I were working there until yesterday,' Dick corrected his grandmother. 'Yesterday I put a hole in one of the pails. It were an accident. But old Tebbit, he turns round, and he says to me, "You again! You're more of a blooming 'indrance than you are an 'elp. Get off with yer. Get out me sight. And don't yer come back!"'

'Thinks it's funny, he does,' said Mrs Turner, shaking her head at her grandson and doing her best to look disapproving. 'What'll happen if they won't have him back? What'll he do then? That's what I'd like to know.'

'Tebbit'll have me back, Granny, once he's cooled off. All bark, no bite, Tebbit — that's what Granddad says, any road.'

'And what'll you do in the meantime, my lad? The devil makes work for idle hands, and don't you forget it!'

'Who you calling idle, Granny? Chance'd be a fine thing! You've had me running errands all morning, and now Ma'll be wanting me; she'll have sewing needs taking round. So I oughtta—' He jumped to his feet.

'Just a minute, my lad. Isn't there summat you'd like to say to Mrs Kaufmann?'

'Is there? Oh, aye. Thank you kindly, Mrs Kaufmann,' he intoned, catching Dorothea's eye and colouring up (he pronounced Kaufmann *Coffman*), 'for all the presents and whatnot — the stuff you sent me.'

Dorothea had all but forgotten — it was part of her old life, the life she'd led before Dr Kaufmann's letter — but she'd always given Dick a little something on his birthday and at Christmas, thinking of herself as a sort of honorary godmother. She'd continued the tradition even after moving to Hamburg.

'That's one of your shirts he's got on,' said Mrs Turner.

'There's me watch, and all.' Dick dug into his trouser pocket, pulled out a small pocket watch. 'Remember when you sent me this? Our Sid were right jealous. I says to him,

"What's the time, our Sid?" And I gets me watch out, and I dangles it under his nose.'

Mrs Turner tut-tutted. 'Torments his brother something rotten, the little monkey.'

'A little monkey. That's me!' Dick broke into a grin that spread all over his face. 'I'm a little monkey, a little monster — int that right, Gran? A scallywag and an 'arf, I am.'

With a cheeky wink at his grandmother, he turned and ran off, heading back down School Street the way he'd come.

Mrs Turner watched him go, indulgent. 'Always in a tearing hurry, he is. Goodness knows what the rush is.' She stirred, easing herself up off the bench. 'Now then. I must get on. And you oughtta get yourself home, Mrs Kaufmann. It's not a day for sitting round outside.'

But Dorothea did not move. There seemed no reason to. Dick Turner, so young and full of life, had brightened her darkness for a moment: a shaft of sunlight on a grey winter's day. But her heart remained frozen, and nothing could warm it — not now Johann had gone.

'I've lost him, Mrs Turner. I've lost him. And I . . . I don't know what to do.'

Mrs Turner sat back down. Turning slantwise, she took Dorothea's hands in hers. 'Yes, dearie. You've lost him. He won't never come back, and it's a crying shame. But afore you lost him, you found him, and you shouldn't never forget it. You've lost him — but you found him first.'

CHAPTER FOUR

She had found him first.

The full implication of Mrs Turner's words only slowly sank in as one day followed another — as (she was dimly aware of it) November gave way to December. She had found Johann once upon a time. Now she must find him again. For it seemed to her she'd been eaten up by loss, and this had left her hollow and empty inside; even her memories had gone.

She would have liked to speak with Mrs Turner again. Mrs Turner was wise in the ways of the world. Mrs Turner could help her. But Dorothea shrank from any idea of going to the village. The risk was too great: the risk of meeting Mrs Adnitt, or Mr Cheeseman, or someone else who'd turned against her.

It was not like her to be afraid of facing people. She'd always made an effort, and had rarely given up on anyone, even Nibs Carter — she'd won Nibs round in the end, back in the old days. But the hostility of a Mrs Adnitt or a Mr Cheeseman was implacable, impenetrable, impervious to reason; she didn't know what she could say to them. And now her old friends were falling away too. Nibs had not spoken to her since he'd turned her out of his cottage back in August.

Dorothea wondered, as she trailed round the desolate gardens, if she would ever dare go to the village again. Today, though, was not the right moment to put her courage to the test. It was too cold and foggy to walk far. Water droplets clung to her coat and to her scarf. The chill air seemed to strike into her very bones. The world was veiled in white.

She went back indoors, took refuge in the nursery. Sending the maid away, Dorothea sat in the day room with just the children for company, little Katherine and baby Laurence, both blissfully ignorant of her suffering; they didn't tiptoe around her. She made up the fire with a shovelful of precious coal, then took a seat in Nanny's chair. Laurence slept unheeding in his cradle. Katherine, on the floor, built towers with wooden blocks, then gleefully demolished them, mumbling under her breath. Dorothea was left undisturbed with her thoughts.

She had letters, photographs — but they weren't enough, just straws to cling to. She wanted more. She wanted to remember him, every detail. His voice: if she could hear his voice again in her mind . . .

She had found him, before she lost him. She must find him again.

She emptied her mind and waited. But it was not Johann's voice that came into her head. It was Roderick's.

Here is Nanny's chair. Funny how it's still Nanny's chair.

Dorothea grew impatient — angry, almost. Why remember Roderick? Why did Roderick still seem so real to her? She had loved Roderick dearly, of course. But she was not sure if she liked him very much, not since that business with Nibs and Susie and Jake.

She banished Roderick from her mind. But — oh, it was typical of Roderick, just typical — he wouldn't stay banished.

She heard his voice again.

I say, Doro, why don't we go on a trip this summer? It would be something to look forward to.

A conversation from years ago. Why think of it now? Yet here it was, clear in her head: Roderick's voice and her own replies.

Why don't we go on a trip this summer? Mother shan't come. It will be a trip just for us.

And Eliza.

If you must.

We couldn't leave Eliza. Oh, Roddy, we couldn't—

It came to her in a flash. Of course! This was the conversation in which the idea of a continental holiday had first cropped up. Roderick was the one who'd suggested it, some six and a half years ago: a trip to France to visit Dorothea's old governess, Mlle Lacroix, and then perhaps on to Switzerland.

Dorothea had been delighted at the prospect of seeing Mlle Lacroix again. For Dorothea, France and the Mam'zelle had been the whole point of the holiday, Switzerland and the mountains merely added at Roderick's behest. Roderick had harboured ambitions of climbing the Matterhorn, an example of what Eliza called Roderick's 'swagger'. Climbing mountains had held no attraction for Dorothea. But—

She had found him first.

And it was in Switzerland she had found him.

Details of the holiday came flooding back. In Switzerland they'd stayed, the four of them (Daisy Turner had been their travelling maid), in a little pension or Gasthaus just outside the village of Anderdorf, near the Rhône valley. Among a handful of other guests had been two young German gentlemen. Dorothea had not been disposed to look too kindly on Germans after her recent visit to Mlle Lacroix. The Mam'zelle had entertained them with tales and incidents from French history. During the Franco-Prussian War forty years ago, the Mam'zelle's father had escaped from the siege of Paris by hot air balloon. ('A likely story!' Roderick had scoffed — but he'd scoffed out of the Mam'zelle's hearing.) The war had ended in defeat for France; the provinces of Alsace and Lorraine had been lost to the rapacious Germans. This dishonour would never be forgotten, Mlle Lacroix had said. France would never rest until Alsace and Lorraine were returned.

Dorothea had considered herself entirely on the side of the French but she'd felt it necessary to compensate for her partisan opinions by being particularly polite and cordial to the German gentlemen: it didn't really seem fair to blame them for the events of forty years ago. They were cousins, the German gentlemen, both called Herr Kaufmann. The elder, married and in his early thirties, had proven an ideal companion for Roderick and they'd spent much of their time climbing together. The younger Herr Kaufmann, however, had been convalescing and under strict orders to avoid all strenuous exercise. Sharing the same Gasthaus, it would have been churlish to have ignored him altogether.

With Roderick and the elder Herr Kaufmann often away overnight in the mountains — and with Eliza early in bed, worn out by the Alpine air — Dorothea and the younger Herr Kaufmann had, on occasion, found themselves alone together after dinner in what Roderick had called 'the common room'. Here, there'd always been a fire, even though it was the height of summer. The flickering flames had cast dancing shadows on the neat piles of sawn logs either side of the grate. Dim lamplight had left the far corners of the room in semi-darkness. The simple wooden furniture was solid and comfortable. Dorothea and Herr Kaufmann had talked together in English and in French. He'd spoken of Germany, and taught her a few words of his language. She'd told him about England and her home. It had seemed a pleasant way to pass the time, nothing more.

While Dorothea had been careful to avoid the thorny question of Alsace and Lorraine, Roderick had not been so scrupulous. But even when presented with this evidence of Germany's infamy, Herr Kaufmann had not taken umbrage. Without jingoism, without rancour, he'd explained the German point of view. Mlle Lacroix would not perhaps have agreed with him, but surely even she could have found no fault in such a fair-spoken, even-tempered, honest young man.

Dorothea, quite unwittingly, had begun to spend more time with him. They'd found themselves thrown together during day as well as in the evenings. They'd walked in the sunshine, though they'd never walked very far, for he was still recovering his strength. She'd taken to calling him 'Herr

Johann', to distinguish him from the other Herr Kaufmann, his cousin Heinrich; it had seemed easier after a time to simply drop the 'Herr'. She'd wished secretly that he would call her 'Dorothea' and not 'Fraulein Ryan', but hadn't liked to suggest it in case he thought her too forward. She'd not wanted him to think badly of her. But there was nothing unusual in that. She always liked to make a good impression.

When first arriving, she expected time to drag in Anderdorf, with Roderick off mountaineering, and nothing much to see except the Gasthaus perched high above the valley and the little village slightly further down. But time did not drag at all. Just the opposite. Before she knew it, they were nearing the end of their stay.

Their last full day arrived, the day before their departure. She'd made a disconcerting discovery. Already she knew that she'd grown very fond of the dear little Gasthaus and would be sorry to leave it behind, but as the last day wore on the thought of leaving made her not just sad, it made her almost unbearably unhappy — so much so that she'd begun to feel unwell. And then, in a blinding flash, she'd realized. It wasn't the Gasthaus she minded about. It was Johann. She didn't want to take her leave of Johann.

This discovery had thrown her into confusion. How could she possibly have such strong feelings for a boy she barely knew? Except that it hadn't felt like that, it hadn't felt as if she barely knew him; it felt as if she knew him better than anyone she'd ever met. She knew him better — *liked* him better — than anyone.

The common room had seemed unbearably crowded that last evening. Even the proprietor had joined the company when he usually kept aloof. Everyone was there — everyone except Johann. Finding small talk all but impossible, Dorothea had gone outside for some air.

She remembered every last detail: a cool, fresh evening, not a breath of wind, the light fading. Small sounds carried clear and far in the still air: the plash of running water, goats bleating, trees sighing in a breeze much higher up. She lingered in the peace and quiet, walking at random, until she found herself following one of several footpaths that had become very familiar to her these last two weeks. She climbed to a little bluff where she could look down on the gable roofs of the Gasthaus, and the twinkling lights of the village further down. The depths of the valley bottom were sunk in shadow, but the mountains opposite were stencilled in a dark jagged line against the paler sky in which the first stars faintly glimmered. It was peaceful, beautiful, but she wasn't able to enjoy it, tormented by her new-found feelings, so very unexpected, so wholly inexplicable. (Looking back now, six years later, she was astonished by her woeful ignorance. She'd not had the first idea about the workings of her own heart.)

A frenzy of wild ideas raced through her mind, as she stood on the bluff. She saw herself leaping from that high place in an agony of despair, she saw her body dashed to pieces on the meadow below — but it was all far too silly to be taken seriously. What did she know of real despair? She was sensible Dorothea, reliable Dorothea — plain and boring Dorothea.

A solitary tear rolled slowly down her cheek. She wiped it briskly away. Silly, it was, and senseless, to get worked up over nothing. She set off, back down the zigzag path. She turned a sharp corner. Suddenly, there he was: he materialized, as if by magic, out of the deepening dusk.

They faced each other on the sloping path, she a little higher, he a little lower down. He made haste to doff his boater. He was always so correct, always so polite. He was wearing a high-buttoned jacket over a shirt and tie. His blond hair, with its meticulous side parting, seemed to glimmer in the twilight.

'Good evening, Fraulein Ryan.' (Sat in Nanny's chair, all these years later, Dorothea tried to remember the sound of his voice, but failed. Why couldn't she remember his voice?) 'Fraulein Ryan, may I walk with you?'

She nodded, tongue-tied. They fell into step. There was a terrible, gaping silence between them. She'd never felt so wretched. She already knew, beyond doubt, that she liked him better than anyone. But it was hopeless to think that he would feel the same. Why would he? She was sensible Dorothea, reliable Dorothea, plain and boring Dorothea. Not the sort of girl who aroused passionate feelings.

She began to shiver. She couldn't stop. Even summer evenings could be chilly in the mountains. But was that all it was, the evening chill?

Johann came to a halt. He took off his jacket. Without a word, he draped it round her shoulders. His hand brushed against her as he did so, making her shiver all the more. He was so perceptive, so kind, so considerate; she'd never met anyone like him.

'Oh, Johann — Johann—' She whispered his name. Desperate. Hopeless. (Sat in Nanny's chair, she found her cheeks burning at the memory of it, so shameless.)

'Fraulein Ryan? What is wrong? Are you unwell?'

'Oh, do please call me Dorothea!'

'Dorota—' His mother's name, the mother who'd died when he was a little boy; his mother had been named after her own mother, who'd come from Silesia.

Johann had told her this. He'd told her so many things. Her days had been rich and full since she met him. Surely it was some sort of sign, that her name was the same as his mother's?

But she was clutching at straws, she told herself severely.

'Dorota. I would like to ask you something. I hope you won't think it impertinent.'

She waited, her heart beating.

He took care over his next words, as if he'd rehearsed them. 'Would you allow me to write to you, when you are back in England?'

'Yes, oh yes!' she burst out. 'There's nothing I'd like more!' It was everything she'd ever wanted. Her heart swelled with joy.

Having reached this understanding, they suddenly became strangely shy of each other, lingering on the path in the growing darkness. Only gradually did she become aware that Johann was now the one shivering.

'Are you cold, Johann? And I have your jacket! Oh, let's go back, quickly. I'd never forgive myself if you got ill again.'

'Illness holds no terror for me, as long as we can stay in touch,' he said.

'Auntie Doro! Auntie Doro!'

A different voice intruded on her memories, a real voice, insistent. Dorothea looked round, startled. She'd been so wholly back on that mountainside that it came as a shock to find herself in the day room of the nursery.

'Auntie Doro!' Little Katherine was tugging urgently at her skirt. 'Auntie Doro, why you crying? Don't be sad! Don't be!'

'I'm not sad.' She picked the child up, gathered her into her arms. 'I'm not sad at all.' And, indeed, she was crying with happiness, infused with all the overwhelming joy she'd felt on that hallowed evening six years ago. 'I was in love, Katherine. I was in love, but I didn't realize. I had no idea what love was like.'

Katherine looked up at her with great interest. She reached out, touched with one curious finger Dorothea's wet cheek. Dorothea smiled at the girl through her tears. Poor Katherine! Poor fatherless child! Motherless, too, now Rosa had gone. (Where was Rosa? There'd been no word.)

But Katherine's father had behaved very badly at the Gasthaus.

'You shouldn't talk so freely to that sausage-eater.'

'I shall talk to whomever I like. Let go of me, Roddy!'

'He's a foreigner and a fraud. He'll probably die of consumption.'

'You're hurting me! I never realized you could be so despicable. I hate you.'

Hate was perhaps too strong a word to have used, but certainly she'd been confused and hurt, she'd been angry and upset. Roderick's words had been spiteful, and they'd been laced with inaccuracies. Johann wasn't a fraud, and it wasn't consumption he was recovering from.

'It doesn't matter what disease he has. Your little friend is so delicate, a sneeze would finish him off.'

'How dare you say that! How can you be so cruel, after what happened to Richard?'

Johann had sensed there was something wrong; he had tried to coax it out of her. But she'd not felt able to tell him of Roderick's nastiness. It would have seemed somehow disloyal. She'd talked instead of Richard — of Richard's all-too-brief life, blighted by illness, and of Richard's death.

Johann had been gentle and sympathetic. 'I think this way of death, Fraulein Ryan. It is as if someone has left the room. Just so, I think of Mutti: that she has gone into another room.'

Now Johann too had left the room. She'd lost him.

But she'd found him first.

She was glad now that she'd not given Johann cause to think badly of Roderick; this mattered all the more, now they were both gone. Roderick had been jealous, of course, at the Gasthaus. He'd been jealous of Johann and that was why he'd behaved as he did. He liked to have his own way. He liked to be the centre of attention. That was where his jealousy had come from. (It was not love, nothing to do with love. He'd not been in love with her; Rosa was quite wrong to suggest it.)

Later, back in England, Roderick had made recompense. He'd come to accept her relationship with Johann; he'd smoothed the way to their getting married, when others doubted the wisdom of it. And he'd done all this because — for all his faults — he'd always been a true friend.

Switzerland was where she'd found Johann. And she'd never have gone to Switzerland but for Roderick.

Sat in Nanny's chair, Dorothea hugged Katherine close and kissed her little forehead. She kissed Roderick's daughter — Roderick, who'd led her to Johann.

* * *

Spots of rain mixed with snow fell from a low and heavy sky as Dorothea, huddled in her coat and scarf, walked round and round the spreading cedar tree in front of the house, her boots crunching on the gravel. She was thinking of the letters she'd exchanged with Johann after they first met in Switzerland and before they were married: nearly two years' worth of letters. When moving to Hamburg after her wedding, she'd taken Johann's letters with her; she'd found that he, likewise, had kept all the letters she'd written to him. They'd put the two sets of letters together in a drawer in their room. She was anxious about them. Were they still safe in the same drawer? She tried to guess what Dr Kaufmann would do, now that his son was dead. Would he clear all Johann's things away, as Rosa had wanted with Roderick's? Or would he keep Johann's room exactly as it was, taking the same attitude as Aunt Eloise? Even though she felt she knew Dr Kaufmann quite well, Dorothea couldn't be sure how he'd react. Grief made people behave impulsively, erratically, out of character. She'd seen it in others. She'd seen it in herself.

'How you manage to fall in love in a letter is beyond me,' Roderick had once remarked, in his inimitable way. But the letters had merely served to nourish and nurture feelings that were already there, that had been there in Switzerland. It was the letters that had made clear to her what she felt she ought to have known all along: that she loved Johann and, incredible though it seemed, he loved her.

Caught up in her thoughts — indifferent to the rain and the sleet — she went through the events of her life with Johann, counting them obsessively on her gloved fingers. One, their first meeting in Switzerland. Two, an exchange of letters — ever longer and more frequent letters, culminating in his proposal. Three, their marriage in St Adeline's on a blazing July day in 1912. Next — four — came their wedding trip; they'd followed the same itinerary as the continental holiday she'd taken with Roderick, Eliza and Daisy. In France, Mlle Lacroix had been delighted with Johann; Alsace and Lorraine had not been mentioned. In Switzerland, they'd stayed at the very same Gasthaus where it all began. They'd revisited the places they'd known so well before: the gentle footpaths on the lower slopes, the common room at evening. They'd laughed fondly at the children they had been — for that was how it had seemed to them looking back, remembering how shy they'd been and unaware, hobbled by their intense and unexpected emotions.

Leaving Switzerland, there'd been a lengthy journey all across Germany to Hamburg: a city of canals and bridges, a busy port; a city with a long and proud history, Johann's city. Her new home was Johann's father's house, also shared with Johann's younger brother, Siegfried, and a cousin, Gerhard, since killed at Verdun. Gerhard was brother to Heinrich, the cousin who'd accompanied Johann to Switzerland in 1910 and with whom Roderick had gone climbing. Both cousins had been partly raised by Dr Kaufmann; he'd taken them in after their parents died. Heinrich had later got married but still lived nearby with his wife and their three children, two adorable little girls and a baby son; Dorothea had seen a lot of them after she moved to Hamburg.

Life in Hamburg was strange and different, not easy to get used to. She'd been homesick. She'd been weighed down, too, by her new responsibilities. Dr Kaufmann's long-standing housekeeper — who'd been with him since before his wife died — had decided to retire. Perhaps she felt herself pushed out, Dorothea had thought, or perhaps she'd taken umbrage at the idea of an interloper challenging her authority after she'd ruled the roost for so long: the head woman in a household of men. Dorothea had worried that Johann's family would resent her for supplanting their beloved old retainer. Also, she would now be mistress; running the house would fall to her. She was horrified. She felt sure that everything would go wrong.

Instead, everything had fallen into place. She was welcomed with open arms by Dr Kaufmann, by Heinrich and his wife, by Gerhard — even by Siegfried. They'd been proud and protective of *die Engländerin*, as she'd been known: 'the

English girl'. (She'd been, for a time, an object of curiosity to the Kaufmanns' friends and neighbours). As for the old housekeeper, no one could have been kinder; she could no longer manage her work, crippled as she was with arthritis, and was much relieved to surrender 'her' family into capable hands. Capable? Well, yes. Dorothea had tempered her sense of panic by asking herself, 'What would Aunt Eloise do?' Magic words. For Aunt Eloise had been mistress of Clifton Park more than twenty years, and Dorothea had watched her deal with every eventuality, from the day-to-day routine of the house, up to and including death and disaster. What better example could she follow?

Dorothea had searched for a new maid to complement the cook and the kitchen maid bequeathed by the old house-keeper. She'd chosen a girl called Lotte, who'd proved so cheerful and practical that even Aunt Eloise would surely not have demurred at Dorothea's calling the girl 'a treasure'.

All of this had made things bearable, even at her lowest ebb, anxious and homesick. But what had made things not just bearable, but wonderful, scintillating — a joy; what had filled her with confidence and made her feel invincible, was Johann. She'd not been able to imagine life without him. It was as if, in some mysterious way, he'd always been with her, as if he'd been waiting in the wings. It was as if, had she only been able to recognize the signs, their eventual meeting had long been foreshadowed. She could not have been happier.

Then came the war.

The war marked a full stop, the end of a chapter. More, it marked the end of the book, the end of her story. All that remained were a few blank pages: the whole of the rest of her life.

She came to a halt and looked around. She had walked unwittingly right to the end of the drive. Sleet was still falling, she was getting soaked, and her fingers were numb with the cold. But as she turned round wearily to retrace her steps, she caught sight, through the bare branches, of the Gatehouse, empty and neglected. She hesitated. She felt somehow drawn to it, she didn't know why. Perhaps because it seemed such a waste, letting it rot.

Here was the garden, gone wild. Without thinking, she set about it, trying to bring some order, trampling down the dead and dying weeds, tugging at the trailing brambles. But the thorns pierced her gloves and pricked her frozen fingers, and the sleet, coming down heavier now, blew in her face, stinging her cheeks and half-blinding her.

Oh, what was the use? Nothing would ever grow here. Spring would never come. This was the endless winter of the world.

Shivering violently with cold, and crushed by a sense of the utter futility of everything, she turned her back on the Gatehouse and stumbled up the drive.

* * *

Remembering caused pain; to forget seemed like treachery. Sleep, when she could find it, sometimes brought temporary release, but on waking she had to face it all over again, as if for the first time, the heart-rending truth. Nowhere in the house could she find any respite. The walls seemed to close in around her, hemming her in. She wanted only to get away, to escape. And so, again, yet again, she pulled on her boots and buttoned her coat and reached for her hat.

She'd had in mind on this occasion a vague idea of trailing round the gardens in the hour or two before lunch, but when she finally looked up and realized where she was, she found she'd come much further than she'd intended and was already near the far side of Horselands. Yet what could be more natural than to walk to the village, especially on a day like today?

And with that thought, she became aware of the weather. For weeks on end, it seemed, the weather had matched her mood, heavy and oppressive: grey skies, mist, rain, snow. Today was utterly different. It was a bright, crisp morning, very cold, her breath steaming, with pale sunshine slanting down out of a high, blue sky. But the sun had no warmth in it, and although the wintry scene had a dazzling surface beauty, she couldn't shake the feeling that there was something false about it. The ground beneath her feet was frozen hard. A glittering frost gilded the leafless trees and hedgerows. It was austere, aseptic, lifeless.

Away across the fields, she could see the crenulated tower of St Adeline's, sharp-lined and solid against the clear sky. She flinched, afraid of the village. Gone were the days when she'd not thought twice about walking there at any time of the day. She'd not been back since Mr Cheeseman chased her out of the shop on the day she'd sat with Mrs Turner on the green, the day she'd lingered in the churchyard looking at the graves: at Uncle Albert's, at Richard's—

Richard! The name clanged in her head like a tocsin. That day in the churchyard she'd been upset, thinking she'd missed Richard's anniversary, when in fact it had been weeks away. But weeks had passed since then, and whatever the date was — she couldn't be sure — she felt quite certain that the twentieth of December had come and gone. She'd thought back then she had forgotten it, and now she truly had.

Richard, oh Richard! How could she have failed to remember? How could she be so thoughtless, so cruel, so selfish?

She went running and stumbling along the footpath, scrambling over the stiles, choked with anguish, half-crazed, desperate, her fear of the village forgotten. She reached the churchyard. She came to Richard's grave. She stood before the headstone, gasping for breath — and she could think of nothing to say, absolutely nothing.

The Lord gave and the Lord hath taken away.

The words formed in her head, a single phrase repeated over and over.

The Lord gave and the Lord hath taken away. The Lord gave and the Lord hath taken away.

The Lord had taken away. He'd taken Richard, Roderick, Johann. They'd all been taken, all of them. Why? Why, why, why?

Her eyes strayed across the frosty grass; reluctant — almost repelled — she looked up at the grey stone walls of the church: the Lord's house.

The Lord gave and the Lord hath taken away.

Placing one foot painstakingly in front of the other, she walked slowly up the path until she came to the porch. Lifting the latch, she opened the heavy wooden door. She stepped inside. It felt like trespassing.

She walked hesitantly up the aisle. The church was deserted. An empty shell. There was nothing here. No presence, no aura — no answers.

'Hello.'

A man's voice rang out in the cold nave. Startled, Dorothea spun round, saw someone framed in the open doorway against the bright winter daylight outside. It took her a moment to recognize him, the young curate whose name was . . . was . . . (she dragged the name out of the fog of the past) was Morgan . . . the Reverend Morgan.

It was happening all over again. Once more, he'd caught her unawares. She shuddered, remembering her violent anger, her abrupt departure. What must he have thought of her?

She clutched the altar rail, watching him warily as he walked towards her. The old vicar had been kind, gentle, understanding, but not all churchmen were like him. The rector of Brockmorton, for instance: when she'd tried to enlist his help in her attempt to get Johnnie Cheeseman discharged from the army, she'd been met by a cold refusal.

'One ought not to stand in the way if a boy wishes to do his patriotic duty. Frankly, I'm surprised that anyone would try.'

Dorothea was sure that a thrusting young man like this curate would be more in the character of Brockmorton's hard-headed rector, and not at all like Hayton's old vicar, a man from an earlier, more innocent age.

'We haven't seen you in church lately, Mrs Kaufmann.'

Her skin prickled at the use of her name. He knew who she was.

'Why . . . why would I come when . . . when I can't find God?' There. She'd said it. She'd confessed. To be clear, she repeated herself. 'I can't find God, Reverend Morgan. He has gone.'

'Please, Mrs Kaufmann, call me Owain. Shall we sit for a moment?'

She couldn't think of any reason not to. They sat side by side in one of the wooden pews. He was silent, as if he expected her to speak first. From a sense of duty, she summoned up a few words.

'I'm sorry.'

'For what?'

But she couldn't explain; it was all too complex and confused, the hatred she'd felt for him at their last meeting, and the remorse she felt now because of it. She searched for something else to say.

'I . . . I've lost him. But I found him first.'

'Him? God?'

'Johann. My husband. He's dead. He . . . he was a German.'

She felt sure the young curate was toying with her, trying to trick her into an admission of guilt. (*Hun-lover . . . traitress . . .*) Once more she repeated herself, but this time clear and defiant.

'My husband was German.'

'So I understand.'

He knew. He knew. How did he know? How else! Village gossip!

She held on to the edge of the pew, waiting — waiting to be confronted with a catalogue of Germany's crimes, for which she must take the blame; waiting to be condemned as a Hun-lover, a traitress — for everyone knew that German nationals in England were spies and saboteurs, looking for any opportunity to deal Britain a death-blow, here at the very heart of the Empire: everyone knew that.

But the Reverend Morgan didn't say anything and she glanced at him, uncertain, unsure, suspicious. He was slender, pale, dark-haired. Very young, he seemed, compared with her, now that she felt so old. Had she heard a faint Welsh lilt to his voice?

She looked away in confusion. What did he want from her — what did any of them want, those people who looked at her with accusing eyes, with hatred in their hearts? What did they want? For her to show shame, remorse; to abase herself, to beg forgiveness — was that it? But she was not ashamed, she never would be, she never could be; she was not ashamed of Johann. As for any crimes Germany might have committed, she knew nothing of that, only what she was told. All she could say with any certainty was that Johann had not asked for war, Johann had not wanted to conquer anybody — nor had his father or Heinrich or Gerhard. Siegfried was all for Germany, it was true. But how did that make him any different to Roderick, who'd been all for England?

She had nothing to offer this silent, solemn young man sitting next to her; she had nothing to say to him. But she couldn't leave without a word, not after last time. He must have thought her incredibly ill-mannered. Perhaps that didn't matter: take no notice, Rosa would have said. It shouldn't have mattered — but it did. It mattered to her. And if she didn't keep her self-respect, then what was left?

Taking a breath, she said, 'I thought he would be safe. He was a doctor, you see, not a fighting man. He was near the front line, but not in the trenches. So I thought he would be safe. But he wasn't. And now he's gone.'

She began to get up. She'd said all that needed saying. But she found that she was still talking.

'I can't remember his voice. Why can't I remember his voice? I remember everything else, I remember it all, I never stop thinking about him; I dream about him, too. In my dreams, he's still alive. He's not dead, but wounded. And he's lost his memory. He's even forgotten his own name. That's why he hasn't come back. That's why he can't come back to me. In my dreams, I know he isn't dead, even though they keep telling me he is. I go in search of him. I walk along endless corridors, and through endless hospital wards, and at long last I find him. He's terribly changed. His face is different. No one else would recognize him. But it's him, I know it's him, and it doesn't matter that he's different, it doesn't matter that he's forgotten everything, all that matters is that he's alive . . . he's alive . . . and I'm with him . . . I'm with him again at last . . . and I feel so . . . so happy . . . so very happy.'

She couldn't begin to imagine where these words were coming from — these words pouring out of her. She'd not told anyone about any of this: her dreams, and the happiness she found in them, and the agony of waking. She no longer talked about Johann at all. Too often she met with hostility, embarrassment, indifference. And even when people were sympathetic, she felt her grief a burden to them.

As she talked, the astounding flood of words seemed to release in her a cornucopia of dammed-up memories. She found herself back in Hamburg, walking hand in hand with Johann on a summer afternoon. She could smell the grass, and the pollen in the air. Sunlight glinted on the waters of the Alster Lake.

She heard herself speaking to him. 'I wish you were coming with me. But some things are more important.' And she knew by these words that she had gone back to their last Sunday, the Sunday before she set off for England.

They had planned for both of them to go to Clifton, but at the last minute an unexpected opportunity had arisen for Johann to advance with his medical training, to catch up on some of the time he'd lost when he was ill, the illness he'd been recovering from when she first met him. He'd hated to change their plans, he'd hated to disappoint her, but she knew how much becoming a doctor meant to him.

'It's not the end of the world, dearest. There's always next time.'

Next time . . .

The scene shifted. It was the day of her departure. They'd said their goodbyes on the quayside. She'd been wearing her travelling clothes: a plain, straight skirt and matching jacket; a cream-coloured overcoat in case it was cool at sea; a hat trimmed with feathers. He'd kept hold of her hand, as if he didn't want to let go.

'How on earth will I manage, *liebchen*, without your common sense to guide me?'

'It's only a month, dearest. I'll be back before you know it. Why not invite Walter to stay whilst I'm gone? Walter will keep you company.' Walter Muller, his friend from university.

He'd slipped a postcard into her pocket at the very last moment. 'Read it after I've gone, *liebchen*.'

She'd caught one last glimpse of him, glancing over her shoulder as she went up the gangway; he'd looked immeasurably handsome in a buttoned blazer, with his tie carefully knotted and his hat in his hands, his eyes a brilliant blue and not a hair out of place.

The scene changed again. The ship had slipped its moorings, was steaming down the Elbe towards the North Sea. She'd stood on deck, watching the city she called home dwindling into the distance, until all she could see of it was the tall, pointed spire of the church of St Nicholas. The ship was an Atlantic liner; her sense of adventure had been sharpened by the thought that many of her fellow passengers would be travelling much further than England, and some indeed leaving Europe for good. Thousands upon thousands of hopeful emigrants from all over Europe set sail each year from bustling Hamburg in search of a better life in the New World.

Even as she was thinking this, she'd suddenly remembered the postcard. She'd taken it out and read the message he'd written, then she'd turned it over. She'd laughed amidst her tears, for there was a picture of the Nikolaikirche, whose spire was just disappearing over the horizon; next time she saw that spire, it would signal her return, and Johann would be waiting for her.

Only a month, they'd consoled themselves. They'd be apart for just a month. But as she stood on deck with the postcard in her hands, she'd wondered how she could possibly manage without him for a whole month.

Now she would have to manage without him for the whole of the rest of her life.

Her memories slowly dwindled and disappeared, like the spire of the Nikolaikirche as she sailed away from Hamburg; she found herself back in the cold and silence of St Adeline's, with the knife-edge pain of loss slicing into her.

But wait — what was that? *Liebchen . . . mein liebchen*: the sound of the German *ch* . . . the sound of his voice . . . his voice . . .

Yes. She could hear his voice. The exact tone and timbre of his voice. There was no other voice on earth quite like it. How could she have forgotten?

His voice. His blue eyes. The touch of his hand. The feel of him. The feel of his skin beneath her fingers, and of his fine, blond hair. The smell of him. The taste of his kisses.

'Oh, how wonderful it was, to be held in his arms—'

She broke off, hearing her voice reverberating around the church; hearing her words, brazen and shameless — and in the presence of a man of the cloth!

But the Reverend Morgan said quietly, 'The flesh is God's creation also.'

The spell was broken. Completely shattered. All her fragile remembrance had vanished like smoke in the wind. There was nothing left, just the grey, desolate church with its empty shadows in the bays and recesses.

'He's gone. He's dead.'

Everything grew blurred. She felt a strange prickling on her cheeks. She reached up to touch. Her fingers came away wet. Tears. She was crying.

She'd forgotten what it was like to cry. Nor could she remember that she'd ever wept for Johann. Until now.

'I'll . . . I'll never see him again.'

'Not in this life,' said the curate softly.

But what other life was there?

'I . . . I used to . . . to believe . . . I want to . . . to believe . . . but what if . . . what if there's nothing . . . nothing at all?'

'That is where faith comes in.'

She tensed up, sat rigid, waiting for what came next: the Resurrection, a reuniting, in sure and certain hope — all those off-the-peg phrases repeated so often and so glibly. To hear them again, now, here — she didn't think she could stand it, she felt she would scream.

But if that was what the Reverend Morgan had in mind, it went unspoken. He sat silent, patient, giving her the space to compose herself, to wipe away her tears with her gloved hands.

What now? What did she do now? She couldn't think. She'd forgotten how to act around people. She'd forgotten how to be Dorothea.

Who was she? How did she fill her empty days?

'I . . . I go walking—' She answered her own question. 'I go walking—' Endlessly tramping the countryside, trying to elude the bitter truth from which there was no escape.

Those solitary treks remained only as jumbled fragments in her mind: apples and plums rotting in the grass; the garden of the gamekeeper's cottage run wild; the silence of Ingleby Wood; a dead pheasant's carcass; the gaping entrance of the canal tunnel, indescribably sinister.

'I saw the sun go down—' From the top of Hambury Hill, a big orange sun with no warmth in it glimpsed amidst the swirling clouds, like a vision of the world's last day.

'There was a meadow—' What had she noticed about it? She furrowed her brow. 'There were bumps — grooves — like stripes—'

She realized now that she'd seen those grooves in other places, other fields. She'd never looked at them closely. She'd never stopped to wonder what they were. A sign, perhaps. Some sort of portent, written into the earth itself.

'Not so much a portent as a message from the past,' said the Reverend Morgan. (Had she spoken her thought out loud?) 'A phenomenon known as "ridge and furrow"; there's another very good example in the field behind the vicarage — Row Meadow, is it called? I'm still getting used to the names.'

He hitched round in his seat so he could face her, warming to his theme.

'It's extraordinary, when you think of it, that we have this evidence of how people used to live, that we can see it for ourselves after so long. Let me explain. In the Middle Ages, every village was surrounded by three big, open fields; there were no hedgerows in those days. The fields were used in sequence. Two were sown each year, and one left fallow for the soil to recover. Each field was divided into long strips that were parcelled out amongst the villagers. Repeated ploughing of those strips over hundreds of years created the pattern we see today. Earth thrown up by the plough formed a series of ridges, with furrows in between. This method of working the land has long been obsolete, of course. The open fields have been cut up and enclosed. But where the fields have not subsequently been ploughed over, where they have been used as pasture, the ridges and furrows remain, testimony to the untiring labour of our forebears, ordinary people whose names are forgotten.'

Their names were forgotten. But Dorothea could see them in her mind's eye. She saw them as tiny figures in a series of stylized and brightly coloured pictures, liked the decorations of an illuminated manuscript.

But was this all that life amounted to: a passing reference in a book, a few grass-grown ridges, some mossy and weathered gravestones? And even these things didn't last. Books were lost and broken, the ridges ploughed over or built on, gravestones slowly crumbled to dust. There was nothing that lasted — nothing.

The young curate seemed to sense that her mind had wandered and he gave a short and self-deprecatory laugh. 'Sorry. I do tend to go on. I'm something of a history buff, you see, only too ready to bore people with it unless I'm put in my place.'

'No, I . . . it's all . . . interesting . . . very interesting.'

She felt she should be the one apologizing, after rambling on and breaking down, imposing herself.

She got to her feet. 'I mustn't take up any more of your time, Reverend . . . er . . . Morgan.'

'That is what I am here for. And, please, call me Owain.'

'Owain.'

He saw her out. At the door, he took her gloved hands in his. 'God bless you, Mrs Kaufmann. And perhaps we will see you tomorrow?'

She looked at him in confusion. 'Tomorrow? But tomorrow isn't Sunday . . . is it?'

'No. Today is Sunday. It is also Christmas Eve. Had you forgotten?'

She made her way outside in a daze, trying to think where the time had gone, how Christmas had crept up on her. For once, it was colder outside the church than in. Frost on the grass and on the gravestones glittered in the thin December sunshine. With a flutter of wings, a robin alighted on a gravestone nearby and watched with proprietary interest as she walked down the path.

Only when she'd let herself out through the lychgate did it occur to her that she had meant to retrace her steps; she should have gone out of the side gate if she wanted to go straight back to Clifton.

She hesitated, looking across the street at the village green, the grass scattered with fallen leaves, brown and black and stiff with frost. A ring of bare earth encircled the syc-amore; its leafless, twisted branches were stencilled against the high blue sky, and they overhung the bench where she'd sat with Mrs Turner — how long ago? A month? More? Incredible to think it was Christmas Eve. And yet, had the Reverend Morgan told her she'd missed Christmas alto-gether, she would not have been entirely surprised. She'd long ago lost all track of time.

After avoiding the village for weeks and weeks, now she was here she found it held no terror for her. She felt as if she'd returned to a place she'd once known well but had long since left behind. She didn't belong here anymore. She didn't belong anywhere.

Aimless, indifferent, she wandered across the green, passed the shop without a glance, and continued down

School Street. The gate of the carpenter's yard was shut fast, but next door Mr Lines the butcher was open for business, selling turkeys at nearly two shillings a pound, an inordinate price. Dorothea turned away from Mr Lines's rather spartan window display to look at the crumbling cottages on the opposite side of the street. They had burned down a dozen years ago during the 'Great Fire of Hayton', as it was known in the village. Once upon a time, the Carters had lived in one of those cottages, but all three cottages were now damaged beyond repair — rather like her friendship with Nibs. No matter. Nothing lasted.

Leaving the ruined cottages, she drifted further down the street, still thinking about the Great Fire, for want of anything else to think about. The fire had started in a hayrick, had gone on to destroy several stables and some outhouses, as well as the three cottages. It remained a notable event in village history, but was hardly on a par with London's Great Fire — or Hamburg's for that matter: there'd been a Great Fire in Hamburg, too, not long before Dr Kaufmann was born. The old church of St Nicholas had burned down and was replaced later by the new building with the tall spire that had been her last glimpse of Hamburg. Hadn't Johann once told her that the new Nikolaikirche had been, for a brief while, the tallest building in the world? But Hamburg seemed a million miles away on this frosty winter's morning, and Johann was—

Well, nothing lasted. Nothing. That was all.

Clang-clang. A metallic sound rang out on the cold, still air. *Clang-clang-clang.* The sound of hammer on anvil. She had reached the Circle, where three streets met in a loop round the duck pond. The school — empty and silent — was on the left, the post office to her right, and straight ahead, across the water, was the smithy, where Mr Atkin must be at work somewhere out of sight. There was broken ice on the pond; there were no ducks.

Dorothea trailed disconsolately round the Circle and turned into Back Lane. *Clang-clang.* The sound of hammering slowly faded behind her. There were other signs of life — smoke curling up from chimneys, the shrill but faint voices of children playing somewhere in the distance — but she'd not met a living soul since leaving St Adeline's. She'd been glad of this at first, not wanting to run into Mrs Adnitt or Mr Cheeseman or anyone of their ilk; but the village seemed so strangely quiet that she began to imagine people were hiding from her, shunning her, watching her unseen with hard, cold eyes. So real did this fancy seem that it made her flesh crawl, and she put on a burst of speed until, with an enormous sense of relief, she came to the end of the village. Here she stopped to catch her breath.

Back Lane ran on between leafless hedges towards the Lawham Road. The way to Clifton seemed long and lonely. All that awaited her when she got back was a house in mourning and the walls that hemmed her in. She turned on her heels, looked at the village. She found herself craving a smile, a friendly voice, some sort of contact with someone — anything.

She began to walk back without really thinking. She walked as far as the first cottages. In the first cottage on the right, the Carters lived. She stared wistfully at this small, square, sandstone building; it was attached to a second cottage, and the pair appeared to be propped up against each other like a pair of doddery, ramshackle old men.

She could expect no warm welcome from the Carters. With a heavy heart, she turned away. Almost opposite, on the other side of the street, were two similar cottages. The one on the left was home to the Turners. Dorothea thought about how kind Mrs Turner had been on the day she'd been turned out of the shop. She had never said thank you. And she'd not seen Mrs Turner from that day to this. On impulse, and giving herself no time to change her mind, she walked up to the Turners' front door and knocked. She waited. Her stomach was in knots.

Mrs Turner herself came to the door, wiping her hands on her apron. Appetizing smells of roasting and baking wafted from within.

'Well I never. Mrs Kaufmann. It's you. Come in! Come in, won't you! Come in out of the cold! You must excuse the state I'm in. I've been seeing to the dinner, and doing a spot of baking for tomorrow — not that there's much to bake with. But I was just this minute about to make a pot of tea and take the weight off my feet for five minutes. You'd like a cup of tea, I'm sure. You look perished. Dad's here, as you can see. I'll be two shakes of a lamb's tail.'

Mrs Turner went bustling off into the back kitchen, leaving Dorothea in the main room. She remembered it well from many past visits — the gate-leg table by the window, the pot of geraniums on the sill, Windsor chairs either side of the fireplace, a glowing fire in the grate; it all looked almost unbearably homely. When she was a little girl, she'd found this a comforting place, for it was much more of a size with what she'd been used to — the lodgings where she'd lived with her papa before she came to Clifton.

Mrs Turner's father, old Noah Lee, was sat in one of the Windsor chairs. In his eighties now, he had a weather-beaten face and white whiskers, and eyes as dark as a crow's. He was watching Dorothea with undisguised curiosity. She felt almost like the little girl of old again, quaking in his presence.

'Now then,' he began without preamble (he was not the type to tiptoe around), 'what's all this I'm hearing about the big house? Is it right that Master Roderick's missus has run off, and left her kiddies and all? And Mistress Brannan's taken poorly, they say, and hardly gets out of bed anymore. What you got to say to that, eh?'

'Let her alone, Dad, for goodness' sake.' Mrs Turner reappeared, carrying a wooden tray on which were cups, saucers and a teapot. 'At least give her chance to get her coat off. You sit there, dearie, by the fire. I'll have this stool. Here's a nice cup of tea for you. And here's yours, Dad. He likes it with plenty of milk — don't you, Dad? Oh, to sit down, what bliss! I've been on me feet since the crack of dawn.' She took a quick sip of tea then continued, 'It's been just me and Dad most the morning. Turner—' She always referred to her husband as

111

Turner. '—He's down the lane, digging Dad's bit of land. Dick and Sid is helping. They're good lads, Dick and Sid.'

'Dunno 'bout that,' muttered Noah Lee. 'They don't dig *proper*, none of 'em. I'd do it meself, if it weren't for me rheumatics.'

'Hark at him! That's what I've had all morning. Miserable as sin, he is.'

'And what you got to laugh about, my girl?'

'Better to laugh than cry, Dad. Least we got each other, if we've got ote else.' Mrs Turner heaved a sigh all the same. 'I'd have liked for us to have been all together for Christmas. It's just one day. But that's too much to ask, seemingly. Ah, well. Worse things happen at sea. And we've Daisy's news to put a smile on our faces. Have you heard, Mrs Kaufmann? Our Daisy — she's expecting.'

'Dint waste much time, did they, her and that Hobson boy,' said Noah Lee bluntly. 'They was only wed September gone.'

'They've taken a cottage in School Street. You know, Mrs Kaufmann, that little terrace opposite the allotments. Our Daisy, she's happy as a pig in muck. The same can't be said of her father. He's never taken to Zack, has Turner. Can't abide those Hobsons. But Daisy were dead set. Times being what they are, who are we to stand in the way of a little happiness? I said as much to Turner. Gave him a piece of my mind.'

With a sense of guilt, Dorothea realized she hadn't given Daisy a thought in weeks — months, even; she was completely out of touch with events in the village.

But if she was out of touch, the village certainly wasn't. A great deal was known about 'the goings-on up the big house' as usual; however — and if Noah Lee was anything to go by — the truth had got mangled in the telling. Rosa had gone away. There was no denying it. She seemed to have vanished off the face of the earth. But to say that Aunt Eloise was too poorly even to get out of bed was far wide of the mark. After her alarming collapse, she had made a full recovery and she'd immediately set about restoring Roderick's room to how it had been before Rosa's 'meddling'. Once her work was done, Aunt Eloise had closed and locked the door, and taken away the key. No one had been in Roderick's room since.

Mrs Turner was still in full flow. '. . . So our Daisy says Zack won't get called up as he works on the land, same as our Jem's let off because of his job at the shoe factory — making boots, they are, at his place, mountains of boots for the army. Shame our Billy dint have a job like Jem or Zack's, then he'd not have had to go in the army. He went off his own bat, of course, but he'd have had to go whether or no, now men are being called up. It does seem hard, though, that he won't be home for Christmas. This is the second Christmas he's missed. He wrote to say his leave's not due. It's been eighteen months now. We've not seen hide or hair of him for eighteen months, and that's a cruel long time. Not that he'll be missing much. It don't seem like Christmas, somehow. No one's making much of a fuss. Ah well. Perhaps the New Year'll bring brighter news. I hear tell as the Germans have offered peace. Summat might come of that. Any road, things'll be different now, with Mr Asquith gone.'

'Mr Asquith? The Prime Minister? Gone?' said Dorothea, startled into speech. 'Where has he gone?'

'Cor blimey. Where you been? Living under a stone?' said Noah Lee. 'Asquith were given the boot. They got shut of him. Mind you, I int too sure about this chap as took his place, this here Lloyd George. Likes the sound of his own voice too much, if you ask me.'

Dorothea was bewildered to find herself so far behind the times. When last had she so much as glanced at the newspaper? This was where Rosa was missed. Rosa had kept them abreast of that sort of news. Who would have guessed that Rosa's departure would have left such a gap in their lives?

'More tea, Mrs Kaufmann?' Mrs Turner was already pouring. 'We'll be having a bite to eat, soon as Turner gets back. You're welcome to join us. It won't be much, mind. We've not had a joint of beef in weeks. Goodness knows how we'll manage for food if this war goes on much longer.'

'Get on with yer!' scoffed Noah Lee. 'There's been hard times afore. Folk always got by. You youngsters don't know what it's like to really go without. Vittles of any sort were hard to come by when I was a nipper. Tis why folk took to poaching. Many's the time I've et pheasant as was bagged by a silver gun — that's snared, missus, not shot,' he added for Dorothea's benefit. 'And why shouldn't we help ourselfs? Why shouldn't we, eh? They helped theyselfs to what little we ever had. They enclosed the fields. They ruined the place with their hedges. They stole all the common land.'

'That's not how they see it,' said Mrs Turner. 'They don't see it as stealing, and they've got the law on their side.'

'Laws is made for their good, not ours,' said Noah Lee, and straight away he launched into some lines of verse.

They hang the man and flog the woman
What steals the goose from off the common
But let the greater villain loose
What steals the common from the goose.'

'They stole our land, I tell you! Why shouldn't we take their game in return? A risky business, mind, poaching. Man-traps, spring-guns, keepers ready to shoot you soon as look at you. And if you got caught, you was hanged.'

'Not in our day, Dad,' Mrs Turner interjected. 'You're talking years back. No one's never been hung far as I can remember, not for poaching.'

'Ah well, mebbe not. But me dad's dad, he remembered it, he knew of poachers what was strung up. Poachers against keepers. That's how it is, how it's allus been, and no love lost either side. That old villain, now, Master Rycroft—' Noah Lee cocked an eye at Dorothea, for he was talking about Aunt Eloise's beloved father, who'd been master of Clifton for forty years — some in the village remembered him rather differently to Aunt Eloise. 'That old villain, he were a menace to poachers. Begrudged every last coney, never mind his birds. A tyrant, he were, and a skinflint. Stopped us fetching wood out Clifton Spinney, and we'd fetched wood out Clifton Spinney time outta mind. But he never got the better of me — not him, nor his lackeys. There was a keeper back then, lived in Keeper's Cottage, what some folk call "the Gatehouse". Gatehouse! Never heard nothing so daft. No gates up the big house, never has been, and I should know. Eighty-five, I am, and I've seen it all, and I've allus got by, hard times or no. I were a totter when I were younger, with a bit of poaching on the side. Made enough of a living to keep meself and me missus, and me two little girls, with a bit put aside. Bought me land with what I saved, an acre of me own. Good bit of land, and all — if they int ruined it atween 'em, your old man, Molly, and that pair of young rascals.'

'You don't half go on, Dad,' said Mrs Turner as she began to collect the cups and saucers. 'I'm sure Mrs Kaufmann's had enough of your old tales for one day.'

But Dorothea had always been fond of hearing about the old days. She still remembered the stories Noah Lee had told her on her first visit here more than a dozen years ago, when she'd come to tea with Nora the nursery maid, Mrs Turner's eldest daughter. Earlier that morning, the Reverend Morgan had talked to her about an even more distant past, a past so remote as to be almost unreal, but Dorothea wondered if perhaps those peasants who'd lived hundreds of years ago had left more of a mark than only the ridges and furrows in the fields where they'd toiled. Perhaps amongst their descendants were men in the village who still worked the land today, Mrs Turner's husband being one of them. Dorothea could not think why she should find comfort in this — the never-ending circles of life — but she did. She found comfort, too, in the hot sweet tea and the glowing fire and this homely little room, just as she had all those years ago when Mrs Turner found her lying on Richard's grave.

She wanted somehow to show how grateful she was. A simple 'thank you' seemed inadequate. But what else was there?

As she got to her feet, Mrs Turner said, 'Now then, Mrs Kaufmann. Are you sure you won't stay for a spot of lunch?'

'I should get back. They'll be expecting me. And after lunch — well, I've bought no Christmas presents at all. I wonder if there'll be any shops open in Lawham?'

'All right for some,' said Noah Lee sourly. 'All right for them as is made of money.'

She did have money, it was true. She'd never thought of the legacy left to her by Uncle Albert as making her rich, but it would seem that way to the Turners. Here was something she could do for them: let them share in her good fortune. Except they'd consider it 'charity', they'd think it an insult. Perhaps, after all, a simple 'thank you' would be best — better than nothing, better than a good deal else.

'Thank you, Mrs Turner. You've been most kind, as ever. And thank you, too, Mr Lee. I always enjoy your stories about the old days.'

Prompted by she knew not what, she quickly leaned down and kissed his wrinkled, weather-beaten old cheek.

As she pulled her coat on, he looked up at her, his mouth wide, his face a picture of astonishment.

'Well, Dad,' laughed Mrs Turner, with the tray in her hands, 'that's the first time in all my days I've ever known *you* at a loss for words.'

CHAPTER FIVE

It was March, but more like the middle of winter, as Dorothea battled through the bitter cold with Eliza at her side, flurries of snow twirling and twisting out of the grey sky. Winter had been hard as well as long. In February, the canal had frozen over, which hadn't happened, said Aunt Eloise, since her brother Frederick died, more than twenty years ago. To Dorothea, it seemed that her worst forebodings were coming true, and that spring really would never come again. She shuddered to think of the poor soldiers, huddled in the trenches, having to live through this.

The weather did nothing to dampen Eliza's spirits. Wrapped up against the cold, she skipped along beside Dorothea as they followed the footpath across the fields towards home, singing under her breath and trying to catch snowflakes on her gloved hands. She was seventeen, bursting with life, resilient, irrepressible. Dorothea, at twenty-five, felt old and worn, numb inside as well as out.

It came as a relief to reach the warmth and shelter of Clifton — to shut out the wintry afternoon that was now fading rapidly into an early dusk. Eliza went stampeding up the stairs, coat tails flying, her scarf trailing behind her; Dorothea followed at a more sedate pace. In her room on the top floor, she began the long process of divesting herself of her out-door clothes. A fire was glowing in the grate. The curtains were half-closed (that would be Tilda, who for some reason thought it saved time when she came to close them fully).

Catching sight of the photograph on the bedside table, Dorothea paused in her undressing and sat down on the edge of the bed. She reached out and touched the picture, caressing with the tips of her fingers Johann's beautiful face. If only he would smile — once, just once — that rare and heart-warming smile which she missed so much. It was silly of her to wish for it: a photograph was a moment frozen in time, unchanging. And yet . . . and yet . . . was it really so fanciful to think that she could see something of it — a trace of his smile? There, at the corners of his mouth, in his eyes too, those eyes staring out so solemnly from the silver frame.

Without warning, the door flew open and Eliza burst into the room. The fragile peace was shattered.

Still wearing her hat and coat, Eliza was in a state of great agitation. 'Doro! Doro! We must go to the village at once!'

Dorothea stared at her in astonishment. 'But we've only just got back from the village.'

'You don't understand. Tilda said that Jeff said—' Eliza's words tumbled out, making no sense. Only gradually did Dorothea get the gist. It was second- or even third-hand news. Billy Turner was rumoured to be on his way home. Billy Turner was coming home on leave. He might even be home already.

'That's most odd!' exclaimed Dorothea. 'We met Daisy in the village and she made no mention of it at all — her own brother, too!'

Daisy had found plenty else to say. The price of bread, a shilling a loaf — it cost more than gold. And what bread it was, so dark and chewy! But oh, her poor feet, and her back, her aching back! She'd never have another child, if this was how it made you feel. All she wanted was to get it out of her as soon as ever she could.

But never a word about Billy.

'Daisy's sly,' said Eliza. 'She wanted to keep it from me.'

'Why would she want to do that?'

Eliza ignored the question. She grabbed hold of Dorothea's hand. 'Please may we go, Doro? *Please!*'

This was Eliza all over, rushing headlong from one thing to another. 'There's no hurry, Eliza. He'll still be here tomorrow.'

'But I want to go now, right away. I have to. I must. I shall go on my own, if you won't come with me.'

'Oh, very well.' With a sigh, Dorothea dragged what she thought of as her old and weary bones up off the bed. 'Just give me a moment to get my hat and scarf and gloves—'

'Yes, but hurry, hurry!' Eliza was hopping with impatience.

They hastened through the gathering gloom, Eliza setting the pace. Because they were heading for the near end of the village, they didn't cut across the fields, but went down Clifton's long drive instead; it seemed like a tunnel this afternoon, a wall of evergreens on each side and the louring sky a roof overhead. The air was icy cold, flakes of snow still drifting down. Mist was rising.

They turned onto the Lawham Road. Eliza raced ahead in her eagerness to reach the village. Struggling to keep up, Dorothea broke into a run. A vague sense of unease took hold of her. She shivered inside her coat.

Tumbledown Cottage loomed out of the gloom and the mist, like the remnants of a world in ruins. Back Lane branched off to the right. Eliza led the way, Dorothea followed. They came first to the Carters' cottage. A dim light showed in the front window. A few steps further and they reached the Turners' place on the opposite side of the street. The little garden that in summer ran riot with flowers lay desolate on this wintry March evening. There were shutters on the windows, no sign of a light. Eliza dashed up the path and rapped on the door. Dorothea joined her by the front step. For a moment, as they waited, Dorothea had the strange illusion that the cottage — the whole village, for that matter

— was completely deserted, that she and Eliza were the only sparks of life on this bleak and inhospitable evening. A shudder went up her spine.

There was a soft click as the latch was lifted inside. The door opened a fraction. Lamplight spilled out through the gap. A face peered out at them. It was Daisy.

'Miss Dorothea. What do you want?' Her tone was guarded; she looked puzzled. Her eyes moved from Dorothea to Eliza. Her expression hardened.

At that moment, a voice from inside said, 'Daisy? Who's there?' Daisy was hustled aside, and suddenly Mrs Turner appeared. She flung the door wide, but not as wide as her smile: beaming, radiant. 'Hello, my dears! Hello! Come in, won't you. Come in. Don't let the warmth out.'

Eliza needed no second invitation but Dorothea, as she stepped over the threshold, found herself strangely reluctant; she was quite unable to explain it. The door clicked shut behind her.

The little front room was full to bursting. Dorothea busied herself taking off her gloves, self-conscious under the scrutiny of so many pairs of eyes. As well as Mrs Turner, smiling all over her face — and Daisy with her swollen belly, easing herself into a chair by the fire — there was Mr Turner, a burly brooding presence by the window; there was Jem, Daisy's elder brother, with his wife, Pippa, and their two boys, Dick and Sid; there was Daisy's husband, Zack Hobson, lurking in one corner and scowling; and, last but not least, old Noah Lee was sat at the gate-leg table, presiding. The table was covered by a pristine white cloth and laden as for a special occasion, with ham and bread, cups and saucers, a bottle with a cork. A leaping fire was devouring a profligate amount of wood.

At least one third of the room was separated off by a folded-out wooden screen. From behind it came the sound of splashing. The way the tableau was arranged made it obvious that the wooden screen had been the centre of attention until a moment ago; all eyes were now on the visitors. Dorothea had never felt so uncomfortable in this room before. She fumbled with her gloves. Even Eliza was silent and subdued.

Mrs Turner bustled round. 'Put the kettle back on the fire, Pippa, there's a love. You'll want tea, my dears. Or shall I open the elderberry wine? Sit down, Mrs Kaufmann, sit down. Make room there, Jem. Would you like a little ham? Or there's bread and dripping?'

Flustered, Dorothea tried to put her thoughts in order, but before she could reply to Mrs Turner, a voice came floating out from behind the screen.

'Who is it, Ma? Who's there?'

It was a man's voice, rather husky and tired-sounding. Dorothea recognized it at once, though she hadn't heard it for over two years. It was Billy Turner. Rumour had spoken true. He was home on leave at last.

Eliza's head snapped up at the sound of Billy's voice. Her eyes shone. She gazed at the screen as if she hoped to see right through it.

'Ma! Who's there?' Billy repeated.

'It's Mrs Kaufmann, Bill. Miss Eliza, too.'

'I . . . I'd best show me face, then.'

'Don't be daft, Bill. They won't mind if you finish your bath first.'

Daisy butted in. 'Filthy, he were, when he first showed up. Stank to high heaven. Covered in lice, too.'

'Honest to goodness, Daisy!' cried Mrs Turner. 'They don't want to hear all that! But it's no word of a lie, Mrs Kaufmann. I put his uniform in to soak straight off, to get some of the mud out.'

Mrs Turner faltered and fell silent. There was an uncomfortable pause. No one spoke, no one moved. Dorothea felt more of an interloper than ever, but Eliza seemed entirely unaware — unaware even of Daisy looking daggers at her (Daisy's hostility seemed inexplicable and out of all proportion).

A sound of splashing broke the silence. Bare feet slapped on the flagstones. Next, a brawny arm snaked round the screen, followed by Billy Turner's head and jutting shoulder.

His hair was wet and plastered down; a growth of whiskers hid the dimple in his chin; a tuft of dark hair stuck out from under his arm. The lamplight, and the light from the fire, burnished his glistening skin, giving him a tanned and healthy look, but there were dark rings round his eyes and his face was pinched and drawn. Colour flushed in his neck as he slowly looked round at them all. Eleven pairs of eyes looked back at him.

'Stone me!' he muttered. 'I've never known such a crowd to watch a chap have his bath!' His eyes for a split second lingered on Eliza and the colour mounted, made his cheeks glow. He quickly ducked down out of sight. 'Where's the towel, Ma? I want the towel.'

Mrs Turner began scouting round at once. 'Now where did I put it? Where's it gone? I had it here a moment ago.'

Dorothea couldn't bear it any longer. She wasn't wanted here, nor was Eliza. They were trespassing on a private family occasion. Mrs Turner, of course — even if she felt that way — was too good-natured to let it show, but the expression on Daisy's face made it plain, and dour Mr Turner was glowering too; even Jem and Pippa seemed perplexed, exchanging questioning looks.

'We'll go now,' said Dorothea, taking Eliza's hand. 'We only looked in to say hello.'

Eliza snatched her hand away. She obviously had other ideas and looked likely to make a fuss about it.

At that point Billy's voice came again, urgent. 'The towel, Ma!'

'I'm looking, Bill, I'm looking. I can't seem to — ah, here it is! You're sitting on it, Daisy. Why didn't you say? Get up a minute.'

As Mrs Turner handed the towel round the screen, Dorothea grabbed hold of Eliza's hand again and this time held it firmly, giving Eliza no choice.

'Lovely to see you all. I hope you enjoy your tea.' Wincing at the false brightness in her voice, she began to drag Eliza towards the door.

Billy sounded anxious as he called out from behind the screen. 'I'll pop up the big house first thing. To see how things are, like; to see how you're all doing, Miss Dorothea and . . . and Miss Eliza.'

Daisy snapped, 'You're to see Annie Britten first thing, Bill. She'll expect it.' Looking at Eliza, Daisy added pointedly, 'Annie Britten's sweet on our Billy, and our Billy's got eyes for no one else.'

Eliza, undaunted by Daisy's open hostility, glared at her, almost snarling; for a second, Dorothea was afraid the two girls would come to blows. She tightened her grip on Eliza's hand. All this seemed inexplicable, as if she'd stumbled into a play halfway through and had no idea of the plot. The air of tension in the room was unmistakeable now. Only old Noah Lee seemed in any way to be enjoying himself: there was nothing he liked more than what he called 'a bit of argie-bargie'.

Dorothea had to almost drag Eliza out of the cottage. Daisy slammed the door shut behind them.

On the garden path, Eliza twisted her arm and freed herself from Dorothea's grasp; she was blazingly angry. 'Why did you do that? Why did you make me leave?'

'It's a special family moment. We were only in the way.'

'But I wanted to see Billy! Billy's *not* sweet on Annie Britten, he's *not*! Daisy's a liar, a dirty liar!'

'Eliza! Please! Whatever's got into you?'

'I want to see Billy! I haven't seen him for such a long time — two years, two whole years! If only we'd waited . . . You've spoiled everything — everything!'

Howling and sobbing, Eliza fled down the path and into the lane.

'Eliza! Wait! Wait for me!'

But it was too late. Eliza had disappeared into the mist. Dumbstruck, Dorothea stared after her, shivering as the chill air began to search through her layers of clothes.

She was about to set off after her cousin, when she heard the door open behind her. Daisy stepped out, holding her shawl close around her and pulling the door to.

'It's not right, Miss Dorothea,' Daisy said bluntly and without preamble. 'It's not right for Miss Eliza to be making eyes at our Billy — making him love her. It's not fair.'

'Making eyes? Oh, but, Daisy . . . surely not . . . you must have it wrong . . . she's just a girl.'

'Beg pardon, Miss Dorothea, but you don't know A from a bull's foot about it. Miss Eliza knows exactly what she's doing. I've watched her. I've seen her. Saw it plain as plain when I worked up the big house. Oh yes, that's no word of a lie: it's been going on all that time. And our Billy, he's a lumbering great lummock and strong as an ox, but underneath he's soft, too soft for his own good. He knows in his heart of hearts it int fitting, a lad like him and a girl like Miss Eliza, but she's got him wrapped round her finger and he'll go running if she asks — he'll go running at the drop of a hat, you mark my words. He's no more sense,' Daisy ended bitterly. 'No man has.'

Dorothea couldn't believe what she was hearing. Daisy had it wrong. She must have. But there was no point arguing about it. 'I'm sorry, Daisy. We shouldn't have come. We never meant to cause any trouble.'

The anger, the bitterness, drained form Daisy's face. She turned pleading eyes to Dorothea. 'We've only got him a few short days. Please don't let Miss Eliza spoil it for us.'

With that, she slipped back inside the cottage and shut the door.

Dorothea stood on the path. Mist was curling round the sandstone walls of the cottage; it was getting dark. Her mind was working overtime. Eliza's insistence on coming to the village, the strained atmosphere in the cottage — what Daisy had said fitted the facts. As well, it was all too easy to forget that Eliza was seventeen now: not yet a woman, perhaps, but more than a girl.

Dorothea stirred. She walked down the path. She made her way up Back Lane through the cold and dark, deep in thought.

* * *

Sat with the newspaper in the morning room after breakfast, Dorothea turned the pages with a curious sense of detachment. She had to keep reminding herself that all this was real, that it was all actually happening: British ships sunk, the Germans in retreat, the never-ending casualty lists. In Russia, it was reported, the Tsar had been overthrown by his own people, while in Germany — if the newspaper was to be believed — the food situation was far worse than it was in England. People were hungry, desperate. Riots had broken out in several places.

Dorothea wondered if there'd been riots in Hamburg, if people were going hungry there too. Johann's cultured father was now in his late sixties; a limited diet would be harder on him than on those younger and more resilient. What about the rest of Johann's family? How were they getting on? The last she'd heard of her brother-in-law, Siegfried, he'd been fighting on the Eastern Front. What would the turmoil in Russia mean for him? There was cousin Heinrich, too, and his wife and children, those dear little girls and the baby boy. But the 'baby', Harald, would be four years old now, and his sisters nine and seven; did they remember their Tante Thea? And what of Lotte, the housemaid, who'd been such a help?

Dorothea sighed. The newspaper told her so little of what she really wanted to know.

She laid it aside. She was alone in the silent morning room. Eliza had not come down for breakfast, sending word by Tilda that she didn't feel well. Aunt Eloise, who never took much breakfast these days, had repaired to the parlour as soon as she'd finished her cup of tea. The parlour — *Mother's Lair* in Roderick's parlance — was where Aunt Eloise conducted all the business of running Clifton Park, but Dorothea had her doubts about how much work actually got done in there these days. Often now, Dorothea found herself importuned by Crompton or Mrs Bourne, seeking clarification when Aunt Eloise's instructions were confused or contradictory, or where there was some pressing matter that hadn't been addressed at all. This would never have happened in the old days. Aunt Eloise had been abreast of everything, down to the finest detail.

Dorothea sighed again. She made ready to stand up. She had things to do. She ought to look in on Eliza, for a start. But the effort to move seemed too great, and after the events of last evening she baulked at the prospect of facing Eliza.

Dorothea wanted to believe that Daisy was mistaken if she thought her brother and Eliza were entangled in any way. Daisy had always been prone to exaggeration; she must have it wrong. Eliza was still very innocent, a young seventeen, and Billy Turner was a grown man of twenty-eight: what could they possibly have in common? But Dorothea could not come up with any other satisfactory explanation for Eliza's wayward behaviour. And she couldn't forget the way Billy Turner's eyes had lingered on Eliza a heartbeat too long, and the way he'd flushed at the sight of her — this couldn't be dismissed as pure imagination.

Dorothea knew she had to talk to Eliza, but not like this, with her mind in such a muddle. She would leave it until later, when she'd worked out what to say. In the meantime, she'd not yet been up to the nursery today, to look in on the children. She wasn't sure that she'd ever promised in so many words to take care of them, but it was what Rosa had wanted, and so Dorothea considered it her duty, as well as a source of joy. The children alone were untouched by all the madness in the world. They were too young to know what was happening — though Katherine did sometimes ask about her mummy. As for her father, she seemed to have forgotten he was dead, or perhaps didn't understand what it meant. 'Daddy is fighting the war,' she announced on occasion, sometimes adding, 'When will Daddy come home again?' Dorothea didn't have the heart to say never: never again.

She sighed once more, and this time made the supreme effort to get to her feet.

In the hallway, she met Eliza coming down the stairs.

'Hello. Are you feeling better?' Suspicion took hold. Eliza was dressed to go out. 'Where are you going?'

Eliza came to a halt three steps up, looked down at Dorothea defiantly. 'I'm going to the village. I'm going to see Billy. He never came like he said he would, so I must go to him.'

'Oh, Eliza! I don't think that's very wise!'

'Why are you being like this, Doro? Why are you against me? I thought you'd understand. You used to understand. This is all Daisy's fault. It's all Daisy, opening her big mouth. I bet she stopped him coming, too. And after everything I've done for her! I taught her her letters. She couldn't even write her own name! She still can't. She writes it back to front. She's so stupid. She's mean and stupid and spiteful. I hate her!'

'That's not a very nice thing to say about poor Daisy!'

'Daisy's all you care about!' Eliza's voice rose alarmingly, until she was screaming at the top of her lungs. 'You don't care about me, nobody does, it's as if I'm invisible—'

Eliza's red-faced tirade was abruptly interrupted. The door to the breakfast room flew open and Aunt Eloise swept into the hallway, spectacles in hand.

'What is the meaning of this? Why are you shouting, Elizabeth? I could hear every word, even in the parlour. And why have you got your coat on?'

Eliza buttoned her lips, glared mutinously at her mother.

'Well? Haven't you got anything to say for yourself?' Aunt Eloise cast a quizzing look at Dorothea. 'Can you explain any of this, Dorothea?'

'She . . . she's going to the village.' Dorothea spoke reluctantly, feeling as if she'd been caught between a rock and a hard place, not wanting to lie to her aunt, but conscious too of Eliza's eyes on her and the expression on Eliza's face that spoke as clearly as words: *Judas! Betrayer!* 'She wants to . . . to see Billy Turner. He's home on leave.'

'Now I understand.' Aunt Eloise turned back to her daughter. 'You are not to go to the village. You are not to have anything to do with Turner. Do I make myself clear?'

Eliza's eyes bulged, her mouth contorted. Such was her suppressed fury, she looked about ready to burst. But few people could outface Aunt Eloise in a determined mood. Lip trembling, eyes brimming, Eliza turned away, defeated, and fled up the stairs, swiftly disappearing round the half-landing. The sound of her stampeding feet faded away.

Aunt Eloise appeared completely unruffled, still gazing at the now empty staircase. 'Oh dear. I thought I'd put a stop to all that silliness.' Catching Dorothea's eye and seeing her look of confusion, Aunt Eloise explained, 'It was when you were away in London last year, Dorothea. I discovered that Elizabeth had been writing to Turner ever since he gave in his notice and joined the army, and he had been writing to her. I made it clear to Elizabeth there must be no more letters. I thought that would be an end to it. But sometimes there is just no telling her.' Aunt Eloise sighed, shaking her head. 'Capricious child! I'm afraid she has no idea about life, no idea what men are like. My own fault, I suppose. But there it is. She will have to be watched whilst Turner is home on leave. It's for her own good.'

Dorothea could scarcely believe that Eliza was in any danger from Billy Turner, of all people; but she didn't think it was worth arguing the point. Clearly, Aunt Eloise had made her mind up on the matter, and that was that.

Rather bemused by events, and not knowing what to do for the best (her unerring instincts seemed these days to have deserted her), Dorothea watched as Aunt Eloise stood silent for a moment, folding and unfolding the arms of her spectacles with a distracted air. Finally, without another word, or even a glance, Aunt Eloise went back the way she had come, leaving the breakfast-room door wide open behind her.

* * *

Tilda came down just before luncheon with another message from Miss Eliza, the gist of it being that Miss Eliza was not hungry and was staying in her room. Dorothea suspected that Tilda had chosen not to repeat Eliza's actual words.

'I'll take a tray up.'

'No, Dorothea,' said Aunt Eloise firmly. 'I have told Elizabeth time and again that there are consequences to her actions. She must learn the hard way.'

Luncheon over, Dorothea was glad to escape into the gardens for a breath of air. It was her old governess, Mlle Lacroix, who'd instituted the habit of a daily walk, a turn around the gardens each afternoon. But Dorothea could not remember that the gardens had ever looked as bleak and wintry as they did today. A biting wind was blowing and there was a dusting of snow.

As she walked along the cinder paths, huddled in her coat, she found herself wondering what had become of Mlle Lacroix. They'd kept in touch for many years by post. There'd also been her two visits to Mlle Lacroix at her home in Jeancourt, first with Roderick and Eliza and Daisy, then with Johann on their wedding trip. That was five years ago now, and it was some time since Dorothea had last received any word from her former governess: the war had swept them apart. As far as Dorothea could tell, looking at the maps printed in the newspapers, Jeancourt was on or very near the front line. Mlle Lacroix had perhaps been forced to move away. Where she might have gone was anyone's guess.

With gloved hands thrust deep in her coat pockets and her scarf up to her chin (either the cold was worse than ever, or she was less able to stand it), Dorothea passed the ornamental pond and took the left-hand path, feeling sad to think that she'd lost touch with someone who'd meant so much to her. When she'd first come to live at Clifton, she'd been like a fish out of water and desperately unhappy. Mlle Lacroix, perhaps more than anybody, had turned things round, made things bearable, helped Dorothea to settle and to think of Clifton as home. But life became ever more dislocated as the war went on. Friendships were mislaid or broken, there were deaths and departures. A sense of loss now haunted her every waking moment — a sense, too, that she was out of touch with the world.

But perhaps she'd never been quite as in touch as she'd liked to think. For instance, she'd known nothing until these last couple of days about what Aunt Eloise called 'that silliness' between Eliza and Billy Turner; nor, whilst Roderick was alive, had any whisper reached her of his entanglement with Susie Hobson. True, she'd spent two years in Hamburg, and more recently she'd been away nursing; but was that any excuse? Roderick and Eliza were, technically, her cousins, but they meant so much more to her than that: they were like a brother and sister to her — or so she'd thought. She couldn't help wondering today if she'd ever really known them at all.

She reached the vegetable garden, where she found Jeff Smith hard at work. He was frowning fiercely as he attacked the half-frozen ground with a fork, trying to dig in piles of compost. He looked perished, his hands white and bloodless, his face pinched and pale.

'Hello, Jeff. You oughtn't to be out in this weather.'

'I have to get on, miss. Everything's behindhand.'

'Where's Becket today?'

'I made him stay indoors. He's a bit out of sorts.'

For a second, Dorothea's heart was in her mouth. She'd got so used to expecting the worst that she could only wonder what fresh tragedy lay in store.

But Jeff said, 'It's just a cough, miss, and a bit of a head cold. It'll take more than a cold to finish the old codger off. Mind you, I knew he weren't feeling too clever when he agreed to stay indoors. Never takes a blind bit of notice of anything I say, as a rule.' Jeff wiped his sleeve across his nose, added, 'This weather don't help none. Enough to make anyone feel out of sorts. We've moved nothing out of the greenhouses yet, and there's not a potato been planted.' He hesitated, glanced at her charily. 'Winny was telling me there's been a spot of bother indoors.'

Winny was Winny Downie, the postmaster's daughter, aged seventeen, who'd been working at Clifton since the end of last year. Her father had been reluctant to give his consent to this.

'I don't want my Winny wasting herself as a housemaid. I want more for her than that. But . . . well . . . I suppose it won't hurt for now — as a favour to Mrs Brannan.'

How times had changed. Once upon a time, in taking the girl on, it would have been Aunt Eloise doing Mr Downie a favour.

'Winny tells me there's been a falling-out: the mistress and Miss Eliza.'

'Just a misunderstanding, Jeff, that's all.'

'If you say so, miss.' Jeff shifted his weight from one foot to the other and avoided Dorothea's eye. 'I don't know nothing about it, and it's not my place to say, but there's been letters coming to the cottage.'

'Letters?'

'Yes, miss. Letters. Letters addressed to Becket, but meant for Miss Eliza. The old devil's been passing them on. I only found out last week, but I reckon it's been going on a lot longer than that.

'"Mrs Brannan oughtta know about this," I says to him.

'"Got nothing to do with the mistress," he says. "It's Miss Eliza's business. She asked me special."

'"Miss Eliza's not the one who pays your wages," I says. "You wanna remember that."

'But he wouldn't have it, the stubborn old goat. Reckon Miss Eliza's got him wrapped round her finger — you know what she's like. I'm not one for telling tales, but Mrs Brannan's been good to me, and I don't want her to think I've been disloyal.'

Dorothea did not know what to say. There seemed little doubt that the correspondence between Eliza and Billy Turner had continued illicitly, despite Aunt Eloise's interdict. Becket no doubt thought it as harmless fun, some sort of childish game. But the deception involved on Eliza's part came as something of a shock.

Jeff burst out, 'It's Bill Turner. He's behind all this, if you ask me. Too big for his boots, always has been. Likes to throw his weight around. I know all about Bill Turner from when he used to work here. I was the chauffeur back then — I looked the part, too — and he was just the stable boy, up to his knees in muck. But since he joined the army, he's in clover. All the girls chase after him now. A girl won't look at a fellow these days, 'less he's in uniform.'

Jeff sounded bitter about it. Perhaps he had good reason. Certainly, having a limp gave him no hope of being a soldier. But surely not all girls were dazzled by a uniform. Dorothea couldn't believe that Eliza would be.

It soon became obvious, however, that Jeff was not thinking of Eliza.

'Annie Britten, she's a fool to herself, chasing after Bill Turner. But why would she look at a cripple like me?' He rammed his fork into the half-frozen ground and then let go of it, blowing on his hands and rubbing them briskly together to restore the circulation. As he did so, he muttered almost inaudibly, 'Bill Turner's been with her, I know he has, and now she thinks she's in with a chance and no one else gets a look-in.'

What a terrible muddle, thought Dorothea. Daisy swore blind that Billy was sweet on Annie Britten, but all the time Billy had been exchanging secret letters with Eliza. Jeff implied the opposite, that it was Annie who was sweet on Billy — and it was only too obvious that Jeff himself had a soft spot for Annie. How long had Annie Britten been a bone of contention between Jeff and Billy? But it had never taken much to set them off; they'd always been at loggerheads.

Dorothea felt like tearing her hair out. Jeff and Billy — it was Roderick and Nibs all over again, another point-less feud, bull-headed men locking horns over nothing. As if there wasn't enough mindless hatred in the world! It was on the tip of her tongue to set Jeff straight, to give him a piece of her mind, but she checked herself just in time, and she began to feel ashamed. What was wrong with her? Why was she so angry all the time? This was Jeff she was dealing with — Jeff, whom she'd known for years. Yes, he could be prickly and pig-headed, and he was never short of things to grumble about, but he was clearly devoted to old Becket, for all they never appeared to stop bickering, and then there was Hecate — the way he'd cared for Hecate towards the end, and then dug her grave after the poor thing died. Jeff's limp, too, couldn't be forgotten. He was obviously still very self-conscious about his limp. ('Why would she look twice at a cripple like me?') Whenever Dorothea thought of it, she couldn't help but feel a twinge of guilt.

She was not to blame, of course. It was not her fault. He'd been hurt in an accident with a motor car just before the war. But she'd been there, she'd witnessed it. And although she'd done everything she could for him in the aftermath, and rushed him to a doctor, she'd had no experience in nursing back then, and she always wondered if she could have done more — saved him, perhaps, from ending up with one leg shorter than the other.

So she did not give Jeff a dressing-down; she tried to be encouraging instead. But her words rang hollow, perhaps because even she no longer believed that things necessarily turned out for the best. She'd lost her sense of optimism, as well as the knack of connecting with people. She was no use to anyone anymore: that was how it felt.

Disconsolate, she took her leave of Jeff and returned to the house. She entered on a scene of chaos.

Aunt Eloise was stood in the middle of the hallway; Eliza and Crompton were there too. Crompton, distinctly ill-at-ease, had hold of Eliza's arms; Eliza, dressed to go out, was struggling to escape his grasp, twisting and turning and trying to wrench her arms free.

'Let go of me, Crompton, let go! I order you to let go of me!'

Aunt Eloise caught sight of Dorothea in the open doorway. 'Ah, there you are, Dorothea. I'm afraid I caught her in the act; she was trying to tiptoe out. Wilful disobedience! She has left me no choice.' Turning to the manservant, Aunt Eloise said firmly, 'Take her upstairs, Crompton, and lock her in her room.'

'Oh, Aunt—' Dorothea couldn't believe her ears: it sounded like something out of a book, to talk of locking Eliza up.

'She has brought this on herself, Dorothea. She has only herself to blame. Crompton, please do as I say.'

It was little to his liking, that much was plain, but he was nothing if not conscientious, and he took his duties seriously. He had a fight on his hands. He wasn't a tall man, and Eliza these days was almost the same height as he was. Exerting all his strength, he dragged her towards the stairs.

'No, no, no! Stop it! Let me go! I hate you, Crompton! I hate you!'

Eliza's heels dragged across the black-and-white tiles. Her hat fell off, and her fair hair hung loose and tangled, falling over her face. Crompton, bright red, began lugging her bodily up the stairs.

It was distressing to watch, and Dorothea turned away. As she slowly closed the front door, the sound of the struggle faded up the stairs. A heavy silence fell in the hallway, broken only by the ponderous ticking of the grandfather clock.

Aunt Eloise appeared to have fallen into a trance. At length, she stirred, frowned. 'It's for her own good. It's all for her own good. She has to be saved from herself.'

Without a glance at Dorothea, Aunt Eloise wandered away down the passage.

Order was restored. But whereas, once, a look or a word had been enough, Aunt Eloise now seemed clumsy and inept, her power sadly diminished, her lightness of touch replaced by a heavy hand.

Times had indeed changed at Clifton Park.

* * *

Dorothea tapped softly on Eliza's door.

'Eliza? Are you there?'

'Is that you, Doro?' Eliza's voice was muffled, the door between them, dividing them. 'Have you come to let me out?'

'I haven't got the key, Eliza.'

'You can ask Mrs Bourne. Mrs Bourne will give you the key.'

'I can't go against Aunt Eloise's wishes.'

'Why can't you? Mama's lost her mind. She's gone mad. Rosa was right about her: she's mean and spiteful and all she ever cared about was Roddy. I'm nothing to her.'

'Oh, Eliza. You know that's not true. Aunt Eloise loves you dearly. She's only doing what she thinks best.'

'She's trying to control me, that's what she's doing. As if I was a servant to be ordered around. But she can't tell me what to do. I don't care what she wants. It's what I want that matters. And I want to see Billy. I have to see Billy. I must.'

'Why is it so important, and why be in such a hurry? You are always so hot-headed, Eliza!'

'Oh, you don't understand, I knew you wouldn't.'

'Then tell me. Explain.'

'I . . . I can't. I . . . I like him . . . that's all.'

'Well, of course you do! I like him, too.'

'But this is different; I like him in a different way.'

'What do you mean?'

'I . . . I used to think I liked him the way you liked him — the way everyone likes him. But when he said he was going away, I . . . I couldn't bear it — I couldn't. And now he's home, and it's been so long, and when he goes away again, if I haven't seen him — if he goes away and . . . and never comes back—'

'You mustn't think like that. Of course he'll come back.'

In a small voice, Eliza said, 'Roddy didn't.'

There was no reply to that: it was the plain and simple truth — the painful and bitter truth.

After a pause, Eliza spoke again, hesitant, and much more muffled now. 'When . . . when Roddy . . . when he . . . died . . . when he *died* . . . nobody cared how I felt . . . Nobody called at Clifton to ask after *me*, nobody wrote letters of condolence to *me* . . . it was as if I didn't count. Billy was the only one . . . the only one who—

'He sent me such a dear letter, about when they were boys, him and Roddy. They used to go around together when they were young; they played cricket in Row Meadow, they snared rabbits, they . . . they did ever so many things. Billy's letter . . . it made me cry . . . It was Roddy, it was Roddy all over, even though I never knew half the things Billy told me.' There was a sound something like a sob from behind the door. 'Billy is *mine*, someone for *me*, and if I never see him again—'

'Don't, Eliza. Don't torture yourself.' Always in the past, when Eliza was hurt or upset, Dorothea had put her arms round her and comforted her, but this was impossible with the door there, keeping them apart. 'All you can do — all anyone can do — is hope, pray, have faith.'

'Pray? Pray! Pray to God, you mean? God doesn't exist. There is no God. Kolya told me that ages and ages ago, and he's right. Only fools believe in God, fools and idiots! How can you, Doro, believe? How *can* you, after Roddy — after Johann? If there was a God — if there was — how cruel . . . nasty . . . *horrible* . . . I'd rather believe in *nothing* than believe in a God like that!'

Dorothea made no reply. There was no reply possible, no comfort she could offer, only well-worn words and empty phrases — just how empty, Dorothea had learned from bitter experience this last year or so. If Eliza didn't believe in God — if she doubted that Billy Turner would survive the war — if she hadn't any faith in anything — who was to say she wasn't right?

Dorothea, these days, found it impossible to be sure of anything. She wasn't even sure if Eliza was still listening on the other side of the door. But in any case, for now at least, it was clear that the conversation was over.

* * *

Dorothea tried to get things straight in her own mind. Eliza could be headstrong, unruly — Rosa's influence, or so Aunt Eloise suggested (but Rosa was no longer mentioned). Eliza, though, had always been like that; she'd been a handful long before Rosa came to Clifton. Aunt Eloise wanted to keep Eliza from harm, which was only natural — laudable. But surely there were better ways of going about it than locking Eliza in her room? And did Eliza really need protecting from Billy Turner?

Billy Turner was a man of few words, as a rule. He kept himself to himself. But he wasn't terse and unsociable like his father. Behind the gruff exterior was a placid and unassuming young man who was possibly even a little bit shy. He was not tall, dark and handsome; there was nothing particularly heroic about him. But he was young, he was strong, and he was far from ugly. Most importantly, he'd always been around: he'd worked 'up the big house' since he was a boy. Was it really so surprising, then, that Eliza should have developed a 'crush' on him? But Billy was a grown man, not likely — Dorothea would have thought — to lose his head over a slip of a thing like Eliza. Dorothea could not discount, however, the way he'd looked at Eliza the other evening — and the way he'd tried *not* to look at her was even more telling.

Where in all this did Annie Britten fit? Daisy insisted her brother had eyes for no one else, whereas Jeff implied it was the other way round. Jeff had also said, *Billy Turner's been with her. I know he has*, leaving little room for doubt as to what he meant. How did Jeff know this? Rumour in the form of village gossip was seldom reliable; if that was where he'd got his information from, then it should be taken with a very large pinch of salt. Or perhaps Jeff had simply been talking out of jealousy, trying to paint Billy in as black a light as possible.

There was only one way to find out, only one way to get to the bottom of this whole sorry saga. She would have to speak to Billy Turner himself.

* * *

In Back Lane, she met Mercy Bates. Grinning and dribbling, Mercy reported that she'd seen 'Birry Turno' going into the 'ale-house'. Dorothea was relieved to hear it. After the other evening, she didn't much want to knock on the Turners' door.

A smile and a kindly word left Mercy bubbling with happiness, and Dorothea continued down the street. The ale-house — the Barley Mow — was located near the far end of Back Lane. Roderick had called it a 'disreputable drinking den'. It was certainly rather more rustic than its rather ostentatious village rival, the Red Lion. In all her years at Clifton, Dorothea had never once been inside.

The doorway was low and narrow. Dorothea ducked instinctively, holding on to her hat. She took it for granted that her visit to the pub would not go unnoticed. Word would soon spread all round the village.

'Well I never. What do you think? Miss Dorothea was seen going into the Barley Mow.'

'Fancy that! Who'd have thought Miss Dorothea would be seen dead in a pub?'

The main room of the Barley Mow proved to be dim and fuggy; there was a pervading smell of beer and tobacco smoke. Small lattice windows overlooked the street, benches lined the walls, horse brasses polished to a shine hung on the walls. There were several stools and a couple of rickety-looking tables. The remains of a fire glowed in the recessed fireplace. The mantelpiece was a rough-hewn lump of wood painted black. Towards the back of the room, there was a bar behind which were some barrels and several shelves stacked with bottles. Mugs dangled on hooks. At one end of the bar, an open doorway led into the private back rooms. There was no sign of the landlord. He was known in the village as Big John, and he was the father of Mr Cheeseman in the shop, just as plain-spoken but rather less acerbic.

There were only two people in the room. They were sat on stools at one of the small tables, hunched over mugs of beer like a pair of old gaffers. Billy Turner was one; the other Dorothea recognized as Harry Keech, younger son of Chips Keech, the village carpenter and joiner. She'd not heard that Harry Keech was home on leave. Time was she'd been up to date with all the village news.

As she walked in, the two young men leapt to their feet and doffed their caps, quickly dispelling the impression of crusty old age. After a moment's hesitation, they pulled up a stool and invited her to sit down, obviously puzzled by her presence. Dorothea found herself rather flustered. She'd planned on talking to Billy one-to-one, in private. Foolishly, she'd not thought to consider how she would manage to get him alone. What she wanted to say to him — to ask him — was personal, intrusive; it couldn't be broached in front of Harry Keech. She doubted now if it ought to be broached at all.

They sat there, the three of them, in awkward silence.

Billy, it was, who finally spoke. He looked more like himself today, clean-shaven, fresh-faced, dressed in ordinary clothes. Scowling into his mug, he muttered something about the beer, how you couldn't get a decent pint for love nor money since the government started watering it down.

'Don't let Big John hear you say that!' laughed Harry Keech. 'He's very particular about his beer, is Big John.'

It had not taken Harry Keech very long to shake off any awkwardness. He was a little younger than Billy. Tow-headed and rather squash-faced, he'd been known in the village since was he was a boy for his chirpiness (some said 'bare-faced cheek' rather than 'chirpy'); he'd always presented a stark contrast to his older brother, serious-minded Nolly.

Asking after Nolly seemed to Dorothea as good a way to break the ice as any.

'Our Nolly? Oh, he's the same as ever, miss — his missus, too, and their nipper. Still grafting for the old man. The old man reckons he couldn't do without him, so there's no soldiering for our Nolly; he gets a badge what lets him off. He don't know what he's missing, do he, Bill? Cushy life, int that right? Always been the blue-eyed boy, has Nolly. Used to get on me wick when we was kids, him being the old man's favourite and the old man making no bones about it. Nolly liked to rub me nose in it, liked to see me jealous.

He still rubs my nose in it, me up to me neck in mud while he lives the high life at home. Good luck to him, I say. Life's too short, int that right, Bill?' Harry got to his feet. 'Who's for another? You'll not say no, Bill. Where's Big John got to?' Standing at the bar, Harry banged his empty mug on the counter. 'John! John! Where you at? Shop!'

'I'll give yer shop, you cocky young—' Big John loomed up, coming from out back, a bull of a man with a grizzled beard. Catching sight of Dorothea, he moderated his language mid-flow. '—Cocky young so-and-so. It's gone two. I'm to shut at half past, case you forgot. And it's "Mr Cheeseman, sir" to you, Harry Keech. I'll have less of yer lip.'

Harry gave him a gap-toothed grin. 'Now then, John. You know us. When've we ever outstayed our welcome? Two more pints, if you'll be so good. And what about you, miss? You'll have a drink with us, won't yer?'

'Nice try, sunshine,' said Big John. 'You know treating's not allowed no more.'

'Do I know? I should say so! I'd never have to pay for me beer again, if it weren't for that daft rule. They all want to buy Tommy a drink. But you'll turn a blind eye just this once, won't you, John? What you got for a lady?'

They settled on sherry, which Dorothea did not really want, but she thought it would be churlish to refuse. The drinks poured and paid for, Big John disappeared out back once more, muttering about cocky young tykes trying to get him in bother.

Harry sat down astride his stool and took a swig of beer, then wiped his mouth with the back of his hand. 'What's up then, miss? You said you was looking for Bill here, but you never said what for.'

'Oh . . . it's . . . I'm not really sure I should . . .'

Giving her a shrewd glance, Harry said, 'Don't tell me he's been setting his cap at Miss Eliza again? Blimey, Bill. I knew you'd get in trouble over it, but would you listen? Not a bit of it.'

'Put a sock in it, Harry. I int set me cap at no one,' growled Billy. But colour was flushing into his cheeks.

Undaunted, Harry went on, 'I done me best to take his mind off her, miss. Been trying for years. "Plenty more fish," I says to him. But our Bill, he's a bit backward in coming forwards around girls. One time, we went to Northampton — do you remember, Bill? It was before the war, miss. The bank holiday weekend. Lots of girls in Northampton, so I'd heard. We went to take a look. Fixed Bill up, I did. What were her name again, Bill? Ethel, weren't it? Mean to tell me you never went back to see her like you promised? Bet she were heartbroken. Took a real shine to you, she did.'

Billy got up abruptly, glowering at his mate; for a second Dorothea thought they might even come to blows. But all Billy said was, 'I'd watch me step, Harry Keech, if I was you. Your great big gob'll get you in real hot water one of these days.'

Harry laughed as Billy went stomping out through a side door.

'You've upset him, I think, Harry.'

'Don't you worry, miss. Takes a lot more than that to get Bill's back up. He's just gone to have a — to blow his nose, so to speak.' Patting his pockets, Harry brought out a rather crumpled-looking packet and drew a cigarette from it. He put it between his lips, then paused. 'D'yer mind if I have a fag, miss? Thought I'd better ask.'

Dorothea had no objections, and he struck a match and lit his cigarette, sliding a metal ashtray across the table towards him. Blowing out smoke, and with his eyes still on the ashtray, he said, 'All jokes aside, I hope Bill's not got hisself in any bother. He's always had a thing about Miss Eliza, don't ask me why, and it's plain as the nose on me face that's what you've come about. Didn't he used to go on about Miss Eliza! Didn't he just! He went on about Miss Eliza more than he went on about them blooming horses, and that's saying summat. But, like I say, he's a bit backward when it comes to girls, and it took a long time for the penny to drop. When I upped and asked him about it, he told me to mind me own business — but I could see I'd hit a nerve.' Harry took the cigarette out of his mouth and studied it a moment, before adding parenthetically, 'Loved them horses, he did. Loved them like they was his own.'

'He was very good with them. Clifton's not the same now they've gone.' Dorothea wondered why they were talking about horses, when they'd started by talking about Eliza.

'He hoped he'd be working with horses when he joined up, that's what he'd have liked. Ended up in machine guns instead. Not what you'd call a cushy number. The Suicide Club: that's the name they go by, the machine-gun lads.' Harry smiled grimly and took another drag on his cigarette.

Billy reappeared and Harry's expression immediately changed. His pensive look gave way to his normal chirpiness as if at the flick of a switch.

With his cigarette clamped between his lips, he spoke out of the corner of his mouth. 'Here he is: Casanova.'

'You'd be a menace, Harry Keech, if you had half a brain to go with yer lip,' said Billy placidly as he returned to his seat.

'Better than being an old grouch, like some people I could mention — eh, Bill Turner?'

Listening as the two young men went on chaffing each other with practised ease, Dorothea nonetheless got the sense that they were watching their words in front of her. She took a sip of sherry, wondering what they'd been talking about before she came blundering in. She was an intruder, surplus to requirements. She ought to leave them to it.

Before she could make a move, however, Harry stubbed out his cigarette, drained his mug, and jammed his cap on his mop of hair. 'Well, that's me, I'm off home. Mother'll be wanting to make a fuss of me. She likes to make a fuss, does Mother, and she's only got till tomorrow. I'll be sure to see you, Bill, afore I leave. Ta-dah, Miss Dorothea.'

Harry departed. A heavy silence fell in the dingy room. Grey daylight seeped in through the lattice windows. Dorothea couldn't think of anything to say. Often these days she found herself at a loss. Common sense had always been her guide, but common sense seemed entirely inadequate in the world as it now was. She looked down at the rickety table, at Harry's empty mug and the little ashtray with his cigarette ends, at Billy's mug still with beer in it, at Billy's scrunched-up cap and her half-finished sherry.

She took a deep breath. Billy opened his mouth at the same moment. They both began to speak at once. They both fell silent.

'Go on, Billy. You first.'

'All I mean to say is, I . . . I never took no liberties with Miss Eliza — never. I wouldn't, miss, not with any girl.'

'But what about—' Dorothea faltered, but she forced herself to go on now she'd started, telling herself she might as well be hung for a sheep as a lamb. 'What about Annie Britten? Daisy says you're sweet on Annie Britten.'

'Daisy knows ote about it. I int never tipped me cap at Annie Britten.'

'Then why did you—' Dorothea stopped short again; she was appalled by what she'd been about to ask, Jeff Smith's words going round and round in her head. (*Bill Turner's been with her, I know he has.*) It was far too indelicate a subject to bring up in the taproom of the Barley Mow, nor was it any of her business.

Billy glanced across at her. He seemed to know by some sixth sense exactly what she'd stopped herself from asking him. He flushed and looked away.

'Who . . . who told you? I've not said ote to anyone — not even Harry.'

He reached inside his collar and scratched his neck, frowning again and avoiding her eyes. A look of understanding came over his face.

'Were Limpalong, weren't it. Limpalong told you. I might a-known. He's always sniffing round Annie. She must a-let something slip, she must a-told him what happened 'tween me and her. Bet Limpalong couldn't wait to open that big gob of his. Bet half the village knows by now.'

'Who is Limpalong?' asked Dorothea, though she already knew.

'Jeff. Jeff Smith. He's Limpalong.'

'Oh, Billy, it's cruel to call him that. How can you be so cruel?'

'It's what everyone calls him. He's called me a lot worse. We don't see eye to eye, him and me. We never have.'

'All this squabbling. All this bad feeling. There's no need for it! You should remember what Harry said: life's too short.'

'That's true, right enough,' said Billy tersely. He took a large swig of beer and swallowed it down, then he grimaced and he scrubbed the table with his knuckles. Suddenly he burst out, 'Never took no liberties? Hark at me! A bleeding lie, that is. Long and short of it, I kissed her — or she kissed me. Either way, I dint put a stop to it like I ought to.'

Dorothea stared at him. She did not know quite what to make of him. The cropped hair, the tanned face, the dimple in his chin — he looked much as he'd always looked, the same as ever. But he'd changed. There was something different about him. She couldn't put her finger on it — unless it was that she'd never really known him at all. She'd always been friendlier with the Turner womenfolk, with Mrs Turner and Nora and Daisy. The men were much less forthcoming and not so easy to get on with — Jem and Billy, their father most of all.

Kissing Eliza; secret letters; a liaison with Annie Britten — was this the real Billy Turner? Dorothea was almost as shocked as when she'd found out about Roderick and Susie Carter.

For some reason, this reminder of Roderick brought back to her a long-ago conversation from the days when they were still children.

Why must you be so horrible, Roddy?

I can't help it. It's in my nature. Slugs and snails and puppy dogs' tails.

And that, it seemed, was the way of boys — all boys.

'When was this, Billy?' she asked sharply, unable to disguise her disenchantment. 'When exactly did you kiss Eliza?'

'A while ago. Afore I went away. She got herself in such a state, crying and whatnot . . . crying her eyes out . . . and all 'cause I was going away. I dint know what to do with meself. Would have seemed mean just to have left her. So I put me arm round her. Next thing, she were kissing me. It just sort of . . . happened.'

'What about Annie Britten? Did that "sort of happen", too?'

'That were different. I met her one night on me way home. I'd been here, in the ale-house—'

'You'd been drinking?'

'I'd had a couple, I reckon, same as usual.'

'Go on. What next?'

'Were like she were waiting for me. She stood in me road, wouldn't let me pass, and she says to me — but it don't matter what she said, it don't need repeating. She oughtn't to stir a chap up that way, is all.'

'So it's Annie's fault?'

'No, miss, course not—'

'And was this before or after you kissed Eliza?'

'Before.'

He looked distinctly uncomfortable — miserable even — as well he might, thought Dorothea.

But it wasn't like her to get so angry, still less to be brusque and tactless. (*Life's too short*, she'd said to him just now; *life's too short*, she'd said to a man fresh from the front.) She'd every right to be concerned about Eliza. As for the rest — was it really any of her business?

Billy, though, seemed to want to explain, to make a clean breast of it. Finding any excuse, she said to herself bitterly. But that wasn't fair, she told herself. Since when had she stopped giving people the benefit of the doubt, the way she always used to? Who'd made her the judge and jury? What was *wrong* with her?

She bit her tongue and listened to him. Slowly she pieced it all together, from what Billy was telling her now, from what Harry had said earlier, from what she already knew. Harry appeared to have been right. Billy had for a long time obviously been unaware of his feelings towards Eliza. And even when he'd begun to realize, he'd assumed that Eliza was too young and too innocent to harbour any such feelings of her own.

'There seemed no harm, like, in just talking to her. I knew nothing would come of it.'

Aunt Eloise, it seemed, had been of a different opinion, which was why she'd tried to put a stop to what she called 'this silliness' between Eliza and Billy.

Billy had not been oblivious. 'She never said nothing straight out, the mistress. But you know how she is. She can freeze the marrow in you with just one look. I tried to put Miss Eliza right out me head after that. I did me level best to keep out her road.

'And then our Daisy turned round to me and says, "Annie Britten's took a real shine to you, Bill."

'And I says to her, "Gerron with you! She's not."

'And Daisy says, "You men! You can't see for looking."

'Then Ma pipes up. "You needn't turn your nose up, Bill Turner. What's wrong with Annie? She's all right, is Annie. And it's about time you found yourself a girl."

'And I says to her, "How many more times, Ma? I'm right as I am."

'And Ma says, "You're too picky, Bill, my lad, that's your trouble."

'Weren't much more than a week or so later when I met Annie on me way home from the Barley Mow. I could have throttled meself after. I dunno what I were thinking. I daresay I was trying to convince meself that Miss Eliza dint mean ote to me. And I knew Ma and Daisy and the rest would've liked to see me and Annie together. But it wouldn't a-been right. It wouldn't a-been fair. Not when I dint like her the way she deserved.

'I made a right mess of things, I know I did. To tell the truth, I were glad to go in the army and get away from it all.'

'Is it true you've been writing to Eliza?'

'Yes, miss. Not that I'm much of a one for writing. But she asked me to, so I did. I meant no harm. I'd never do nothing to hurt Miss Eliza. I'd not hurt a hair on her head. Truth is, Miss Dorothea . . . letters from home . . . they mean everything . . . they keep a chap going. And Miss Eliza, she, she—' He broke off, scowling fiercely.

Watching him, Dorothea was reminded of Roderick again — something Roderick had said last May (only last May).

It's hell out there, Doro, I can't tell you.

All her doubts, her disapproval, were suddenly swallowed up by a feeling Dorothea didn't quite understand. Hesitantly, she said, 'It must be . . . hell . . .' Roderick's word, *hell*, sounded glaringly incongruous coming from her lips and she blushed.

'It int so bad, miss, once you get used to it; you can get used to anything. Worst part is thought of it beforehand — before you go up to the front line. It's never as bad once you're there — except I can't never get used to the cold. It's been perishing cold. Sometimes I've thought I'll never get warm again.'

He fell silent, staring at the table with furrowed brow. She had a strong impression that he'd not said everything he wanted to say, that there was something of which he wanted to unburden himself.

He suddenly took hold of his cap with both hands and twisted it savagely before, just as abruptly, letting it go.

There was an inescapable air of tension in the room. Dorothea dared not make a sound. She hardly dared look at him. Slowly his hands curled up, bunched tightly into fists; his knuckles had turned white.

'One time—' He stopped, swallowed, began again. 'One time, in the line, Jerry had a crack at us. Jerry came over. We knew he were coming. We was waiting for him. The second he stopped shelling, we was up and ready. There's five of us, the team I'm with. We had our gun all set. Jerry came on. All strung out in a line, they was. We . . . we knocked 'em down. We knocked 'em down like skittles. More come. They kept on coming, line on line. We knocked 'em down and we knocked 'em down. We went on firing till our gun were so red hot it wouldn't work no more. Were all over by then. Finished. Jerry'd given up the ghost.'

Billy paused, hunched over, eyes fixed on the table, on the space between his fists, as if he could see there in miniature the events he was describing.

'Don't get me wrong. I'm not a nesh sort of a chap. I've seen pigs stuck, I've wrung the necks of rabbits. But that day . . . the way they fell over . . . seeing them all lying there, one atop the other . . . I won't never forget it. I felt sick to me stomach. I spewed me guts up. I spewed me guts up right next to the gun. I was sick as a dog.'

He fell silent once more and they sat there, frozen in place.

Dorothea, while she was listening to his gruff, staccato voice, had felt a creeping horror come over her, making her skin crawl. She tried to shake it off now. Reaching out, she touched with hesitant fingers Billy's tightly clenched fist.

Billy snatched his hand away as if he'd been burned. He looked around with wild eyes, as if he'd forgotten where he was; he seemed reassured to find that he was still in the bar of the Barley Mow and he relaxed a little.

His eyes briefly met hers and he said, 'I've never told no one . . . I don't know why I told you, miss . . . I just seemed to feel as if I could—' He broke off, grabbed hold of his empty mug and peered into it. A look of puzzlement came over his face, as if he couldn't understand where the beer had gone.

Dorothea sat back. She was ashamed of herself. How could she have doubted him? This was Billy Turner; she'd known him half her life. He'd worked for fifteen years in the stables at Clifton, longer than she'd lived there; he'd loved the horses, had often said they were a lot less trouble than people. And when the head groom had handed in his notice many years ago and was never replaced, Billy had been left to run the stables single-handed, a heavy responsibility for a lad of seventeen. But he'd managed, because that was the sort of man he was: steady, dependable, as honest as the day was long; even Roderick had been known to say that Turner 'wasn't a bad sort'.

Dorothea went back to the long-ago conversation with Roderick she'd remembered earlier. She reminded herself how it had ended.

Why must you be so horrible, Roddy?

I can't help it. It's in my nature. Slugs and snails and puppy dogs' tails.

That's what you'd like people to think. But it's not true. Underneath, you're . . . you're nice!

Nice!

He'd been affronted. He'd considered it an insult. But that didn't make it any the less true. It was, if anything, even more true of Billy Turner — and she'd known that all along. Why had she not trusted her instincts, the way she used to? Whatever Aunt Eloise might say, Billy Turner was not some-one Eliza needed protecting from.

Billy reached for his cap, shook it out, put it on. He got to his feet. 'We'd best go, miss. Big John'll want rid of us. It's way past closing.'

They found the front door locked. Only then did Dorothea recall that, as they were talking — engrossed — Big John had come out of the back room and watched them for a while from behind the counter, before going over to lock the door. He'd disappeared back where he'd come from without a word. She'd hardly noticed.

He'd left the key in the door. They let themselves out. A bitter wind was whipping along the street. They stood for a moment outside the pub. They were both a little tongue-tied, Dorothea felt, both a little shy of each other.

It was Billy who spoke first. 'Better go, miss. Promised I'd call on Grandpa, see if there's ote he needs. He can't do as much for hisself as he used to. Goodbye, then, miss. I'll see yer.'

'Goodbye, Billy.'

Even as the words left her lips, Dorothea reached a snap decision. She would go against Aunt Eloise, if that was what it took; she would set Eliza free. Why shouldn't Eliza and Billy meet up, if that was what they wanted? What harm could come of it? There was enough misery in the world, without adding to it.

She took hold of Billy's hand. 'Dearest Billy. Goodbye — and good luck.'

He was overcome by embarrassment — *didn't know where to look*, as they would have said in the village — but he let her hold his hand for a heartbeat, before stepping back and harrumphing loudly, shrugging inside his jacket. He went tramping off, hands deep in his pockets, shoulders hunched against the wind. Rounding the corner of the building, he took the path that ran between the Barley Mow and Frank the waggoner's place, a path that led out of the village and across the fields to Manor Farm. But Billy would only be walking a few dozen yards or so, as far as old Noah Lee's little cottage.

Shivering, Dorothea turned up the collar of her coat. Now that Billy had gone, she set off to return to Clifton.

She had not gone far up Back Lane when she met Mrs Turner and Daisy coming the other way. Dorothea faced them in the middle of the street.

'What you doing in the village?' Daisy was cold and suspicious. It was almost as if she knew that Dorothea had been talking to Billy — or *poking her nose in*, as Daisy would have put it.

If Dorothea expected Daisy's mother to be less hostile, she was swiftly disillusioned. Mrs Turner wouldn't even meet her eye.

Apologetic but unwavering, Mrs Turner said, 'Were you coming to see us, Mrs Kaufmann? It might be for the best if you didn't call round for the time being. After the other evening, Turner, he said—'

'He called you a Hun, a Hun's wife,' said Daisy, with a little too much relish.

'That's enough, Daisy! But you see how it is, Mrs Kaufmann. With things the way they are, and with all this to-do over Miss Eliza, it would be better all round if you stayed away, at least until the dust settles.'

Dorothea felt Mrs Turner's words like a slap in the face. It seemed even the Turners were now against her. Stood half-way up Back Lane in the bitter wind, she felt as if the very last vestiges of her old life were crumbling away before her eyes.

Mrs Turner's once-rosy face was grey and desolate. 'Billy's going back the day after tomorrow. He's going back.'

Without another word, Mrs Turner and Daisy went on their way.

* * *

Dorothea stood at the window in the morning room watching snow come down, a blizzard of white specks swirling in a gusting wind. It had been the coldest Easter anyone could remember, and still there was no break in the weather. The green shoots of spring, such as they were, seemed no more than a mockery.

She thought back to last Easter, less than a year ago. Johann had been alive, Roderick too. She'd been working at the hospital, enduring long, exhausting hours of drudgery in the most gruesome surroundings, confronted daily by blood and gore and suffering, and by endless transports of men in pain, aware of continuous whispering behind her back and having her name — Nurse Kaufmann — thrown at her like an accusation. But she'd felt useful, she'd felt she was doing something worthwhile, and she'd known it wasn't forever. She'd had hopes back then, even though she'd not really had time to think about them; she'd had hopes of a brighter future, however remote it might be.

Last Easter now seemed like a lost paradise.

Snow continued to fall, lashed by a squalling wind. She wondered if it was also snowing in France — snowing on the trenches, on Billy Turner, who would be shivering with cold and thinking he'd never be warm again. It was nearly two weeks since she'd sat with him in the Barley Mow. That same afternoon, she'd gone to Mrs Bourne and asked for the key to Eliza's room. Mrs Bourne had handed it over without comment. If the housekeeper had informed Aunt Eloise — and it wasn't certain that she would have — nothing had come of it. There'd been just over a day left of Billy's leave. Perhaps he and Eliza had contrived to meet in that time. Dorothea didn't know for sure. She had not asked, and the name 'Billy Turner' had not passed Eliza's lips from that day to this. Billy Turner had gone, Harry Keech too; Dorothea, avoiding the village this last fortnight, heard news second-hand from the housemaid, Winny Downie.

It just so happened that the day of Billy's departure would have been Johann's twenty-ninth birthday. A few days later, three inches of snow had fallen. The snow had lingered all week; there'd been snow on the ground on Good Friday. The following day, the newspapers had announced that the United States had entered the war on the side of the Allies, provoked into it by the German policy of indiscriminately sinking ships. The newspapers had trumpeted this development. People had talked of little else. 'Now we're bound to win,' they said, 'and there will be peace before the end of the year.'

That was on the Saturday. In the early hours next day — Easter Sunday — the clocks had changed, moving to summer time. But summer seemed as far off as ever; summer was impossible to believe in, with snow falling in April. Nor was Dorothea excited by the Americans joining the war. She did not believe in the mirage of peace.

Stood at the window in the silence of the morning room, with the wind whining and moaning outside, Dorothea watched the snow come down.

CHAPTER SIX

Working steadily and methodically in the hot May sunshine, Dorothea cleared one patch of ground at a time, pulling up weeds and digging down to get at their roots, attacking trailing brambles and spindly invasive saplings with her spade. She wore a wide-brimmed hat to keep the sun off, held in place by ribbons tied under her chin. Her long skirts — trailing in the dirt, snagged by thorns — were stained and torn and dusty; she was glad she'd remembered to put on an old frock before setting about the task of clearing the long-neglected keeper's garden. But even if she managed to get on top of it, would anything much ever grow here? Becket, when she consulted him (she'd had to raise her voice to make herself heard), had regarded her dubiously; it would take a deal of elbow grease to make anything of *that* wilderness, he'd said, and she ought to have started before now. All the same, he'd added, it was a late season this year — unusually late — so she might, *might*, just be in luck. He would see about letting her have some of his seedlings by and by, if there were any to spare (his seedlings were as precious as children to him).

Perspiring in the heat, Dorothea paused to wipe her face and surveyed her handiwork. She'd made a promising start, but there was still much to do. And she couldn't help feeling a nagging sense of guilt at spending so much time on something that might come to nothing.

She looked all around. It was a perfect morning, warm and sunny with barely a breath of wind. Sparrows hopped and twittered on the sloping roof of the Gatehouse; a robin darted in and out of the undergrowth, and eyed her magisterially. She cocked her head, listening for the waffling call of a green woodpecker — she'd seen one earlier, flitting high up in the shade of the trees — but all she could hear was the occasional faint cawk of a pheasant deep in the gloomy brakes of the Spinney on the other side of the drive.

As she stood there, she found herself by force of habit thinking up words and phrases she could use later to describe the scene in a letter to Johann, a habit she'd still not shaken off even after six months and more. She knew very well that she could write as many letters as she liked, but that he would never read them. She wondered what on earth he would have thought of her, could he have seen her now, the sweat pouring off her, her frock torn and grubby, dirt under her fingernails.

'*Du bist sehr schön.*'

A thrill shivered through her, remembering those words and the tone of his voice, and the touch of his hand as he gently brushed the curls off her forehead.

'You are very beautiful.'

She'd laughed at herself — at her own vanity — she who'd always been plain and ordinary and unassuming. Yet he'd seen her otherwise. He had really seen her otherwise. There was no room for doubt about that. And always a secret thrill had run through her when he told her so — that she was *sehr schön*: very beautiful.

They'd spoken to each other in English, then in German, swapping and changing. She'd never been able to decide which she liked best: to hear him speak freely and easily in his native tongue, or to listen to the great pains he took with his English pronunciation; he'd aimed to speak English like a native, but he'd never been entirely able to disguise his crisp German accent. He'd practised his English by reading the Beatrix Potter books she'd brought with her as gifts for Heinrich's children (Beatrix Potter had been a great favourite with Eliza in her nursery days).

'"A tale about a tail." This is most amusing, yes? But how are you saying this word here?'

'Squirrel. Squirrel Nutkin.'

'*Skvill. Skvirl.*' He'd done his best to get his tongue round the word. '*Was? Was ist so lustig?*'

'You. You are funny. Oh, Johann, I'm sorry! I didn't mean to laugh!' But he had been laughing too.

People had thought him a solemn, serious-minded, rather shy young man — all of which he was. But there was much more to him: so much warmth and laughter, so much kindness and compassion.

His brother Siegfried, four years younger, was very different: much more reserved, much more stiff and formal. Though he'd always been perfectly polite, Dorothea could not help wondering if he entirely approved of her. But by the summer of 1914, when she departed for England, she'd felt she was beginning to win him round. He'd gone so far as to shake her hand and wish her a good trip. And when, in return, she had kissed his cheek, she'd sensed he was pleased, and perhaps even a little moved. Siegfried, she rather suspected, was a young man of deep emotions who kept himself carefully in check. There was no reason why they shouldn't become friends, she'd felt. In those days, she'd been confident in her ability to make a friend of almost anyone, if she put her mind to it. All it needed was time.

Even scrupulous Siegfried had been known to unbend at times, when egged on by his cousin Gerhard. *Die Jungen*, Dr Kaufmann had called them, 'the boys' — they'd both been in their early twenties.

They'd made fun of her and her foreign ways. 'Is it "tea time", Frau Kaufmann? We want our English "tea time"!'

She'd taken their raillery in good part; it was no more than she expected, living in a house full of men (apart from the servants). Gerhard had been the ringleader in the jokes and japes — happy-go-lucky Gerhard, so clumsy and untidy, with his tie crooked and hair that never lay flat. How had he got on in the disciplined German army? His talent for making people laugh had no doubt served him well. But had there been anything to laugh about in the mincing-machine of Verdun?

She shied away from such morbid thoughts. They seemed out of place on this bright May morning. She turned to happier memories. Sunlight glinting on the waters of the Aussenalster. Trams rattling and clanging on Jungfernstieg. Ships in Hamburger Hafen, gateway to the world, their funnels silhouetted against the sky. But even such innocuous memories as these brought tears to her eyes, reminding her of her new family whom she'd left behind one July morning three years ago: scruffy Gerhard, prickly Siegfried, Lotte who was such a treasure. She could never go back. For all that was gone, gone for good, Gerhard dead, and Johann—

'Good morning, Mrs Kaufmann.'

The unexpected voice caught her completely off-guard and made her jump. Wrenched out of her reverie, she quickly turned round to see who it was.

An old stone wall ran alongside the Lawham Road for several hundred yards either side of the entrance into Clifton's driveway. Here by the Gatehouse, the wall had crumbled and partly collapsed, leaving a jumble of fallen blocks and a gap big enough and low enough to step through. The Reverend Morgan — or Owain, as he liked to be called — was standing on the grass verge on the other side of the wall. He was dressed in black and holding his bicycle. *New-fangled* they called him in the village: 'That there new-fangled vicar' (they made no distinction between a vicar and a curate).

'A lovely morning to be out and about, Mrs Kaufmann.' He filled the silence as she gathered her thoughts. 'Almost impossible to believe there was snow on the ground not much more than a month ago.' Glancing at the patch of earth she'd cleared, he added, 'You're busy, I see. I shan't interrupt.'

She'd not made him welcome. He was on the point of wheeling his bicycle back onto the road and pedalling away. But she could tell he was only trying to be friendly, and he'd called her 'Mrs Kaufmann' without an edge to his voice.

'Wait. Please. I was about to take five minutes. Won't you join me?'

They sat in the sunshine, perched on the ruined wall. Owain's bicycle lay flat amongst the primroses in the long grass of the verge. There was nothing on the road.

Dorothea tried to think of something to say. Suffused still in the afterglow of her memories, she was tempted to talk about Hamburg. But what did Owain know of her life there, or of the people and places she'd been thinking of? She baulked at the idea of trying to explain. And so they sat in silence.

It was Owain who, at length, found his voice. 'You've become something of a stranger again of late.'

'I am not welcome in the village.'

She was aware that, in days gone by, she would not have let this put her off. As she'd done with Siegfried — and with Nibs Carter too, for that matter — she'd always believed she could change people's minds and win them round. But these days—

'There's nothing I can do. I am the enemy, and that's that.' She spoke dispassionately, merely stating the facts. 'Even people who don't know me are ready to condemn me.'

'There's nothing personal in it. You are the victim of circumstances, that's all. Not much by way of consolation, I'm afraid. But there's plenty for which to be thankful.'

'Is there?'

'Well, we are both here, sitting in the sun. The birds are singing, flowers are in bloom, the miracle of spring is all around us.'

It really did seem like a miracle. Winter, at long last, had released its vice-like grip, and the blazing sun was warming her very bones. But her heart was still frozen. That was how it seemed, anyway. Not that she could say this out loud. It would sound far too histrionic.

Owain glanced at her keenly, as if he had a shrewd idea of what she was thinking, but he said nothing and, after a moment, looked away. He shaded his eyes with his hand, gazing along the deserted road as it ran down the gentle incline towards the half-glimpsed canal, and then on to Lawham, and on again to still more distant places: Leamington, Oxford, London — the wide world.

Following the road with his eyes, staring into the distance, Owain said in a conversational way, 'I know something of what it's like to be an outcast. I can't claim to have suffered as you have suffered, but I am the black sheep of my family. I am a recusant: I chose Church over Chapel, and that is unforgiveable.' He paused, then continued by way of explanation, 'I say "chapel" — singular — but there are, of course, many different versions. I have always found it disconcerting: the rivalry, the in-fighting. Even my own parents are caught up in it. They go their separate ways every Sunday, my father to one chapel, my mother to another. I could never convince myself that it was a state of affairs of which God would approve. I listened to my heart, and my heart led me to the Church of England. I felt I had a . . . a calling, a vocation — if one can say such a thing in this day and age without sounding precious.'

Precious, he most certainly wasn't; if anything, the opposite. She warmed to him, felt there might even be the beginnings of a connection between the two of them.

'I also followed my heart,' she said. 'I followed my heart when I married Johann.'

'And your family disapproved?'

'They didn't understand. I was marrying a foreigner, moving to another land. They thought me terribly misguided.'

'But you've no regrets?' It wasn't really a question.

'I would do it all again. I wouldn't change a thing.'

'Even if you knew what lay ahead?'

'Even then,' she said, without hesitation. She added, 'And you? Has your family forgiven you?'

'Let's say I remain something of a disappointment to them.'

She felt bitter on his behalf — or was it her own family she felt bitter towards? She had good reason, or so it seemed to her just then, after all the trouble Eliza had caused with the Turners, and Aunt Eloise's insistence on seeing Jake Carter which had earned Nibs's ire. As for Roderick, she could not entirely forget his appalling behaviour in Switzerland, not to mention his fathering a child of Susie Carter when he had a pregnant wife at home.

'He didn't always behave very well.'

'Your husband?'

'No, no, not Johann. My cousin, Roderick. He could be so selfish at times, so very selfish—'

She stopped abruptly, shocked by her own words, the vitriol in them. 'I can't . . . I mustn't . . . not now he's dead . . .'

'The way we feel about someone doesn't change just because they've passed on. You used to get angry with your cousin, I take it, when he was alive?'

'Yes, oh yes! He could be *infuriating*—'

She stopped herself again. Even if this was true, she felt disloyal, saying it to Owain, a stranger.

'It's quite in order for you to get angry with him — as angry now as you did before. He's still the same man, even if he's with you now only in memory and not in person.'

'But I never used to get angry quite like *this*! I get angry all the time now.' She was thinking of the way she'd lost her temper with Billy Turner in Barley Mow.

'You lost your husband in the most tragic of circumstances. It is only natural you should feel anger — resentment, even.'

'But that's not me. It's not who I am.'

'You shouldn't be too hard on yourself. No matter how well we think we know ourselves, none of us can be entirely sure how we'll react in a time of adversity.'

There was something both soothing and reassuring about Owain Morgan, and he was surely right about remembering Roderick as he really was — hadn't Rosa said something similar on the day of the memorial service? Oddly enough, Dorothea was struck by how similar they were, Rosa and Owain, both calm and measured and methodical, though there was a spiritual side to the soft-spoken Welshman that was absent in Roderick's widow.

Dorothea was taken aback by how much she missed Rosa and she said so, though she assumed Owain would have little idea who Rosa was. But it seemed he'd heard all about her in the village.

'She sounds a most intriguing character,' said Owain. 'I should have liked to have met her.'

'Perhaps you'll still get the chance, if she ever comes back. But I'm afraid Rosa did not have much time for God.'

'I'd argue His case, of course, but I like to think there's more to me than my dog collar.'

'Oh, there is, and I'm sure Rosa would see it. She's very open-minded, very level-headed — or at least she was, until she went away so suddenly. Her poor children! I don't mind looking after them — I love them dearly — but I can't help thinking that they need their mother. Oh, Owain, I'm sorry! I keep bringing the conversation around to me and my troubles. You must get tired of listening to other people's problems.'

'It goes with the territory, rather.' He hopped down from his seat on the wall. 'Now, alas, I must go. I have other calls on my time. But infrequent though our meetings are—' (If he was chiding her for her sporadic attendance in church, it was gently done.) '—I always enjoy our discussions.' As he picked up his bicycle, he added, 'I think you'll find, if you look, Mrs Kaufmann, that you have rather more friends than you realize.'

Perhaps that was true. On a morning like this, she could almost believe it. There was Nettie Thomson, for one.

'I'd almost forgotten. Nettie's coming on a visit next week. She's been a good friend to me. I don't know how I'd have coped at the hospital without her.'

'There's me, too,' said Owain, getting astride his bicycle. 'I'd like to think you consider me as a friend by now. Well, until next time!'

Dorothea watched him cycle away, rising half out of the saddle as he built up speed, toiling up the gentle incline. He dwindled, then disappeared, where the road dipped towards the village.

He'd looked more boyish than ever today, sat on the wall kicking his heels. But she felt he was wise beyond his years, and there was a strength in him that belied his slender frame. She liked him. If, as he said, he was a friend, then he was a nice friend to have.

As she looked along the empty road, shielding her eyes from the blazing sun, Dorothea's thoughts turned back to Nettie and suddenly she realized just how much she was looking forward to Nettie's visit.

* * *

'Such a wonderful view!' said Nettie Thomson, sat on the terrace sipping her tea.

It was what people always said, when visiting Clifton for the first time. They always praised the view. Partly its impact came from being so unexpected. Approaching the house up the tree-lined drive a visitor got the impression of a place tucked away out of sight; there was no far horizon at the front of the house, just lots of trees and the green slopes of Rookery Hill in the distance. Having arrived, you entered the house, you made your way along the passage, you stepped out onto the terrace — and suddenly there it was, a breath-taking panorama, the land sloping gently into a wide, shallow valley, with a great space of ever-changing sky overhead. The view was at its best this afternoon, blazoned with spring green and bathed in sunshine. Nettie Thomson had arrived at just the right time.

Dorothea had met her off the train. She'd noticed at once how pale and tired Nettie looked, with dark rings round

161

her eyes: evidence that the hospital routine was just as gruelling as ever. But Nettie had begun to relax almost at once, had slowly come alive in the short time it took to get from Welby to Clifton.

Her first sight of the house had left her open-mouthed. 'It's so big — enormous! Why didn't you tell me it was so big?'

'I suppose it is rather bigger than most houses, but it's hardly a palace.'

'It looks like a palace to me.'

Shown to her room, Nettie had stayed upstairs just long enough to unpack and change out of her travelling clothes, then she'd come down for afternoon tea. She was sat now on the terrace next to Dorothea, Aunt Eloise presiding, Eliza a little apart. There was some colour in Nettie's cheeks now. Her russet-coloured and rather wild hair, usually tamed and hidden under her nurse's cap, was this afternoon shaken free and gleaming in the sunshine.

'Such a wonderful view!'

Nothing was more certain to win Aunt Eloise's approval than to praise the house and the grounds, and Nettie was rewarded with a warm smile as Aunt Eloise passed her a slice of cake.

'More tea, Miss Thomson? I'm so glad you like the view, though it is not quite as intended when Clifton was built. The landscaping, you see, was never completed.'

Dorothea did not need to listen to Aunt Eloise's words, she knew it all by heart: how an old manor house had once stood on this very spot, how the manor house had been demolished and the present house built to replace it, how the money had run out so that very little work was ever done on the grounds. Aunt Eloise never tired of repeating this tale; she never tired of introducing newcomers to her beloved Clifton Park.

She had come alive this afternoon, seemed almost her old self. Roderick had sometimes called his mother 'the perfect hostess', and at moments such as this, that was exactly what she was. She put guests at their ease. She made them feel welcome. She kept up all the proprieties.

As they lingered over afternoon tea, talk eventually turned to hospital matters. Dorothea's memories of the place had been coloured by the dreams that had haunted her after coming back to Clifton, dreams in which she had never left south London and was toiling at the hospital still, weighed down by her workload and always behindhand, scurrying feverishly from one task to the next, but never quite able to complete them, whilst in shadowy beds on every side faceless men kept up a ceaseless refrain: 'Nurse! Nurse! Please, Nurse! Please!' Those dreams had given her a horror of the place, but as she listened to Nettie's news, Dorothea began to feel an unexpected nostalgia for her former life as a nurse.

The idea that she might go back had crossed her mind once or twice. Her disturbing dreams had not made it a particularly welcome prospect, however, and she'd always told herself that her duty now lay at Clifton in any case. Also, since Johann's death, nursing had lost what had always been to her its primary purpose: to feel closer to him, to try to get a better understanding of his work, to equip herself for her future role in supporting his career. None of that mattered now. All the same, nursing had made her feel useful, had made her feel she was making a real difference, and she liked to think she'd been good at it. Certainly she'd proved equal to its vicissitudes. And even the frosty-faced matron did not seem so terrible, looking back today, on this serene and sunny afternoon.

The afternoon really did seem idyllic. Almost it was as if the war had never happened, as if time had stood still at Clifton. As they lingered just a little while longer over the last of their tea, the illusion was almost complete.

* * *

Ingleby Wood in late May could hardly have presented a greater contrast to when Dorothea had seen it last, on the day of her long and desolate trek more than six months ago, when she'd walked as far as Hambury Hill before returning in the teeth of a blizzard. The trees now were green with new leaves. Sunlight spilled through their branches; sunlight splashed the woodland floor with pools of dazzling brightness. Pale anemones raised their shy heads above the burgeoning foliage. Climbing honeysuckle was in full bloom. Dorothea and Nettie walked side by side, following a beaten track, whilst Circe ran ahead snuffling in the mould and barking at a sudden squirrel seen only as a flash of russet-red, almost the exact same colour as Nettie's hair.

A pattern had developed since Nettie's arrival. A leisurely breakfast was followed by conversation in the morning room and perhaps a quick glance at the newspapers, before taking a turn around the gardens before lunch. Each afternoon they went roaming further afield, returning in time for tea. A quiet interlude followed, a chance to read or to write letters, or to simply sit outside in the sunshine (the weather remained perfect), until it was time to go up and dress for dinner.

'It's another world here,' said Nettie wonderingly. 'I thought people only lived like this in books.'

The hospital was only ever mentioned now in passing. The war, too, was kept at bay — though Dorothea had fallen back into her old habit (or obligation, as she thought of it) of reading the casualty lists each morning.

'Why do you torture yourself?' Nettie admonished her. 'I think it's macabre. Imagine how you'd feel if you saw a name you knew!'

Nettie steered clear of the newspapers. She steeped herself in the past instead. She'd developed quite a taste for Aunt Eloise's tales of days gone by. No one knew more about the age-old chronicle of Clifton Park than Aunt Eloise. She never tired of reciting the annals of its long-time owners, the Massinghams — her own ancestors.

'Aren't you lucky, Doro, having grown up amongst all this!' Nettie exclaimed. 'The house and the sense of history — you must have felt like royalty!'

Eliza mostly kept to herself and showed little interest in their guest, which was most unlike her.

'She's at the awkward age,' said Aunt Eloise, excusing her daughter's behaviour. 'What she needs is something on which to set her sights. Marriage and motherhood: that's what girls her age should be thinking of.'

'Marriage!' exclaimed Dorothea. 'Oh, Aunt! Eliza's far too young for that.'

As she guided Nettie through Ingleby Wood on this perfect May afternoon, Dorothea found herself thinking of the beech woods of the Harz Mountains where she'd gone on holiday with Johann in the summer of 1913, their only holiday together apart from the wedding trip with which they'd begun their married life. Johann, that summer four years ago, had shown her all the places where he used to go hiking with his good friend Walter Müller in his university days at Leipzig, and Dorothea had hoped in return to bring him here one day, to Ingleby Wood in full leaf. But that would now never be, and it was Nettie Thomson she was showing round all the places she'd hoped to show Johann — the village, Rookery Hill, the bridleway to Brockmorton.

Calling to Circe, they began to retrace their steps, leaving the dappled shade under the trees and joining the Lawham Road where it crossed the canal by a humpbacked bridge. They followed the road as it began to climb gently between thick, leafy hedgerows to the top of the rise. They paused where an entrance opened off the road into a sloping meadow strewn with yellow buttercups. A glimpse of grey stone through the trees away to their left was all that could be seen from here of Clifton.

A flicker of movement caught Dorothea's eye and she pointed out to Nettie two boxing hares on the other side of the meadow. They were dancing on their hind legs and flinging their paws at each other, their shadows shimmering on the grass. Nettie watched in silence, swinging her hat by its ribbons, until the hares suddenly took fright at something and fled towards the far hedge.

Still gazing at the now deserted meadow, Nettie said suddenly, 'I've put my name down for overseas service.'

'Nettie! Why didn't you tell me? If you're selected, we shan't see each other again for goodness knows how long.'

Nettie turned to face Dorothea, leaning back against the gate. 'Why not come with me? I'm sure it could be arranged, if you put your name down too. I'd feel so much better if I was going with you! I can see you're tempted.'

'Oh, Nettie, I can't, really I can't. Aunt Eloise relies on me. There's Eliza too, and the children. Rosa asked me to look after the children. I can't let her down.'

'Rosa should look after her children herself.' Nettie had heard all about Rosa and didn't think much of her behaviour.

They walked on again in silence to the top of the rise. Passing the place where Dorothea had sat with Owain Morgan last week on the tumbled wall, they turned into Clifton's long driveway, Circe now trailing in their wake, tongue lolling. Dorothea was deep in thought. She had to admit that it was an enticing prospect, the adventure of overseas service and a chance to work with Nettie again. They might even be sent to France where she'd be that much closer to the places in which Johann had served as a doctor. She'd be doing the same sort of work as he had, too. She'd found comfort in that before. Might she not find comfort in it again?

There was little doubt she was needed. 'When I think of all those poor wounded men . . . But I'm needed here as well. I can't simply abandon everyone. Oh, Nettie! It's like being torn in two!'

'You can't do both. Even you can't manage that, Doro. But you shouldn't feel guilty about it. You must do what you think is right.' Nettie shook her head in gentle disapproval. 'You take too much on yourself, Doro. Haven't I always said so?'

'I like to keep busy, Nettie. I have to keep busy. If I sat down and thought about everything that's happened this last year or so, I don't think I'd have the heart to ever get up again.'

'Yes, I see. I can understand that. I'm sorry, Doro. I didn't realize.'

'Oh, take no notice, Nettie. I'm just feeling sorry for myself. There are lots of people far worse off than me.' But Dorothea felt she'd rather cast a pall over the perfect afternoon.

Circe alone seemed untroubled, ambling to catch them up. Her tail began to wag as the house at last came into view. They were back in time for tea.

* * *

The days simply flew by; Nettie's visit was almost over. It was her last evening. They were up in the nursery. Dorothea always looked in on the children before dinner and this evening Nettie had accompanied her. Nettie was sat in Nanny's chair, with little Laurence on her knee. Katherine stood four-square at a distance, watching impassively.

'You're a bonny wee man! What a bonny wee man you are!' Nettie looked up. 'How old did you say he was, Doro?'

'Ten months, more or less.' Dorothea paused in the task of putting toys back on the shelves: the nursery maid was apt to let the place get rather untidy, but it wasn't fair to berate her as Katherine was a handful at the best of times and Laurence now at an age where he needed constant attention. 'He was born just a few weeks after his father died.'

'So Roderick never knew him?'

'No.'

'I'd have liked to have met Roderick. Your aunt obviously doted on him.'

'He was her only son and her heir.' Dorothea sighed.

'What is it, Doro?'

'I was just thinking. It was a year ago. It's a year since his last leave.'

'I seem to remember you had special leave of absence.'

'Matron was angry about that when I broke my contract less than two months later. My name must have been mud after I left.'

'Actually, I don't believe she ever mentioned you again. You were sterilized out of existence.' Gently jigging Laurence on her knee, Nettie looked at Dorothea over the top of the child's head. 'I've an idea, Doro. You want to go back to nursing, but you don't want to leave Clifton. So why not have men here?'

'Wounded men, you mean? Here?'

'They needn't be the worst cases. You could have convalescents. I believe lots of stately homes have been turned into hospitals since the war started.'

'Clifton is hardly a stately home.'

'It's plenty big enough to hold a fair few patients. Why don't you look into it?'

'Oh, Nettie, whatever would Aunt Eloise say, turning the place upside down and filling it with grime and gore? She'd never give her permission.'

'Dearest Doro,' said Nettie severely. 'Worthy as you are, even you can't hope to please everyone all of the time. There comes a point when one has to be true to oneself, even if it inconveniences others; one simply has to make a stand.'

Dorothea smiled fondly at her forthright friend. 'How very no-nonsense you are, Nettie! I wish I had you here with me all the time, to point me in the right direction. I shall miss you when you've gone.'

* * *

'A most agreeable young lady, your friend Miss Thomson. I was sorry to see her go.'

Aunt Eloise announced her approval as she walked with Dorothea in the gardens after lunch, Nettie having left that morning. It seemed to Dorothea that the visit had worked wonders with Aunt Eloise. Called on to play the role of perfect hostess, she had risen to the occasion with all her old sangfroid.

Seeing her aunt restored to something like her old self, Dorothea felt encouraged to raise the subject of having convalescents at Clifton. Aunt Eloise might be more amenable if she knew it was Nettie's idea, Nettie being so much in favour. But she'd only just begun to broach the subject when they reached the ornamental pond, where there was a meeting of ways. A little way along the path to the left, which led to the vegetable garden, Eliza was chatting and laughing with a boy dressed in corduroy trousers and a shirt with the sleeves rolled up, his cap tilted back on his head.

Aunt Eloise gripped Dorothea's arm. 'Who is that Elizabeth is talking to? Who is that boy?'

'It's Jack Britten, Aunt. Jack Britten, the gardener's boy. Surely you recognize him?'

Jack was a village lad, the younger brother of Annie Britten who'd been such a bone of contention between Billy Turner and Jeff Smith. Jack had worked in the Clifton gardens for a number of years, on and off, earning himself a few shillings whenever he was needed.

'Britten? Ah, yes. Of course. One tends to forget about Britten.' Aunt Eloise relaxed her grip on Dorothea's arm. 'We must keep an eye out, Dorothea. We must be vigilant. We don't want a repetition of that business with Turner.'

'Oh, Aunt, I hardly think . . . I mean to say . . . there's no need to worry . . .'

Dorothea was incredulous. She might even have burst out laughing had she not been able to see that her aunt was deadly serious. But Eliza and young Britten looked such children together, it ought to have been obvious that the relationship was entirely innocent. Eliza had long enjoyed lording it over Jack, acting as if she was a lot older than him (in fact it was Jack who was the elder, by just a few months); as for Jack, he'd always been somewhat ingenuous and it was difficult to believe he'd be eighteen in a matter of weeks.

'Jack will be leaving us before long,' Dorothea added, offering her aunt further reassurance. 'He'll be called up.'

'It's not just Britten we have to worry about. There is danger on every side. Yesterday, I caught Elizabeth talking to a delivery boy.'

Dorothea was at a loss. To talk of *danger* seemed to her excessive. Perhaps there had been a little childish flirting with the delivery boy but Eliza, for all her skittishness, was unlikely to do anything silly. If anything, Dorothea was encouraged to see Eliza laughing and joking with Jack Britten. She'd been far too quiet and withdrawn since Billy Turner's leave ended; it was most out of character.

Was Aunt Eloise really still brooding over what she called 'that business with Turner'? And it was difficult to believe that she'd actually forgotten who Jack Britten was: Aunt Eloise paid all the staff weekly by her own hand and Jack's name was in the ledger.

Putting all this aside for the time being, Dorothea tried to steer the conversation back to the subject of convalescents at Clifton.

'Nettie suggested that we—'

'Not now, Dorothea. I have to decide what to do about Elizabeth. I have to give the matter some serious thought.'

Without another word, Aunt Eloise went wandering off. Watching her go, Dorothea could only think that, for all her aunt had seemed like her old self recently, things were not yet quite back to normal.

* * *

Working in the keeper's garden, Dorothea did her best to prepare a patch of earth to receive the seedlings Becket had bestowed on her. It was slow going. The ground was hard as iron, the soil compacted. Much effort was needed to force in her garden fork. She found it difficult to keep her mind on the task in hand; as the dry soil crumbled through the tines of the fork, she thought of the tortured earth across the Channel, where the war still raged unabated.

Today was the 309th day of the third year of the war — the newspapers kept a tally — and there'd been reports this morning of a new British attack. The main objective, a place called Messines Ridge (Dorothea had only the vaguest idea where it was), had been taken in the first assault, which was being hailed as an unprecedented success. But Dorothea seemed to remember other such triumphs that had come to nothing. Would this latest success also prove to be a chimera?

The attack had opened in a particularly gruesome manner and it was this which had stuck in Dorothea's mind. Large mines had been laid under the enemy lines. They had all been detonated at zero hour. Dorothea had read in the newspaper how the ground had shaken and trembled as if in an earthquake, how sheets of flame had blotted out the sky; the deafening sound such colossal explosions would make could only be guessed at. Tons of earth had been hurled in the air, to rain back down on the newly mutilated landscape. In light of such gruesome details, it seemed gratuitous to point out — though the newspaper had been only too ready to do so — that any German soldiers caught in the cataclysm would have been instantly blown to atoms.

To think of it made Dorothea feel queasy. She wished that she'd never read the reports. But she *had* read them, and she couldn't put them out of her head. It seemed almost beyond belief that so much time and effort, and so much invention, went into dreaming up ever more appalling ways of killing the piteous young men caught up in the war. And this grisly conflict had been going on now for three years and 309 days, which gave a total of over one thousand: one thousand days of war.

'D'you want any help, miss?'

She was jolted from her macabre train of thought by a bright and cheerful young voice. Dick Turner was climbing over the gap in the wall. He was dusty and grimy and wearing his work clothes with a pair of hobnailed boots. He snatched his cap off and presented himself, providing a welcome distraction.

'Why, hello, Dick! What are you doing here?'

'Come to tell you about the new-born. Auntie Daisy's had her baby, miss. Little girl, name of Daisy, same as her mum. We'll get mixed up with two Daisies. But that's Uncle

Zack for you. Mum said you'd want to know about the baby, so I promised to drop by the big house if I got chance.'

'That's very good of you, Dick. Thank you. How are they, Daisy and the baby?'

'Oh, aye, right as rain, both of 'em.' He nodded at the garden fork Dorothea was still holding. 'I'll give you an 'and, Miss Dorothea, if you like.'

'Don't you need to get back to work? I wouldn't want you to get in trouble with Mr Tebbit again.'

'I won't be missed for half an hour or so. They's having their bait. That's how I was able to come. You sit down, miss, and have a bit of a rest. Let me do a spot of digging.'

She didn't like to refuse so generous an offer, though she thought it hardly worth his time to indulge this whim of hers to bring the keeper's garden back to life (it would never come to anything, like as not). He took his jacket off and flung it down, tossed his cap on top, and she handed him the fork. He threw himself into the task, bursting with energy, full of boyish enthusiasm, attacking the dry ground and turning big clods of earth and breaking them up with the tines of the fork, bending down every so often to pick out stones and throw them aside: 'digging proper', as his great-grandfather, old Noah Lee, would have said. Perched on the crumbling wall, where she'd sat with Owain Morgan just a few weeks ago, Dorothea watched Dick at work. He carried on talking as he was digging. His voice had broken a while ago but it was still rather husky-sounding, as if he'd not yet grown into it; at times it cracked if he got too animated.

'Beats me why Uncle Zack was so keen to call the little one Daisy. Mum told me folk often name their kids after theyselves.

'Says I, "You dint name me after no one. Int no Dicks in our family."

'And she says, "Was Miss Dorothea as suggested 'Richard'. Yer dad and me, we liked the sound of it, so we used it."

'Great-Grandpa, he turns round and he says, "There was me thinking yer lad were named for Dick Turpin!"

'And Mum says, "Don't talk wet, Grandpa! As if I'd name any lad of mine after a highwayman!"

'And Great-Grandpa says, "Ote wrong with Dick Turpin, my girl. One of us, Dick Turpin. All for the common folk, he were."

'But Mum, she wouldn't have none of it. "Dick Turpin, my eye!" says she. "I'll call the lad by his right name from now on, see if I don't, and we'll have no more of Dick."

'And Great-Grandpa, he dint say ote, he just looks at me and he winks — like this — when Mum's not watching. He don't half egg her on! He's an old rogue, if ever there was one, and never mind Dick Turpin.'

Dick paused in his work, wiping the sweat off his brow with the back of his hand. Glancing at Dorothea a little shyly, he said, 'You've not been in the village lately, miss. Mum were only saying the other day. That's why she sent me to tell you about the baby.'

Dorothea wasn't quite sure how to respond to this, and Dick flushed a little as if he feared he'd made some sort of *faux pas*. He busied himself with his digging.

But he must know she wasn't welcome in the village, thought Dorothea, surely he must know. She still found it painful to remember her last encounter with Mrs Turner and Daisy, on the day she'd talked with Billy in the Barley Mow. But she could hardly say this to Dick when his own family was involved.

Perhaps Dick's mother Pippa thought more kindly of her. There seemed some hope of it. Why else would she have sent Dick with news of the baby? Pippa was a Turner by marriage but a Cheeseman by birth, the daughter of Big John at the Barley Mow and sister to John Cheeseman in the shop. Pippa had married Billy and Daisy's elder brother, Jem, in the autumn of 1901. Dick had come along nearly a year later, on a day Dorothea was unlikely to forget — for she'd been present at the birth.

Dick had been born on the day of the Great Fire of legend. Amidst all the chaos and confusion of that day, pregnant Pippa had gone missing. Whilst taking a shortcut home through the thicket between School Street and Back Lane — 'the Wilderness', it was called — she'd tripped and twisted her ankle, leaving her stranded. Dorothea had been the first to find her, by which time Pippa was in labour. Everything had happened in a rush. There'd been no time to go for help. Dorothea remembered as if it were yesterday her shock and terror at seeing the baby come squelching out to lie unmoving on a bed of the previous year's withered leaves: a scrap of flesh, he'd been. Just skin and bones. Dead, she'd thought. And yet here he was, almost fifteen years later, the scrap of flesh having grown into this strapping lad who was digging her garden.

How tough and resilient they were, human beings, but terribly fragile, too — as fragile in the face of war as that help-less scrap of flesh lying on the dead leaves. She thought about the newspaper report she'd read earlier, the German soldiers blown to atoms. Just a few short days ago, they'd been as real as Dick here, and in the prime of life. Then — in one horrible, sickening moment — they'd simply ceased to exist.

Was it wrong to feel sorry for them? Mrs Adnitt would say it was. So would Mr Cheeseman in the shop. To feel sorry for German soldiers was to be disloyal to England. Had compassion, then, become a sin?

She couldn't help wondering — 'torturing' herself, as Nettie would have it — if Johann too had been blown to atoms when the bomb landed on his field hospital. But that was too horrible to think of, his beautiful body torn and mangled, or perhaps utterly destroyed: his handsome face, his strong arms, his agile fingers, his gentle mouth, his warm skin. How she longed for him — ached for him — to be able to touch him, hold him, caress him. How it tormented her, wanting him.

She felt her cheeks burning, self-conscious and rather ashamed by the turn her thoughts had taken — such naked desire, with Dick just inches away. But why should she be ashamed? 'The flesh is God's creation,' Owain Morgan had said. And Johann had not been ashamed. Johann had shown her how the daunting mysteries of physical love could be simple, natural, beautiful.

But now he was gone, and there was nothing left of him — not so much as a corpse, perhaps. And what seemed so cruel — what seemed cruellest of all — was that she'd not been granted the consolation of having given birth to his child. *In sorrow thou shalt bring forth children*, said the Bible, the Book of Genesis. But what about the sorrow of *not* bringing forth children? What of that?

'There.' Dick thrust the fork deep into the ground. 'That'll have to do for now. I oughtta get back afield.' He pulled on his jacket, jammed his cap on his head, hesitated. 'I . . . I could come another time, if you want. Help out, like.'

'Well, if . . . if you're sure . . . that would be . . . would be . . .'

She found herself flustered, brought back to the present moment after being lost in deep thought. His generous offer had caught her unawares. But she could see that he meant it. He was not just being polite. And this little kindness went straight to her heart, seemed indescribably precious amidst all the pain and the suffering and the inexhaustible hostility.

She knew she would only embarrass him if she made too much of it, so she simply said, 'That would be a great help, Dick. Thank you.'

He broke into a grin. 'Well, then. I'll see yer again.'

He'd already taken to his heels and the last of these words were flung over his shoulder as he ran down the road. His grin seemed to linger in the air behind him like the Cheshire Cat's.

Dorothea had to wipe her eyes as the sound of his boots on the tarmac faded away. He was always so full of life. He was so young, too, not yet fifteen. King and country had no claim on him for now. But the war, she reminded herself — and how could she forget, with the newspapers keeping careful count — had already lasted a thousand days, and still there was no end in sight. In a thousand days more, Dick would be old enough to fight. Would the war then devour him too, as it had devoured so many others?

Lunchtime was at hand. Dorothea decided to abandon her gardening for now. Walking slowly up the drive, she was bewildered by her changing moods, couldn't keep track of them. One moment everything seemed hopeless, the next — well, it was impossible to be entirely cast down, when the sun was shining and the birds were singing, and she was surrounded by all the simple pleasures of a beautiful June morning. Dick, too, had been a breath of fresh air, and he'd made short work of the digging. Perhaps there was some hope, after all, for Becket's seedlings in what had seemed such unpromising ground. Daisy's baby was also a sign of hope, a reminder that life sprang ever anew. Dorothea dared to wonder, if she sent a little something for the baby — it would also serve by way of an olive branch — whether Daisy would accept it.

As she let herself into the house, Dorothea found Aunt Eloise standing in the hallway, almost as if she'd been waiting. There was a piece of paper in her hand.

'Ah, Dorothea. There you are. I was about to come and find you. This has just arrived, a message from Brockmorton Manor. Viola Somersby has passed away.'

* * *

'It is much to her credit that she held out for so long, far longer than anyone expected,' said Dr Camborne, as he helped himself to more new potatoes. 'I gave her six months myself, no more — not that I was privy to the details of her case. But there's very little one can do under such circumstances. Even the finest Harley Street specialists are powerless in the face of cancer.'

They were not long back from the funeral at Brockmorton and were now sat round the table eating a late luncheon. There were four of them: Dorothea, Aunt Eloise and Eliza had been joined by Dr Camborne, whom they'd met at the funeral and who'd accepted an invitation to Clifton. Knives and forks scraped on the best china. Crompton hovered in the background. The windows of the dining room were wide open on this sultry afternoon.

The village doctor looked no different now to how he'd looked seventeen years ago, when Dorothea had first seen him, leathery skin stretched over his balding and bony skull, and only a hint of a wrinkle on his desiccated face. As usual, he was far from being at a loss for words.

'Excellent lamb, this, Eloise. From your Home Farm, I presume? I thought as much. But where was I? Ah. Yes. Cancer. Now, cancer is an insidious disease. It takes people before their time. Viola Somersby was only fifty-seven, no age at all. But — dare I say it? — even cancer has its uses. I have been told on good authority that the Kaiser is being eaten away by cancer, by cancer of the throat — or is it his ear? I forget. Either way, he'll be dead before the year's out, the prognosis is quite certain — and not a moment too soon, as far as I'm concerned. Ah, well, there you have it. *Pallida mors aequa pulsat pede, pauperum tabernas, regumque turres.*' The doctor turned to Eliza. 'Now, young lady. Are you up on your Latin? Let us see if you can construe what I've just quoted. *Pallida mors*, of course, is "pale death". What about *pauperum tabernas*? Any ideas? Come along now! Think of "pauper", think of "tavern", and work sideways.'

Eliza had been pushing her food around her plate for the last ten minutes. Giving Dr Camborne a withering look, she ignored his question and said bluntly, 'Why was Giles Milton not in uniform? Does a lisp make him exempt?'

As if snubbing the doctor was not bad manners enough, Eliza's sarcastic question sounded horridly callous, asked of a man who had just buried his mother-in-law. There was an awkward silence round the table. Even Dr Camborne seemed, for once, at a loss for words.

In days gone by, Aunt Eloise would never have allowed the conversation to lapse like this. She'd have quelled Eliza with one look, then gone on to say something brightly and in passing about the weather or the Home Farm lamb, before introducing a new topic for discussion. As recently as Nettie Thomson's visit, Aunt Eloise had shown signs of her old self, but the perfect hostess was entirely absent today. Dorothea was not even sure that her aunt was aware of what Eliza had said.

But if Aunt Eloise was distracted, she had every reason. Though she gave very little away, Mrs Somersby's death must surely have come as a blow. Aunt Eloise and Viola Somersby had known each other for years. To all appearances, they'd been the best of friends, though they'd perhaps not exactly been confidantes; Dorothea wondered if Aunt Eloise had ever truly been intimate with anyone. Certainly, she was very reserved. 'Cold' and 'aloof' were words sometimes used of her, though Dorothea felt this was not entirely fair. 'Poised' and 'dignified' would be more accurate; 'poised' and 'dignified' described her precisely today.

Watching her aunt all in black sat in Brockmorton church — composed, arresting, immaculate — Dorothea had found herself curious about the events that had shaped her, that had made her the woman she was today. Much of Aunt Eloise's past was a mystery, and likely to remain so. Her stories of bygone days were rarely of a personal nature. On the surface, Aunt Eloise looked much the same as ever. She never seemed to change. To the other mourners, it really must have seemed that way. But they didn't see her at more private moments. There were occasions, these days, when she would sit for perhaps an hour at a time, simply staring into space, and this would never have happened in the old days. Aunt Eloise had always been a woman who liked to make the most of every waking moment.

Brockmorton's tiny church had been full today: a very respectable turnout, people said, under the circumstances. The funeral had been entirely fitting; everything had been correct and proper. Yet Dorothea had been unable to shake the feeling that there was something ad hoc and perfunctory about it, a long-expected event that had come at the wrong moment, or too late. It ought to have been Mrs Somersby's final fanfare. She should have taken centre stage one last time. But she'd been overshadowed, pre-empted. There was nothing unusual anymore about an untimely death. Death before its time had ceased to be shocking, or even very poignant. Death had become commonplace since August 1914.

A widow, Mrs Somersby was survived by three children, all of whom had been in attendance today. The elder daughter, Julia, was married to Mr Giles Milton, the man with the lisp Eliza had just mentioned. Giles Milton was uncle to Roderick's Oxford friend Gerry Milton, while Julia had once been dubbed 'Horse Face' by Roderick, as Eliza had reminded them in church in an all-too-audible whisper. The younger daughter, Cecily, was yet unmarried and lived at home, along with Eileen, the wife of Mrs Somersby's soldier son Mark: he'd come hotfoot from a staff posting in France to attend his mother's funeral.

The rector of Brockmorton had chosen, in his eulogy, to highlight Mrs Somersby's long battle with the disease that killed her. He'd compared her courage and tenacity to the fighting spirit of the nation. Dorothea could not be sure, but it seemed to her that the rector had fixed his eye on her at this point in his speech, remembering perhaps how she'd tried to enlist his help earlier in the war in her unavailing attempts to get Johnnie Cheeseman out of the army, an enterprise of which he'd not approved. Briefly departing from his written words, the rector had made a topical reference to the 'beastly crimes of the Hun' (he'd characterized England's enemy as 'this cancer on the face of the world'). Only yesterday, he'd said, there had been a 'despicable attack on the innocent civilians of London, cowardly airmen dropping their ungodly bombs from their flying machines, and killing women and children indiscriminately'.

After the service, Giles and Julia Milton had supplied further details of the raid. They lived in town and had experienced it first-hand, just as they were making ready to leave for Northamptonshire. At least a dozen German aeroplanes had been involved. 'They came buzzing like a swarm of angry bees,' was how Julia had put it.

The first bombs had fallen around midday. 'There was such a banging and crashing,' said Julia, 'worse than the worst thunderstorm one could imagine. The fact it was such a beautiful morning only made it all the more awful.' In all, over one hundred people were reported to have been killed.

'And where were our own airmen in all this?' Giles had demanded, holding court after the funeral. 'Why weren't they there, in the skies over London, protecting us? What are the generals thinking of — our blundering government, too — keeping all our aeroplanes in France, and leaving women and children in England at risk? A disgrace, that's what it is. An absolute disgrace. Someone should pay dearly for such a blunder. As for the Hun, I'll tell you what must be done. Give him a taste of his own medicine! What he metes out to us, repay him in kind. Repay him tenfold — twenty — a *hundred* times. Make him suffer, I say. And I'm sure you all agree with me.'

No voice had been raised in dissent. Dorothea, too, had kept silent. There'd seemed no point in drawing attention to herself by swimming against the tide. She felt sure that Giles Milton approved even of the dropping of bombs on German hospitals. He would say that killing German doctors was the reckoning they deserved. He would think it entirely justified. Nor would he be alone in that.

A heavy silence had fallen on the dining room. The silence seemed even to weigh on Dr Camborne. He had nothing more to say.

Dorothea picked at the Home Farm lamb on her plate. She'd begun to feel, lately . . . well, 'hope' was too strong a word, but certainly the days had seemed a little less dark. High summer in May had been followed by this heatwave in June. Winter was a fading memory. She'd been heartened by Nettie's visit, by Owain's friendship, by unquenchable Dick Turner. With Dick's help this last week, she'd cleared nearly all the keeper's garden and planted out Becket's seedlings.

But now, with Mrs Somersby's passing and today's difficult funeral, death — pale death — had returned to haunt them.

Death was not done with them yet.

* * *

There'd been so much heat in recent days that thunder seemed inevitable. On Sunday evening, the storm duly came. Dorothea was in her room just after seven tidying her dressing table, as it was not yet time to go down for dinner. There was still an hour to sunset, but a grey gloom had fallen like the onset of dusk. She could hardly see what she was doing.

She crossed to the window and looked out. Louring clouds were swirling in a threatening sky, a downpour imminent — indeed, it was already raining in fits and starts. The gloom deepened. The rain grew heavier; it quickly became torrential. Water streamed down the window; it cascaded from the drooping branches of the cedar tree, it bounced up off the gravel below. A vivid flash of lightning ripped the sky apart. Thunder cracked and boomed directly overhead. More thunder rumbled ominously in the distance. Watching the deluge, Dorothea was reminded of Julia Milton's description of the air raid on London: 'It was worse than the worst thunderstorm one could imagine.' But terrible as were the works of man, nature could never be outmatched.

Dorothea became aware, through the blur of rain, of a trudging figure that had just come round the corner from the drive, hands in pockets, head bowed, wet, bedraggled — the only sign of life. Who was out in weather like this?

The figure hesitated near the cedar tree and looked up at the house as if undecided whether to go on. Dorothea recognized Dick Turner. Why had he come? Surely not to work in the Gatehouse garden.

She was seized by the sudden certainty that he was here on some important errand; he mustn't be allowed to leave until she'd learned what it was. As he hesitated, she left her room and ran downstairs. She opened the front door just as

Dick was climbing the steps; he'd obviously nerved himself to go on. She ushered him inside and shut out the storm. He stood there in the hallway, drenched from head to toe, water running off him and forming a puddle on the black-and-white tiles at his feet.

'Oh, Dick, look at you! You're soaked to the skin! Why ever did you come out in this?'

'Mum sent me, miss. She said you'd want to know. A letter come. A letter about Uncle Billy. He got hit. Wounded. They tried to save him, the letter said, but they couldn't.

'He's dead, miss. Uncle Billy's dead.'

CHAPTER SEVEN

'I wrote to Lieutenant Cartwright some time ago and invited him to Clifton when he next had leave,' said Aunt Eloise at breakfast, looking up from a letter she'd been reading. 'He has sent word that his leave is due and he would be delighted to come. I must reply at once and make all the arrangements. I wonder, Dorothea, as it's urgent, if you'd be good enough to take the letter to the post as soon as I've written it?'

'Who is Lieutenant Cartwright?' asked Owain Morgan later, as Dorothea sat with him in the churchyard; they'd happened to meet in the street when Dorothea was on her way back from the post office, Aunt Eloise's letter safely despatched. 'I've not heard you mention a Lieutenant Cartwright before.'

'He's a friend of Roderick's — was a friend.'

A very good friend: that was how Aunt Eloise had described him at breakfast. This was not entirely accurate. Roderick had met Lieutenant Cartwright in May last year; they'd been crossing the Channel together, going on leave (Roderick's last leave, as it turned out). Learning that Cartwright had nowhere much to go 'back in Blighty', Roderick — on the spur of the moment, characteristically off the cuff — had asked him along to Clifton. Lieutenant Cartwright had been something of a hit, as far as Dorothea remembered, though she was ashamed to say she'd not really taken much notice of him. It wasn't that she'd deliberately ignored him; there'd simply been too much else to fit in on her flying visit. The matron at the hospital had allowed her a few days' leave under special dispensation in view of Roderick being home. She'd not seen Roderick for more than six months, and she'd been away from Clifton for even longer, so she'd had much to catch up on. Lieutenant Cartwright had not been her priority.

Sat with Owain on a bench in the lee of the church tower, Dorothea furrowed her brow as she watched two spotted orange butterflies flickering over a bed of nettles in the fitful sunshine: she was thinking of the matron, who'd been so accommodating when Roderick was on leave, yet after Roderick's death just a few short weeks later had been cold and disapproving as she faced Dorothea across her cluttered desk.

Really, this is most inconvenient. To leave now, when we are at our busiest. I find it incomprehensible.

Harassed and overworked — everyone was overworked at the hospital — perhaps the matron had felt she'd been taken advantage of, having granted Nurse Kaufmann special leave of absence only for that same Nurse Kaufmann to quit her post not much more than a month later. Was it this that had prompted the matron's harsh words about divided loyalties, that had led to her threat to make sure that Dorothea never worked in a hospital again? If so, thought Dorothea, it might be that the threat had come out of a sense of resentment and frustration, and her German connections had been seen by the matron not so much as a mark of Cain but more as a convenient stick with which to beat her.

Nothing was as clear-cut as it seemed, thought Dorothea as the sun went behind a cloud and the butterflies disappeared over the churchyard wall. Roderick's inviting Lieutenant Cartwright to Clifton, for instance. On the surface, this seemed a kind and generous act, but Roderick was far too complex a character for that to have been all there was to it. There was even a possibility that kindness had very little to do with his motivations. Perhaps Roderick had invited Lieutenant Cartwright to deflect attention from himself. On the face of it, this seemed unlikely — Roderick had hardly been shy and retiring — but there were certain things he'd definitely been reluctant to talk about: anything to do with the war, for a start. (*Mother hasn't the first idea . . . nor Rosa . . . you're the only one I can really talk to, Doro . . .*) All the same, if he'd intended Lieutenant Cartwright to serve as a decoy, Roderick could not have foreseen how popular the visitor would prove to be, and he must have felt as if he'd been rather hoisted by his own petard.

None of this could Dorothea say to Owain; it was all too complicated to put into words, like trying to undo a knot tied up too tight. She stuck instead to simple facts about Cartwright.

'He was a schoolmaster before the war. Aunt Eloise has kept in touch with him since his visit. She writes to several of Roderick's old friends.'

'Perhaps she finds some measure of consolation in it.'

'Perhaps.'

The conversation lapsed. There was nothing more to be said about Lieutenant Cartwright.

The clouds parted and the sun shone brightly for a moment. The churchyard was a haven of tranquillity, the only sound that of birdsong and the buzzing of bees. The grass had not been cut for some time, so was scattered with daisies and primroses, and with the drooping stems of flowering sorrel, swaying in a faint breeze. The weathered gravestones, leaning at different angles, were stained by lichens that showed up in the sunshine white and grey, brown and pale yellow.

One of the orange butterflies came fluttering back into view. Following its dancing progress along the top of the churchyard wall, Dorothea tried to put a name to it. Roderick would have known. He'd have told her in an instant. He'd collected butterflies as a boy, had considered himself an expert. But Roderick was gone, and gone with him was his great store of knowledge, gleaned so assiduously over the twenty-three years of his life. She felt sad to think of the waste of it, when he'd had so much to offer.

She glanced at Owain, sat companionably beside her, a very different sort of man to Roderick. It was odd how quickly she'd grown to feel at ease with the young curate. They could sit here in silence without the least awkwardness. He was thin, pasty-faced, very young-looking — though she had an idea that he wasn't actually very much younger than her. Yes. He was undoubtedly very different to Roderick. Perhaps a little more like Johann. But whereas Owain leaned towards the spiritual, Johann had been logical and rational, though never in a cold or clinical way. *Civilized* — that was the word that most readily sprang to mind when thinking about Johann: he'd been a very civilized man. Even though he'd been convalescing when she first met him, there'd still been something vigorous and vibrant about him, whereas Owain . . . was the right word *brittle*? Was there a certain brittleness to him? He reminded her a little of Richard, perhaps, Aunt Eloise's ill-fated nephew and heir to Clifton Park. Dorothea could imagine that Richard, had he lived, might have grown into just such a man as Owain.

But all comparisons were entirely superficial and — ultimately — pointless. Owain, Richard, Roderick, Johann: they were all so very different, and she felt about them differently, so that it was impossible to say that she loved one more than the others — except that Johann came first, would always come first: no one would ever take Johann's place in her heart.

She suddenly went rigid, as if she'd only just realized the full significance of this, though in fact she'd always known that no one would ever take Johann's place, nor did she want them to. Which meant — what? A life spent alone? A future in which she had no family of her own — perhaps even no friends, the way things were going?

She quickly corrected herself. It wasn't true to say she had no friends. There were still people who wished her well. She was sitting next to one of them. And in the post office earlier, Mr Downie had been courtesy itself. But she couldn't help thinking about something that had happened a few weeks ago, soon after she'd first heard of Billy Turner's death.

She'd been anxious to offer her condolences. Surely all differences would be put aside at a time like this. But her knocking had gone unanswered at the Turners' cottage in Back Lane, and in School Street Daisy had stood on her doorstep frosty-faced, with her arms folded; Dorothea's words of sympathy had run off her like water off stone. Making a last attempt, Dorothea had gone round to the cottage opposite the Barley Mow, where Dick Turner lived with his parents and younger brother.

Pippa Turner had not been unfriendly; she'd been apologetic, even. 'It's very good of you to call, miss. I'd ask you in, only I . . . I don't think Jem'd like it.'

'Oh, Pippa, all I want is . . . I'm sorry, that's all. I'm so sorry. Sorry about Billy. Sorry about everything.'

'I know, miss. I know you are. But they're not ready to hear it yet. It's . . . it's too soon.'

Too soon — or too late? Would this rift ever be repaired? She wasn't even sure what she was supposed to have done. They seemed to think, the Turners, that she'd colluded with Eliza, and that Eliza was some sort of siren who'd been luring Billy to ruin, instead of a slip of a girl with a silly crush.

'A penny for your thoughts?'

She found Owain watching her, the way he sometimes watched people: silent, observant, tactful.

'I was thinking—'

But where could she begin? And wherever she began, she always ended up at the same place.

'Nothing will ever go right while the war lasts. How much longer can it possibly last?'

'Until one side or the other gains the victory — and that is in God's hands.'

'But you pray that the victory will be England's?'

'I'd rather it was England than not.'

'I'd rather there wasn't a war between England and Germany at all.'

'War is an evil best avoided. There's no argument there. But sometimes war cannot be avoided. Sometimes war is the only course of action.'

'But was that really the case this time?'

'Well . . . when one thinks of Belgium—'

'So you believe Germany is to blame for the war?'

'Germany must take her share of the blame. They are a martial race, the Germans.'

'But they aren't warmongers, not the ordinary people — no more than the English. The Germans I knew in Hamburg weren't.'

'I expect they were patriots, nonetheless.'

'Well . . . yes,' Dorothea admitted, thinking of Siegfried's ardent devotion to the country of his birth: no doubt Siegfried had been only too willing to fight in its defence. Then there was happy-go-lucky Gerhard. For all his levity, Gerhard had been an honourable man and would have wanted to do what he thought was right. The same applied to Roderick: love of his country, wanting to do what was right. Also, Roderick had thought of war as an adventure, at least to begin with.

Patriotism, duty, a sense of adventure: she had seen where it all led. Shattered limbs. Broken minds. Death. Yet even this didn't stop men wanting to go.

'Jack Britten couldn't wait,' she said. 'He hated to think that he might miss out.'

'Jack Britten? Let me see. He's the baker's son — am I right?'

'Yes. The second son. He worked at Clifton, in the gardens. He's only just turned eighteen.'

'I've heard that Dixon Carter has also been called up.'

'Dixie? But surely he's exempt?'

'It's my understanding that, this time, the tribunal turned him down.'

'What were they thinking? How will we manage if all the men are taken off the land?'

'Obviously Dixon was not thought indispensable.'

'Everyone is indispensable, one way or another. All those names in the casualty lists, each one of them is someone's son, brother, husband. When I think of all the suffering, I feel so . . . so *helpless*.'

'All we can hope to do is play the part allotted us. How is your plan to turn Clifton into a hospital coming along?'

Eliza had said, *Mama will never agree to it*, and Dorothea had been inclined to think she was right. But Aunt Eloise had surprised them both by not dismissing the idea out of hand.

'We are to be inspected, to see if the house would be suitable.'

'That's a first step.'

'Yes. I suppose so.'

But nothing would happen for months and months, and in the meantime she grew ever more impatient to be doing something — anything.

She sighed and got to her feet. 'I sometimes wonder, when it's all over, if we'll have forgotten how *not* to hate.'

Owain had no answer to this.

Taking leave of him, she let herself out of the churchyard by the side gate and joined the path that led across the fields to Clifton. As she climbed the first stile, she saw those fields laid out in front of her. Horselands, in the distance, was a sea of green wheat only just beginning to turn gold. In Row Meadow, right in front of her, haymaking was coming to an end. The field in between, Coney Close, had been ploughed over, something she could never remember happening before.

When she reached the next stile, she paused and looked back, watching the haymakers awhile; they had only one small section left to cut, right over by the brook. She picked out the figure of Nibs Carter, working with his back to her, a scythe in his hands. Now that Dixie was in the army, it would just be Nibs, Susie, Jake and Ned in the cottage in

Back Lane. Dorothea wondered how they were getting on. Jake must have grown a lot since she'd taken him to Clifton to be inspected by Aunt Eloise.

As Dorothea lingered by the stile, she almost convinced herself that Nibs knew she was there, knew she was watching. Any second now, he would turn round and their eyes would meet, and then—

But he never so much as paused in his work — the rhythmic swinging of the scythe — and at last she turned away and climbed the stile into Coney Close. Slowly, she trudged along the path back to Clifton.

* * *

Dorothea, a week later, joined Aunt Eloise and Eliza in the hallway as they waited to greet their guest. In he came, a tall figure in khaki, Crompton trailing in his wake lugging a battered valise.

Lieutenant Cartwright was lean and strong, with brown eyes and a rather wispy moustache, a man in his thirties who looked both older and younger than his years. His face was pale and drawn, his smile a little forced; there were dark rings round his eyes, he'd not shaved, his uniform was crumpled and dirty. He took off his cap, ran a gloved hand through his tousled, mousey-coloured hair, looked round at them.

Aunt Eloise stepped forward, the unfailing mistress of Clifton Park. 'Lieutenant Cartwright, welcome.'

'How do you do, Mrs Brannan. I must thank you again for inviting me. You don't know what it means to be back here.'

Aunt Eloise smiled at him. 'I'm glad, Alexander.' The practised warmth of her smile brought an answering warmth into Lieutenant Cartwright's tired face.

Eliza, who might once have been expected to thrust herself forward, stood today expressionless, waiting her turn. Since the news of Billy Turner's death, she had withdrawn more than ever into a world of her own.

Lieutenant Cartwright turned to her.

'Hello, Alex,' she said.

'Hello, Helena.'

She laughed — rather weakly it was true, but laughter nonetheless.

Lieutenant Cartwright brought out his wallet and opened it. He took from inside something which he lay on the palm of his hand and showed to Eliza. 'Do you remember this?'

Dorothea, looking over Eliza's shoulder, saw resting on Lieutenant Cartwright's long hand a small dried flower in a scrap of tissue paper.

'Is it . . . ?' Eliza looked up at him, questioning.

'The very same: the daisy you gave me the day I left.'

'You . . . you kept it . . . all this time?'

'I keep it with me always. It's my lucky charm.' Slipping the pressed flower back into his wallet, Lieutenant Cartwright greeted Dorothea last of all. 'Mrs Kaufmann. Delighted. We met only briefly on my previous visit. I hope to get better acquainted this time.'

Dorothea acknowledged him politely, then Aunt Eloise took charge. 'Tea is ready, Alexander. Or perhaps you would prefer to go to your room first?'

As Aunt Eloise led the guest away, Dorothea turned to Eliza, who hadn't moved, was still standing there with a far-away look in her eyes.

'Why did he call you Helena?'

'Why . . . ?' Eliza's eyes slowly focused. 'But you must remember, Doro. It happened last time. Alex said something about Helen of Troy, and in my ignorance I thought he'd said "Helena Troy". He started calling me Helena after that. It was a sort of joke. He's very nice, isn't he, Alex. I'm glad he's not dead. I'm glad he's not dead, like all the others.'

* * *

Dr Camborne came to Clifton that evening. A small dinner party, Aunt Eloise called it, in honour of their guest. But at one time even a small dinner party at Clifton would have seen eighteen or twenty people sitting down to eat, not a mere five; Mrs Somersby, in all likelihood, would have been there, Colonel Harding too. Dorothea forbore from asking if the Colonel had been invited this time; she preferred not to know, in case the Colonel had stayed away because of her.

Cook's chicken was on the menu, always a favourite, and there was no danger of a lag in the conversation with the doctor present. As usual, he knew everything worth knowing, including all the latest war news. He had it on good authority that the first American troops had already landed in France, and that the long-awaited Russian offensive was progressing well; Germany was most definitely on the way out.

'Her submarines were her last, desperate hope. But they have failed her: they can't sink enough of our merchant ships to bring us to our knees. There's no chance now of our being starved into surrender, no chance at all.' Accepting from Crompton a second helping of chicken, Dr Camborne continued, 'But when I think what the war is costing us . . . the cost is beyond computation.' He gave a sorrowful shake of his head, but it was soon obvious that he was measuring the cost not in men's lives but in monetary terms. 'The government is spending millions of pounds on the war every single day — every single day. The national debt, by now, must be quite staggering; we'll be paying it off for the rest of our lives. Already we are being squeezed for all we're worth. You don't know how fortunate you are, my dear Eloise, having your late husband's businesses to fall back on. You made a very wise move when you turned them over to war production. Your factories in Coventry will be working flat out, where they'd be standing idle otherwise. No one wants motor cars these days. Motor cars are a luxury no one can afford, with petrol on ration and costing the earth — a shilling per gallon in tax alone, I understand! Ah, well. What can't be cured — (First rate chicken, this. Delicious.) — must be endured. Despite our trials and tribulations, we aren't finished yet.' He turned

192

to Lieutenant Cartwright and said brightly, 'I daresay morale is very high at present amongst fighting men such as yourself — am I right?'

'Word is, we're in for another big show,' said Lieutenant Cartwright, not exactly answering the doctor's question.

'Another big attack? That's just the ticket! Keep the enemy on his toes! You can be sure, Lieutenant, that we at home are right behind you. If I may say, our humble village has already played a distinguished part in the war: many of our finest boys are overseas as we speak. Lambell — he's the village headmaster, don't you know — Lambell has three sons serving king and country. His charming wife was telling me only the other day how her youngest boy took part in the capture of Baghdad. That was a telling blow to the enemy, the capture of Baghdad, make no mistake about it. I can't see the Turks holding out much longer. Always has been the sick man of Europe, the Ottoman Empire, everyone knows that. But as I was saying — what was I saying? (More chicken? Don't mind if I do. Shame to waste it, in these frugal times.) Ah, yes, now I remember: our humble village, playing its part. We have our share of fallen heroes, Lieutenant, of whom we are justly proud: young Roderick here at Clifton, of course, so sadly missed; Turner, too, who worked in the stables here; then there's young Cardwell, the shopkeeper, killed at Loos. Cardwell, Turner: I can remember when they were born, seems only yesterday. Never thought I'd live to see them in their graves. Trying times. Trying times. But there you have it: *forsan et haec alim meminisse iuvabit* — eh, Lieutenant?'

Lieutenant Cartwright looked at him blankly. 'I'm sorry, sir. I don't understand.'

'Virgil, my dear boy, Virgil! Surely you know your Virgil?' Dr Camborne peered at the lieutenant expectantly. When no response was forthcoming, he spoke slowly and clearly, as if to a child, his knife held poised in one hand, his fork in the other. '*Forsan et haec*, et cetera, et cetera. "Maybe one day we shall be glad to remember even these things." Rather apt, I thought. Yes. Rather apt.'

Lieutenant Cartwright gave a perfunctory smile. The doctor nodded loftily, before turning his attention back to the last of his chicken.

Dorothea had already finished her own helping. As she watched Dr Camborne clear his plate, she recalled that Roderick, in private, had been wont to pour scorn on the doctor's habit of quoting Latin. There were times, however, when the doctor's aphorisms had a certain resonance. *Maybe one day we shall be glad to remember even these things*: it would be comforting to think so. But for now that remained a hope for the distant future.

Dinner finally over, they all retired to the drawing room, Lieutenant Cartwright showing no sign of wanting to linger with the doctor over port and cigars. As she sat down on the settee, Dorothea found Dr Camborne easing himself into the place beside her. He leaned across a moment and murmured out of the side of his mouth, 'Whoever heard of a schoolmaster who didn't know Latin! Where did you say he taught, my dear? It can't be much of a place.'

'It's—' But Dorothea realized she could not say for sure. She remembered now that there'd been some confusion last year over Lieutenant Cartwright's school: after he'd departed, no one had been quite sure if it was in Gloucestershire he taught, or Worcestershire.

Dorothea glanced across the room to where the lieutenant was sat with Eliza on the couch. In truth, they knew very little about him; she doubted that Roderick had known much more. A chance encounter, a spur-of-the-moment invitation, had brought Lieutenant Cartwright to Clifton last year. This was only his second, very brief, visit. Before the war, he would have counted as a stranger.

Dorothea tried to hear what was being said over on the couch, a quiet conversation *à deux*. (Would Dr Camborne expect an accomplished schoolmaster to know French as well as Latin?) Eliza, it seemed, was reminding the lieutenant of an occasion during his previous visit when he'd sung to them. Dorothea had no memory of this, but Eliza insisted that the song had been 'Keep the Home Fires Burning'. Would Alex sing it for them again, now?

'You will have to excuse me, Helena. I am not much in the mood for songs these days. Too many of the men who used to sing them are no longer with us.'

The lieutenant always spoke very well. He sounded urbane and educated. But as she listened to him, it seemed to Dorothea's ear that there was a trace of an accent, an accent she felt she recognized, an accent that had once been very familiar to her, living with her papa in poverty in east London before she ever came to Clifton.

But what did it matter if Lieutenant Cartwright had an accent? She would be turning into a snob if she wasn't careful. She'd probably imagined it, in any case. And it was the lieutenant's words that mattered, not the way he said them. The lieutenant's words and the sentiment behind them — his empathy for the men who were gone — seemed to shine a light on her suspicions and show them up for what they were: unworthy of her. Whatever would Johann have thought? He'd have been ashamed of her!

* * *

Sat on the terrace with her aunt, Dorothea watched Eliza and Lieutenant Cartwright walking together on The Park, the neat, mown meadow at the back of the house, which — as Aunt Eloise never tired of pointing out — would have looked very different if the landscaping had ever been finished according to plan. This was the third morning of the lieutenant's visit. The day had begun clear and bright, but in the distance, away to the right, clouds were gathering over Hambury Hill and beginning to advance in serried ranks across the wide blue sky. For now, however, the sun was still shining on Clifton and it glinted in Eliza's fair hair, worn today in a bun. Eliza seemed more animated than Dorothea had seen her in weeks, talking volubly to the lieutenant, who looked very different in civilian clothes, nothing of the soldier about him. He even looked a little less tall, seen from up here on the terrace.

'It seems almost providential,' murmured Aunt Eloise, 'as if Alexander had been sent especially to solve the problem of Elizabeth.'

'"Problem", Aunt?' Dorothea gently questioned her aunt's choice of word. Eliza was young, impressionable, could be headstrong and impulsive, but *problem* seemed too strong a term.

'Elizabeth must be saved from herself. She is a precocious child, and the world a perilous place.'

'But she has us to look after her.'

'You don't understand, Dorothea. I failed with Roderick. I failed to keep him safe. If I fail with Elizabeth too, whatever will Albert say?'

'What happened to Roderick wasn't your fault, Aunt. There was nothing anyone could have done. Uncle Albert would understand that.' (Did Aunt Eloise believe her dead husband was looking down on them? Was she preparing for a reckoning in the afterlife?)

'If Albert were here, things would be different,' said Aunt Eloise. 'But he's gone, and there's nothing to do but make the best of it. And, on the whole, I think that this will be best for Elizabeth.'

'What will? What do you mean, Aunt?'

'My understanding is that Alexander is going ask Elizabeth to marry him.'

'He . . . he's going to do *what*?' Dorothea was stunned. 'Marriage? Are you sure?'

'He hinted as much. I made it clear I would have no objections.'

'But . . . Aunt . . . they hardly know each other . . . they've only met twice . . . I can't believe it!'

'I think Alexander eminently suitable.'

'But we don't know anything about him!'

'We know he's a gentleman. We know he's been awarded the Military Cross. And he was Roderick's friend. What more do we need?'

This last consideration obviously trumped all: if Lieutenant Cartwright had been worthy of Roderick's notice, that put him beyond reproach. But Roderick had not really known Cartwright any better than the rest of them.

Aunt Eloise appeared surprised that Dorothea should harbour any doubts. 'It is true they have not been much in each other's company, but they have been writing to each other regularly since last year. You know better than anyone, Dorothea, how real intimacy can arise through correspondence. It is how your own marriage came about.'

But that was different, completely different. The two years' worth of letters she'd exchanged with Johann had shown her that she knew him better than anyone she'd met, that she liked him better than anyone; this, however, had been clear to her in Switzerland, and the letters had only confirmed what she was already sure of. Did Eliza feel that way about Lieutenant Cartwright? Did she even write to him with any regularity? She'd barely mentioned him from one month to the next.

But it was almost impossible, these days, to guess what Eliza was thinking and feeling: she was a closed book. True, she'd never spoken of Billy Turner either when he was alive, but she'd gone out of her way to keep up a clandestine correspondence with him and she'd been desperate to see him when he came home. This surely militated against any idea of Cartwright being at the centre of her thoughts — unless she'd been toying with them both, Cartwright *and* Turner. But Dorothea couldn't believe that of her.

Dorothea could draw only one conclusion from all this: that it was something Aunt Eloise had concocted in her own head. If the idea behind it was to 'save' Eliza from any more crushes on unsuitable boys, then the solution seemed out of all proportion — like amputating a leg to treat a broken toe. Dorothea's only consolation was that nothing would come of any of this. How could it? Even if Alex Cartwright was romantically interested in Eliza — which was open to question — there was surely no chance of Eliza going along with any plan of her mother's to marry her off. Eliza had made it her vocation to rebel against her mother.

No. Marriage was out of the question. It would never happen.

* * *

'It's happening,' said Dorothea to Owain Morgan. 'It's actually happening. Words fail me. It's beyond all understanding.'

She had lingered outside St Adeline's after the Sunday service, saying she had errands to run in the village; Aunt Eloise, Eliza and Lieutenant Cartwright had gone on without her. Now that the congregation had finally dispersed, Dorothea had made her way back inside the church, where Owain was collecting hymn books from the pews. She felt she had to talk to someone, and Owain was the only person she could think of.

'How can they get married? How *can* they? Aunt Eloise could put a stop to it even now, but she won't listen to reason. It's as if she's taken leave of her senses.'

Owain paused in his task, balancing a pile of books on his arm. He said cautiously, 'Do you mean to say that you think your aunt is of unsound mind?'

Dorothea stared at him in astonishment. 'No, of course not! It's just a figure of speech.'

'Ah. It's just that I've heard Mrs Brannan was . . . indisposed for a time last year.'

'But she wasn't seriously ill, or anything like that. She was suffering from nervous exhaustion, Dr Camborne said, brought on by Roderick's death.'

Privately, Dorothea was convinced that Aunt Eloise's collapse last September had been caused as much by her clash with Rosa as by Roderick's death, but she'd not said anything about that to Dr Camborne at the time, and she didn't mention it now.

'A stroke, they say in the village,' said Owain. 'Mrs Brannan suffered a stroke.'

He'd been listening to village gossip, it was obvious. This was how they twisted things in the village, exaggerating Aunt Eloise's natural grief into some terrible affliction that left her prostrate — almost as absurd a story as that old chestnut about Aunt Eloise keeping Richard locked in the attic at Clifton until he starved to death. In days gone by, Dorothea would simply have shaken her head at such silliness, but today she found herself exasperated — annoyed even. She'd always been fond of the village; it was like a second home. But just recently her feelings had become more ambivalent — and she felt she had good reason, when she considered the persistence of village gossip and the harm it did. Even someone as sensible as Rosa had repeated the old calumny about Richard (whether she'd actually believed it was another matter). And now here was Owain questioning Aunt Eloise's health, all because of mindless tittle-tattle.

'Aunt Eloise isn't ill, wasn't ill; she never gets ill,' said Dorothea firmly. 'Nor is she someone likely to lose her reason, even in bereavement.'

'I see. I'm sorry.' Owain at least had the good grace to look sheepish as he reached for another hymn book.

But if Aunt Eloise hadn't lost her reason, what other explanation was there for her behaviour? Dorothea had racked her brains. She wondered if Alexander Cartwright represented in some way a replacement for Roderick, a surrogate. Or was it that Aunt Eloise was a little in love with Alexander herself? She was acting blindly, on impulse — just like someone in love.

Dorothea shook her head. The very idea was preposterous — though not much more preposterous than attempting to marry Eliza off to a stranger.

'To your aunt it may appear perfectly logical,' said Owain. 'After all, as you say, neither Eliza nor Lieutenant Cartwright seem averse to the match.'

'But Eliza's so young, just seventeen.'

'Juliet was thirteen.'

'Juliet?'

'Shakespeare. Sorry, I can see I'm not helping.' He put the hymn books aside, invited her with a gesture to sit in a pew, took the place beside her. 'Please. Go on. I'm all ears.'

'It's all happening in such a rush.'

'That is not exactly unexpected, under the circumstances. There are a lot of hurried marriages these days.'

'He's twenty years older than her.'

'Does that matter, if they are in love?'

'How can they be in love? They hardly know one another.'

'There is such a thing as love at first sight, it's well attested. But I see you are not convinced. Is that because you think they are unsuited in some way? He seems perfectly pleasant on first acquaintance. Your aunt introduced me to him just now.'

'Oh, he's pleasant enough, he's very nice.'

'I sense a "but".'

'No. You're right. I have no reason to doubt him. It's me. That's where the problem lies: with me. I used to see the good in people; now I expect the worst. I'm so suspicious all the time. It's not very nice to be so suspicious. I can't think what is wrong with me.'

'I don't think there is anything wrong with you. If you're a little more wary these days, it's only to be expected, given everything you've been through. I don't suppose for one moment that you've really changed, not deep inside. People don't.'

'Not ever?'

'Not in something as fundamental as an inherent belief in the goodness of human nature. I'm sure you will find it's still there, deep down, just waiting for a chance to blossom again.'

'I wish I could believe that. I wish — oh, I don't know what I wish! All I can think about is this intended marriage. It doesn't seem real somehow.'

'Have you talked to them about it: your aunt, your cousin, Lieutenant Cartwright?'

'No. Not really. At least, I've spoken with Aunt Eloise, but not with Eliza or Alex.'

'Perhaps if you talk to them, it will set your mind at rest.'

'It can't hurt, I suppose. Yes. That's what I'll do. I'll talk to them. Oh, Owain, thank you! I can't tell you how grateful I am. Nothing ever seems quite so hopeless after talking to you!'

* * *

As luck would have it, an opportunity for a quiet word with Lieutenant Cartwright presented itself that very afternoon. She found him alone in the library after lunch. He'd opened the glass front of the Chippendale bookcase and was running a finger along the rows of books, reading the titles on the spines.

'Hello, Mrs Kaufmann. I hope you don't think I am prying. I couldn't help myself. I find books irresistible. I suppose it's because there weren't a lot of books around me when I was growing up.'

'Where was it you grew up, Lieutenant Cartwright?'

'Please do call me Alex.' He'd taken a book off one of the shelves, began juggling it from hand to hand. 'I grew up in London, Mrs Kaufmann: that's where I was born. I shan't pretend we were exactly well-to-do.'

'We?'

'Mother and I.'

'And what about your father — if you don't mind me asking?'

'I never knew my father. Mother raised me single-handedly. She died before I was fifteen. I had to fend for myself after that. I believe you, too, are an orphan?'

'My mother died when I was born; I was raised by my papa until I was eight, when he brought me here, to Clifton. I don't know what became of him after that. Papa and I, we weren't well-to-do either. I don't see there's any shame in it.'

But she could scarcely believe that Alexander Cartwright had known poverty as she had known it, living hand-to-mouth in the East End of London; at times, her papa had even struggled to put a roof over their heads.

Dorothea checked her wandering thoughts. Somehow the conversation had veered off course. They were talking about her, when it was Lieutenant Cartwright she wanted to know about.

What had she learned so far? Some things were obvious. His mother had brought him up to be well-spoken, well-mannered; he must be well-educated, too, to have secured a post at that school of his — wherever it was (Gloucestershire or Worcestershire?). He was thirty-six years old, she knew that too. But she still felt very much in the dark; his life was still very much a mystery. So much could happen to a man in thirty-six years.

She shrank from firing questions at him. She didn't want to turn the conversation into an interrogation. Not that the conversation had proceeded very far. It had lapsed altogether now, as she racked her brains for something to say. All was quiet, except for a faint fluttering sound that she couldn't immediately identify.

It was Lieutenant Cartwright who broke the silence. 'Mrs Kaufmann—'

'Dorothea,' she interrupted automatically. 'You should call me Dorothea — especially if we are to be family.'

His eyes lingered on her. 'You . . . you have your doubts about that, I can tell.'

'Lieutenant Cartwright . . . Alex . . . I only want—'

'I don't blame you in the least for having doubts.' He was now the one interrupting, cutting across her confusion. 'If I considered it at all sensibly, soberly, I'm sure I'd have second thoughts too. But now is not the time to be sensible and sober. We must seize every opportunity, make the most of every minute, because tomorrow—'

He stopped abruptly and turned away, his hand jerking out and putting the book back in its place. After a pause, he slowly closed the glass front of the bookcase. His fingers lingered on the polished wood of the frame.

'If I have someone to come back to — a rock, an anchor — it would make all the difference; it would get me through, I honestly believe it would.'

There was no mistaking the pent-up emotion in his voice. She could understand his point of view, too — even if she thought it a bit far-fetched. She thought of Roderick, who'd also had a presentiment. (*I have this feeling I'll pull through. I really think I shall.*) Less than two months later, he'd been dead. There was no rhyme or reason in war. There was no surety to be had. There was only chaos, fear, superstition.

Dorothea laid her hand on the Hepplewhite desk beside her, as if to gain from the hard and unyielding feel of it the strength to hold to her purpose. She said, 'Love cannot be had to order. Eliza deserves better than that.'

'I'm awfully fond of her.'

'Fond?'

'More than fond. I've thought of her a lot, since my last visit. Her innocence. Her spirit. She . . . she's the opposite of everything we have to endure out there — an antidote.'

'But you hardly know her!'

'I feel there's a connection between us.'

'What sort of connection?'

'You sound sceptical. That's understandable. I can't explain why I feel as I do. I'm under no illusions, either. I know she's too good for me. In any other circumstances, I'd never presume to . . . to . . . But then again, under any other circumstances we'd never even have met. The war has made all sorts of things possible that weren't possible before. These things happen for a reason. There's some sort of purpose behind our coming together — there has to be.'

Superstition again, thought Dorothea. And yet . . . wasn't this how she'd felt about Johann, that somehow she'd always known him, that they were meant to be together?

Alex said, 'She tells me it's what she wants.'

'She's very young.' Too young to know her own mind?

Alex was silent for a moment and ran his fingers through his thick, mousey-coloured hair, making it stand on end before smoothing it down again with the palm of his hand until he had restored his neat side parting.

Finally he said, 'I believe you know Helena — Eliza — better than anyone. Do you think her feelings are real? If you have any misgivings . . . if you do . . . I mean to say, the wedding could always be postponed.'

This was what she'd wanted, for everyone to take a step back and consider things properly. She had only to say the word, it seemed.

But it was unfair of him to put this on her — unfair, when there was no knowing what tomorrow might bring. For Johann, for Roderick, for Billy Turner, there was no tomorrow.

She tried to convince herself that it wasn't Alex Cartwright's best interest she should be concerned with. She had to think of Eliza, and only Eliza. She had to do right by her cousin. But even as she was debating in her own mind, a flicker of movement caught her eye, distracting her. Suddenly she understood where the fluttering noise was coming from. A butterfly — a Red Admiral — was trapped inside the window, beating its patterned wings against the glass, beating its wings and beating its wings.

The butterfly was beautiful, fragile, helpless. Watching its fruitless quest for freedom, she found herself faced with the utter futility of life, a feeling she'd come to know only too well this last year or so. Her thoughts went back to the men she'd nursed in London: men with closed-up faces and haunted eyes; men who slept uneasily at night, tossing and turning, muttering, moaning, dreaming strange dreams — as trapped and helpless as the butterfly. She knew almost nothing of what they'd been through. Billy Turner had given her a glimpse into that other world, Roderick too with his hints and allusions (*It's hell out there, Doro, I can't tell you*). But it was like peering through a frosted window, seeing forms and shadows she could only guess at.

She glanced at Alex, almost afraid of him suddenly, for he'd seen both sides of the glass; he knew what it was like, the hell out there. But if she'd had any idea at all of asking him about it, the impulse died in an instant. Alex was no longer looking at her. Whether he'd seen the butterfly for himself, or whether he'd followed her lingering gaze, she couldn't say, but it was the butterfly which now held all his attention.

He suddenly jerked into life. He crossed the room in a few lengthy strides and threw open the casement. With his long-fingered hands, he gently guided the fluttering insect towards freedom. The butterfly escaped through the gap and flew off. Dorothea followed it briefly with her eyes until it vanished into the brightness of the wide world beyond the ivy-framed window.

She expected to feel joy at its release. Instead, and inexplicably, she was overcome by a sense of loss — a sense of loss so strong and so poignant that it brought a lump to her throat. She knew in that moment that she couldn't bring herself to say anything more, to raise any more objections. Not when it mattered so much. Not when she was so unsure of Eliza's feelings. She didn't trust herself to get it right. She simply didn't trust herself.

Without another word, she turned and left the room.

* * *

It was the morning of the wedding.

Dorothea could scarcely believe it had come to this. Apart from anything else, it had all been arranged with such unseemly haste. Yet how could things be otherwise, when Lieutenant Cartwright's leave was so brief? As Owain had pointed out, this would by no means be the first hasty wedding of the war.

Eliza had her breakfast upstairs. Dorothea found her in her room, sitting up in bed with a tray on her lap, picking at her food. Her face was rather flushed, as if she was running a fever, but otherwise there was a calmness about her that seemed out of place at this most pivotal moment in her young life. Her new frock was set ready, draped carefully over a chair. Tilda would come soon to help Eliza dress, and Aunt Eloise's own maid was going to do Eliza's hair. For now, though, it was just the two of them alone together, as so often in years gone by; they'd lived in their own little world up in the nursery all through Eliza's childhood.

Sitting on the edge of the bed, Dorothea took Eliza's hands in hers. Thinking of everything they'd been through together — and despite the nagging suspicion that she couldn't get things right anymore — Dorothea found it impossible not to make one last appeal. Looking into Eliza's eyes, she said, 'Are you sure, dearest? Are you sure this is what you want?'

'Yes.'

'But . . . but you don't even know him! I can't understand you, Eliza!'

Eliza took her hands away, as cold and implacable as Aunt Eloise.

But, as she put the tray aside — her half-eaten breakfast — a troubled look came over Eliza's face. She turned away, staring at the open window and the fine July morning outside. Dorothea bit her tongue, waited, watching Eliza closely.

After a time, without looking round, Eliza said slowly, 'Do you know when I last left Clifton Park? Do you know how long it is since I went anywhere further than the village or Lawham, or Northampton at best? It was when we went to look for your papa in London. That was the last time — the very last time I went anywhere. I was twelve. It was five years ago. Five years since I went anywhere. I can't bear it anymore. I can't bear being kept a prisoner here.'

As gently as she could, Dorothea said, 'Dearest Eliza, I don't think you are being entirely fair. Clifton is not a prison. It's your home. I know that Aunt Eloise can seem a little . . . stern . . . at times. But that's just her way. She always has the best of intentions. She's a good woman at heart.'

'Then her goodness is suffocating me! She won't let me *live*! Rosa saw it. Rosa knew how I felt. She was the only one who knew. But Rosa's gone. She escaped. Now it's my turn. Mama thinks she's getting her own way with this wedding. She thinks she's getting her own way, as usual. But I am the one who is getting what I want. I'm escaping, like Rosa. I'm escaping at last — escaping from Clifton!'

'That's no reason to get married!' cried Dorothea, appalled. It seemed to her that everyone was looking at this marriage in the wrong light. Aunt Eloise saw it as a device for securing her daughter's safekeeping; Alex seemed to want to win a lady's favour, to be her champion, like a medieval knight going into battle; and, for Eliza, it was simply an escape route. Eliza appeared to think that Alex would set her free, as he'd set the butterfly free in the library. But where did she think she could fly to? She was marrying a man who would go back to war almost at once, and he had no home of his own as far as Dorothea was aware. Presumably, before he'd joined up, he'd lived in rooms at the school where he taught. But even if his position was being kept open for him (was it?), Eliza could hardly wait for him there. So she would have to return to Clifton after her wedding trip with Alex. She had no choice. And all this would have been for nothing.

'You've not thought it through, Eliza, you're not being—'

'I've heard all that already,' Eliza interrupted. 'I know you don't approve. I don't care.'

'But it's not fair on Alex to use him in this way. You don't love him. He should know that, he should be told.'

Eliza sat bolt upright, said fiercely, 'If you say anything to him, I'll never forgive you, never. If you try and stop me—' She let out a long breath. 'But you can't. It's too late.' The fierceness in her died away. She reached out a hesitant hand, touched Dorothea's arm. For a split second, the old Eliza was there, guileless, gentle at heart. 'Don't be angry, Doro. Don't be angry. It's what I want. And Alex is a nice man. I like him very much.'

'And what about Billy Turner? Have you completely forgotten him? How can you be so fickle!'

Dorothea was taken aback by her own vehemence, but she felt slighted on Billy's behalf, as if she stood proxy for him now he was not here himself to be hurt by Eliza's behaviour. Eliza's giddy nature had always been part of her charm, but today it seemed only cruel and heartless.

Faced with Dorothea's clear reproval, Eliza shut down at once. She gave Dorothea a distant glance, then turned away, looked towards the window again.

'Billy is dead,' she said in a toneless voice.

At that moment, the door opened. Tilda had arrived to help Eliza get ready. She was followed, seconds later, by Aunt Eloise's maid. Dorothea slipped away, the private interlude over. In any case, she could only think that anything else she said would simply make things worse. She'd never felt so angry with Eliza as she did at that moment. All she knew was that, if she'd dismissed Johann from her thoughts after he'd died as readily as Eliza appeared to have dismissed Billy, then there wouldn't have been any words to describe how mean and detestable that made her.

But as Dorothea climbed the stairs to the nursery and to her own room, all her anger drained away. If Eliza really had loved Billy — if she'd felt for him even one tenth of what Dorothea felt for Johann — then of course she couldn't turn her feelings off like a tap, however much she might want to now he was dead. If Eliza was grieving inside for Billy, it might go some way to explaining her wayward behaviour. The problem was, Dorothea couldn't be sure anymore exactly *what* Eliza felt.

You know Eliza better than anyone, Alex had said. How ironic that sounded now!

Dorothea was no longer angry. She was just terribly sad — all the more so when she compared today's unhappy charade with her own wedding day five years ago. Everything then had been perfect, a week of warmth and sunshine in the otherwise dismal summer of 1912. She'd been driven to St

Adeline's in the Clifton motor, Roderick sitting beside her. He'd been so proud to give her away — though of course he'd covered it up in his inimitable style.

'What if I don't give you away?' He'd said this in the porch before they went into the church. 'What if I keep you for myself?' The usual raillery. A boy's bluster, to cover his emotions. Roderick had always been such a typical boy. (His words were not to be taken seriously — of course not. Dorothea was quite sure that Rosa was wrong to suggest Roderick had been in love with her.)

Getting ready in her room, Dorothea allowed herself to remember that perfect day. She'd walked up the aisle on Roderick's arm. The genial old vicar — such a dear man — had been waiting for her, the Bible open in his hands. But she'd had eyes only for Johann. He'd looked so elegant in his frock coat, a radiance all about him, sunlight streaming in many colours through the stained-glass windows and glinting in his golden hair. He'd glanced over his shoulder, immeasurably handsome. His blue eyes — his beautiful eyes — had widened at the sight of her; they'd shone with an inner light. One of his rare, shy smiles had passed across his face for a fleeting moment before he became stiff and solemn again, anxious to play his part to the very best of his ability, anxious to get everything right for her sake — for Dorothea.

As she put on her best frock and did her hair, Dorothea thought of something else Rosa had once said.

Mrs Brannan wants to wrap Eliza up in cotton wool. But if Eliza's to learn about life, she must be allowed to make her own mistakes.

But that seemed hard — it seemed callous — to simply sit back and let Eliza sink or swim.

Rosa's rebellious example, Aunt Eloise's unyielding strictures: between them, they'd led Eliza to this, a hasty marriage for all the wrong reasons. But Dorothea didn't think it right to hold others responsible when some of the blame was hers. She'd played a big part in raising Eliza. For a large part of Eliza's childhood, she'd been nurse, nanny and governess rolled into one. That she'd never asked for such a role was no excuse. She'd been lax, let Eliza run wild. Eliza had spent too much time playing with the village children, not enough time at her lessons. There'd been no beatings like with Nanny in the old days. But at least Nanny's beatings had kept Roderick in line.

But what good had it done him, except to leave Roderick feeling there was something broken inside him? Perhaps Rosa was right after all. Perhaps Eliza had to learn for herself.

Dorothea pinned her simple hat into place, inspected her reflection in the three-folded mirror on her dressing table. It occurred to her as she did so that, now Roderick was gone, there was no one to give Eliza away. But it wasn't that sort of wedding, to be married at Lawham register office.

She was ready. She looked round her room one last time to make sure there was nothing she'd forgotten, then she went downstairs.

* * *

All the formalities were over. They left the register office and walked the short distance to Lawham's recreation ground. A photographer had been commissioned to record the happy event. He arranged them against a backdrop of trees. The groom was in uniform, his face tanned yet pale beneath his cap, his tie perfectly knotted, jacket buttons polished to a shine, the leather of his belt and his boots gleaming. The bride was almost unrecognizable in a straight-cut cream frock, with a half-length overskirt, a high-waisted jacket, a hat with a turned-up brim; she clutched a modest posy with both hands, the only flowers. Dorothea stood next to Aunt Eloise; Cecily and Eileen were also there, daughter and daughter-in-law to the late Mrs Somersby, and still in mourning: Aunt Eloise had enlisted their help as bridesmaids alongside Dorothea.

Once the photographs had been taken, they had to hurry to the sleepy station on the edge of town. In days gone by,

Lawham had been an important staging post on the old coaching routes, but as first the canal, then the railway, passed it by, it had dwindled to a backwater and was served only by a single-track branch line, an afterthought. Eliza and Alex were going by train on their wedding trip to Great Yarmouth. (Why Great Yarmouth? Dorothea had no idea.) The trip would be necessarily brief: Alex's leave was almost up. He would go straight from Yarmouth back to France. Eliza would have no alternative but to come home, her short-lived moment of freedom swiftly over.

Dorothea gave her cousin a hug and gently kissed her cheek, as a whistle sounded in the distance, signalling the approaching train. 'I will see you soon, dear Eliza.'

'Perhaps.' Eliza turned hurriedly away.

The train steamed out of the station. The sound of it faded. The half-dozen passengers who'd alighted melted away. A somnolent silence descended on the station once more.

Aunt Eloise lingered on the platform near the steps of the footbridge, gazing along the empty tracks into the distance, as if she could still see the vanished train, as if she was watching it get smaller and smaller until it was no more than a point on the far horizon.

Standing a little apart, Dorothea watched and waited. She found herself taken back seventeen years, to the night when she'd first clapped eyes on her aunt. There'd been a party in full swing at Clifton, to mark the New Year; led into the midst of it by her papa, eight-year-old Dorothea had been confused and half-asleep. She'd felt horribly conspicuous, the centre of attention, so many eyes on her. Gradually, she'd become aware of a woman in the background who nonetheless stood out from the crowd, poised, dignified, coldly beautiful; she was like a statue, Dorothea had thought. Here, all these years later, was that same woman, stood straight and unbending on the platform at Lawham station. Aunt Eloise had barely changed in all that time, or so it seemed. She was immutable, timeless. Dorothea, for a moment as she looked on, felt like a little girl again, silent and solemn, staring up in awe as if at a vision.

Aunt Eloise stirred at last. She turned. There was a strange, blank expression on her face.

'And so all is settled,' she said, 'and the old life has come to a close. Here, now: this is the end.'

CHAPTER EIGHT

'Mrs Kaufmann. A word, if I may.'

Dorothea, pushing wearily past the curtain in the side corridor — the curtain that divided the ground floor in two — was met by the advancing figure of Mrs Bourne.

'Those men, Mrs Kaufmann: they've been playing billiards again. I found four of them in the billiard room — four of them! I had to remind them that the billiard room is out of bounds. It is not the first time I have had to remind them.'

Those men were patients, mostly convalescents on the road to recovery, though some were further down that road than others. One half of Clifton, in this fourth autumn of the war, had been given over to them. Here on the ground floor that meant the morning room, the dining room and the library; the blue room, in the same half of the house, was being used to store various items of furniture and such valuables as the ormolu clock from the dining room, and the painting of a racehorse that used to hang in the morning room — the painting that Aunt Eloise said was a Stubbs, but that Roderick always insisted wasn't. Some rooms of the upper storeys also formed part of what had become known as 'the hospital wing', set aside for the use of the patients and staff. Dorothea numbered amongst the latter.

Having been up half the night and busy most of the morning, Dorothea was too exhausted now her shift was finally over to dissemble with the forbidding figure of Mrs Bourne. She found herself admitting, rather guiltily, that she'd told one or two of 'those men' that they might play billiards now and then, as long as they were careful.

'But they aren't careful, Mrs Kaufmann. They aren't careful at all.' The housekeeper's tone was one of reproach. 'They are bulls in a china shop, the lot of them. When I think of the damage that's been done since they came — all the things that have been chipped and broken, the scuff marks on the walls and on the furniture — when I think of all that, I could cry, I really could. And they've not yet been here much more than a month. I shudder to think what the place will look like in six months' time.'

Anyone would have thought it was *her* home, Mrs Bourne's; she carried on, thought Dorothea, as if she owned the place. Fighting a growing need to yawn, Dorothea tried also to stifle her resentment: she was sure it had more to do with being tired than with any real sense of injustice. In all fairness, Mrs Bourne could be said to have a claim on the place. She'd been here longer than anyone, except Aunt Eloise (and Becket, of course, in the gardens: he'd been at Clifton forever). These days, Mrs Bourne seemed to think it beholden on her to play the role of Clifton's chief protector, now that Aunt Eloise concerned herself much less with the minutiae — all those little details that had once been so important to her. Not that Aunt Eloise had given up on Clifton. That was plainly impossible, when Clifton was in her very blood. But it was true to say she had a new perspective now. Preserving the house in amber no longer seemed a priority, which was why, in the end, it had not proved overly difficult to persuade her to turn part of the house into a hospital.

'If Roderick had been badly wounded instead of killed in action,' Aunt Eloise had said, 'I like to imagine he might have come to a place like Clifton to get well again.'

Aunt Eloise had not even demurred when Dorothea expressed a preference for other ranks over officers. Johann had always been of the opinion that medical science should benefit everyone, regardless of wealth and privilege. He'd have said that boys from the village, such as Harry Keech and Dixie Carter, deserved as much consideration as Roderick and his ilk.

As for the catalogue of damage, the items chipped and broken and — so Mrs Bourne had darkly hinted before now — even lost or stolen, Aunt Eloise merely said, 'It would not be the first time. Lady Emerald was little better than a thief, and she had fourteen years in which to rifle the place.' Thus Aunt Eloise referred to her long-dead sister-in-law, who had once been mistress of Clifton Park. According to family lore, Lady Emerald had mislaid or otherwise misappropriated various items of jewellery and several heirlooms, including a Persian carpet.

How much truth there was in those old tales, Dorothea couldn't say. The facts of the matter were lost in the mists of the past. Meanwhile, here in the present, Dorothea's way was still barred by Mrs Bourne.

'Will you have a word with those men, Mrs Kaufmann? Will you *please*?'

'Yes, Mrs Bourne. Of course.' Dorothea was too tired to argue but her easy acquiescence only led the housekeeper to look at her doubtfully.

Dorothea stifled another yawn. Nursing at Clifton was very different to what she'd been used to at the hospital in south London even though much of the drudgery was the same. The men she was nursing now were, in the main, nothing like the men she remembered in London — terrible cases, those, often limbless and contorted, subject to panic attacks and violent tremors, many of them clinging on to life by their fingertips. The men here at Clifton were nearly all of them on the road to recovery; there was real hope for them — if it could be called *hope* when the ultimate objective of all this nursing was to pack them back off to the front. Dorothea, at times, was overcome by a sense of guilt at the thought of making them well again for *that*.

But it was for this very purpose that the system had been put in place, as Sister Elliot often pointed out. 'These men are desperately needed, Nurse Kaufmann. It is our duty to get them fighting fit. We simply cannot afford to lose the war at this late stage for the want of men.'

All this, however, was neither here nor there. Dorothea's immediate problem was how to placate Mrs Bourne without making impractical promises. She couldn't help wondering if Mrs Bourne, for all her complaints, secretly enjoyed lording it over the wounded men. Amongst Clifton's other servants she'd long been known, behind her back, as 'Bossy Bourne'; even the male staff had never been a match for her. Now that the only indoor manservant was poor, downtrodden Crompton, this steady influx of rough-and-ready — and sometimes boisterous — young men must seem like grist to Mrs Bourne's mill.

Or was that being unfair?

Havering over how best to deal with Mrs Bourne, Dorothea recalled Nettie Thomson's words from as long ago as last spring: *Dearest Dorothea, you can't please everyone all the time.*

Dorothea took a deep breath and did her best to be firm. 'I think, Mrs Bourne, we must make some allowances when it comes to "those men".'

Mrs Bourne looked even more dubious, but all she said after a meaningful pause was, 'Very good, Mrs Kaufmann. But on your head be it.'

Off she swept, a stern and upright figure all in black, the ubiquitous bunch of keys jangling at her belt, a sound that had sent waves of terror through Dorothea as a child. It almost raised a feeling of nostalgia in her now.

Tempting as it was to fall straight into bed, Dorothea knew she'd never sleep without a breath of fresh air first to clear her head. She crossed the hallway, opened the front door, stepped out into a grey October day. It was early afternoon, and it had been raining again; the sky was still heavy with cloud. There was a smell of damp earth, there were puddles in the gravel, water slowly dripped from the flat, spreading boughs of the cedar. Over by the red-brick garden wall Annie Britten, on her way to the house, had stopped for a word with Jeff Smith, who was leaning against the frame of the garden door. He would catch it hot if Becket saw him idling, thought Dorothea. The ever-expanding vegetable garden was winding down now with winter fast approaching but, as Becket never tired of pointing out, there was 'no rest for the wicked', and among the hundred and one other daily chores, there were now a dozen hens to look after brought in from Home Farm. All this Becket and Smith had to manage between them, now that Annie's brother, Jack, had gone to do his bit for king and country.

Annie caught sight of her and came hurrying over, after taking her leave of Jeff.

'Not late, am I, miss? I thought I left home in plenty of time.'

'Don't worry, Annie, the clock in the hallway hasn't chimed the hour yet. They've all had their lunch; there's not much else to report. But I ought to warn you, the Ranee is on the warpath again. She's just given me a dressing down.'

They called Sister Elliot *the Ranee* because she'd nursed in India sometime in the last century — or was it in Africa she'd nursed, during the Boer War? Perhaps both. Nobody was quite sure. It was Sister Elliot who was in charge of all things medical.

'It's shameful, the way she talks to you in your own home,' said Annie.

'Oh, I don't mind. That's just her way.' Dorothea had known worse during her time at the London hospital.

Annie sighed. 'Well, I suppose I'd best brave it. Don't go telling her I went in by the front door, or I'll never hear the last of it!' She slipped into the house.

Dorothea still had half an eye on Jeff. All this time, he'd been watching Annie from under the brim of his oversize cap, and as Annie disappeared indoors it seemed to Dorothea that she could hear, even at this distance, a heartfelt sigh. Jeff stopped slouching and straightened up, and he seemed about to return to his work, but as Dorothea made her way across to him he paused, waiting.

Jeff was never one to start a conversation but today he couldn't contain himself. 'Don't she look a picture, Mrs K!' He glanced at the front door where Annie had passed from sight, a wistful look in his eye. 'That nurse's uniform suits her just fine. An English rose, that's what she is. I think just lately she's grown to like me a little bit more. I really think she has.'

Was it true? Had Annie transferred her affections to Jeff, now that Billy Turner was dead? Dorothea felt a pang for poor Billy, who seemed to have been abandoned by Annie as well as Eliza, though she knew very well that Billy had not been interested in Annie. Nor, for that matter, did she know how deep Annie's feelings for Billy had been. Annie Britten was a girl who attracted comment. Some in the village had expressed cynical surprise when she took up nursing. She thought too much of herself to make a go of it, they said. She was not a girl who, by nature, put others first. Dorothea felt this was unfair. Apart from anything else, Annie was just nineteen, barely grown up, her personality not yet fixed. And she'd proved so far a most competent nurse. She did not always live up to Sister Elliot's exacting standards — did anyone? — but she was quick and willing, and she had a good rapport with the men.

Jeff sighed again in a very un-Jeff-like way (nor was it in character for him to wax lyrical and use such poetic language as 'an English rose'). 'I'd best get on, Mrs K, before old Misery Guts starts mithering me.'

Dorothea watched through the garden door as Jeff walked off along the cinder path — could a man with a limp ever be said to have a spring in his step? She hoped for his sake that Annie really had grown to like him 'a little bit more'.

Lingering a moment, Dorothea gave thought to Jeff Smith who'd first come to Clifton aged sixteen as the new chauffeur, not long before she got married. After the accident two years later in which he'd acquired his limp, he'd returned home to Coventry to recuperate, but after a time he'd come back to Clifton at his own request. She'd been nursing in London by then, but she'd learned that he'd found chauffeuring too much with his damaged leg, and Aunt Eloise had offered him instead a role in the gardens. By all accounts, he'd not taken to it at first; he thought he'd come down in the world, swapping his smart chauffeur's uniform and the modern Clifton motors for muddy boots and old-fashioned manual labour. 'That there boy had rage in his heart,' was how Becket had put it to her recently. She'd been stood with the elderly gardener watching Jeff dig up a crop of carrots with unexpected finesse. 'He had rage in his heart when he first come to work under me. He's a different lad now, Miss Dorothea. A different lad altogether.'

He would turn twenty-two in a few days' time. Oddly, it was Aunt Eloise who'd remembered. She seemed to take an interest in Jeff Smith, whether from a sense of responsibility after his accident, or for some other reason, Dorothea was not sure. Certainly, the accident had hit Jeff hard and he'd been very bitter for a time about his limp, all the more so when it led to him 'missing out' (his own words) on the war. A blessing in disguise, some might have said. But that was not how a young man of Jeff's mould saw it. Amidst all these tribulations, he continued to work in Clifton's gardens and it appeared to suit him. He seemed to find it — was 'soothing' the right word? 'Cathartic', perhaps?

Johann would have known what she meant. Johann would have supplied exactly the right word. What was the right word in German? *Beruhigende*? Was that it?

She found she wasn't sure. How quickly she was forgetting all the German she'd once known! It made her feel sad, to find she was forgetting.

She turned away from the garden door and began to walk slowly back across the gravel. The wind was getting up, shaking a shower of raindrops from the boughs of the cedar;

the trees of the Pheasantry, almost bare now of leaves, were seething and swaying; heavy, louring clouds swirled in the grey October sky. Dorothea felt tired but was still not ready for bed. She never could get used to sleeping in the daytime when she'd been on duty all night. Rather than tossing and turning, it would be better to stretch her legs. A quick turn down the drive, perhaps. She could take a peek at the keeper's garden while she was at it. She'd done a lot of work in the keeper's garden back in the spring, but just lately she'd been forced to neglect it, having so little time to spare.

Bit by bit, she picked her way along the drive, which was wet from recent rain, the ruts and potholes full of water. Weeds were encroaching at the edges. The wind was sighing through the tall evergreens that marched on either side.

Her thoughts turned to Eliza, as they often did. Why didn't Eliza come home? It was three months and more since Eliza had set off with Alex on their brief wedding trip to Great Yarmouth. From Yarmouth, Alex must have gone straight back to the front — that had been the plan, anyway. He would have re-joined his battalion just in time for the great Allied offensive at Ypres. Eliza, meanwhile, instead of returning to Clifton as expected, had gone to London — to the house at 28 Essex Square that Uncle Albert had purchased in 1904, somewhere for the family to stay when they were in town. In recent times, number twenty-eight had been shut up and left unused, and it was more than five years since any of the family had been there. Now, Eliza had taken up residence and she refused to come home. Had this been her plan all along? Under the terms of Uncle Albert's will, her allowance had increased now that she was married and this seemed enough for her to live independently at Essex Square. She'd written home perhaps half a dozen times, saying almost nothing about herself. She'd signed the letters *Helena Cartwright*: Helena, Alex's name for her, after the mix-up over Helen of Troy. Helena Cartwright. It made her sound like a stranger.

'Absurd behaviour.' Aunt Eloise could be dismissive at times, judging people by her own high (Rosa would have said 'hidebound') standards. 'Eliza doesn't know what's good for her. She never has. Well, she is Alexander's responsibility now. If he wishes to pander to her every whim, then we must accept that.'

But Dorothea had her doubts that Alex had played any part in Eliza setting herself up at number twenty-eight.

What sort of life would Eliza have in London, so far from her family and friends? By the time it became clear that she would not be returning, Clifton had been in upheaval as it was readied for its new role as a hospital. Dorothea had felt it wouldn't be fair to leave Aunt Eloise to deal with all the chaos, and ever since there'd been so much to do that she still hadn't found time to visit Essex Square. It was October now, Eliza's wedding as long ago as July.

Dorothea sighed and came to a halt. She felt she really ought to go back to the house and write another letter to Eliza, begging her to come home. But what good would it do? If Eliza replied at all, she would be as vague and elusive as ever. As Dorothea stood hesitant, shivering in the gusting wind (why did the wind always feel so much colder when you were tired?), she thought again of the neglected keeper's garden. She was almost there. She might as well take a look at it, as she'd intended. To abandon her purpose midway would be like an uncomfortable echo of those dreams that still sometimes troubled her, the dreams in which she was inundated with tasks needing her attention, whether it was nursing duties or keeping up the routine of the house, and yet somehow nothing ever got done, no task was ever quite completed. She would wake in a sweat of panic, weighed down by a sense of failure. Well, she could at least see this through. She would visit the Gatehouse, even though it wasn't really important, and even though she knew she'd only feel disheartened to see the derelict old cottage and the sadly neglected garden.

But when she reached the end of the drive, she was taken aback to find the keeper's garden in much better order than she remembered, and she was even more surprised to see

Dick Turner there in muddy boots and with mud halfway up his trousers, busy digging. The warm winter scarf she'd given him on his last birthday was wrapped round his neck, the ends tucked inside his waistcoat.

He paused in his work when he caught sight of her, resting his foot on his fork so that he slowly trod it into the miry earth. 'How do, miss. Just cleared away these bits of cabbages and whatnot, and now I'm digging the ground over. Hope you don't mind, like.'

'Oh, Dick, of course I don't mind! I've not had time to keep the place tidy, and I've been fretting about it. But by the looks of things, this isn't the first time you've stopped by.'

'I've been here on and off, doing what I can. Peaceful place, this. A place I can be on me own. I like time to meself now and then.' He coloured up and added hastily, 'Not you, miss. I don't mind you being here.'

'That's all right, Dick. I quite understand. I like to get away too, sometimes.'

Dick broke into a grin. 'Ma reckons I take after Grandpa. He's an old misery guts and all, she says.'

'That's not true of you, Dick, you're not a misery guts. But I hope you're not neglecting your other responsibilities by coming here. Aren't you needed elsewhere? What about work?'

'There's not much doing down the farm and old Tebbit says he can't afford to keep me idle.' Dick's grin faded. He knitted his brows. 'I were thinking, miss, whilst I were digging. I might chuck the farm. I've had enough of it. I reckon I might be able to get some sort of situation at the shoe factory — you know, miss, the one in Lawham where me dad works. I wouldn't mind making boots for a bit, till I'm old enough to fight.'

Till I'm old enough to fight . . . There was something chilling about the way he said this, so matter-of-fact. Back in June, she'd tried to work out how long it would be before the army claimed him. Not for a while yet, she'd calculated. But the war showed no more sign of ending now than it had in

June, and Dick had turned fifteen in the meantime. He still had two years before he'd be called up. But two years was nothing.

Dorothea shuddered, thinking of the patients up at the house. Private Bamford, blind. One-armed Private Wilson. And then there was Private Sutton, who stammered so badly he could hardly talk — as if, after all he'd been through (wounded in the chest, shell-shocked), his brain refused to let him speak about it. But they were the lucky ones. There were many more who were dead. She saw Death in her mind's eye, cloaked and hooded and wielding his terrible scythe, waiting to cut Dick down.

'You all right, miss?' Dick was peering at her with shy concern. 'You gone white as a sheet. You look almost as badly as Mrs Carter. Death warmed up, Mum called Mrs Carter. Are you cold, miss? Shall I borrow you me scarf?'

'I'm tired, Dick. Just tired, that's all. But what's wrong with Susie Carter? I do hope she's not ill.'

'She's been up nights with that lad of hers. Got a fever, he has.'

'Jake, you mean — Jake's not well? What's the matter with him?' But Dick could tell her nothing more.

She'd not seen Jake in months, and it was more than a year since she'd held him in her arms on the day she'd taken him to Clifton, a barefoot and snotty-nosed little boy. *If there's ever anything he needs*, Aunt Eloise had said that day, *I know I can rely on you.* Tired though she was — exhausted — Dorothea knew she wouldn't rest until she found out how Jake was doing. Leaving Dick to his digging, she set out for the village.

The crumbling sandstone wall, partially collapsed on the Gatehouse side of the entrance to Clifton's drive, was in better repair on this other side and it ran along the verge for a hundred yards or so as the road headed towards Hayton. Only when the wall came to an end did she really feel she'd left Clifton behind. She hurried on between the faded hedgerows, trying to recall when last she'd walked this way. She'd not been to the village much of late; when she did venture there she nearly always took the shortcut across the fields. But she felt sure she must have come this way at least once in the last month or so, because she distinctly remembered meeting children from the village school picking blackberries.

'To make jam for the soldiers,' they'd told her; they'd been let out of school especially.

How anyone could find sufficient sugar to make jam was a mystery. There was barely enough these days to sweeten a cup of tea. Cook despaired. She had baskets full of apples from Clifton's long-neglected orchard, and there were plums in profusion this year too, but most of them would go to waste if they couldn't be preserved. Sugar wasn't the only thing in short supply: tea, bacon, butter and margarine were all hard to come by. Food of any sort was now highly prized, hence the conscientious harvesting of apples, plums and blackberries that might once have been left to rot. Not that anyone was starving quite yet. The shortages were inconvenient more than anything. No doubt old Noah Lee could remember harder times. *You don't know what it's like to go without*, he'd said last Christmas, back in the days when she was still welcome at the Turners'. *You don't know what it's like*, he'd said. But perhaps a time was coming when they would all find out.

With this sobering thought, she reached the turning to Back Lane. Before long the Carters' cottage came into view. Susie answered the door. Wan and drawn, she looked even more exhausted than Dorothea felt. Guessing, perhaps, the reason for the visit, she let Dorothea in without a word.

Jake, wrapped in a rag rug, lay in a battered old cot in the main room. He had red-rimmed eyes and a runny nose, was coughing repeatedly — but the sound of his coughing was to Dorothea's ears ominously feeble, as if the last of his strength was ebbing away.

She took a hold of herself. There was no need to be melodramatic. She seemed to have lost all sense of proportion in her state of fatigue, but she'd be no help to anyone if she got overwrought.

Susie said, 'We fetched the cot down 'cause his coughing were keeping Nibs awake. Nibs needs his rest. He's got work. I sit up with Jakey. But — oh, miss — I dunno what to do! He's burning up, and nothing seems to make no difference.'

'What does Dr Camborne say?'

'We don't need the doctor. Leastways, we can't afford him.'

'Don't worry about that, Susie. Don't worry about it now. Dr Camborne's very good, he won't expect to be paid all at once.'

'Nibs won't have it. Well, he won't, miss, you know how he is.'

'Listen, Susie. What's more important? Jake — or Nibs's stubborn pride? I'll go for the doctor myself, I'll go right away. You can tell Nibs it was all my doing.'

Dorothea let herself out of the cottage. Dr Camborne's house, Maybank, was at the other end of the village, out on the Welby Road. But Dorothea had only got as far as the junction of Back Lane and the Lawham Road when she saw Dick Turner swinging along from the direction of Clifton. He'd obviously finished his digging and was heading home. She waved to him and he came running. He was only too pleased to do her another good turn; he said he'd fetch Dr Camborne at once. He went haring away towards the High Street. Dorothea went back to the Carters'.

Susie was in a terrible state, which could not be having a soothing effect on Jake. Dorothea prevailed on her to sit down and then made her a cup of tea, before doing what she could to settle the fractious child.

Dr Camborne arrived. Dick came in with him and loitered by the door. The doctor, in his professional capacity, was very different to the bon viveur of Clifton dinners. Brisk and to the point, he examined Jake and made a speedy diagnosis.

'Measles. Most definitely measles. Has he been in contact with anyone infected?'

'Dunno,' said Susie miserably. 'I . . . I did take him with me the other day when I'd washing to deliver in Brockmorton.'

'There we are, that'll be it. There are at least half a dozen cases in Brockmorton, so I'm told.' The doctor turned to Dorothea. 'Let me show you, Mrs Kaufmann. You can see — here, and here — the rash starting behind his ears — and there on his face, too. It will spread before long over the rest of his body. Have you had measles yourself?'

'I'm not sure. I don't know.' No doubt she'd been exposed to any number of contagious diseases when she was a child living in what Roderick had called 'the slums of London' but — ironically — the only time she could remember being seriously ill was after coming to Clifton, when she'd caught diphtheria aged thirteen. Although not unduly worried about herself, she realized what it meant to have come here. 'I can't go back to Clifton now I've been near Jake. I might infect the men, or Katherine and Laurence.' But if she had to stay for now, that was all to the good. She felt she could be of some use here. Her only worry was what the Ranee would have to say about her playing truant.

'Don't concern yourself with Sister Elliot,' said Dr Camborne. 'Let me deal with her. I'm due at Clifton later, on my regular round. I'll talk to her then.' He snapped shut his black bag, pulled on his hat and coat. 'I'll take my leave. I'll call again tomorrow. Remember, the patient must have plenty of rest. I have prescribed something to cool him, and something to relieve his cough. Try to make him eat if you can, anything light and nourishing. The room must be kept at a comfortable temperature, too. And let's not have the whole village traipsing in and out,' he added, cocking an eye at Dick. 'Even the family should stay away as much as possible. We don't want the infection to spread, if we can help it.'

Dr Camborne made his exit. As soon as he'd gone, Dorothea despatched Dick to the shop with a list and the few shillings she had in her pocket. She guessed that Susie would not have much in by way of supplies, living hand-to-mouth as the Carters did. Whilst waiting for Dick to return, Dorothea lit a fire in the grate.

Susie stood wringing her hands. 'What you doing, Miss Dorothea? That firewood, and the bit of kindling — that's all we got to last us. And we've got no money for medicines and all the rest of it.'

'You heard what Dr Camborne said, Susie: the room must be kept warm. Remember, we're doing this for Jake — it's all for Jake. Come and sit with him whilst I tidy round. I expect you've not had time to breathe, with him being so poorly.'

'I've been worried sick, miss, I can't tell you. But — oh, miss — what am I gonna do about Nibs's tea? He'll be wanting his tea when he comes in, and he's so very particular.'

'Never mind about Nibs and his tea. I'll see to all that. Sit down a bit, Susie. Shut your eyes for ten minutes, if you can. You look about ready to drop.' Dorothea found it disconcerting to see Susie so weak and ineffectual, and not her brash and fiery self.

Dick came back. Dorothea met him at the door. 'You'd best not come in, Dick, after what the doctor said.'

'Right-oh, miss. You can always send for me, if there's ote you need. I'll pop round later, any road, just in case.'

Dorothea swiftly got organized, transforming the little front parlour into a sickroom; it came as second nature after all her months at the hospital in London and working more recently under Sister Elliot. She rather dreaded the inevitable meeting with Nibs, however. As Susie had pointed out, she knew what Nibs was like, and she knew the way things stood between them. They'd not exchanged a single word since the day she'd taken Jake to see Aunt Eloise, and that was over a year ago. She braced herself for the inevitable.

He came stomping in with muddy boots, a little knapsack and a savage look on his face; his brother, Ned, came in at the same time. They were not big men, but they seemed to fill the tiny front room, and Dorothea felt hemmed in. She stood her ground, nonetheless, determined not to be bullied.

Nibs turned his back on her, growled at his wife, 'Why'd you let *her* in?'

'She's come to help,' said Susie in a small voice.

'I don't want ote to do with her — I told yer. I don't want ote to do with any of 'em, them busybodies up the big house. You done this deliberate, to get me back up.'

Ned involved himself. 'Don't get on at Susie!'

Nibs glowered at his brother. 'Keep out of it, you. It's none of yer business.'

Ned glowered in return. 'Why are you like this, Nibs? Why are you so obstropulous? Yer always in a bate the whole time, yer always rubbing folk up the wrong way — I have to make no end of excuses for you and I'm fed up of it!'

'I'm fed up and all — fed up with the lot of yer, hanging round me neck.'

'I don't hang round no one's neck. I pay my way — and don't you forget it.'

'This is my house and you'll show me some respect, all of yer. And put that bleeding fire out. It's sweltering in here.'

'The fire's for Jakey.' Susie began to sob. 'The fire's for my little boy.'

It was Ned who moved to comfort her, putting a consoling arm around her and looking daggers at his brother.

'There, now. There, there. Come along now. Come and dry yer eyes a minute.'

With a last reproachful glance in Nibs's direction, Ned led Susie through to the back kitchen.

Dorothea was now alone with Nibs (Jake didn't count in a situation like this). She held her breath, waited.

He did his best not to look at her. 'You can clear off and all. We don't need none of your charity.'

'Charity!' She was stung by the word and it fuelled her anger. Nibs had been downright nasty ever since he came in, throwing his weight about and upsetting everyone. She could only wonder what good she'd ever seen in him. 'Charity is something given to strangers, Robin Carter.' She called him by his right name, as she'd always done when taking him to task. He hated being called Robin. 'It's not charity when its

kindness between friends. That's not charity. All I want is for
. . . for Jake to . . . to get better—'

She never finished her sentence. She found herself sobbing — sobbing far worse than Susie. She had broken down,
and it had taken her completely by surprise.

She was dismayed. She couldn't understand it. What had
brought it on? Not Nibs. Not Nibs alone, anyway. Nibs was
just the last straw. Tired all the time, and rushed off her feet,
and weighed down by her responsibilities: that explained some
of it. But there was also the fact that it was a year since Dr
Kaufmann's letter. A whole year had passed since she'd learned
of Johann's death, but it still felt just as raw. And what made it
worse was that no one mentioned Johann anymore. He'd been
forgotten by everyone — everyone except her.

She was being silly, she told herself severely. Why should
anyone remember Johann? Most people in Hayton had never
heard of him, let alone met him. And even at Clifton it was
five years now since his one brief visit, before the time of
such servants as Crompton and Tilda Johnson. Getting upset
because no one remembered Johann was just silly. And sillier
still was to have let herself down in front of Nibs — Nibs,
of all people! He'd only despise her all the more for making
such a spectacle of herself.

As she fought to regain some semblance of self-control,
however, Nibs seemed more taken aback than anything.
Indeed, there was an expression on his face that — had it
been anyone other than Nibs — she might almost have said
seemed *humble*.

'Give over now,' he grunted. 'Stop this carry-on. It's not
like you, all this blarting.' Frowning fiercely, he fumbled in
his pockets, then thrust at her a screwed-up handkerchief.
'Here. Dry yer eyes. Dint mean to upset you and all that.
Gets on me wick, is all, folk sticking they nose in. Can't abide
it, being obliged to folk.'

She all but groaned with the frustration of it. How many
times had she heard this? Too many times. Too often down
the years she'd found herself banging her head against the

brick wall of his stubborn pride. Well, this time she was not going to let him get away with it.

Twisting in her hands the filthy, fraying handkerchief she would not have dreamt of having anywhere near her face, she did her best to keep her voice steady and matter-of-fact.

'I've always been very fond of you, Robin Carter, and all your shouting and bawling won't change that. You might have decided not to be my friend anymore, but I am not so fickle. If you won't accept my help for your own sake, you can at least do so for Susie and Jake. I'd never forgive myself if anything happened to Jake — if anything happened, and I'd stood by and done nothing! So if I hear any more talk of you being *obliged* to me, I'm warning you, I'll . . . I'll . . .' But she didn't know what she'd do and she stumbled into silence, flinching a little as she readied herself for one of his devastating broadsides.

When the expected outburst didn't come, she dared to glance across at him. She found he wasn't looking at her at all. He was staring instead at the cot, and at the wheezing, coughing child within it.

Finally he tore his eyes away. He shot her a dark, unreadable look. 'Do what yer want,' he muttered. 'You always do.' With that, he pushed past her and went into the other room, slamming the door behind him.

A fragile peace descended on the tiny cottage. While Susie in the back kitchen served up the meal that Dorothea had prepared for Nibs and Ned, Dorothea sat with Jake in the main room. Nodding in her chair, sleeping in snatches, she saw to the fire in between times and tended to Jake, and she watched as the room sank into shadow, dusk giving way to dark.

She went on sitting there long after Nibs and Ned had gone to bed. She had Susie for company. In the flickering candlelight, and in the glow from the fire, they watched in helpless silence as the red rash spread slowly but inexorably across Jake's face and neck and arms.

There was nothing they could do to stop it.

* * *

Dr Camborne called the next day, after Nibs and his brother had left for work. A frown came over his face as he examined the patient.

'I rather suspect there's some inflammation of the lungs,' he said in an undertone to Dorothea.

'His fever's not dying down, Doctor.'

'That is also cause for concern. In my opinion, the next forty-eight hours will be critical. I'll not presume to issue any orders, Mrs Kaufmann. I can see you're doing sterling work. Carry on as you are and I'll be back by and by.'

As soon as he'd gone, Susie asked anxiously, 'What did he say, miss? It's bad, isn't it, real bad.'

'He's worried, Susie, I won't deny it, but he's satisfied we're doing all we can. There's every chance Jake will begin to get better in a day or two.'

'But he looks so poorly, miss. He looks sort of helpless. It's like he can't hardly breathe. And he's messed hisself again.'

'I'll see to that, Susie.'

'Oh, miss, you shouldn't have to—'

'I've coped with a lot worse. I've seen it all since I started nursing, and it doesn't worry me one little bit. Go and lie down for a while. Get some rest. Then you can sit with him later, whilst I have a nap.'

Susie wouldn't go upstairs to sleep. She nodded off where she was, sat in one of the rickety old chairs. Dorothea cleaned and changed Jake, found fresh bedding, settled him as best she could, put the soiled things in to soak. She had just finished washing her hands when there was a knock on the door. Opening it just a fraction — to keep the warmth in — she found Dick on the doorstep. He'd come to see if he was needed.

'I heard what the doctor said, miss, yesterday. I heard him say as it were measles like they got in Brockmorton. It's spread to Broadstone now, and all. A kiddie's died of it in Broadstone — a little girl it were — and there's others took badly. Mum heard it from Mrs Franklin. Mrs Franklin's got a brother what lives in Broadstone.'

Dorothea found herself trembling at this news, and she glanced behind her at the battered little cot. But there seemed no point in fearing the worst. There was little enough she could do, but anything was worth a try. She decided then and there to make a start by cleaning the room from top to bottom. She wouldn't disturb Jake or Susie, as long as she was careful. If nothing else, it would reduce the risk of infection; it would also keep her busy and stop her brooding.

She sent Dick to fetch what she needed from the shop, then she set to work. On her hands and knees, quietly scrubbing the floor, she tried to banish all gloomy thoughts and think about something else. What did the maids at Clifton think about when they were scrubbing the floors: Tilda Johnson and Winny Downie, and Ada Walker, the most recent nursery maid? Dorothea was taken back to her earliest days at Clifton, when she'd often watched an earlier nursery maid doing the same job: her very first friend at the big house, Nora Turner. The smell of carbolic had been strange to Dorothea in those days and had made her wrinkle her nose; the series of rented rooms in which she'd lived with her papa up until then had not been noteworthy for their cleanliness.

Dorothea paused in her work, sitting back on her haunches. For her, the smell of carbolic was forever evocative of her first weeks and months at Clifton. For Johann, it had held very different associations.

Dorothea furrowed her brow. How did she know this? How on earth had they ever come to be talking about the smell of carbolic? But was there anything during their all-too-brief time together that they *hadn't* talked about? They'd spent so much time talking that she'd never be able to remember even the half of it.

Johann had been four years old when his little brother was born. That same summer, there'd been a deadly outbreak of cholera in Hamburg. Thousands had perished in the space of a few weeks. The panic-stricken population, desperate to keep the disease at bay, had resorted to vast quantities of carbolic and Lysol, and soon the whole city had reeked of disinfectant. Among those struck down was Johann's mother. She'd died barely a fortnight after giving birth; her sister — Johann's Aunt Ana — had also died. Aunt Ana's two sons, Heinrich and Gerhard, had already been bereft of their father (he'd succumbed to throat cancer four years before); with their mother gone too, they'd been left orphans. That was when the two boys had been taken in by Dr Kaufmann, who was newly widowed and already had two young sons of his own.

Only once had Dorothea heard Dr Kaufmann refer to that time, and even then merely in general terms: the overcrowded hospitals, the untold suffering and death, the dead bodies shovelled into hastily made 'nose-squasher' coffins. An endless procession of hearses, vans and carts of every sort had rolled from the hospitals to the city cemetery. Gravediggers had worked round the clock. This atmosphere of terror and panic, the sense of doom as the death toll mounted, the alarming behaviour of the adults around him: all this had been engraved on Johann's memory. But he'd not liked to dwell on it. He'd tried to block it out — just as Dorothea had tried to block out some of the more uncomfortable memories from her own early childhood (sleeping in doorways with her papa when they couldn't afford a room for the night, her papa's chaotic approach to life, his drinking). But there was always something that brought these deep-buried memories to the surface, there was always a trigger. For Dorothea, it was whenever she thought about the time when she'd gone in search of her papa after she'd grown up, returning to the places where she'd lived as a child and learning more about her past. For Johann, on the other hand, it had been certain sounds, certain smells — among them the smell of carbolic.

Johann, without a doubt, had been proud of his hometown: the fiercely independent Hanseatic port and Free City of Hamburg. But he'd not been blind to its faults. The Alley Quarters, for instance, were such pernicious slums that one distinguished visitor, on seeing them, had been heard to remark, 'Gentlemen, I forget that I am in Europe'; the Alley Quarters had been in the process of demolition when Dorothea moved to Hamburg, but she'd seen enough to recognize a similarity to some of the places she'd known in her childhood (she wondered if perhaps such places existed in every city). Then there was the question of Hamburg's water supply. After a previous outbreak of cholera — Dr Kaufmann had lived through it as a young man — the city's ruling Senate had taken the decision to introduce filtration into the water supply in the hope of making it much safer to drink. But progress had been painfully slow. Many powerful senators begrudged the expense, and some even questioned the need. They'd produced 'experts' ready to attest that filtration was unnecessary, because disease did not spread in water but through the air, by a miasma. Dr Kaufmann had disagreed with this point of view but he'd found himself in a minority — with bitter personal consequences. When cholera returned to Hamburg some twenty-eight years after the previous outbreak, the improvement works had still not been completed. The endless procrastination and the imperfect theories about disease led directly to the deaths of over eight thousand people, his wife among them.

While reluctant to spend money on public health, the Senate had not been nearly so parsimonious when it came to building a new and grandiloquent city hall.

'The Rathaus is a magnificent building, *liebchen*, do you not agree?'

They'd been standing, Dorothea remembered, her and Johann, in the square called Rathausmarkt, looking up at the ornate facade of the city hall on one of their tours of Hamburg, by which Johann introduced her to his hometown in the weeks and months after her arrival.

'A magnificent building, yes. But what is the use of it? Does such ostentation serve any purpose beyond vainglory? The money lavished on it would have been better spent improving the city's sanitation — or in founding a university.'

Hamburg's rulers, down the years, had been steadfast in their refusal to fund a university — again, they'd baulked at the expense — and so, in pursuing his medical studies, Johann had been forced to go elsewhere.

It wasn't so very surprising that Johann should have chosen a career in medicine. Sons often followed in their fathers' footsteps and took up their fathers' professions. But for Johann, it was his mother's death that had settled the matter.

'I could do nothing for Mutti. I was only a little boy and I couldn't save her. But now I want to help others, for her sake and in her memory.'

How many wounded soldiers had Johann treated before his hospital was bombed? How many young men owed their lives to the untimely death of a thirty-four-year-old woman over two decades ago? But all Johann's hard-won learning — all his skill and dedication, all his youthful energy and enthusiasm, all his high ideals and the promise of more to come — all that had been lost forever when the bomb fell. It seemed such a waste. Such a senseless waste.

Dorothea, on her haunches, brushing back her limp curls from her forehead with the back of her hand, felt a wave of hopelessness wash over her. Was there any point in all this cleaning? Was there any point in *anything*?

But she couldn't just sit here and do nothing.

She went back to it.

* * *

Nibs and Ned used the back door when they came in from work, and they stayed in the back room all evening until it was time for bed. The sound of their heavy tread on the stairs woke Dorothea, who'd been nodding in her chair. She stirred herself, yawning, and got up.

Popping out for a breath of air, she stood on the doorstep on this cold autumn evening. Wisps of fog were drifting in the fields beyond the village, but the sky above was clear: there was no moon, but many stars. No lights were showing in any of the nearby cottages. The residents of Back Lane did not stay up late, it seemed.

As she took a last look round, she caught sight of a solitary bat flitting round the roof of the Turners' cottage like a splinter of shadow, before disappearing into the darkness. She shivered and turned to go back indoors, but even as she did so, there came a faint sound on the very edge of hearing — a sound like distant thunder — and it seemed to her that the cottage windows rattled for a moment. She stood frozen in place, straining her ears. After a long pause, she thought she heard another faint *boom*, but this was even more remote than the first, and she could not be sure. And then — nothing. Just the misty darkness and an empty silence.

She went inside and shut the door.

* * *

The night wore on. Dusk began to seem a very long time ago. Dawn was a far-off dream. Susie was fast asleep, but Jake was restless and he started to grizzle, a thin and sickly sound; he scratched himself repeatedly with feeble fingers. Dorothea did her best to soothe him, leaning over the cot.

'How is he?'

The hoarse, muttered voice, complexly unexpected, made her jump nearly out of her skin. She'd not heard Nibs come down, but there he was, large as life, stood at the foot of the stairs. He was wearing a crumpled, half-open shirt that hung down over a pair of grubby long-johns; his feet were bare.

'Can't seem to drop off.' He sounded almost apologetic, as if he felt he had to account for his presence, and he remained where he was, uncharacteristically hesitant.

Dorothea, with a gesture, invited him to approach: it really did seem to her that he was waiting on her permission. They stood side by side, looking down at the child in the cot. Jake took rapid, shuddering breaths that rattled in his throat; the red rash looked worse than ever tonight.

Remembering her duty as a nurse, Dorothea said, 'You shouldn't get too close, Nibs. Not unless you've had measles yourself.'

'Must have, some time or other. Got the lot, we did, when we was kids. Caught everything going.' Suddenly he scowled and turned abruptly away. 'What you doing here? You'd not make this fuss if Jake weren't *his* child.'

Dorothea sighed. She made no attempt to hide it. 'Believe what you like, Nibs. I'm too tired to argue.'

She put a lump of wood on the embers in the grate, then sat down. Nibs also took a seat. They didn't look at each other, Dorothea watching the fire, Nibs staring at the floor. All was quiet except for the crackling flames and a sound of breathing: Jake loud and laboured, Susie soft and slow.

After a time, Dorothea found her eyes drawn inexorably towards Nibs. He was sat hunched over on a little stool in a brooding silence, his hair tousled and five days' growth of beard on his face since his Sunday shave. His threadbare shirt hung open, affording a glimpse of his pale chest with a scattering of black hair. His big feet were firmly planted. She found herself comparing this man of twenty-seven with the scrawny boy scrumping apples from the old orchard at Clifton — Nibs as she'd first met him. He'd never been tall or particularly well-built, but he was strong and wiry and dour. And he'd always been intimidating — now as much as ever.

He glanced up, met her eye briefly, then looked away, scowling more fiercely; but when finally he spoke, his tone was almost conversational, or as conversational as he could get in his gruff, rough-and-ready way.

'Aye. Got the lot, us kids. Never did us no harm. Mum and Dad, though — they weren't so lucky. Snuffed it. Cottage were to blame. Unwholesome place. When it burnt down, that were best thing for it.'

The cramped cottage where the Carters had lived was one of three in a row in School Street that were now half-destroyed and derelict. Nibs's parents had died in that cottage within a year of each other, just before Dorothea first came to Clifton. Arnie, the eldest child — he'd been seventeen back then — had done his best to raise his six siblings on his own, until disaster struck and their home was gutted by fire — the Great Fire of legend. Dorothea had been moved by their plight. She'd appealed to Uncle Albert. He'd agreed to help. There was nothing wrong, he'd said, in helping those who were willing to help themselves; it wasn't charity, he'd said, it was a helping hand, it was giving a leg up. And so Arnie Carter had been offered a position in one of Uncle Albert's Coventry factories on far better wages than he'd earned as a farm labourer, and work had been found at Clifton for Nibs and his second sister, Milly (the elder girl, Becky, had her hands full with her younger siblings). With what Nibs and Milly earned, along with contributions from Arnie in Coventry, the Carters had been able to scrape by and even afford the rent on this place, the cottage where Nibs still lived. With Arnie gone, there'd been six of them, and only two bedrooms, but rudimentary though it was, this cottage was a big improvement on the decaying hovel in School Street. The Carters' situation was not unique, or even uncommon. Dorothea knew from her own experience that countless people lived in similar conditions, or worse. She herself, when she first came to Clifton, had left behind a single room shared by five people.

To keep the conversation going — such as it was — Dorothea asked for news of Nibs's brothers and sisters.

'Int seen our Arnie in ages,' said Nibs, glowering at his own feet. 'He's too busy slaving up in Coventry to find time for us. Making stuff for the war, they are, at his place. Making a packet for the profiteers, and all.'

Dorothea shot him a glance, wondering if the remark about profiteers was a dig at her. She received an annuity under the terms of Uncle Albert's will — an annuity no doubt paid out of the proceeds of the Coventry factories. But Nibs didn't know this — how could he? — so she guessed that he was railing against profiteers in general, which didn't surprise her in the least. He'd never been a respecter of rank or privilege.

Arnie Carter had done well for himself 'up in Coventry', as Nibs freely —if sourly — admitted. Their brother-in-law, Linus Young — he was married to Becky — had done even better. Once the blacksmith's apprentice here in the village, Young had risen high in Uncle Albert's engineering concern; so high, indeed, that he'd recently taken over as general manager of Brannan Engineering, following the death of Mr Simcox, Uncle Albert's right-hand man in days gone by. Dorothea knew all this from Aunt Eloise, who ensured she was kept informed about her husband's businesses.

Nibs, it seemed, was not unaware of Linus Young's new standing. He gave a snort of disdain at mention of Becky's good fortune.

'Living the high life, her is, up in Coventry. Come to see us a while back. Told us all about it. You should have seen her, the way she came swanning in, stinking with pride. Forgot where she's from, has Becky.'

Of Nibs's other siblings, Milly was now married to Nolly Keech, son of the village carpenter, one-handed Ned worked alongside Nibs at Home Farm, and Clover, despite Susie's doubts a year ago, had contrived to hold on to her post as kitchen maid at Hayton Grange.

'She were here last Wednesday, her half-day, was Clover. Said she'd seen you up the Grange, hobnobbing with that dotty old bird and her cripple of a son. Int there cripples enough for yer up the big house? Stuffed full with cripples, I've heard.'

The *dotty old bird* was Lady Fitzwilliam, mistress of Hayton Grange; her *cripple of a son*, Henry, was paralyzed from the waist down after a motoring accident four years ago. It was on the tip of Dorothea's tongue to rebuke Nibs for referring to Henry — and the patients at Clifton — as cripples, and in such a disparaging tone of voice. But she half suspected he'd only done it to get a rise out of her, and she wouldn't give him the satisfaction.

'Henry is my friend,' she said, 'one of my oldest and dearest friends.' She added pointedly, 'I don't abandon my friends — even when *they* abandon *me*.' If her words hit home, Nibs didn't let it show, but sat stolidly on his stool.

They went back to the subject of Nibs's siblings. Arnie, Becky, Milly, Ned and Clover: that was five accounted for. Only Dixon was left. Dixon was Clover's twin and the youngest of them all by a couple of minutes. He was eighteen now, and Dorothea remembered Owain Morgan telling her that Dixie was in the army. He'd been 'combed out', as it was called; a desperate need for more men at the front had led to many of those men who'd been working in scheduled trades to be reassessed and conscripted, and Dixie was one of them.

'More fool him,' said Nibs.

'He had no choice. He wasn't exempt anymore. He wasn't exempt the way you are.'

'Think I'd go in the army? I'd not go even if they said I had to. Sooner be locked up than fight for that lot. This bleeding war, it's toffs' business. Only toffs will get ote out of it.'

Dorothea said nothing. Perhaps he had a point. Perhaps not. She couldn't say. Immense, pervasive, endless, the war passed all understanding.

The fire crackled and spat. Its dancing flames cast shadows on the walls. Dorothea glanced again at Nibs on his stool, hunched over, brooding. She almost had to pinch herself that she was actually here, in his cottage, talking to him. A year ago last August, he'd thrown her out and told her not to come back. That was when their estrangement had begun. Was it over now? Or was this just a temporary truce, this dreamlike interlude in the middle of the night?

They sat on in silence for a while. The flames slowly died. Her eyelids began to feel heavy. She stifled a yawn. More to keep herself awake than anything else, she got up to check on Jake.

'He's asleep,' she said in answer to Nibs's interrogative look. Sitting back down, she tested the extent of their rapprochement by asking how his work was going at Home Farm.

He stared at the glowing remains of the fire. Times were hard, he said. The wet weather held them back. Animal feed was becoming scarce, too, and the livestock were of an inferior quality. They grew, but they didn't fatten. And almost all the working horses had been requisitioned (he pronounced *horse* as *hoss*).

'Only two now left up Home Farm, and one of them's lame. Daresay *they* think men can pull a plough same as an 'orse. That's all we are to *that* lot, beasts to make use of.' He added darkly, 'There's *women* working up Home Farm, if you can believe it. Women working the land,' as if this was the last straw, as if it was a calculated insult to his masculinity.

Yet why not, thought Dorothea: why shouldn't women work the land? Rosa, surely, would be in favour. Rosa believed that women could do anything that men could do.

Dorothea was struck by a sudden thought. Both Rosa and Nibs were rebels in their different ways. Nibs had always been scathing about *them*, *that lot* — the toffs, the bosses, the do-gooders — while Rosa decried unearned power and privilege, and saw herself on the side of the oppressed. Rosa sometimes spoke of the 'dignity of labour'. But would she see much dignity in Nibs's stiff-necked pride? As for Nibs, Dorothea could just imagine what he'd make of a 'toff' like Rosa, a mere woman; he'd not take kindly to her having the brass neck to think she knew the first thing about *his* life.

Dorothea glanced across at Nibs and found him watching her suspiciously.

'Love it, don't you,' he said. 'Love it when you think folk can't do without you.'

Dorothea was much too tired to pretend that his words didn't exasperate her. 'I want to help, that's all. What's wrong with wanting to help?'

'Who said we need *your* help?'

'Shush, Nibs! You'll wake Jake and Susie.'

He glowered at her. 'This is *my* bleeding house, case you forgot. I'll say what goes here. Mind you,' he added, 'her's as bad.' He jerked his head at the sleeping form of his wife.

'Her and that bleeding cripple upstairs, ganging up together, taking each other's side.'

'Why must you be so horrible to poor Ned? It's not his fault he lost his hand.'

'That's all you know. If he'd not been playing silly buggers — playing silly buggers with one of them new-fangled machines — it needn't never have happened.'

'However it happened, he's done his very best to cope with it. I think he's been very brave.'

'Huh. You'd not be saying that if you'd seen him after his hand first came off. You dint see him like I did, hiding hisself away, blarting over his stump. They was after giving him the sack up Home Farm and all. I wasn't having that. "He'll be right in a day or two," I says to them. "Least give the daft bugger chance to pick hisself up." And they did — grudging, like.'

'That was good of you, getting them to keep him on. I didn't know you'd done that.'

Nibs shrugged. 'You work, else you go hungry — and he knew it. His stump don't bother him so much now. He's gotten to be nifty too, I'll give him that. Does more with one good hand than most folk do with two. It dint come easy, mind. Bloody useless, he were, to start with. Wouldn't even try half the time. Nearly ended a cripple meself, doing his work as well as me own, so they wouldn't sack him.'

'Oh, Nibs, I'm sorry! I had no idea you'd done so much for him!'

'Had no choice, did I, seeing as I was lumbered with him.'

But not everyone would have made such an effort, thought Dorothea, not even for their own brother.

There was no point heaping praise on Nibs, however. He'd only think she was trying to butter him up. All she said was, 'You helped Ned when he needed it. Can't you accept a little help yourself, now that you're in need?'

'Charity, you mean.'

'Call it charity if you must. Call it whatever you like. The simple truth is that people are ready and willing to help you, if only you'd let them. How much is it worth, your stupid pride? What price is this boy's life — your son's life?'

Nibs glowered fiercely at this, and she knew at once what he was thinking: that she'd called Jake *your son* to be provoking — which, of course, she hadn't.

'He int, though. He int my son.'

'You are the one bringing him up. You are his father. The only father he'll ever know.'

'If it had been anyone but *him* . . . why'd it have to be *him*? Eats me up that *he's* Jake's dad.'

'Roderick is dead. You must forget about Roderick.'

Looking at Susie, still fast asleep, Nibs growled, 'I wish to goodness she'd never clapped eyes on him. I wish to goodness she never had.' His gaze lingered, his eyes dark and impenetrable. 'It were *him* more'n *her* — *he* led her on and *she* dint know no better. Dint help that she's a Hobson. Everyone knows what the Hobsons are like. They've diddicoy blood, so folk say. Not that it makes a blind bit of difference to me where she comes from. And folk — folk'll say anything.' Nibs's eyes narrowed, as if boring into Susie's very soul. 'If I'd had any sense, I'd not have gone near her. But I were just a lad, greener than grass. She got under me skin afore I knew it. Led me a merry dance, she did. I ate me heart out over her. I were so far gone, I even scratched our names on the old plank bridge over the runnel by Row Meadow—'

He stopped abruptly and sat up straight on his stool, scrubbing his face with his hand. 'Dunno what I'm jabbering on about. Take no notice. Don't mean ote.'

'Nibs, I—'

'Daresay you've troubles of your own. Yer old man—'

'Johann,' she blurted out, taken by surprise that Nibs had mentioned him. 'His name was Johann,' she repeated. She found she could say his name quite calmly, without so much as a tremor in her voice.

'Foreign sort of chap.'

'German.'

The enemy. But so was she.

'You'll get a reputation,' she said, a feeling of bitterness welling up in her, 'harbouring one of the enemy. Mr Cheeseman calls me a "Germ-Hun".'

'Load of bleeding nonsense. And he's a fool, old Cheeseman, always has been. This chap of yours. He must have had summat about him, for you to . . .' Nibs left the sentence hanging.

'He did. Oh, he did!'

She'd been thinking about Johann a lot today — even more than usual. She couldn't help wondering if they'd have got along, Johann and Nibs. Johann wouldn't have been put off by Nibs's prickly manner, nor by his poverty; Johann would have seen the man himself. As for Nibs — well, he wasn't the most sociable of men, it was true. But it would have been entirely in character, he who made enemies of so many of his neighbours, to have made a friend of his enemy.

But she would never know for sure. She would never know.

A wave of weariness washed over her and she yawned, covering her mouth with her hand. Nibs was watching her again, his dark eyes unfathomable.

'You look done in.'

'I do feel rather tired all of a sudden. I can't keep my eyes open. I shall have to wake Susie.'

'Leave her be. Get some kip. I'll sit with *him*.'

'But you've work in the morning.'

'Only end up tossing and turning if I go back to bed. Might as well make meself useful.'

'Are you sure?'

'Do as yer told, woman, can't you, for once in yer bleeding life?'

Even couched in those terms, it was far too tempting an offer to refuse in her exhausted state — though it was unexpected, too, and she wasn't quite sure what to make of it. For a moment, as she settled back and surrendered herself to sleep, her brain continued to niggle away at this question. She found herself wondering if — hoping that — something of their old friendship might be rescued out of all this. The fleeting thought came and then it went, and her mind shut down.

She had one last, brief moment of consciousness as she drifted towards oblivion. Her heavy eyelids half-opened, and in the dim light from the glowing fire she saw Nibs bending over the cot and reaching down to soothe the restless child. In the very final second before sleep took her, it seemed to her that she saw on Nibs's tanned and hard-bitten face a look of such solicitude and tenderness that, when she woke some hours later in the pale light of dawn, she felt sure she must have dreamt it.

* * *

There followed another anxious day. Dr Camborne called mid-afternoon. He wore a frown of concern as he examined the patient. Finally, he stepped back from the cot and snapped his bag shut. As he put his hat and coat on, his frown was partly smoothed away. Jake was no worse, he said, which was something. Possibly — just possibly — there were even signs of improvement, but it would be best not to get the family's hopes up (he made sure to speak out of Susie's earshot, confiding in Dorothea as a fellow professional).

Later, Dick Turner came knocking. He'd taken a message to Clifton earlier for Dorothea and was back now with a bag of clean clothes for her, and some other bits and pieces. He'd also heard some news that explained the mysterious sounds of the previous night, the sounds like distant thunder. Rumour had it there'd been a Zeppelin at large. The 'Zepp' — as Dick called it — had dropped bombs on Northampton; according to at least one version of the story, there'd been several casualties, even some deaths. Dick was breathless with the excitement of it. Just think! The Zepp might have flown right over Hayton itself!

Dick didn't stay long. He had errands to run for his mother. As he went scampering off, Nibs and Ned came home from work and he dodged round them on the garden path. Dorothea lingered a moment on the doorstep. Ned nodded to her on his way round to the back door, but Nibs paused on the path. As she stood there holding the door almost shut, Dorothea felt they were a little shy of each other. Nibs avoided her eye. He watched Dick Turner instead, racing away down Back Lane in a tearing hurry as always.

'That lad's took a real shine to you,' said Nibs.

Without another word, he disappeared round the side of the cottage.

* * *

'He's ever so much better.'

Susie spoke cautiously. Even so, it was obvious that she was allowing herself to hope for the first time. Jake's rash had faded from red to brown, his breathing was much easier. He was still pale and thin, but he had strength enough now to make his presence felt and was growing ever more noisy and fractious.

'Out of danger,' Dr Camborne announced when he called.

Dorothea had been nearly a week at the Carters' but now her help was no longer needed: the crisis was over. Susie was duly grateful for everything Dorothea had done, but did not seem overly sorry to see the visitor go — which was only to be expected. Susie wanted to get back to normal. She wanted to be mistress in her own house once more.

Dorothea packed her bag, said her goodbyes, and stepped out of the cottage into a grey and gloomy afternoon, the ground still wet from recent rain. She found she was strangely reluctant to go straight back to Clifton; almost without realizing, she turned right into the village, instead of left and the way back. She'd felt indispensable this last week and as if she belonged — she'd begun to feel part of the family. But Nibs's family wasn't her family. She didn't have a family, never would now that Johann had gone. Also, she reminded herself, she wasn't welcome in the village. She didn't want to run the risk of meeting someone and being snubbed: that would shatter the fragile sense of acceptance she'd gained over the last few days.

She decided to turn back, leave the village without delay — but it was too late. Old Mrs Harrison was outside her cottage beating her rugs and mats against the wall with great vigour; catching sight of Dorothea, she paused in her work and waited. Dorothea felt she had no choice but to go on and face her.

Mrs Harrison spoke first. 'Afternoon, miss.'

'Oh . . . yes . . . good afternoon.'

'Looks like rain again.'

'Yes. Yes, it does.'

'Ah, well. No rest for the wicked.'

Mrs Harrison went back to her rugs.

Dorothea walked on down Back Lane. She almost hugged herself in her sense of relief. The commonplace little exchange seemed everything she could have hoped for. All the same, it would have been less of an ordeal to have gone straight back to Clifton. Her heart was hammering inside her chest.

Almost at once, she was faced another nerve-racking moment. She had reached the Circle, where the duck pond was and the Jubilee Oak. Walking down School Street towards her was Mrs Atkin, the blacksmith's wife; Mercy Bates was lolloping along beside her.

'Miss Doppoppy! Miss Doppoppy!'

Mercy came leaping and bounding down the street, a huge, beaming smile all over her face. Dorothea couldn't help but smile too. Here was one person at least only too delighted to see her.

Mercy grabbed hold of Dorothea's hand and launched into a breathless account of her many adventures.

'. . . And den I went up *dat* way . . .' Pointing wildly. '. . . And den I seed the flappy thing . . .'

Dorothea understood less than half of it, but a nod and a smile every so often was all the encouragement Mercy needed. As more and more words tumbled from Mercy's mouth, Mrs Atkin joined them, a mild-mannered woman in her late fifties.

After a while, Mrs Atkin caught Dorothea's eye. 'You've the patience of a saint, bless you. But she'll keep you all day if you let her. Come away, now, Mercy. Leave Mrs Kaufmann alone. She's got things to do, I'm sure.'

Laughing and looking back over her shoulder at Dorothea as if she couldn't keep her eyes off her, Mercy allowed herself to be led away by Mrs Atkin. They rounded the duck pond and went into the blacksmith's house, next to the forge.

Alone once more, Dorothea set off up School Street. She soon came to the derelict cottages. The Carters had lived in the middle one of the three: *unwholesome*, Nibs had called it. All three cottages had been abandoned after the Great Fire and left to slowly crumble away. The decaying walls were slowly sinking into the grass and had been climbed all over by ivy and trailing brambles. Dorothea remembered standing on this very spot last Christmas Eve and thinking how sad and gloomy the ruins looked: a salutary reminder that nothing lasts forever, her friendship with Nibs included. But now, and even though it was mid-autumn and the fading time of the year, she couldn't help thinking that this little wilderness had a certain bedraggled charm, a haven of peace and quiet reclaimed by nature. As for her friendship with Nibs — well, she wasn't quite sure what to think. At the time of the Great Fire, they'd been children, eleven or twelve. She'd helped Nibs rescue what they could of the Carters' belongings from the flames. Up until then, she'd been terrified of Nibs, and Nibs had always poured scorn on her, the la-di-da rich girl. But that day had seen a change; a friendship had been forged in the Great Fire that had endured over many years. Was it too much to hope that it wasn't beyond repair?

As she lingered by the ruined cottages, Dorothea was hailed from across the street, and she turned to find Milly Keech standing in the half-open gateway to the carpenter's yard. Milly was daughter-in-law to the carpenter, Chips Keech, and she was also Nibs's sister: the middle sister, the one who'd once worked in Clifton's kitchens.

'I saw you out the window, miss, and I had to pop out and ask how Jake is. How is he, miss? How's my poor little nephew?'

'He's much better, Milly. On the mend.'

'Oh, that is good news! Oh, I'm ever so glad! They tell me you've been a godsend, miss. You've helped Nibs and Susie no end.'

'I don't know about that. I did what I could. It wasn't much.'

'A regular Florence Nightingale. That's what I heard.'

Milly couldn't be disabused of this notion and they parted on the best of terms, Dorothea feeling that the plaudits were undeserved but grateful for the outpouring of Milly's goodwill. Dorothea's spirits rose as she cut across the green where the grass was littered with fallen leaves and seeds from the twisted branches of the sycamore, but almost at once they came crashing down again. The village was very quiet this afternoon and the High Street was almost devoid of life; there was just one solitary figure walking towards her.

It was Mrs Adnitt.

They both stopped in their tracks. They stood frozen, confronting each other across a no-man's land of several unbridgeable yards. Milly's praise, Mercy's smiles, the sense of relief at Jake's recovery: all this withered to nothing in the face of Mrs Adnitt's implacable hatred, clear on her face.

Mrs Adnitt was the first to move. She turned away, turned her back. Stiff and bristling, she retraced her steps along the High Street and went in at her gate.

Dorothea let out a shuddering breath, badly shaken — although she'd at least been spared this time Mrs Adnitt's verbal vitriol. Summoning what felt like her last reserves, she crossed the street and started up the path between the churchyard and the wall of the vicarage garden. She told herself that for every Mrs Adnitt there was a Mrs Harrison, a

Mrs Atkin, a Mercy Bates, a Milly Keech. What did it matter if Mrs Adnitt turned her back? There were others who didn't.

A strange mood took hold of her, a swelling sadness; one in which the thought of all the kindness and consideration she'd encountered this afternoon seemed to cut into her more sharply, more deeply, than any ill will. She couldn't imagine why this should be. It was unfathomable. She didn't understand herself at all.

Still a little shaky, she climbed the stile into Row Meadow and left the village behind. Where the path divided the other side of the stile, she took on impulse the right-hand way, the path that led in due course to Home Farm in its little hollow beneath the slopes of Rookery Hill. She followed this path only a short distance, as far as the edge of the meadow where grass gave way to rushes bordering a little brook: 'the runnel', as Nibs had called it. A rickety gate led onto the old plank bridge. Water ran clear in the channel beneath. Searching along the handrail, Dorothea found what she was looking for, weathered initials carved deep into the wood: *R.C.+S.H.* — just as Nibs had described it.

With one finger, she traced the lines and curves of the letters. Nibs had used the R of his real first name, if any more evidence was needed of how in earnest he'd been. She pictured him in her mind's eye, the scrawny boy he'd been, loitering here day after day on his way to work and on his way home, frowning fiercely as he scratched the wood with his knife, carving a little more of the careful inscription each time: a lovelorn and lonely figure. Lonely was the right word, too, for though this spot was only a stone's throw from the village, it felt remote, forsaken — more so than ever today, on this dull grey autumn afternoon. Nibs had waited a long time for Susie. Susie had kept him hoping and guessing all those years. And when finally he'd won her hand, she'd been carrying another man's child.

Why was it — why must it be — that love brought with it such pain amidst the joy?

Dorothea ran her hand one last time across the carved initials, then she turned away. She closed the little gate behind her. She cut across the meadow in order to re-join the path to Clifton. Startled rabbits scattered ahead of her, whisking into their burrows. Above the hedgerow, the branches of the tall elm trees, laden still with fading leaves, bent and seethed in a rising breeze. Her mind was a tangled mess, all manner of thoughts tripping over themselves. Sadness swelled within her breast and sharpened into something more, something beyond all description. She stopped and looked all round. The green meadow, the white-tailed rabbits, the tall elms etched against a louring sky, the swirling grey clouds: how beautiful it all was, so very beautiful.

Her vision grew blurred from the tears brimming in her eyes and it seemed to her that, if her heart had not been broken already, then seeing the world as it was this afternoon — so sad, so beautiful — would surely have broken it now.

CHAPTER NINE

Sat at the round satinwood table in the breakfast room, Dorothea carefully wrapped the carved wooden figures of the Christmas crib in old newspaper, whilst listening to the sound of singing from the drawing room next door. Private Glasspool could play the piano by ear and had begged permission to trespass in the forbidden part of the house. Other men had added their entreaties to his, for there was nothing they liked better than a good old sing-song. Dorothea felt sure that doing something they enjoyed could only speed their recovery, and to her surprise Dr Camborne, on one of his regular visits to Clifton's makeshift hospital, had agreed, thereby overruling the Ranee. And so this morning, a morning off from her nursing duties, Dorothea had been entertained as she wrapped the wooden figures by the tinkling piano and a chorus of rather raucous male voices that were only slightly muffled by the door separating her from the drawing room. She'd been regaled with 'Tipperary', diverted by 'Goodbye-ee', and was now being treated to a heartfelt rendition of 'Take Me Back to Dear Old Blighty'.

Picking out a delicately carved and painted Joseph, Dorothea reached for another sheet of newspaper in which to wrap him. Doing her best, just before Christmas, to bring some festive cheer to the rooms in the hospital side of the house, she had suddenly remembered the old crib, which in days gone by had played such an important part in Christmas in the nursery. A long time ago, it seemed now — so far in the past that it was almost as if it had happened to someone else.

She had found all the pieces of the crib jumbled in a canvas bag and stuffed at the back of the toy shelves in the day room. There'd always been much excitement when first setting it up each year, for it had meant Christmas was almost upon them. Every year, Roderick had turned his nose up, professing to have no interest in such 'kids' games'; every year it had not been long before he came prowling round, hanging back at first before pushing in, taking charge. He'd been a stickler for setting it up exactly the same as last year, as every year, which was why, having searched it out, Dorothea had arranged all the pieces as Roderick would have wanted. She'd positioned the crib where the men could see, hoping to brighten their days a little and to create some Christmas cheer.

Christmas Day, when it came, had been bright and sunny but bitterly cold, with frost on the ground and flurries of snow. That was three weeks ago now: Christmas 1917 had come and gone. And it was three *months* since Jake Carter's illness, though it seemed only yesterday: time simply flew by when you were always rushed off your feet. Jake was now back to his old self, restored to health if not to happiness — for who could be truly happy in times like these?

The sound of the full-throated singing formed a backdrop to her thoughts as Dorothea picked up the last of the carven figures, Baby Jesus himself. She readied a sheet of newspaper, then hesitated, inspecting the tiny wooden figure in all its meticulous detail; she wondered if, next year, it might be Katherine and Laurence setting up the crib in the nursery, as she used to with Roderick and Eliza: history repeating itself.

Whilst she was lost in these speculations, her eyes strayed from Baby Jesus to the sheet of newspaper beneath, seeing it as a blur of closely packed print.

253

Suddenly, a word — a name — leapt out at her.

CARTWRIGHT

Her eyes focused. Yes. It was most definitely Cartwright.
How odd. But there must be hundreds of Cartwrights.

She looked at the page more closely. The words *Roll of
Honour* were printed at the top, the sub-heading *Killed* underneath. It was one of those casualty lists that Nettie Thomson,
last June, had frowned on her reading. *Why do you torture yourself?* And indeed, these days, Dorothea didn't torture herself:
she'd not so much as glanced at the casualty lists in ages; there
simply weren't enough hours in the day.

Nettie's remembered voice echoed in her head. *Why do
you torture yourself? I think it's macabre. Imagine how you'd feel if you
saw a name you knew!*

A cold hand took hold of Dorothea's heart. She looked
more closely at the printed page.

CARTWRIGHT, Lt A.

The right name. The right regiment. But this newspaper
was weeks — months — old. Surely Eliza would have sent
word if Alex had been killed. It had to be a coincidence.

Well, it did . . . didn't it?

The cold hand gripped tighter. There was only one way
to find out for sure — and that meant going to London.

For a moment she baulked at the thought, but quickly
got a grip of herself. She must go and see Eliza, she simply
must — she had put it off for far too long. Now there could
be no excuse. She would leave for London at once.

Abandoning Baby Jesus, she hurried upstairs. The sound
of the men's singing faded away behind her.

* * *

She walked up and down the platform at Welby station —
up and down, up and down, never at rest. A train was due
— but when would it come? Half a dozen other people were
also waiting, huddled in winter clothes. It was cold, it was
windy: a bleak January day.

As she waited, Dorothea grew ever more nervous, half expecting at any moment to feel a heavy hand fall on her shoulder: the long arm of the law. There'd been no time to go to the police and arrange a travel permit; she wasn't even sure if such restrictions still applied. 'Some things are more important,' she had told herself firmly, as she got ready to go. She repeated it now, but with less conviction.

She tried to reassure herself. Nobody would know, to look at her, that she was an enemy, a German. But that didn't assuage her feelings of guilt. Roderick would have mocked her — Miss Goody-Goody, always so compliant — but she hated going against the rules, she simply hated it, and she couldn't help how she felt.

She did her best to distract herself, wondering if she'd been missed at Clifton yet. Only two people knew she'd gone. She'd decided not to worry Aunt Eloise, not until she had the facts at her fingertips. Part of her was still convinced that it was nothing more than a coincidence, a different Lieutenant Cartwright. So after packing a small bag she'd sought out Crompton, whom she judged least likely to ask awkward questions. 'Tell Mrs Brannan, if she asks, that I . . . that I've been called away . . . called to the village.' It had the ring of truth to it, after her sojourn with the Carters, but she couldn't help but feel guilt-ridden about this too, telling such fibs. More guilt, yet more guilt. Why, oh why must she be such a Miss Goody-Goody?

The Ranee, to Dorothea's surprise, had raised no real objections to her playing truant. Then again, Dorothea reasoned, no one could have done more than she had to make reparation after abandoning her post to look after Jake Carter: she'd worked her fingers to the bone ever since — and it had not gone unnoticed, seemingly.

'You may go, Nurse Kaufmann, if it's an emergency, as you say. But do please try to be back tomorrow at the latest.'

Pausing only to snatch up today's paper for something to read on the train, Dorothea had fled from the house.

A whistle sounded, faint, far-off. The train was coming at last; it must just have steamed out of Duncan's Hill Tunnel.

Puffs of smoke appeared in the distance, rising then fading into the grey sky. There was a stir and bustle on the platform.

The train arrived, crawled into the station, panting like an old man. Brakes squealed. The plum-and-white carriages came to a ponderous halt; vast clouds of steam belched from the black locomotive. Dorothea fought her way on board. The train was very crowded; all seats were taken. Tommies in uniform lolled on the floor in the corridor, so you even had to watch where you trod. They all looked very young. Was it her imagination, or were they younger than ever?

There was no Ernest Grimshaw ready to offer up his seat. She found a corner to stand in, and braced herself against the walls as the carriage jolted and the train got under way. Running through her mind were the sounds of a tinkling piano and rowdy male voices.

> *Take me back to dear old Blighty*
> *Put me on the train for London town . . .*

The train for London town.
And what would she find when she got there?

* * *

It was mid-afternoon when the train finally steamed into Euston station. She joined the flood of people streaming out of the carriages and swinging along the platform. She surrendered her ticket. Her senses quickened. She was back. Back in London. Back for the first time since quitting the hospital. A lot had happened in the eighteen months since. She could scarcely believe she was the same person.

She squeezed onto an omnibus, preferring it to the tube. As on the train, there was nowhere to sit. Clinging to the back of a seat amidst the press of passengers, she glimpsed shifting scenes through the windows as the bus lumbered down Tottenham Court Road and turned into Shaftesbury Avenue. The pavements were seething with pedestrians;

traffic clogged the streets. People were dressed in long buttoned coats, or jackets with high collars, or ubiquitous khaki; they were wrapped up in scarves and gloves and furs; they sported hats of every description, carried bags, clutched parcels, wielded black umbrellas. Horse-drawn hansom cabs had reappeared in numbers, mingling with modern motor cars; one of these she saw with a strange tent-like sack on its roof, and she was reminded of something she'd read, that coal-gas was being used for fuel now that petrol was rationed and in short supply — that sack on the roof must be full of coal-gas. She wondered what Uncle Albert would have made of such a contraption, he who'd carved a career out of making motors. Dear Uncle Albert! He'd not lived to see any of this, coal-gas cars, overcrowded trains, the war, Roderick's death, Eliza's precipitous marriage.

The bus crawled on, passing queues outside shops, passing statues piled with sandbags, passing a giant gun set amidst the windy wastes of Hyde Park. Cold and dismal though it was, and worn down by years of war, London still teemed with life.

She got off the omnibus on the Fulham Road and walked the last part of the way, leaving the busy streets behind. As she neared Essex Square, with its quiet terraces of white-fronted houses and neat black railings grouped around a central private garden, she remembered that Uncle Albert had always spoken of his town house as being in Chelsea, and she'd taken him at his word; but this was South Kensington, rather than Chelsea — surely this must be South Kensington? Why had she never realized before? Uncle Albert must have been mistaken — unless he'd had some other reason for disowning South Kensington; some sort of reverse snobbery, perhaps? More or less a self-made man, and coming from somewhat humble beginnings, Uncle Albert had always been a little sensitive about his ambivalent position in society. Like me, thought Dorothea: the girl from the slums of London who'd gone to live amidst the opulence of Clifton Park; the English girl who'd become a German by marriage.

Number twenty-eight Essex Square looked the same as ever, indistinguishable from the houses either side. Dorothea stood across the street, by the railings of the garden, looking up at the tall facade, the pillared entrance, the blank windows. The last time she'd come here was nearly six years ago; she'd been in search of her papa, hoping to track him down. But the trail was long cold, and she'd finally begun to accept that she would never see him again, would never know what had happened to him. One chapter had closed back then, and another had opened: for it was here, also, that she'd decided to accept the proposal of marriage she'd received from Johann by post; and though that chapter, too, was now over, she'd never regretted her decision made just before Easter in the year 1912 (another time, another world).

Heartened by the warm feeling swelling inside her — because she'd made the right decision all those years ago — she crossed the street, climbed the steps and rang the bell.

There was a long pause. She began to think that she'd made a mistake, that Eliza wasn't here at all. The thought of the long and weary journey back to Clifton, with nothing accomplished, snuffed out the warm glow inside.

The door opened abruptly. A middle-aged woman in a black dress with white cuffs and a white collar, and with a black cap on her head, stood looking at her suspiciously.

'Yes? What can I do for you? What do you want?'

'Is . . . is Eliza here? Mrs Cartwright, I should say. I'm Mrs Kaufmann — Dorothea Kaufmann, her cousin.'

'Her cousin, you say?' The cold, suspicious look began slowly to thaw. 'So she has got friends, she has got family — I did wonder. No one visits, you see, and she never speaks of anyone. I thought she was all alone in the world. Come in, won't you? I'm Mrs Moss, the housekeeper. Come in out of the cold. Don't forget to wipe your feet.'

Dorothea obeyed; she would not have dared do otherwise. It was this acquiescence on her part, as much as anything, that seemed to accelerate the thaw, as Mrs Moss shut the door on gloomy London.

'I'm so glad you've come, Mrs Kaufmann, you don't know how glad. I've been that worried about her. So quiet, she is, so down-in-the-mouth. This way, ma'am; the sitting room is up these stairs.'

But Dorothea did not need to be told: she remembered this house in every detail; nothing had changed. She allowed herself to be led nonetheless. Mrs Moss was in full flow.

'She's no appetite at all, eats no more than a sparrow; it can't be good for her, nor the baby.'

Dorothea was stopped in her tracks by this and Mrs Moss looked round at her.

'Oh! You didn't know? You didn't know about the baby? Well, it's true. She's with child. Six months gone, I'd say, at a guess. Another poor mite who'll grow up without a father.'

So that was true, thought Dorothea, even as she was trying to recover from the shock of learning Eliza was pregnant: Alex was dead.

'This war!' Mrs Moss went on up the stairs. 'It's a crying shame! There'll be no young men left, the way things are going; there won't be any young men left at all. But she never talks of him — her husband, I mean. And she won't — she simply won't — wear mourning. Peculiar, I call it. But you'll see for yourself. Here we are. She's in here.' Mrs Moss opened the drawing-room door. 'A visitor, Mrs Cartwright. A Mrs Kaufmann come to see you. Shall I fetch up a pot of tea, ma'am? You'd like some tea, I'm sure, Mrs Kaufmann.'

Mrs Moss bustled off, closing the door behind her. Dorothea hesitated, standing just inside the room. It was strange to be here again, like stepping into the past: before the war, before her marriage, all those Easters and the weeks in summer when they'd come here as a family, her and Aunt Eloise and Eliza, Uncle Albert and Roderick too. The curtains, the carpet, the Boulle cabinet: it was all exactly as she remembered. The carriage clock was still keeping time on the mantelpiece. And there, across the room, was the window seat where Eliza had so often sat in the old days.

She was not sitting there today. Dorothea's eyes came to rest on her cousin, whom she hadn't seen for the best part of half a year. Eliza looked up at her from the settee, listless, her fair hair hanging limp, dark rings round her eyes, her expression blank. Her swollen stomach was barely noticeable. (Six months, had Mrs Moss said?)

'Doro? Doro, is it really you?'

'Oh, Eliza—'

'Helena. My name is Helena now.'

Eliza's gaze drifted away, wandered round the room. Removing her gloves, Dorothea sat down on the settee next to her cousin, watching her anxiously.

Shock, said the nurse in her: surely Eliza was showing the signs of shock.

Dorothea said gently, 'Dearest, why didn't you let us know about Alex, about the baby? Why didn't you come home?' It was on the tip of Dorothea's tongue to call her cousin Eliza again, but she stopped herself; there was no point in causing unnecessary vexation. But Helena just didn't seem to fit; she couldn't call her cousin Helena.

'The baby?' Eliza's eyes came to rest on her stomach. 'Oh, yes, the baby.' She laid a hand there. '*His* baby.' She took her hand away. 'I don't want it. What would I do with it?'

'You don't have to go through all this alone. You have us to help you: me, and Aunt Eloise.'

Dorothea tried to keep the conversation going but Eliza was distant and distracted. It was like talking to a stranger.

Perhaps 'Helena' did fit, after all.

Dorothea was still trying to gather her thoughts when Mrs Moss reappeared with a tray. There was a pot of tea, cups and saucers, milk in a jug, a basin with a sprinkling of precious sugar; there were also slices of bread and butter (or more likely margarine), but there was no cake.

Mrs Moss lingered a moment. 'Beg pardon, Mrs Kaufmann, but will you be staying for dinner?'

'Yes. Yes, I think I shall.' Dorothea could see she had her work cut out with Eliza. 'I hope it's not too much trouble, Mrs Moss.'

'Why, it's no trouble at all, Mrs Kaufmann! Easy to cook for two as one. I'll get started straight away. I'll be down in the kitchen, Mrs Cartwright, if I'm needed.'

The 'housekeeper', it seemed, was more by way of being a cook-general. Had it just been the two of them, Dorothea wondered — Eliza and Mrs Moss — all this time?

Dorothea poured tea. She handed a cup to Eliza. Eliza sipped it disinterestedly. Choosing her words carefully, Dorothea tried once more to engage her cousin in conversation. She felt it best to stick to neutral subjects until she'd had a chance to fully gauge Eliza's state of mind. There was no shortage of things to say; so much had happened since Eliza set off on her wedding trip last July. But every topic Dorothea started on seemed to lead inexorably back to the war.

The war dragged on and on. Less than a month after Eliza's marriage, another great offensive had opened on the Western Front — the 'big show' of which Alex had given them advance notice. The newspapers had immediately trumpeted a decisive victory, but the 'show' had continued all summer with scant evidence of any real progress. Autumn had brought disquieting news from other fronts. The Italians had been routed at Caporetto. The Russians had stopped fighting altogether (the new Russian government was said to be negotiating a separate peace with the Germans). Jerusalem, it was true, had been captured from the Turks just in time for Christmas, but for all its symbolism this did not appear to have brought the end of the war appreciably nearer. As for the big show itself — begun with such fanfare at the end of July — it had reached a muddy conclusion in late autumn with the capture of Passchendaele Ridge — wherever that might be.

Passchendaele: an oddly spelt and somehow sinister-sounding name. Was it where Alex had fallen? When exactly had he been killed? But Dorothea felt it too soon to press Eliza about Alex and the baby.

What was there left to say? Plenty. But nothing safe, nothing suitably anodyne. News of Clifton required an account of how it had been transformed into a hospital with an endless procession of patients: blind Private Bamford was long gone, but Private Sutton was still in residence, his stammer as bad as ever, and Private Glasspool, who could play the piano by ear, had undergone surgery on his left leg on four successive occasions, more of it amputated each time until he was left now with a short stump.

But this was too sombre a subject. To mention Jake Carter would be more hopeful. He was in fine fettle, as if his life had never hung in the balance — and he would soon have company, a little brother or a sister, for Susie was expecting again. All talk of babies, however, was probably best avoided, given Eliza's condition.

Growing desperate, Dorothea settled on the only other topic she could think of: the crippling strike in Coventry last November that had disrupted many local factories, Uncle Albert's included; Dorothea could only imagine that it was thinking of Uncle Albert earlier which had brought this to mind. Even though it could hardly be of much interest to Eliza, Dorothea pressed on with her tale, for want of anything better. The strike had been roundly condemned in the national press; questions had been asked in Parliament. Aunt Eloise had grown very agitated.

The workers never went on strike when Albert was alive. Albert never had trouble of that sort. What should I do, Dorothea? What would Albert want me to do?

Aunt Eloise could do nothing, of course, nor would Uncle Albert have expected her to. His trusted deputies had been more than capable of running the businesses since his death eight years ago and, even though one of them, Mr Simcox, had now passed on, Linus Young was reportedly a worthy successor: Linus Young and Mr Smith could be relied on to take all necessary measures to deal with the crisis.

It was symptomatic of the change in Aunt Eloise that she'd become obsessed with events outside her control; her sense of proportion — her sense of what was possible — had always, until now, been her greatest strength.

But Dorothea did not mention Aunt Eloise for the moment.

'I remember . . .' Eliza frowned, as if dredging something up from the distant past.

'What is it?' Dorothea prompted. 'What do you remember?'

'I remember that Roddy was going to run Daddy's businesses.'

'Yes, that's right, it was all mapped out: once he'd finished at Oxford, he was to go to Coventry each day to learn the ropes. But then—'

'Then the war began.'

Dorothea surrendered to the inevitable, as the conversation came round to the war again. It really wasn't possible to avoid it. Everything spoke of the war — even the sprinkling of sugar in the sugar basin, and the margarine scraped thinly over the untouched slices of bread.

'Roddy is dead,' said Eliza, her voice flat and expressionless. 'Roddy, Johann, Johnny Cheeseman, Joey Atkin.'

'Billy as well.' Dorothea bit her tongue, but too late, taken unawares by her niggling resentment that she'd thought she had got over; her niggling resentment at the way Billy had been dismissed, forgotten, in the run-up to Eliza's wedding.

Eliza turned her head away, just as she had when Dorothea mentioned Billy on the morning of her wedding. Dorothea was seized by an almost overwhelming urge to take hold of Eliza and shake her — shake some sense into her. But it wasn't just Billy who was side-lined now; Eliza had made no mention of Alex, either, and she seemed utterly unconcerned about anything that had happened at home, back at Clifton.

Dorothea was still trying to recover her composure — what good would losing her temper do? — when suddenly

Eliza turned towards her. For the first time, cracks showed, her eyes moist, her lips trembling.

'I thought one of them, at least, might have lived: one, just one. But they've gone. They've all gone, and we'll never see them again. How can they all be dead — everyone we've ever cared for?' A single tear spilled from her eye and rolled down her pale cheek.

Dorothea was stricken with remorse. How could she have doubted Eliza? Of course Billy wasn't forgotten. Eliza wasn't callous, wasn't cruel. She was lost and alone, and desperately unhappy.

Dorothea took Eliza's cup and saucer, and put them aside, then she enfolded her cousin in a warm embrace, as she had so often down the years. Eliza gave a single, convulsive sob, then was still; her body was stiff and unyielding, as if frozen solid. Dorothea sought words of comfort. There were none. But it seemed wrong that Eliza should have to face all this on her own.

Stroking Eliza's fair hair, Dorothea murmured, 'Oh, Eliza, dear Eliza, you should be with the people who care about you. Why didn't you come home when you heard about Alex? You could come home now, with me. Won't you come back to Clifton, dearest, dearest Eliza?'

Eliza said nothing, made no sound. After a moment she broke away, tearing herself out of Dorothea's embrace. Her face was blank once more, as if a mask had fallen back into place. The glittering track of her single teardrop was like water running down hard, cold stone.

'Helena,' she said in her flat, empty voice. 'My name is Helena. And it's not my home. Clifton is not my home anymore.'

* * *

Dorothea found she was mistaken to have thought that Eliza had only Mrs Moss for company. A maid, a young girl, appeared at dinner to help Mrs Moss serve. The dining room was at the back of the house, overlooking the garden and the buildings in the mews beyond. Dorothea remembered family dinners here long ago: happy times. There was no happiness now at number twenty-eight. It was a lonely, cheerless place.

'What made you think of coming here?' Dorothea asked as they ate.

'I didn't want to go back to Clifton. I promised myself I wouldn't go back. Essex Square was the only other place I could go.'

Eliza had stuck stubbornly to her plan. There'd always been a headstrong side to her, even as a child. She wasn't much more than a child even now: just eighteen. But in the way she'd gone about all this there seemed something cold and calculating and very grown up.

'Did you come here with Alex?'

'There was no time. He went off in a rush.'

'He left you in Yarmouth?'

'Yes.'

'Did he know you weren't going back to Clifton?'

'Not until afterwards. I wrote and told him.' Eliza fell silent, picking at her food.

Dorothea did not want to keep firing questions at her cousin, but there seemed no other way of getting her to talk.

'What happened after you left us in July?'

'We travelled to Great Yarmouth by train. We stayed the night at a hotel. Next morning, Alex had to leave.'

'Next morning? But weren't you meant to stay two nights at Yarmouth? Alex had one more day before he had to go back.'

'Word came. He was summoned.'

'Summoned by his regiment?'

'Not his regiment.'

'Then who? It can't have been his family. He doesn't have any family. A friend, perhaps? What was so urgent that he had to change his plans? Why won't you tell me, Eliza!'

'Helena. My name is Helena.' Eliza cut the conversation short. Silence fell again.

Dorothea was annoyed with herself; she had pressed Eliza too hard. But just when it seemed Eliza would remain tight-lipped for the rest of the meal, she suddenly began to talk again, continuing the story of her sojourn in Great Yarmouth as if there'd been no interruption.

'After he'd gone, I walked along the parade. The sea was very blue, very calm. I sat on a bench and looked at the place where the sea met the sky. I sat there a long time. Then I went back to the hotel. The room was booked and paid for, so I stayed a second night. Next day, I took a train to London. I had the keys to this place. I got them from Mama's bureau. I thought it would be a nice place to live. I always liked coming here in the old days.'

Eliza hesitated, seemed lost in thought. She'd put her knife and fork down. She'd eaten less than half of what was on her plate. It was obvious she would eat no more.

She looked up, caught Dorothea's eye; there was a strange, faraway expression on her face. 'Do you remember the old days, Doro? And the time when we came to London to look for your papa — do you remember that? We stayed here, just the three of us: you, me, young Stan; no servants. At Clifton, Stan was only the chauffeur; here he was one of us. He ate with us, he went everywhere we went. That's what I wanted: I wanted to live like that again, to make my own dinner and do just as I pleased. I thought it would be easy. It seemed so easy before. But it wasn't easy at all. I couldn't manage on my own. I know nothing, you see. I know nothing about anything. I can't even boil an egg. I made such a mess, trying to boil an egg.

'*He* saw it; *he* knew. "How innocent you are," he said to me in Yarmouth. *Ignorant*: that is what he meant. I'd been kept in ignorance, because I was to be a lady, that was all Mama wanted of me. Nobody asked what *I* wanted.'

A shudder passed through her and a look of pain showed briefly on her face before the mask came down once more. When at length she spoke again, her voice was flat and lifeless.

'I found an agency. They sent Mrs Moss. But something was wrong with me, something didn't feel right; I kept being sick. Mrs Moss told me why. "It's a baby," she said. "A baby is growing inside you." I didn't know it could happen like that — so soon, so quickly. I didn't know what to do. Mrs Moss said I should write to Alex. Alex should be told. So I did. Alex wrote back. He said he was glad. That made me feel better. I knew when Alex came home, he would look after the baby. Then a telegram came. Alex wasn't coming home. Alex had been killed. So the baby is not needed now and . . . and that's all.'

A heavy silence descended on the dining room. They were alone, the two of them; Mrs Moss and the maid had cleared the table and gone.

The meal had been very welcome after Dorothea's long journey. She was no longer hungry. But she was far from satisfied. *That's all*, Eliza had said. Only it wasn't. It wasn't the half of it, Dorothea was quite sure of that.

What was it Eliza wasn't telling her?

There seemed no point, however, in sitting in silence at the table. Dorothea got to her feet. 'Shall we go back up?'

* * *

Mrs Moss had made up the fire and closed the curtains, and the drawing room felt almost snug. Eliza returned to her place on the settee. Dorothea crossed to the window and opened a gap in the curtains. She looked out at the dark and silent square, and at the black sky above the rooftops. There were no street lamps, no stars; the young moon, a white sliver, had slipped below the horizon some hours ago. Dorothea was mesmerized by the strange and eerie sight, as if the city was deserted. Why were there no lights? Then she remembered. She remembered the distant explosions she'd heard in October when the Zeppelin came to Northampton. She remembered Giles and Julia Milton describing the air raid in June, the German aeroplanes 'buzzing like a swarm of angry bees'. The aeroplanes in particular Dorothea hated, those demons of the air responsible for Johann's death.

She let the curtain fall back into place. 'Aren't you ever frightened?' she asked Eliza. 'The aeroplanes. The Zeppelins. Don't they frighten you?'

'There is always a warning now, when there's a raid,' said Eliza. 'I go to the basement with Mrs Moss and the maid.'

This was not exactly reassuring. Eliza seemed to accept air raids as a matter of course. But despite Dorothea's unease, there appeared to be no immediate danger, so she did her best to put it out of her mind. She sat down in a chair by the fire. Greedy flames were licking the few coals, hissing and crackling. The gentle ticking of the carriage clock was loud in the quiet room. On the mantelpiece, next to the clock, was a vase with an arrangement of dark green leaves, but no flowers.

Eliza gave the impression that she would sit there all evening without saying a word. Dorothea was tempted to do the same: it would be so much easier. But that was not why she'd come, to sit silent with Eliza and ignore all unpleasantness.

She roused herself with an effort. 'How . . . how did Alex die?'

Eliza answered mechanically, without any trace of emotion. 'He was shot in the head. It was instantaneous; he did not suffer. Someone wrote and told me, one of his men, I think, I forget the name; I still have the letter somewhere. Later, they sent me his things, Alex's things. It was the day the bells rang: joy-bells, Mrs Moss said, because of the great victory.'

'Cambrai,' said Dorothea.

She remembered the electrifying headline in the newspaper: *HINDENBURG LINE SMASHED!*

But the Battle of Cambrai had been weeks and weeks ago, a month before Christmas. And despite the victory bells, it had proved another false dawn.

'Mrs Moss took his uniform away,' Eliza continued. 'It was cruel of them to send it, she said. It was cruel of them to send it, when it was covered in mud and blood. There was a strange smell, too. I don't know what Mrs Moss did with the uniform. The other things I put in the cabinet over there.' Eliza hesitated, then added quietly, 'He was not who he said he was.'

Dorothea looked up, startled. 'What do you mean?'

'There was no school in Gloucestershire, or anywhere else. He was not a schoolmaster.'

'He . . . he wasn't? Then why did he say he was? How do you know he wasn't a schoolmaster?'

'He told me. He told me in Great Yarmouth, the evening we arrived. I deserved to know the truth, he said.'

'What else did he tell you?'

'He was a clerk before the war, an ordinary clerk in an ordinary office, right here in London.'

'But that's incredible! To tell such fibs — what extraordinary behaviour! Was any of it true, any of the things he told us? His name—'

'His name really is — was — Alexander Cartwright. His mother really did die when he was fifteen. He was left all alone after that; he never knew his father.' Eliza gave these details in the same flat, toneless voice she'd used almost the whole time since Dorothea had arrived, as if what she was saying could have no real interest for anyone.

Dorothea struggled to comprehend. 'I don't understand why he lied. What did he hope to gain? Unless—' Suspicion darkened Dorothea's mind as she groped for some sort of explanation, however unpalatable. 'You said he only stayed with you for one night?'

'He left directly after breakfast next morning.'

By which time he'd got what he wanted: Eliza's condition proved that. Had that been the plan all along, to abandon Eliza after one night?

'Didn't he give you any explanation as to why he had to go?'

'He said he'd tell me later. He was going to tell me everything, once we were together again. He asked me to forgive him — for lying, for leaving. He . . . he told me he loved me.'

The way Eliza spoke of it, anyone would have been forgiven for thinking it had all happened to someone else, a stranger.

'Did you believe him? Did you believe any of it? But how *could* you believe him, after all the lies he'd told. The school he worked at, his being a teacher — lies, all lies!'

'I didn't marry him for any of that.'

'I don't know how you can be so . . . so *calm* . . . when he betrayed you.'

'It doesn't matter anymore. It's over. He's dead. I just want to forget now. But I can't forget. I have his baby inside me. I wish I didn't. I wish it wasn't there. Why won't it just go away?'

The poor, unwanted child — how could Eliza be so unfeeling?

But she wasn't entirely blameless in all this. She'd not been truthful either. She'd lied too. Had she loved Alex? Had she loved him at all? Dorothea couldn't even begin to guess. Eliza was so very changed. There was no anger, no bitterness, just a blank acceptance.

Mrs Moss was right to be concerned.

Dorothea's heart softened. 'You look tired . . . Helena. Why don't you go to bed? You need plenty of rest in your condition.'

'I won't sleep,' said Eliza. 'I never do.'

She obeyed nonetheless, something she would never have done in the old days — not without protest. This only served to make Dorothea all the more anxious.

Eliza paused in the doorway. 'I nearly forgot. Mrs Moss has made up a bed for you in your room, the room you always had.' She hesitated. The mask of her face seemed to crack a moment; a vague and wistful expression showed through. 'Do you remember . . . we used to come here when Daddy was alive . . . we were all together in those days . . . we were . . . happy . . .'

She drifted from the room, leaving the door wide open.

Dorothea sat unmoving. She didn't know what to think. Mostly she felt a failure, an abject failure, because she'd not seen Alex for what he was. Alex had been—

But it wasn't right to speak ill of the dead.

She sighed and got slowly to her feet. It was late, she'd had a long day, she was tired. Perhaps things would look brighter in the morning.

She could only hope so.

* * *

Dorothea was awake early. She found Eliza already up. In the old days, they'd have sat in the morning room on the ground floor; the drawing room had been set aside for afternoons and after dinner. But Eliza seemed to have a new routine. The drawing room was her place; she had settled there.

She sat in the same spot on the settee as yesterday, wearing the same frock, her hair pinned untidily. A newspaper was open on her lap, the newspaper Dorothea had brought with her to read on the train, though she'd never actually looked at it: she'd had to stand all the way to Euston.

'Good morning.' Dorothea was as bright and breezy as she could manage. 'Is that tea I can see?'

'Oh. Yes. It might still be warm. I will ring for Mrs Moss to make breakfast.'

But Eliza didn't move, staring into space as Dorothea poured herself a cup of tea.

'Were you reading the newspaper?' Dorothea prompted.

'What?' Eliza came back to herself, glanced down, seemed surprised to find the newspaper there. She ran her hand across the printed page. 'Oh, yes, I remember now. There's been an accident, an explosion in a coal mine. I was reading about it. The colliers were trapped underground. One hundred men and boys crushed, suffocated, dead.'

Dorothea, sipping her tea, had the strangest feeling that Eliza was talking not about the mining accident, but about herself: crushed, suffocated, dead — dead inside. A shiver went up Dorothea's spine. She wished she'd left the newspaper on the train.

Eliza furrowed her brow, as if trying to remember something. 'Kolya once said to me . . . he said miners are heroes.'

'Kolya?' Dorothea cast her mind back. 'Roddy's Russian friend — is that who you're talking about?' She'd not seen the young Russian since August 1914, his last visit to Clifton. She'd barely given him a thought since then.

'His name was Nikolai Antipov, but he said I could call him Kolya; his friends called him Kolya. He was nice to me. He talked to me. He told me things. He didn't treat me like a child. He said that a change was coming — a new dawn, he called it. Things would be different — for women especially. Women's lives would at last be their own, that was what he said.'

'He was always saying things of that sort, as far as I remember. Such an odd young man. What did he mean, I wonder, about women's lives being their own? Perhaps he was talking about the vote — so I suppose he was right, in a way. Parliament is going to give women the vote. Rosa must be glad — wherever she might be.'

'Perhaps she's gone to look for Kolya.'

'I don't think that's very likely.'

'Kolya was in love with her.'

'Mr Antipov? In love with Rosa? Where did you get such an idea!'

'But it's true. Kolya loved Rosa, and Rosa loved Kolya.'

'Don't be silly, Eliza. Rosa loved Roddy, you know she did.'

Dorothea bit her tongue — but too late. She had rather snapped at Eliza, and she had made it worse by saying *Eliza* instead of *Helena*. The conversation came to an abrupt end, as she might have expected. Eliza turned her face away.

But Rosa and Mr Antipov — in love? It was absurd. A ridiculous thing to say. Eliza had always had a vivid imagination. Sitting here alone, day after day, brooding, her imagination had obviously taken a morbid turn.

And yet — Dorothea furrowed her brow — hadn't Aunt Eloise once hinted at something similar? Yes. She had, she most definitely had: in September 1916 during that awful confrontation with Rosa in Roderick's room. She'd accused Rosa of planning to run away with the Russian.

Dorothea shook her head. Words spoken in the heat of the moment could hardly be taken seriously. And Rosa wasn't her concern right now. She was here for Eliza — to be of some help to her cousin.

'Dearest Helena.' She spoke as gently as she could, careful to use the name Eliza had chosen for herself. 'I know everything looks bleak just now, and you can't see a way out, because that is exactly how I felt after Johann died. The world seemed to me a shabby, worthless place; I wanted things to go back to the way they were. But you can't go back, you can't change what's happened. That's not much comfort, I know, but the way you feel now, it won't last forever. You might not believe me, but it's true, I promise you. All you need is a little faith.'

'Faith!' Eliza turned to her, and for the first time showed some real animation. Her eyes glinted; she seemed almost feverish in the sudden intensity of her emotion. 'Faith in what? In who? In God? But even if there was a God, I'd not worship him. I'd curse him. I'd curse him for what he's done to us. But — but there is no God. There is no God. It's not God who's done this to us. We've done this to ourselves. Mankind is responsible for all of it. Man's own wickedness has torn the world apart. Kolya said to me once, a long time ago, he said, "We must fight the tyranny of our own nature before we fight the tyrannies of the world." He thought that could be done. He believed in us. But we have failed his trust. We have failed. The tyranny of our own nature has overmastered us and we have destroyed everything — everything.'

* * *

Over lunch, Dorothea said, 'I wish I could stay.'

She felt she was needed here. She felt it more than ever now she knew of Alex's duplicity and she'd seen for herself just how despondent Eliza was. But she was needed back at Clifton, too. Poor Private Sutton! His stammer would be getting worse again; she was the only one with the patience to help him coax his words out. Private Glasspool, too, so dexterous on the piano, so clumsy on his crutches: he needed every encouragement. She had given her word. She had promised faithfully that she would only be away one night. The Ranee would be expecting her. And there was Aunt Eloise: Aunt Eloise relied on her.

'I wish I could stay, but I can't. I simply must go back to Clifton. You could come with me, Eliza. Why not? You needn't move back permanently, not if you don't want to. But you could stay until the baby is born. You could stay until then. Clifton is your home, it will always be your home. Dearest Eliza, won't you come home with me?'

Eliza was unmoved. 'I am not Eliza Brannan anymore. My name is Helena Cartwright, and my home is here. I can never go back.'

Dorothea could see it was no good pressing the point; she might even make things worse if she did. She didn't like to leave Eliza in this state, she didn't like it one little bit, but what else could she do?

Luncheon over, she went upstairs and packed her little bag, got ready to leave, torn in two by her conflicting loyalties.

'I will come again soon — as soon as ever I can.' She stood in the drawing room in her hat and coat, saying good-bye. Eliza was in her customary place on the settee. 'At the very least, I hope to be here when the baby comes.' She sighed. 'And now I must go. I really must, if I'm to get back this side of midnight. Don't come down. Stay here in the warm. Well, goodbye. Be sure to look after yourself, dearest . . . dearest Helena.'

The housekeeper saw her out. Dorothea turned to her on the front steps. 'Will you look after her, Mrs Moss? I should feel so much better if I knew you were watching over her.'

'I shall do my very best, Mrs Kaufmann,' said the house-keeper stoutly, 'I can't say fairer than that.'

* * *

274

Dorothea had lingered after lunch far longer than she'd intended, finding it difficult to tear herself away. The grey January afternoon was already fading to an early dusk as she caught an omnibus and sat looking out at the passing streets. The street lamps were not lit, but shop windows blazed brightly, splashing pools of light on the busy pavements. It was an ordinary Tuesday, people going about their usual business. To see life carrying on, despite all the hardships of war, bolstered Dorothea's spirits, made the prospect of the long journey ahead of her somehow less daunting.

Euston was teeming. She had half an hour to wait for the next train. When finally it steamed in, there was a stampede for the doors. By pure luck, she snared a corner seat in one of the compartments and sank into it thankfully, with a feeling that half the trials of her journey were over already. All she had to do now was sit back as the train whisked her through the gathering gloom to distant Welby.

* * *

They were somewhere near Wolverton. The train had been at a standstill for some time. Outside, it was pitch dark. Pressing her face against the cold glass of the window, Dorothea could make out swirling snow falling from the unseen sky. The ceaseless movement of the millions of small white flakes was mesmerizing. A mysterious world was starting to take shape, as a white veneer slowly settled on trees and fields and hedgerows.

'A regular blizzard,' said a lugubrious man sitting opposite in the crowded compartment, addressing no one in particular. 'We shall be stuck here for good, snowed in I shouldn't wonder, if we don't move soon.'

The end of her journey, which had seemed so near when she got on the train at Euston, now felt distant, remote, almost unattainable. This seat up in a corner, which had been such a godsend, now held her like a trap. There was nowhere to escape to on the congested train, and now this talk of getting stuck in the snow filled her with dread.

She turned back to the window, tried to lose herself in the darkness and the hypnotic, falling snow, but her mind, in turmoil, gave her no rest. She had put on a brave face for Eliza, and in doing so had almost convinced herself that things weren't as bad as they seemed, but on this endless journey all her fragile optimism had slowly withered away; it was as if, instead of bringing comfort to Eliza as she'd intended, she'd been infected with Eliza's despair.

How can they all have gone . . . how can they all be dead? Eliza's words haunted her, and brought to mind the phrase that had repeated over and over in her head when she'd stood by Richard's grave on Christmas Eve over a year ago: the day she'd talked to Owain Morgan in the church. *The Lord gave and the Lord hath taken away.*

She'd little known, back then, just how many the Lord would take — so many of the people most dear to them, to her and Eliza and Aunt Eloise. It seemed exceptionally cruel and unfortunate, as if they'd been singled out. Surely no other family had suffered so much loss. There couldn't be anyone in this compartment — anyone on this whole train — who had been quite so unlucky. The alternative — that it wasn't bad luck, that it wasn't some peculiar misfortune, that it was the same for everybody — didn't bear thinking about.

Rosa, on the day of Roderick's memorial service, had likened the war to a nightmare from which one never woke up. But the war was horribly real, and there was no getting away from it. The old life, life before the war: it was that which seemed like a dream, a fading dream. The war had become immeasurably vast and impersonal and greedy; the war was unquenchable, grinding on and on without end. And all this had come about, Eliza said, through man's wickedness.

Was she right? Was mankind really so irredeemable? Dorothea knew that, once upon a time, she would have denied it. *You always see the good in people*: how often, down the years, had she heard this said of her? And even now, she still shied away from condemning anyone outright. Faced with the full extent of Alex's deceit, her first thought was to find some excuse for his behaviour, some extenuating circumstances. He'd not been a single-minded seducer, he'd not intended to have his way with Eliza then leave; if he'd left before time in Great Yarmouth, perhaps he really had been called away (but to where?). And he'd kept in touch with Eliza, even after he'd returned to the front. He'd been pleased about the baby, he'd written to say so. There was no good reason to doubt that he'd cared for Eliza.

But did any of this really absolve him?

Gullible, Dorothea said to herself. A word Roderick had delighted in using when he was a boy, a word he'd applied to her. Oh, but he was right, he was right! All this time, she'd been fooling herself, and a boy of ten had seen through her years ago.

She shivered, pulling her coat closer round her, but there was no hiding from it, there was no avoiding the cold and uncomfortable fact of her gullibility. She had to make a change. She had to stop fooling herself. It was time to harden her heart, and accept that some people were simply wicked, and that there was no helping it.

The time had come to stop being so gullible.

The train, with a jerk, began to move. Inching forward at first, little by little it gathered speed. Faint and muffled came the sound of the locomotive, labouring through the blizzard.

The journey continued. Roade, Blisworth, Weedon all came and went. An end was now in sight. Dorothea took hold of her bag. The train began to slow once more. Here, at last — at long last — was Welby.

She got out and slammed the door. Glancing along the platform, she saw that only one other passenger had alighted, a shadowy figure walking towards her through the thickly falling snow. She suddenly remembered that she was travelling without a permit — and the half-seen figure was wearing a uniform. But it was a soldier's uniform, not a policeman's, and she let out her breath.

Her sense of relief was short-lived. The crowded train now seemed a haven of warmth and light; she was almost tempted to get back on, where she'd be safe. But it was too late. The train had already begun to move.

She turned hastily away and battled along the platform, her booted feet sinking into the snow, her skirts dragging, snow blown in her face by the gusting wind, her breath steaming. She was uncomfortably aware of the soldier somewhere behind her. There was no sign of the stationmaster.

Wheezing and clanging, the train rumbled slowly past her, picking up speed. It rattled out of the station and was swallowed up by the blizzard, the sound of it fading rapidly into the dark. She was alone now — alone with the khaki-clad figure she felt was bearing down on her, though she dared not look back.

She hurried down the steps, stumbling in her haste. She passed through the desolate booking hall and came to the little concourse out in front. She looked along the road. The lights of the Railway Inn, away to her right, were all but veiled by falling snow; but she had to go the other way, to the left, where the road passed under the railway and on into utter darkness. She tried to encourage herself. Twice before she'd made it all the way to Clifton at night: eighteen months back, on a balmy July evening after Roderick was killed; and eighteen long years ago, as a girl of eight, with her papa, her first arrival. But this time, with snow falling heavily and the night black as pitch, the journey looked likely to defeat her.

Crunching footsteps sounded behind her. She felt a shiver of fear. With great reluctance, she turned to face the stranger from the train — there was nothing else she could do.

He was almost upon her.

A muffled voice said, 'Is that you, Miss Dorothea?'

She strained to see through the falling snow. The soldier drew nearer. The shadowy shape slowly resolved into someone familiar. Squash-faced, and with a gap-toothed grin, it was none other than Harry Keech — Harry Keech, whom she'd not seen since last March, in the Barley Mow with Billy Turner.

'Harry! Oh, Harry, you're—' She was going to say *you're alive, you're still alive*, but she stopped herself just in time, not at all sure it would be tactful. 'You're home, you're back!'

There was no mistaking it. He was solid and real — large as life and twice as ugly, as he might well have said himself.

He seemed somewhat taken aback by her excessive delight at this unexpected meeting. 'Yes, miss, it's me all right. John Harrison Keech, at your service. Or—' He drew himself up, saluted, his grin growing wider. 'One-six-seven-six-five Private Keech, I oughtta say.'

'Are you home on leave, Harry?'

'That's about the size of it, miss. A stroke of luck, really. Some sort of cock — er — mix-up, I reckon: it's not twelve months since my last leave. Mind you, they could have picked a better time to send me. Lousy weather.' He held out a hand. 'Let's cop hold of yer bag, miss. I'll carry it for yer.'

He was already heavily laden, with a haversack and his tin hat dangling, and all sorts of other paraphernalia strapped to him, half-seen in the gloom; there was his rifle, too, jutting above his shoulder. But she surrendered her bag, because he insisted, and because he seemed so strong and doughty; he was a heartening companion to have on this bleak winter evening.

But the snow was still coming down and the night was as dark as ever. She thought again of the long, weary miles still to go, and the brief spark of joy that had flared inside her on meeting Harry was quickly snuffed out.

'Oh, Harry! We'll never get to Hayton in this!'

'Course we will, miss. After all what I've been through, it'd take more than a spot of snow to keep me from home. We'll get there, miss. We'll get there in the end, you see if we don't.'

CHAPTER TEN

She had promised to visit Eliza again as soon as ever she could but, day after day, week after week, Dorothea found she hadn't the time. Two months elapsed in the blink of an eye. Eliza's baby would soon be due. Now was the time to return to Essex Square; it couldn't be put off any longer.

But just as Dorothea was planning her trip, a new complication arose, with the abrupt departure of the nursery maid, Walker.

'One simply can't rely on staff these days,' said Aunt Eloise. 'I don't know what I'm to do.'

Always such a capable woman, Aunt Eloise seemed curiously helpless these days in the face of adversity.

Dorothea's main worry was that, with the servants already overstretched and the medical wing only adding to their workload, Katherine and Laurence might find themselves neglected. She couldn't guard against this if she was in London, nor would she be able to help out around the house where needed. She simply couldn't see how she could be spared.

One possible solution was for Aunt Eloise to go to Essex Square in her place, but Aunt Eloise was adamant: she wouldn't go.

'Elizabeth hasn't sent for me. If she needed me, she would send for me.'

How deeply Aunt Eloise had been hurt by Eliza's apparent spurning of them all was impossible to say; she had never been one to discuss her feelings. All Dorothea knew for sure was that it was pointless to try to change her aunt's mind. Which meant — for now at least — Eliza would have to work out her own salvation. Dorothea's only consolation was that Eliza was not entirely on her own. She had Mrs Moss to rely on. Mrs Moss had seemed a very capable woman.

By now the end of March was already in sight. Johann's birthday fell this year on Maundy Thursday: he would have been thirty years old. Thirty was just another number, Dorothea had told herself. But it seemed to her, all the same, that a great gulf of time now separated her from Johann, a gulf that would never cease to widen. For she could only picture Johann as she'd seen him last, when he was twenty-six; Johann stayed the same, while she grew ever older and more careworn, the years taking their toll. Would Johann have looked very different at thirty? How would he have looked at forty, fifty, sixty? There was nothing she wanted more than to have grown old with him.

She could only properly think of Johann in moments of peace and privacy, when she could be sure of no interruption — last thing at night, or first thing in the morning. The rest of the day, even if she wasn't nursing, there were a hundred and one other calls on her time. She was, this afternoon, in the nursery, getting the children ready for a walk outside. She liked to take them for a walk whenever she could, remembering congenial afternoons with her governess long ago (very long ago, it seemed to her today — to a woman whose husband would have been celebrating his thirtieth birthday). She was wrapping up the children in their coats and hats, for it was cold outside. The previous week, a burst of spring had made it pleasant to be out in the fresh air but at the weekend, when the clocks had changed, the weather had changed too and winter had returned.

Laurence, aged twenty months, was no trouble at all, placid and cooperative. Katherine was a different matter.

'Please don't undo all your buttons, Katherine, I've only just done them up. Here, let me help you with your mittens.'

'I don't want my mittens, I don't *want* them!'

'But your hands will get cold without them.'

'I shan't put my mittens on. I shan't, I shan't, I *shan't!*'

Katherine stamped her foot with rage, and Dorothea sighed. How was it that a little girl of three and a half could be more trouble than all the wounded men downstairs together?

Outside at last, Katherine ran ahead across the space of gravel in front of the house and through the doorway into the gardens. Laurence tottered after her but found he could not keep up, so he came tottering back, holding out his arms to be carried. Scooping him up, Dorothea followed Katherine through the doorway and along the cinder path, turning right through the opening in the privet hedge that led onto the lawn. Katherine had made a bee-line for the old swing, rather decrepit these days, but — typical Katherine — she quickly lost interest in it. Her attention was drawn to Private Chambers, one of the more recent arrivals, who was limping doggedly round and round the mulberry tree in his hospital blues.

She pointed. 'Why has that man got a stick?'

'He has a poorly leg.'

'Why has he got a poorly leg?'

'Because he has been in the war.'

'What's the war?'

'It's when men go away and fight.'

'Mummy went away. Did Mummy go to the war? When will Mummy come back? Will she have a poorly leg, too?'

'I don't know, Katherine. I don't know when Mummy will come back. Come on. Let's go this way.'

Dorothea shepherded Katherine away from poor Private Chambers, who could not have failed to hear the child's shrill voice, and who was self-conscious enough as it was about the difficulty he had in walking: he seemed to think it was something for which he had to repeatedly apologize. Leaving the lawn, Dorothea led the way across the cinder path and through an opening in the opposite hedge, shifting Laurence from one hip to the other as she did so.

Old Becket and Jeff Smith were at work in the flower garden; Circe, lying prone with outstretched paws, was watching Jeff's every move with doleful eyes.

Laurence stirred. He took his thumb out of his mouth. 'Doggy!'

Dorothea set him on his feet and he went wobbling off in his sister's wake, for Katherine, as usual, had gone racing ahead. As they both bore down on Circe, the dog raised her head, then got to her feet, eyeing them warily; Circe was something of a timid animal, quite unlike her mother, Roderick's spirited Hecate, who had died so soon after her master. Jeff stopped what he was doing, straightened up, went across to reassure Circe, directing Katherine and Laurence as they stroked and patted the trembling animal. Jeff was rather good with the children, thought Dorothea; surprisingly patient.

Stiff and slow, puffing and blowing, Becket made his way over to her. 'Afternoon, Miss Dorothea. You've got Master Laurence with you, I see, and Miss Katherine. Breath of air'll do them good.' Holding the small of his back with both hands, he cast a critical eye around the flower garden. 'Doing me best to put this place in some sort of order, whilst the rain holds off. Overrun with nettles, it was, end of last year. But we don't have so much time to spend on the flowers these days. It's one thing after another, and them there hens on top of all else. Vittles: that's all you want up the house now — and that means fruit and veg. Flowers won't serve — nor weeds for that matter. Mind you, saying that, mari-golds'll always brighten a salad, and country folk used to eat nettles when I was a youngster; they ate nettles as a vegetable. But that's going back a bit.'

'We shall all be eating nettles before very long, the way things are going,' said Dorothea with unwonted fatalism. She noted, too, that she referred to the war only obliquely — *the way things are going* — which seemed to be the way everyone spoke of it these days, when they spoke of it at all.

But even if people didn't talk of it, it couldn't easily be forgotten. There'd been disquieting news this week. The Germans, who were said to have been on their last legs, had suddenly launched a big offensive completely out of the blue. They had broken right through the British lines and forced the British back; much ground had been lost in a disconcertingly short space of time, including the old Somme battlefields where Roderick had fallen in 1916. The names of such places as Péronne and Bapaume had begun to appear in the headlines again; just this morning, the newspaper had announced the loss of Albert. Paris, meanwhile, was being bombarded by a long-range gun.

'A grave situation', the newspaper called it, and for *The Times* to have lost its bullish tone showed how serious things were. An air of tension, of suspense, had been building all week, growing ever more oppressive — impossible to ignore. Easter would be both cold and cheerless this year.

'Who's this now?' Becket interrupted Dorothea's thoughts, peering short-sightedly. 'Is she coming or going?'

'It's Tilda — Tilda Johnson, one of the maids. Yes, Tilda? Are you looking for me? What is it?'

'Please, ma'am, it's Cook. Mrs Bourne asks please will you see to her. Mrs Bourne says there's nothing more she can do. Cook's leaving, ma'am.'

Dorothea was startled and, indeed, rather alarmed. Cook leaving? Could it be true? To lose the nursery maid was bad enough, but Cook's departure would be nothing short of a disaster. They all relied on Cook — not just the family, but the wounded men and the hospital staff, too.

'I'll go at once, Tilda. If you could just take the children up to the nursery for me . . .'

Dorothea made her way swiftly round to the stable yard and the side door of the house. She hurried down the back stairs. A long, dingy, white-tiled corridor ran the length of the basement, the electric lights on night and day; the kitchen, first on the right, was not much brighter, having only high, narrow windows. Cooking utensils of every description were stacked on shelves or hung from hooks; warmth radiated from the range. In the midst of it all, Cook, incongruous in a hat and coat, was scrubbing the big centre table; a shapeless and bulging carpet bag had been set down near the door.

'No one can't say I never left the place spotless,' said Cook tersely, not looking up as Dorothea came in. Even more than the way she was dressed, her manner was at odds with her usual self.

'What's wrong, Cook? Whatever's happened?'

'I'm sorry, Mrs Kaufmann, but I've had enough, and that's an end to it. I'm going away. I shall go to London and stay with my sister, Grace.'

'You're going now, right away?'

'Yes, I am. I know I ought to work my notice — *that woman* made it quite plain — but I don't care about what I'm owed or about my particulars, I don't care about — about—' Her voice faltered and she broke off, scrubbing furiously.

That woman was Mrs Bourne. Cook and the housekeeper did not get on. Both of them formidable in their different ways, the friction between them had long been part of the pattern of life at Clifton. Cook was more than capable of holding her own — the kitchen was the one part of the house where Mrs Bourne did not reign supreme — so it hardly seemed likely that anything the housekeeper had said or done could have precipitated a crisis like this. In fact, Dorothea had long suspected that, at some level, the two bitter rivals rather enjoyed locking horns and defending their territories.

But if it wasn't that, then what?

'Dear Cook. Please tell me how we've upset you. Please tell me what it is we've done.'

'It's not you, ma'am. It's not you at all. It's . . . it's everything. Everything.' Dropping the cloth with which she'd been scrubbing the table, with a sudden jerky movement Cook swept the cover off a platter on the sideboard, revealing a chunk of raw meat standing in its own blood. 'Look at this joint. Just look at it. What am I meant to do with *this*? Why, it's all gristle! It's not fit to eat! But that's what we get now, it's what they send us — when they send us anything at all. There's never enough of what they send, neither. We go short. Here, for instance: this is all the butter I've got; I'm to use margarine. But margarine is not the same. It's *not* the same. It just isn't. As for the bread — don't talk to me about the bread! It's so poor now, so very dark: it's not like bread at all. Seven years I've been at Clifton — more than seven years — and I'm sure in all that time I've never given any cause for complaint. But the food I send up now . . . I'm ashamed. Ashamed. I can't imagine *what* you must think of me upstairs.'

As she spoke, tears brimmed in Cook's eyes and then spilled over, rolling one by one, unchecked, down her plump cheeks. Dorothea found it heart-wrenching to see, in so able and no-nonsense a woman as Cook.

That Cook took pride in her work was obvious to anyone — obvious, but all too easy to forget. In fact, Cook was often overlooked altogether, buried down here in the basement; if not exactly the bowels of the earth, the kitchen certainly had a subterranean feel to it, with no sign of the outside world apart from a tiny patch of sky seen through the high, narrow windows. Cook spent most of her time down here, lovingly preparing the meals they ate. Day after day she slaved at it: day after day, week after week, month upon month, for seven long years. To have kept her standards so high amidst all the shortages and hardships of war was testament to her skill and dedication — yet what thanks did she ever get?

Humbled by these thoughts, Dorothea said, 'Dearest Cook, of course we don't think badly of you — just the opposite. We may not say it — and we should, we really should — but we know how difficult things are, and the pressure you're under, and it's nothing short of a miracle, the way you provide for us all — the family, the staff, the hospital contingent — not to mention so many wounded men.'

'But that's no hardship, Mrs Kaufmann, no hardship at all! It's no more than they deserve; it's the least I can do for those poor creatures, after everything they've been through.'

'I can't tell you how much of a difference your meals make in speeding their recovery. We nurses can only do so much.'

Dorothea hesitated. She sensed that she hadn't yet got to the crux of the matter; this wasn't a crisis that had come about all at once.

'Are you quite sure you want to leave us, Cook? Are you really so unhappy here?'

'Lord bless you, Mrs Kaufmann,' Cook exclaimed, 'but I've loved every minute of working here; it's the best situation by far what I've ever had. Still,' she added, pursing her lips as if suddenly remembering her resolve to leave, 'all good things must come to an end. I'll not be sorry to see Grace again, I don't mind telling you — Grace and her kiddies. You don't know how worried I've been, what with the shortages and the price of everything — and those bombs you hear of in London, those air raids. It's been a struggle for poor Grace to make ends meet, ever since her worthless excuse of a husband ran off and left her. Oh, if I could only get my hands on him! I'd give him what for, and no mistake!'

Was this, then, the straw that broke the camel's back, her sister's plight?

'Why didn't you tell me this before, Cook? You should have come to me at once, if you were worried.'

'I couldn't very well . . . What's Grace to you? . . . I'm sure I don't . . .'

'Now, Cook. You know you can always talk to me. You know that. But never mind. At least now I understand. Of course you must go to your sister, if you think it best, but that doesn't mean you have to give up your position here. I'm sure we can come to some arrangement. In the meantime, why not send Grace a few odds and ends to tide her over: some groceries and so on? We must be able to spare some of our food. We're better off here, in the country, than people in town.'

Cook stiffened a little. 'I don't think Grace would . . . well, she wouldn't take kindly to charity.'

'It wouldn't be charity — not if it was your own food you were sending. I believe you must be due a rise — I'm sure all the staff are due. Why not take your rise in kind? There's plenty you could send by post.'

'Well . . . I don't know . . .' Cook furrowed her brow.

Dorothea felt the situation was hanging in the balance. At this most delicate of moments, an interruption was the last thing needed, and her heart fell when she heard hesitant footsteps out in the basement corridor. She glanced round, saw a pale face peering in at the door, a face that drew back the instant it saw her.

Cook had noticed the face too, and it had a strange effect on her. She began at once to bustle round, taking off her coat, reaching for her apron, drying the last of her tears on the hem.

'Here's Leonard, now, come to peel the potatoes and lend a hand, and I've nothing ready.'

'Leonard?' Dorothea was puzzled for a moment. 'Oh, of course, it's Private Sutton!' Private Sutton with the incurable stammer, who'd almost become a fixture at Clifton. 'How silly of me. I ought to have recognized him at once.' Curious, she asked, 'Does he often come and help you? I didn't know.'

'Well, yes, to speak the truth he does — and why shouldn't he? That Sister Elliot, she tried to put a stop to it, told him the kitchen's out of bounds. I said to him, I said, "Don't you take no notice! You can come down here, my love, any time you like. An extra pair of hands is always welcome."' Cook paused in the act of tipping some potatoes from a sack into a bowl. 'Do you know, Mrs Kaufmann, it's the funniest thing. If you pass the time of day with him, he can't hardly get a word out, poor lamb. But as soon as I set him to work, it's like he forgets himself. I can ask him how he's doing with the peeling — or whatever it is he's doing — and he'll answer straight off, no trouble at all; or he'll call for help if he needs it, and he don't trip over his words at all. And there's that Sister Elliot saying too much effort's not good for him! Huh! Shows how much *she* knows! Who does she think she is, anyway, telling me what I can and can't do in my own kitchen!'

Cook, it was very apparent, had taken possession of the kitchen once more, and was ready to do battle to protect her domain. She was also, suddenly, much more like her old self: she'd always been intolerant of those who might be categorized as petty tyrants and she numbered Mrs Bourne chief amongst them; Sister Elliot, it seemed, also came under that heading.

There was no more talk from Cook of her imminent departure. For now, at least, the crisis had been averted. And that left Dorothea to face her next task: persuading Aunt Eloise to raise the servants' wages.

'I'll get out from under your feet, Cook. I'm sure we'll be able to come to some arrangement that will suit everybody.'

'I shall think it over, ma'am. I'm not making any promises, mind. But I really must see about dinner. I'm behindhand as it is. Send Leonard in, would you, Mrs Kaufmann, on your way out? And where's that Merrells when you need her? Calls herself a scullery maid, she does. Huh!'

If Dorothea was a little hurt by Cook's brusque manner — a summary dismissal, it felt like, though she told herself she was being over-sensitive — that all changed a moment later. Cook suddenly turned to her as she was leaving and said, with one of her familiar beaming smiles, 'Bless you, Mrs Kaufmann! It's good of you to listen, and offer to help Grace and all. There's not many who'd be so understanding. But that's you all over. You're an angel, that's what you are: a proper little angel!'

* * *

There was no more talk of Cook leaving, nor did Aunt Eloise quibble over the matter of a rise in the wages. She couldn't deny that what the staff were paid hadn't kept up with the ever-increasing prices.

'I'm sure Albert would have agreed,' she said. '"A fair day's work deserves a fair day's pay": that's what Albert always said.'

Just a week after her conference with Cook, Dorothea finished a long stint in the hospital side of the house and happened to glance out of the window. It had been raining most of the day, but now there was a break in the weather, and she at once threw on her hat and her coat and set out for the village, hoping to get to the post office before Mr Downie closed for the day. As she sped down the drive, she looked up at the sky dubiously; she was not hopeful of the rain holding off for long.

There'd been much rain and drizzle in the week since Easter — hail and thunder, too. The sun had briefly shown itself once or twice but mostly the sky had been completely overcast. It did not feel much like spring.

Dorothea slipped a hand inside her coat pocket, making sure she'd remembered to bring the letter she wanted to post. Yes, it was there; she hadn't left it behind. Sometimes, lately, she felt she would have forgotten her own head if it hadn't been screwed on.

The letter she was sending was in reply to one from Nettie Thomson. Dorothea had been glad to hear from Nettie the other day after a long silence. Writing from the base hospital in France where she'd been posted, Nettie had dashed down a few lines so brief and slapdash that they spoke more eloquently than any words of the strain she must be under. The German offensive had brought the base hospital near to breaking point. The wards were overflowing, the work never-ending, the sound of the guns crept ever nearer. Nettie had her box packed and ready, should the Kaiser's army break through. Dorothea could only guess what it must be like. Her own tribulations seemed nothing in comparison.

A few spots of rain began to fall as Dorothea hurried towards the village. But what was a bit of rain, when not three months ago she'd walked along this same road with

Harry Keech in the teeth of a blizzard? He'd insisted on seeing her right to Clifton's front door, when all he really must have wanted was to get home. He'd carried her bag the whole way.

'I'm sure I can manage it, Harry. You've enough to carry.'

'Don't fret, miss, I'm used to carrying stuff. That's what us privates are for: something to hang things on.'

Harry had been indomitable, undaunted by the cold and dark. They'd talked in snatches, battling through the snow on the long and difficult trek from Welby station. Much of what they'd said had, like the snow, long since melted away, but with her visit to Essex Square still very much on her mind at the time, it was only natural that she had mentioned Eliza, and Dorothea remembered that part of the conversation. She remembered lamenting the fact that Eliza and Aunt Eloise were at loggerheads at a time when they needed each other.

'That's families for you, miss. Look at me and Nolly. We're brothers, but we can't abide each other. I reckon there'd have been murder afore now, if it weren't for Mother keeping the peace.'

Harry was back in France now, his leave long over. Dorothea wondered if he'd been caught in the chaos of the retreat these last couple of weeks. On Friday, there'd been ominous reports of the enemy in Amiens — as far forward as Amiens. Since then, the newspapers had been rather more sanguine, even suggesting that the offensive might at last have run out of steam. But it wasn't the offensive Dorothea was thinking of as she hurried towards the village. She was thinking instead how Harry's kindness and cheerful companionship on that January evening had undermined her new resolve to harden her heart and stop being so gullible — to stop being such a wide-eyed goody-goody. Indeed, her resolve might have crumbled altogether, had Harry not happened to mention the long-running feud with his brother.

Everyone knew that the Keech boys didn't get on. They were worse by far than Nibs and Ned Carter, who were at least civil to each other most of the time. But the feuding didn't end with the Keech brothers, for Harry had been pals with Billy Turner, a long-sworn enemy of Nibs Carter, and Nibs at one time had been thick with Harry's detested brother, Nolly (these days Nibs said Nolly was 'up himself' and not worth the bother). And while the Keech boys and the Carters and Billy Turner never ceased to fight amongst each other, they all of them shunned the Hobson boys, who formed a gang of their own. So it went on, all round the village, the lads scrapping, the women tittle-tattling, the old gaffers bearing grudges over half a century and more. If ever Dorothea needed to remind herself what people were really like — if ever she needed to stiffen her resolve — she had only to look at the village.

But here she was at the post office, and she'd arrived in the nick of time.

'Well, Mrs Kaufmann, what can I do for you? I was just this minute about to bolt the door. Another for your nurse friend, is it?'

Her letter stamped and handed over, Dorothea took her leave of Mr Downie. As she walked round the duck pond and turned into Back Lane, she had to admit — even with her heart properly hardened — that Mr Downie was never less than courteous and polite. How different he was to dour Mr Cheeseman in the shop!

The threat of rain had lifted. There was even some evening sunshine slanting out of the cloud-strewn sky as Dorothea walked up Back Lane. Reaching the last cottage on the right, she came across Mrs Turner at work in her little front garden. The ground had been dug all over; there was no sign of Mrs Turner's renowned spring flowers. This seemed such a desecration that Dorothea, without thinking, stopped and spoke, forgetting how things stood between them.

'Your poor garden!'

Mrs Turner did not exactly meet her eye. 'We're planting vegetables front as well as back this year.'

'No flowers?'

'Needs must.'

'You're right, of course. All the same . . .'

A little bit more colour had been lost to the world.

There was an uncomfortable silence. Mrs Turner stood inspecting the freshly dug earth. With a heavy heart, Dorothea made ready to pass on.

Suddenly, Mrs Turner turned to her, faced her across the rickety old fence. As if making a snap decision, she said, 'Won't you come in and have a cup of tea, Mrs Kaufmann?'

'Oh, I . . . I'm not sure . . .'

'This has gone on long enough, all this cutting each other dead. Plain daft, is what it is.'

'But Mr Turner—'

'Turner won't disturb us. He'll not be back a good while yet. They're busy down Manor Farm this week.'

Dorothea had yearned so much for this moment, a chance to be reconciled with one of her oldest friends in the village, but now that the moment had actually come, she found herself strangely reluctant. Why? Was she worried that the breach might be beyond repair, and that this attempt to mend things would only go to prove it? Or did she mistrust Mrs Turner's motives?

To be suspicious of people — that was good, it was what she'd decided, not to be so gullible. But that didn't mean she had to be rude.

'A cup of tea would be nice.'

Dorothea did her best to raise a cautious smile, disguising her hardened heart. Mrs Turner nodded briefly and led the way into the cottage.

While Mrs Turner made tea in the back kitchen, Dorothea stood and looked round the little front room, which she'd first seen aged eleven. She'd come that day with Nora, Mrs Turner's eldest daughter and back then the nursery maid at Clifton. It had seemed a wonderful treat, going to tea at the Turners'. How easily pleased she'd been, that girl of eleven, bursting with happiness on such a memorable day.

A long time ago.

Mrs Turner reappeared. She had put on a clean apron and was carrying a tray. They sat down at the gate-leg table next to the window. Sixteen years ago, there'd been geraniums in a pot on the sill; today the sill was empty, and the window looked out at the desecrated front garden.

Mrs Turner poured. Dorothea sat waiting, still with her hat and coat on.

'I'm sorry, but we've got no sugar. I've grown used to taking my tea without. There's a little honey, if you'd like something to sweeten it.'

'Thank you, no. Tea without sugar will be fine.'

So stiff, so formal. They sat facing each other across the little table, like strangers in a tea shop.

'How is—'

'I heard that—'

They both began to talk at once; both stopped and looked away. There was a long pause. Mrs Turner toyed with the handle of her cup. Dorothea looked out of the window. The evening sun was casting long shadows in the lane.

At length, Mrs Turner opened her mouth as if to speak, but no words came, and abruptly she took a sip of tea instead. Dorothea, too, was tongue-tied; she suddenly couldn't think of a single thing to say. She had never had this problem in the past. She was turning into someone she didn't recognize.

Looking down at her tea, she realized that she'd hardly touched it. The sooner she finished it, the sooner she could go. She picked up the cup and gulped, making ready with her excuses.

Mrs Turner got to her feet. Dorothea watched her. Going to the plain and sturdy dresser opposite the fireplace, Mrs Turner opened a drawer and took something out. She came back to the table and sat down. She placed whatever it was she had fetched on the tabletop between them. Dorothea realized it was a tiny photograph with uneven edges: it appeared to have been cut from a larger picture. It was a photograph of Eliza.

Mrs Turner spoke at last. 'We found it in amongst Billy's bits and pieces. They sent them to us. This was the only photo — the only photo he took with him.' She paused, then added, 'He . . . he must have been ever so fond of her.'

'Eliza was fond of him, too.'

'It didn't take her long to marry someone else, once he'd gone.'

'I don't think she really knew what she was doing.'

'Let's hope she doesn't live to regret it. "Marry in haste, repent at leisure."'

'Too late for that. Her husband is dead.'

There was a moment's silence, then Mrs Turner said, 'I'm sorry to hear it. I didn't know.' She picked up her cup, but it was empty, and she put it down again. Positioning it carefully on the saucer, frowning a little, she said, 'Now don't get me wrong. I've nothing against Miss Eliza. But her and our Billy — it would only have ended in tears. I knew it. Turner knew it. Turner called Billy a bloody fool for not putting Miss Eliza straight. They had words. Said things they shouldn't have. And then . . . afterwards . . . well, they're as stubborn as each other, dint part on good terms. I needn't tell you where Turner lays the blame for that: not just on Miss Eliza, on all of you, everyone up the big house. You bring nothing but trouble, he says. He's not a forgiving man, Turner. And our Jem and our Daisy, they take after him. But this time they was right, that's what I thought, that's how it seemed to me.'

Mrs Turner hesitated, fingering the little photo with its uneven edges that looked like they'd been cut by scissors.

'I'd no idea, you see, how much she meant to him. I thought it was all the other way, her chasing him. He'd never shown much interest, never bothered with girls. And he kept things close to his chest. He was always the same, right from when he was a very little boy. But then . . . when I found this . . . when I found it amongst his bits and pieces . . . well, it set me thinking, that's all.'

She looked at the photograph a moment longer, then put it down. Getting to her feet again, she went this time to the mantelpiece, where there was a photograph in a simple wooden frame. She brought it over to the table, lowered herself back into her seat. She placed the photograph in the frame next to the photograph of Eliza. Dorothea, from her place opposite, was looking at the pictures upside down, but she saw at once that the photograph in the frame was of Billy in uniform.

'The only picture we have of him,' said Mrs Turner, her eyes focused on the slightly blurry black-and-white image. 'He never did like having his picture took. I went once with all four kids to a man in Lawham, a proper photographer with a studio and all. I saved up to get them all done. Jem, he'd have been about twenty, Nora seventeen, Daisy just four. Billy was nine, and he wanted none of it, wouldn't sit still for love nor money. In the end, I just gave in, let him have his way. That's why I've pictures of the others, but only *this* of him.'

With the tip of one gnarled finger, she stroked the edge of the frame. Softly, she said, 'Such a good boy, he was. Strong as an ox, mind, but he'd not hurt a fly. Always gave me his wages, he did, right up to the time he left the village. Gave me his wages same as he did when he was a boy, even though he mostly slept up the big house by then — a room above the stables — and he ate most of his meals up there too. "You don't want to be giving your money to me, Bill," I said to him. "You ought to be saving up, for when you get wed." But he wouldn't have it. There was never a lad who looked after his mother so well as my Bill.'

She picked up the photograph in its frame, studied it closely. 'I don't like to see him as a soldier. It's not how I want to remember him. But this picture — it's better than nothing.'

Laying the photograph back on the table, she continued after a pause, 'Turner don't like to talk about it. "No good crying over spilt milk, woman. Lad's dead and gone, and that's an end to it. Least said, soonest mended." By which he means he'd like to put Billy away, the way he did with our Ivy.' Mrs Turner looked up, caught Dorothea's eye. 'Don't suppose you know about Ivy. Daresay you've never heard of her. She was my other girl, the middle child, two years younger than Nora.

Ivy passed on, the same year Bill was born. Scarlet fever, it was. She was five years old.'

Dorothea was utterly taken aback by this unexpected revelation; she was speechless. In all her time at Clifton — in all the years she'd been coming to the village — she'd never so much as heard a whisper about a girl named Ivy Turner. The Turners had four children: Jem, Nora, Billy, Daisy. The Turners had four children, that was set in stone. Except there'd been a fifth. How, Dorothea asked herself, could she not have known?

'We don't talk of her,' said Mrs Turner. 'It was "least said, soonest mended" with Ivy, too. But I won't have Billy put away. I won't have it. I want him where I can see him, there on the mantelpiece.'

'Well, of course you do,' said Dorothea, thinking of Johann on her bedside table, and Roderick, too, on the sideboard in the drawing room at Clifton.

But there were so many pictures on so many mantelpieces and on bedside tables and in pride of place on sideboards; there were so many pictures of the fallen that it had become commonplace. How long before these pictures became part of the furniture, to be dusted and put back, and never really noticed anymore? And there were some whose pictures would never be put on display (Mr Turner was surely not alone in wanting no reminder of his loss), and still others who had no picture at all, who'd never been photographed, who were all but forgotten already. Oh, if only—

But all the 'ifs' in the world added up to nothing.

She remembered sitting with Billy in the Barley Mow a year ago. She remembered what he'd told her about scything down the onrushing Germans with his machine gun. It wasn't something she could tell Mrs Turner. He wouldn't have wanted his mother to know, Dorothea was sure of that, just as she was sure he'd never told anyone else, that no one else in the world would ever now know. He'd needed to get it off his chest, and she'd been there. But would he have confided in someone who had hardened her heart, who took a step back from people?

Mrs Turner reached across the table suddenly, laid her hand on Dorothea's, bridging the gap. 'I just wanted to say, before you go—' (The tea was all gone, time was ticking on.) '—That I know what you did for Billy—'

Dorothea gave a start, thinking for one minute that Mrs Turner had read her mind. But Mrs Turner's next words showed she was thinking of something else; it was nothing to do with the Barley Mow.

'—The parcels you sent him. Not just Billy, as I've found since. The other boys, too: all the village boys. Socks and cigarettes and cake and sweets.'

'It . . . it's nothing . . . not worth mentioning . . .'

'Our Billy didn't think so. Not that he'd have let on, of course. He'd not have told me, if I hadn't picked up on summat he let slip. Meant a lot to him, what you did; I'm his mother, I could tell. But no one in the village knows, they've no idea; they mightn't be so quick to judge, if they did. It's high time we learned to appreciate the people round us. Maybe we'd not feel so bitter then, when some of them are taken away.'

Mrs Turner squeezed Dorothea's hand, just once, then got quickly to her feet. She busied herself, collecting the cups and saucers: it was the best china, Dorothea now noticed.

She had to go. Mr Turner would be home soon, and she was due on duty back at Clifton before long. Mrs Turner saw her out. The setting sun was now veiled in cloud. Back Lane lay deserted under the patchwork grey sky.

'Dear Mrs Turner — I'm glad we made the time to talk.' This was all she could find to say: there were no words for the rest.

'And I'm glad you didn't just walk by. I was in two minds, seeing you come up Back Lane, you know how it is. But when you stopped and spoke, I realized all of a sudden what I should have realized before, what's only right and proper. We'd no business falling out, Mrs Kaufmann, not me and you. Our Billy wouldn't have wanted it, I know that much. Well, goodbye, dearie. Goodbye, for now. You take care of yourself.'

'Goodbye, Mrs Turner. Thank you for the tea and — and for everything.'

* * *

It was early, barely light. Tossing and turning in bed, Dorothea, having woken, could not get back to sleep. Her mind ran ahead, already up and about. It was Sunday. She'd not have time to go to church. But she'd see Owain Morgan later when he came to visit the men, as he always did on Sundays. He was very good with the men, taking his time, talking or listening, or both, as required.

But even he might struggle to raise their spirits after the deep gloom of yesterday. The Germans were on the offensive again. The first intimation of their new and violent onslaught had come last Tuesday, the day after Dorothea had taken tea with Mrs Turner, and before long it had become clear that fierce fighting was in progress somewhat north of the previous assault. Once again, the Germans made startling advances. Within a matter of days, they'd crossed the River Lys and the Allies had evacuated Armentières. Messines Ridge looked likely to fall — Messines Ridge, captured with such fanfare, and in such gruesome circumstances, last June. As Private Chambers had pointed out yesterday, the Germans were now within forty miles of Calais. 'If the Channel ports fall,' Private Chambers had begun. Then he'd fallen silent, shaking his head.

Far from being on their last legs, the Germans had confounded all expectations by launching two major offensives in the space of a month. There seemed little doubt that they'd been bolstered by their peace treaty with Bolshevik Russia. Divisions freed from the Eastern Front were now available for operations in the west. Did this mean, Dorothea wondered, that Johann's brother Siegfried, last heard of in the east, had been sent across Europe to kill British soldiers in Flanders? Nettie Thomson would certainly be rushed off her feet again, with a fresh flood of wounded pouring into the base hospital.

Yesterday's sombre mood had been compounded by newspaper reports that all men up to the age of fifty were to be called up and conscription extended to Ireland, whilst a tightening of the rules would see even more men 'combed out' who had previously been exempt. What would all this mean to middle-aged men like Crompton, and like Mr Downie at the post office? Would Nibs have to fight for the toffs, despite himself?

Where would it all end?

Dorothea sighed and sat up; there was no point lying in bed with the same bleak thoughts going round and round in her head. She got out of bed, dressed, drew back the curtains. She was met with a blank wall of thick grey fog. The upper branches of the cedar tree showed as mysterious shadows in the murk. Nothing else was visible. The weather these last few days had certainly matched the prevailing mood, being grey and damp and oppressive with no hint of spring. And now the world lay under a pall of impenetrable fog.

Dorothea turned away from the window. She touched for a moment, with the tips of her fingers, the photograph of Johann in its silver frame, then she went downstairs. She made her way, by force of habit, to the breakfast room, but it was far too early for breakfast; the table wasn't yet laid, the curtains still closed. If any of the servants were up, there was neither sight nor sound of them. The house was as still and silent as a morgue.

Yesterday's paper lay open on the table where someone had left it. Dorothea lingered a moment, slowly turning the pages. She could only just make out the printed words in the dim light. Her eyes came to rest on a report of General Haig's order to the army; his portentous words had added in no small amount to yesterday's gloom.

There is no course open to us but to fight it out. Every position must be held to the last man; there must be no retirement. With our backs to the wall, and believing in the justice of our cause, each of us must fight to the end.

To Dorothea it seemed clear that a crisis had come, a turning point, perhaps the supreme moment of the war. You could see it in people's faces. They were thinking the unthinkable. They were facing up to it for the first time. Even General Haig seemed to have in mind the unspoken word: defeat.

But to Dorothea it felt as if she'd had her back to the wall from the war's very beginning. She'd faced defeat after defeat. She'd faced defeat on every side. She was a widow. She was childless. She was an alien in her own land. She'd lost everything: hope, happiness, her future — she'd even lost faith in herself. She was alone now in a cruel and pitiless world. That was why she had to harden her heart, be gullible no more. It was her last defence.

Except she wasn't alone. She'd never been alone. She knew that now. She had Aunt Eloise, she had Katherine and Laurence, she had Eliza and the unborn child. There were others, too, all manner of friends and acquaintances: Nibs and Nettie Thomson, Mrs Turner and Owain Morgan — to name just a few.

Nor could she harden her heart the way she wanted. Her great resolve to change was crumbling already. It had been crumbling ever since she'd taken tea with Mrs Turner — no, before that, long before, going right back to when she'd first decided to make the change, on the long journey home from London. She'd made up her mind to do it on the train, then almost at once she'd met Harry Keech.

Harry Keech, people said, had a lip on him. He swore like a trooper since he'd been in the army, and he made no bones about the fact that he hated his own brother. But he'd always been perfectly polite to her, and she'd seen for herself what a good friend he'd been to Billy Turner. And on a dark and snowy night in January, he'd walked back with her all the way to Clifton, when there was no earthly reason why he should. As they walked through the blizzard on the long, dark Welby Road, talking in snatches of families at loggerheads — of Aunt Eloise and Eliza, of Harry himself and Nolly — suddenly

Harry had said, 'I'll tell yer a funny thing, miss. I were in front line, we was standing-to like we do of a morning, case Jerry comes over, and I were thinking of Nolly back home, Nolly snuggled warm in bed with his missus — and there was me, up to me knees in muddy water and freezing me b — fingers, freezing me fingers off, and didn't I wish Nolly had been there getting a taste of it, and his teeth chattering like mine; didn't I wish Jerry really would come over and stick his bayonet in Nolly's lousy, scrimshanking guts. I could just see it, the look on Nolly's face, and Jerry's bayonet sticking out of him. And this is the funny bit, miss. Right then, all in the blink of an eye, I knew I'd never let it happen; I knew I'd rip Jerry's throat out sooner than let him anywhere near Nolly — our Nolly, who's been on me back all me life! If that int arse-about-face, then I don't know what is, 'scuse my language.'

He wasn't all bad, Harry Keech. There was more good in him than bad. There was good and bad in everyone — in Alex Cartwright, for instance, who'd deceived them all, who'd been calculating and callous, but who'd simply been dreaming of a different life, perhaps, a better life. He'd shown the other side to himself in winning his medal for bravery, and when he'd set the butterfly free in the library.

People might scoff (a butterfly!), but Dorothea knew better, for these little acts of kindness happened everywhere and all the time: Cook taking so much trouble with Private Sutton, Mr Downie always so courteous in the post office, Ernest Grimshaw giving his seat up on the train.

Ernest Grimshaw! How long since she'd last thought of Ernest Grimshaw? She didn't know him from Adam, of course; he might now be dead. But she would never forget that crowded train out of Euston on a day when she'd felt ground down by events. She would never forget how he'd offered up his seat, how he'd told her his life story, how he'd fallen asleep with his head against her knee, young, innocent — good. Yes, she'd seen the good in him. She had an unerring instinct for it. She had an unerring instinct that she had never really lost. All she had to do was trust herself.

It came to her then in a flash. Everything suddenly became clear. She'd made a mistake. She'd made a dreadful mistake. Trying to change who she was: that was her mistake.

Let people call her gullible. Let people call her what they liked. It didn't matter. To see the good in people, not to judge, never to turn away: this was *her* cause, the cause she believed in — a cause she would fight for, fight to the end. It was everything Johann had most admired in her. It was why he'd loved her. And even though he was gone, she must keep faith with him. She had been — she was — she would always be — the woman he'd loved.

Slowly she folded the newspaper. She left it on the table where she'd found it. Her mind was clear now. All that was needed was to blow the last of the cobwebs away.

She left the breakfast room. She crossed the hallway. She opened the front door and looked out. Thick, swirling fog blotted out the world. But the fog was paler now, less grey. There was a glimmer in it, almost imperceptible, yet there nonetheless: the first, faint presage of the new day.

Taking a deep breath, Dorothea stepped out to meet the white dawn.

THE END

THE JOFFE BOOKS STORY

We began in 2014 when Jasper agreed to publish his mum's much-rejected romance novel and it became a bestseller.

Since then we've grown into the largest independent publisher in the UK. We're extremely proud to publish some of the very best writers in the world, including Joy Ellis, Faith Martin, Caro Ramsay, Helen Forrester, Simon Brett and Robert Goddard. Everyone at Joffe Books loves reading and we never forget that it all begins with the magic of an author telling a story.

We are proud to publish talented first-time authors, as well as established writers whose books we love introducing to a new generation of readers.

We have been shortlisted for Independent Publisher of the Year at the British Book Awards three times, in 2020, 2021 and 2022, and for the Diversity and Inclusivity Award at the Independent Publishing Awards in 2022.

We built this company with your help, and we love to hear from you, so please email us about absolutely anything bookish at feedback@joffebooks.com

If you want to receive free books every Friday and hear about all our new releases, join our mailing list: www.joffebooks.com/contact

And when you tell your friends about us, just remember: it's pronounced Joffe as in coffee or toffee!